A Place to Call Home

Evie Grace was born in Kent, and one of her earliest memories is of picking cherries with her grandfather who managed a fruit farm near Selling. Holidays spent in the Kent countryside and the stories passed down through her family inspired her to write her Maids of Kent trilogy.

Evie now lives in Devon with her partner and dog. She has a grown-up daughter and son.

She loves researching the history of the nineteenth century and is very grateful for the invention of the washing machine, having discovered how the Victorians struggled to do their laundry.

A Place to Call Home is the third and final novel in the Maids of Kent trilogy, following on from *Her Mother's Daughter*.

Also by Evie Grace

Half a Sixpence
Her Mother's Daughter

EVIE GRACE

A Place to Call Home

arrow books

1 3 5 7 9 10 8 6 4 2

Arrow Books
20 Vauxhall Bridge Road
London SW1V 2SA

Arrow Books is part of the Penguin Random House group
of companies whose addresses can be found at
global.penguinrandomhouse.com.

First published in Great Britain by Arrow Books in 2018

www.penguin.co.uk

A CIP catalogue record for this book is available from
the British Library.

ISBN 9781784756246

Typeset in 10.75/13.5 pt Palatino
by Integra Software Services Pvt. Ltd, Pondicherry

Printed and bound in Great Britain by Clays Ltd, Elcograf S.p.A

To Tamsin and Will

1876

Chapter One

A Patchwork Family

'You look well, my dear Rose.'

As Aunt Marjorie spoke the marble clock on the mantel in the dining room chimed four. It was a warm summer's afternoon and the sunshine had roused the dumbledores into a frenzy on the fragrant honeysuckle outside the half-open window.

Rose caught a glimpse of her reflection in the mirror. She had pinched her cheeks to add some colour to her complexion and bound her dark brown hair up to the back of her head in a heavy plait.

'I've always said she's quite the aristocrat,' Aunt Temperance joined in as they stood waiting to be seated. 'With those cheekbones and striking blue eyes she could easily pass as a baronet's daughter.'

Rose turned towards her tall, brown-eyed father who was giving his sister a look, meaning *don't give her ideas above her station.*

Dear Pa, she mused fondly. He was the head of their family, their rock. Rose considered him a very handsome man for his age, with his loose curls of dark hair, side-whiskers and beard, run through with sparse strands of silver.

'I remember the day you were born, Rose,' Aunt Marjorie said. 'The most angelic child has grown into a refined young lady. How time flies!'

Sixteen years had passed since her parents had blessed their tiny infant with the name of Rose Agnes Ivy Catherine Cheevers. She didn't know what they'd been thinking of, but her parents said that they were family names and it was important to keep them alive. Her elder brother was plain Arthur Cheevers, and her younger siblings had but two forenames each.

'I'm sorry that Mr Kingsley couldn't join us,' Pa said. Mr Kingsley was Aunt Temperance's husband, and Rose's uncle, but no one ever called him anything but Mr Kingsley.

'He is sadly indisposed.'

This was Aunt Temperance's usual response. Rose smoothed the front of her new dress made from pale muslin decorated with woven pink and green sprays of flowers. She knew that Mr Kingsley was more than likely to be in one of the local taverns.

'It is unfortunate that he is some years my senior and not in the best of health,' Aunt Temperance went on.

'He is a little liverish again, I expect,' Aunt Marjorie said with a wicked glint in her eye.

'He is suffering from a touch of gout,' Aunt Temperance responded sharply.

'An affliction worthy of our sympathy. You must convey our best wishes for a full and prompt recovery – I hope to see him in the office as usual on Monday,' Pa interrupted as Rose's younger sister, Minnie, entered the room, her face flushed from the heat. 'Please, do sit down.'

As the aunts took their places at the table, Rose watched and waited.

The dining room at Willow Place was roughly square, the outer wall sloping out at an angle as though, like Mr Kingsley, the builder had partaken in too much liquor when erecting the timber frame for the wattle and daub infill. The window with its diamond leaded lights was set deep into the wall, and an oak bookcase stood alongside it, crammed with leather-bound tomes on subjects ranging from natural history to travel and exploration, and Sir Walter Scott's *Ivanhoe, The Lady of the Lake* and his *Waverley* novels. On top of the bookcase was a stuffed pike that Pa had caught from the river, and a medal presented to him by the dignitaries of Canterbury for rescuing two men from drowning.

Rose often wondered how Pa had felt risking his life in the filthy waters of the Stour.

'Rose,' Aunt Temperance said, jolting her from her reverie, 'you would do well to remember in future that there is nothing wrong in marrying an older man – he is more likely to be settled in his preferences, financially solvent and grateful. It helps, of course, if it is a love match.'

Rose didn't know how to respond. Family folklore said that her aunt had chosen her husband because she had thought the name Kingsley a great improvement on Cheevers. Rose couldn't help thinking that Aunt Temperance, who was two or three years older than Pa, could have done much better for herself. According to Ma, she had been quite a beauty, with delicate features and chestnut hair.

Aunt Marjorie was in her fifties and had never married. Rose wondered if it was because she was rather plain. She had hair of silver and sienna, wore serge skirts and horn-rimmed spectacles that kept slipping down her nose.

'Sit down, Rose,' Pa said, gesturing towards the far side of the table where he had suspended a plank between two of the stick-back dining chairs to provide an extra perch.

She moved round and sat down on one of the chairs on which Pa had placed a cushion for extra padding. Minnie took the other chair and left the plank for Donald.

The aunts sat opposite with Arthur between them, while Ma and Pa sat one at each end of the table. Arthur had stuck his forelock of sandy blond hair to his forehead with Pa's Macassar oil.

From Rose's vantage point, she could see the globe, a beautifully decorated map of the world on a stand in the corner of the room. Pa had bought it as a present for Ma, but she had judged it too fine to be exposed to her pupils' grubby fingers and had instead kept it in the house. Some evenings, she wheeled it on its castors into the parlour and made a game of finding the different parts of the British Empire, naming their capital cities.

She glanced towards Arthur who rolled his eyes in her direction. She smiled, sympathising for his plight.

'Arthur, dear boy, you seem a little out of sorts,' Aunt Marjorie observed, although he was a young man of twenty-three, not a boy any more.

'He is missing his sweetheart,' Ma said cheerfully. Her mouth was wide, her nose small, and she was beginning to run to fat. Sometimes her eyes looked green, sometimes hazel, depending on the light. She had tied her greying hair back, which had the effect of making her look rather austere. 'I told him he must spend some time with us for a change. He will have plenty of time with her when they are married.'

'I can speak for myself, Ma,' Arthur countered.

'He will go out later,' Minnie chuckled. 'He's oiled his hair. Look how it glistens. And he is wearing his Sunday best on a Saturday.'

'Do I hear the sound of wedding bells?' Aunt Marjorie said, smiling, and Arthur blushed.

'You have been walking out with the apothecary's daughter for over a year,' Aunt Temperance said. 'Mind she doesn't tire of you.'

6

'Leave the young man alone. Marry in haste, repent at leisure. There's no rush. You need to be sure that you can face Miss Miskin every day for the rest of your life, treating her with love and respect and without wearying of her.' Pa looked fondly at Ma who smiled in response. Rose couldn't imagine her parents ever tiring of each other's company.

'I can't see any reason to delay once one has made the decision to enter the state of holy matrimony,' Aunt Temperance said.

'If you must know, we've been saving up for our future,' Arthur said.

'I'm delighted to hear it. Miss Miskin is a very lucky woman. You will make an excellent husband.' Rose couldn't help feeling that Aunt Marjorie was aiming this comment at Aunt Temperance, who pursed her lips as if she was sucking a lemon. Aunt Marjorie wasn't their aunt by blood, but Pa's cousin once removed. It wasn't her only connection to the family – she had once been Ma's nanny and governess. She'd aged considerably since she'd last visited Willow Place, and Rose couldn't see how she could manage to care for her current employer's children with her stoop, shuffling gait and stiff fingers.

'I love a good wedding,' Aunt Marjorie sighed.

'Where is Donald?' Ma changed the subject abruptly.

'Have you seen your brother recently?' Rose asked her little sister, except that Minnie wasn't little any more. She was twelve and growing fast with dark brown eyes like Pa's and hair that fell around her shoulders in soft blond ringlets.

'Why is he always my brother, not ours, when he's in trouble?'

'I told him not to be late – I'll have his guts for garters,' Ma said.

7

'I hope he's here soon. I'm looking forward to my tea,' Aunt Marjorie said.

'I'll go and find him,' Rose offered.

'Arthur should go, but thank you, Stringy Bean,' Pa said before lowering his eyes in apology for calling her by her pet name in company.

'Where can he be?' Aunt Marjorie asked just as an object came flying through the window. Minnie screamed as it whistled past her ear and landed in the middle of Rose's plate. Pieces of china flew in all directions and the object – a dark red ball – rolled to a stop in front of her. She grasped it and held it up, the leather smooth under her fingertips.

''Ow is that!' said Arthur.

'Donald!' Pa stood up and roared through the open window. 'Get yourself indoors this minute!'

'Be gentle with him, Oliver,' Ma said. 'I'll make sure he pays for what he's broken. I'm sorry for his behaviour, but boys will be boys.'

'There is a balance to be struck between allowing children to express themselves in order to develop their characters, and spoiling them, Agnes,' Aunt Marjorie said, taking Pa's side.

'Indeed,' Aunt Temperance agreed and Rose wondered how she knew when she had no children of her own. Aunt Marjorie had none either, but she had had plenty of experience of bringing up other people's offspring.

'I would make an example of him if he were mine,' Aunt Temperance opined. 'A beating would soon l'arn him to stop his impetuous ways.'

'I'm not a believer in corporal punishment,' Pa said firmly. 'The expectation of a good hiding makes one more apprehensive of a repeat performance, but it doesn't address the cause of the problem.'

'Well, that boy is trouble. He's already in training for the treadmill and oakum shed.'

'Oh, Temperance,' Ma sighed. 'You do exaggerate. He's in high spirits, that's all. He knows very well the difference between right and wrong.'

Donald was slow to answer Pa's call. Eventually, he sauntered into the dining room, wiping his hands on a white shirt that sported several grass stains. He was Minnie's twin, and the younger one by virtue of having followed his sister into the world two hours behind, after midnight. Minnie was born on Tuesday, and, as the rhyme said, was full of grace, while Donald, born on Wednesday, was full of woe, although Rose felt that it was truer to say that Donald could create woe wherever he went.

'Well, what do you have to say for yourself?' Pa barked from where he sat in the oak carver at the head of the table.

Donald looked at him sheepishly, gazing through a fringe of sandy-coloured curls. 'I'm sorry, Father. Joe and I were practising.'

Joe was one of Donald's friends. Rose had thought of him as a calming influence, but now she wasn't so sure.

'If it wasn't for the presence of your mother and aunts, I would banish you to your room. Rose, give me the ball, please.'

Rose handed it over, aware of Donald's frown of disapproval as Pa turned and placed it carefully in the bonbon dish that stood on top of the dark oak court cupboard, a hefty, Gothic-looking piece of furniture which used to belong to Pa's grandfather.

'When shall I be allowed to have it back?' Donald asked, his brow furrowed.

'When you've cleared the broken plate and paid for a replacement.' Pa smiled ruefully. 'Mr W. G. Grace has much to answer for.'

'He is becoming a legend in his own lifetime,' Aunt Marjorie said. 'I've read that he's the first man to pass a thousand runs and a hundred wickets – that must have been last year.'

'He's a giant,' Donald said, his eyes filled with admiration. 'Literally.'

'I've heard that he's a large man with a fair bird's nest of a beard, but I don't hold with cricket,' Aunt Temperance cut in. 'It's a game that's played by any Tom, Dick and Harry on the streets, and a complete waste of time. I don't know how many winders have been broken around here because of it.'

'It's become the sport of gentlemen,' Ma said, putting on a cut-glass accent.

'When will we expect to see you playing at the Beverley Ground?' Aunt Marjorie asked.

'As soon as I'm old enough. There's a lime tree there and I'm going to be the first cricketer to clear the tree to score a six.' Donald tweaked the braces holding up his brown moleskin trousers as he moved round to sit with his sisters. The plank creaked ominously with the extra weight and Rose moved as far away from him as possible. She admired his ambition, but his clothes reeked of perspiration and a hint of the tan yard.

'What's for tea? I'm starving,' he whispered, his dark brown eyes settling on the slices of fresh bread, cheese and jars of pickled onions, eggs and cucumbers. A grin spread across his face. 'Oh, I can guess.'

'We thought we would have ox tongue for a change,' Ma said, straight-faced.

Rose glanced at her Aunt Marjorie, whose expression changed from joyful anticipation to consternation. Rose was confused, too, because she knew that Mrs Dunn, the housekeeper, had bought a pig's head and soaked it in brine – she had shown Rose how to check the strength of the solution by floating a potato in it. Then she had drained the head, put it into a stew-pot with the ears, some chopped onions and herbs, covered it in cold water and brought it up to the boil, simmering it for hours and skimming off the scum, until the meat fell from the bone. She had let it cool, chopped the meat, added parsley and stirred it together with a little of the cooking liquor before placing it in a mould with a muslin and brass weights from the kitchen scales on top.

Rose remembered how there had been some discussion between Ma and the housekeeper about the best way of keeping it cool, the pantry being considered too warm. It had been placed in the cellar, but perhaps that hadn't been right for it either. Had the brawn failed to set?

'There is no brawn?' Aunt Marjorie enquired.

'I'm afraid that it's gone off.' Rose caught Ma smiling at Pa.

'That is a disaster. Oh, what a terrible shame.' Aunt Marjorie sounded distraught.

'Do not distress yourself,' Pa said, chuckling. 'Of course, there is brawn.'

'Thank goodness,' Aunt Marjorie sighed. 'I've been so looking forward to it.'

'It's the only reason she calls on us,' Donald whispered.

'Hush.' Rose nudged him with her elbow. It wasn't true.

'I will do the honours,' Pa said, getting up from his seat and disappearing from the room. He returned shortly afterwards, carrying a plate on which sat the trembling mound of brawn. He placed it in front of him, took up the carving knife and fork and began to slice it, the blade slipping through it as if it were butter.

'Pass your plates. Ladies first, Donald,' he said as Donald raised his platter.

The maid, dressed in her dark uniform and pristine white apron, came into the room with a replacement plate for Rose. Jane was eighteen and had been at Willow Place for six months. She was tall and slender with long, pale blond hair plaited and coiled beneath her cap. Ma and Mrs Dunn had found her to be kind, hard-working and quick to learn, and the family were already quite attached to her.

Once the brawn was served, they sat waiting for Jane to finish pouring the lemonade and beer into their glasses. Rose could hear Donald's stomach rumbling. She could see Aunt Marjorie's fingers hovering over her cutlery as she tried to restrain herself.

'Thank you, Jane. That will be all for now,' Pa said.

Jane gave a small curtsey – Pa had tried in vain to train her out of the demeaning habit which she'd learned at her previous place – and left the room.

As Pa said grace, Rose noticed how Donald's eyes darted furtively around the room. She wondered what he was thinking, what he was plotting next.

'Amen,' she said, joining in with the others. Aunt Marjorie's fingers made contact with her knife and fork, but flew off again when Pa said jovially:

'I believe that a toast is in order. We're very pleased that you have chosen to spend some of your precious annual holiday with us, Aunt Marjorie. And I'm delighted you were able to grace us with your presence, Temperance. Let's raise a glass and drink to health and happiness, and the jolliest of times.'

'To health and happiness,' Ma echoed.

'And the jolliest of times,' Pa repeated, beaming widely as he drained his glass.

'Thank you very much for your hospitality. It's lovely to be back in the family fold, albeit for a brief visit,' Aunt

Marjorie said before Pa finally released her from her misery, saying, 'Let's eat.'

Rose helped herself to bread and butter and a pickled onion before trying the brawn. It was delicious, the meat soft and flavoursome and the jelly succulent. Aunt Marjorie could certainly tuck it away, she thought as she watched Pa serve her a second helping.

'The sea air seems to agree with you, Marjorie,' Ma said eventually. 'How are your charges in Ramsgate?'

'They are well, thank you, although I find it more tiring chasing after them now – I'm not getting any younger. Occasionally I think of retiring, but I enjoy being a governess too much to give it up just yet, and besides, what would I have to talk about? I can't imagine myself settling to a daily routine of a little light gardening and games of Patience.'

'It's a shame that one has to work to make oneself interesting,' Aunt Temperance observed.

'How is the school, Agnes?' Aunt Marjorie went on, ignoring the slight.

'It's much the same,' Ma said. 'Rose is a willing and able pupil teacher.'

'Thank you,' Rose said, her cheeks growing warm at Ma's compliment.

'She will be ready to take it on when I retire,' Ma said.

Rose felt awkward on hearing the pride in her mother's voice. She liked teaching the younger children, but she didn't see education as her future. She would like a husband and family of her own, and it would take a very special man to allow his wife to work instead of keeping house, as Pa did with Ma. Equally, she didn't want to end up on the shelf like her spinster aunt.

'Tell me, Oliver, how is business at the tannery?' Aunt Marjorie asked.

'Ah, life is good. The leather market is as buoyant as a cork – the butts are selling more briskly than ever.' Pa grinned and Rose smiled back. 'Our leather is always in great demand, and only yesterday, I met with two potential new customers. In fact, I'm looking to increase the supply of hides as a consequence. We can't depend on our local suppliers to keep pace with our requirements.'

'Mr Kingsley says that the availability of imported hides threatens to wreck the home market,' Aunt Temperance said.

'I have no issue with it. I've heard that the hides from Argentina are bigger and of better quality than those I can get here. Our grandfather would have embraced change if it was for the good of the business.' Pa smiled again. 'I'll never weary of seeing the butts lifted out of the pits and hung up to dry until they're ready to be made into boots fit for our beloved Queen Victoria, and portmanteaux fit for gentlemen.' He looked at Minnie and Rose, his expression suddenly stern.

'Remember, my dears, that there are true gentlemen and then there are those who purport to be gentlemen.'

'How do you tell the difference, Pa?' Rose asked.

'Well, it isn't as simple as looking at the label on his luggage to see where it was made and by whom. Having the means to purchase a luxury item made by royal warrant is no guarantee of a person's manners and character. You have to observe how he interacts with his acquaintances and treats his servants. You have to take time to dig deep and find out what's really in his heart.'

'Well said,' Aunt Marjorie exclaimed, clasping her hands together.

'They are wise words,' Aunt Temperance agreed. 'I disagree, though, on using one's attitude to one's servants as a measure of manners. One shouldn't treat servants as friends. There should always be a respectful distance maintained between employer and maid.'

'They are people, made from the same flesh and blood as anyone else,' Ma said. 'I shall treat our servants as I see fit. I must be doing something right, mustn't I? Mrs Dunn has been housekeeper at Willow Place since Evie left.'

'How long ago was that? Remind me,' Aunt Marjorie said.

Ma paused to think for a moment. 'Evie married and moved away to be nearer her family when Rose was about three, if I remember rightly. We're still in touch.'

Rose had a vague recollection of their previous housekeeper, a kind woman who had spoken with a country accent.

'Please may I trouble you for a little more brawn?' Aunt Marjorie asked.

'Of course.' Pa served her two more slices. 'Minnie?' The brawn was soon demolished.

'Mrs Dunn has done us proud,' Aunt Marjorie said, scraping her plate.

'What shall we do tomorrow after church?' Pa asked, changing the subject and reminding Rose that her aunt was staying for two more nights before returning to Ramsgate by train.

'Oh, you must come with us to worship at the cathedral,' Aunt Temperance said. 'You don't want to go to St Mildred's. Oliver, I have no idea why you continue to frequent that church when you have your position to maintain.'

'What position?' Pa said, trying not to smile.

'You are an esteemed member of society – look at your medals and the recognition you've received for your charitable deeds – your work for the Sanitary Society, for

15

example. You should make the most of it.' Her voice rose with excitement. 'You could end up an alderman of the city, even mayor.'

'I like St Mildred's. It's where our grandfather worshipped and where he took us every Sunday when we were younger and before you got this bee in your bonnet about the cathedral. I feel welcome there. One may worship wherever one feels close to God.'

'Oh, suit yourself.' Aunt Temperance shrugged her bony shoulders. 'You are a fool.'

'And you are misguided in thinking that I would seek fame in return for my services to the poor and disadvantaged in our society,' Pa said a little sharply.

Arthur started to choke. Ma patted him on the back and he coughed up a pickled onion.

'You two are like Minnie and Donald, always bickering,' Ma observed cheerfully. 'Let's have some cake. Mrs Dunn has been busy baking.'

Their attention turned to fruit cake with almonds, cups of tea and the gifts Aunt Marjorie had brought for their curiosity cabinet in the parlour at Willow Place. She fetched them from her luggage and passed them around the table: a tiny silver thimble; a jar of shells; a fine geode filled with rose quartz crystals. She brought sweets too, rose rock and mint drops, which they shared between them.

Pa always said they were a patchwork family stitched together by circumstance, and people could say what they liked about them because there was nothing wrong in that. The presence of her aunts, sparring like two gamecocks, their words like spurs, reminded Rose that they were a happy family, but no ordinary one.

Chapter Two

Making the Ordinary Extraordinary

Aunt Marjorie went back to Ramsgate and life returned to normal. On the first Monday morning of July, Rose was standing in the hall at Willow Place, waiting for Donald as she had on so many other Monday mornings in the past.

Minnie would never win a prize for attendance, nor would Donald win one for punctuality, she thought. He had disappeared after breakfast with Pa and Arthur while Ma had gone ahead to open the school. Eventually she gave up on him and went into the parlour to say goodbye to Minnie.

'Donald is green with envy,' Minnie said from the window seat where she was sewing buttons on to one of Arthur's shirts. 'He wishes Ma had given him the day off school.'

'He's a lazy tyke,' Rose said. 'Minnie, what's wrong with you? Are you in pain?'

'Ma said I looked peaky. She thought it best that I had a day off, although for my sins, she has left me with a pile of mending and socks to darn.'

Minnie had given them many frights: the ague, quinsy and croup. She had always been delicate, more fragile than the rest of them, and a little slow of thought, a feature that Ma had mourned for many years. Rumour had it that she had been dropped on her head on the day she was born. Rose suspected that it had been one of those

17

mysteries created by families to cover up a weakness, a difference. No one had actually confessed to dropping her. Had it been Ma, under the influence of the chloroform she had been given for the pain of childbirth? Or had the doctor been so busy looking out for Donald that he had omitted to take proper care of Minnie?

'Is Ma going to send for the doctor this time?' Rose asked, throwing a shawl over her modest blue dress and tying the ribbons of her bonnet.

'I told her she mustn't.'

'And I concur,' Rose smiled as she fastened the buckles on her fine leather shoes. The last time Doctor Norris had attended her sister, he'd diagnosed lack of blood and costiveness. The cure for the former was a diet of meat and for the latter, a weekly laxative purgation. It was no wonder Minnie didn't want to see him again.

Rose left her sister threading her needle. She walked out of the house and down the drive, glancing back briefly at the black and white timber-framed building. Willow Place had three storeys stacked unevenly on top of one another, giving the impression that they might topple over at any moment.

Rose crossed the street into the yard, passing the sign that read in freshly painted gold lettering on black: *Cheevers' Tannery: Estd 1798 for the best leather, natural and dyed. Enquire within*, and slipped in through one of the high gates which had been opened for deliveries.

Two workers, dressed in stained leather aprons and carrying pipes and tea cans at their waists, were unloading hides from a cart, sending up clouds of flies. Rose pressed a handkerchief to her nose. She had never become completely accustomed to the smells and sights of Pa's business.

Treading carefully across the slippery stones, she caught sight of Arthur who was tipping a bucket of powdered bark into one of the pits. Donald was there too, stirring the bark into the water with a wooden pole a head taller than he was.

'Donald,' she called. 'It's time you weren't here.'

He paused, looked up and gave her a rueful grin.

'Donald!' she repeated more forcefully.

He laid down the pole and ambled across to her with his hands in his pockets.

'Arthur said I could help him today,' he muttered as she gently cuffed his ears.

'Well, he shouldn't have done,' she said loudly for her elder brother's benefit.

Arthur glanced at her, a glint of humour in his eyes.

'Give the lad a break.'

'You know what Ma says. The three R's come before anything else.'

'I can read and write, and recite my times tables,' Donald said. 'In't that enow?'

Rose frowned at him and he quickly reverted to the Queen's English.

'I'm twelve years old and I'm ready to work all hours like Pa and Arthur here,' he went on.

'I think Ma places too much store by it,' Arthur contributed. 'I can't see the point in l'arning unless it serves a purpose. I've never been asked to multiply seven hides by seven, for example. Although I'm sure Pa would appreciate it – if it were physically possible.' He chuckled.

'You see. Arthur agrees with me,' Donald piped up.

'You're both wrong.' Rose shared Ma's view that you never knew when you might need a little learning. Her eyes settled on Donald's collar. 'Look at your shirt. It's filthy.'

'Who cares when I have to mix with the maggoty boys at school?' he said, setting his mouth in a stubborn straight line.

'You mean the boys from the Rookery? Baxter and his brothers?'

Donald nodded.

'You mustn't speak of them like that,' Rose said.

'It's the truth.'

'They are boys, the same as you, but they haven't had much luck.' Rose knew that their mother was a lunatic and their father was struggling to keep them fed and clothed with his meagre takings as a bone-picker and rag-gatherer.

'You must go to school to learn to be kinder, Donald,' Arthur said softly. 'I remember being like one of those boys, starvin' and without hope. I started work when I was seven, helping my dearly departed mother by collecting and delivering laundry, cutting the trimmin's from the hides here at the tannery and selling them on, and running errands for the Spodes.'

'Who were they? I don't recognise the name,' Rose said, shading her eyes from the sun.

'They were screevers. They had years conning money out of innocent people with fakements and petitions, signed with false names. Anyway, what I'm trying to say is that if it hadn't been for Ma and Pa taking me in when my real ma passed, who knows what would have happened to me?'

'I'm sorry,' Donald said, apparently contrite. He did have a heart, Rose thought fondly. He just found it harder than some to show it.

'My older brother Bert started out the same before Pa gave him a proper job as a tanner.'

'What happened to him then?' Donald said, squinting.

'He's a few years older than me. There was some kind of trouble and he went to London to make his fortune out of bricklaying,' Arthur said wistfully.

'Did he succeed?' Donald asked.

'I think he must have done very well for himself with all the building works going on, but I haven't heard from him – he isn't one for writing letters.'

'I'm sure that I'd make my fortune if I went to London,' Donald said, rather too full of his self-importance. Ma spoiled him, in Rose's opinion, or maybe being the youngest of the Cheevers family, he felt that he had to make himself noticed.

'There's no need for you to go running away to London, or anywhere else,' Rose scolded him. 'You and Arthur will end up running the business—' After Pa has gone, she was going to add, but that seemed an impossible thought. 'Come along.' She held out her hand, but Donald didn't take it. He was too old for that now, she thought with regret. She had helped Ma bring the twins up since they were infants and couldn't count how many times Donald had linked his sticky fingers through hers. 'Quickly.'

'I'll see you both later.' Arthur picked up the pole that Donald had laid down. 'I'd better stir my stumps.'

'So you had. Never a truer word has been spoken.'

Rose turned at the sound of Pa's deep guffaw. He was striding across the yard towards them, wearing a white coat over his suit.

'Oh, here's the gaffer,' Arthur said. 'Morning, Pa.'

'What's all this? Shouldn't you and Donald be at the schoolhouse by now?' their father went on, addressing Rose.

'I'd have been there already if it wasn't for this one.'

'You've been of great help, Donald, but it's time you left,' Pa said. 'Arthur, I need you in my office – I'd like you to sit in on this morning's meeting with Mr Kingsley and the agent who's calling to discuss the supply of hides from Argentina. Off to school, you two.'

'I suppose we have to,' Donald sighed.

'Yes, we do,' Rose said firmly, and they made their way back across the yard to the gates.

As they headed along the street, Donald – fearing Ma's wrath – ran off around the corner towards number 4 Riverside, one of the terraced cottages that belonged to the tannery. Rose followed him, but the sound of conversation caught her ear.

A woman's voice drifted from a narrow passageway between two of the unkempt houses on the far side of the road.

'I've always found it odd that a wife goes out to work when she has a husband who makes a good living.'

'If I were her and I had the chance of being a lady of leisure, I'd take it,' came another voice.

'She should be at 'ome with 'er children. That boy of theirs has been allowed to run riot on the streets for years. 'Is parents are far too soft on 'im.'

'Perhaps Mrs Cheevers don't want to spend more time than is necessary with 'er husband.'

'Oh, I don't know about that. He's a handsome man with a fine countenance.'

'Don't let 'er hear you say that, Mrs Couch. She's an uncommon woman,' said the other.

'Do you mean rare in respect of being employed, or refined? For she is most respectable in her appearance and manners, and she speaks like a lady.'

'It was strange how she ended up here with Mr Cheevers.'

'Oh, you are a tattletale.' Both women paused. 'Go on.'

'She fell on some kind of hard times – she were in the family way when they picked her up from by the Westgate.'

'Really?'

'You must have 'eard.'

'It's history. I don't like to hear anyone talk badly of her when she's bin so good to us. Our Michael couldn't

22

add two and two together before she gave him a place over the way there.'

'Letters and numbers don't mean nothing. What use is l'arning? While your Michael is in the schoolroom, he could be earning a few bob with his father on the barrer.'

'He does his bit when he i'n't at school. Mrs Cheevers said she'll borrer us the money for 'im to buy a decent suit in future so he can apply to become a clerk. Just think of that.' The women emerged from the passageway and Rose hurried on, feeling guilty for eavesdropping.

She knew her history. Arthur was adopted, while the twins were the offspring of Pa's loins, and Rose was their half-sister. Ma was the common thread running through the fabric of their family.

Having arrived at school, Rose pushed the door open and walked straight into the classroom where the girls sat on one side and the boys on the other. The pupils, aged between five and fourteen, looked up from their slates and papers and Rose did a quick head count – there were only ten of the fifteen registered children there.

Ma tapped her stick against the blackboard.

'Look this way,' she ordered. 'You're supposed to be practising your letters.'

Rose noticed Donald pick up his pencil and start to write. When she had been a pupil of about ten years old, Ma had employed another teacher to work alongside her. Miss Clements's cane had come down on the back of Donald's hand with a loud crack for writing with his left hand, and Ma had sent her packing, saying it was in some people's natures to be back to front.

'It would be much to their advantage if you would assist the younger ones, Miss Cheevers,' Ma said.

'Of course.' Rose removed her hat and shawl and hung them on one of the hooks at the far end of the schoolroom before joining her pupils. She helped them clean their slates with a rag, and started them off on writing their names in their best handwriting.

'Well done, Ada,' she said, admiring her copperplate letters. 'There is definitely some improvement here, Baxter.' She pointed to his letter B, feeling sorry for him because it wasn't really very good. She was about to ask him to rub it out and start again, but stopped when she noticed his skinny arms, the nits crawling through his hair, and an angry purple bruise on his cheek. 'Oh,' she gasped. 'What happened to you?'

'Nothing, miss,' he whispered.

'Somebody has hurt you.'

'I fell over.' A tear rolled down his cheek.

''Is pa thumped him one,' Ada interrupted. 'I sin 'im.'

'Hold your tongue! 'E told me not to say nothin',' Baxter snapped furiously.

'Is everything all right, Rose?' she heard Ma ask from the front of the room.

'Yes, thank you,' she said, not wanting to draw any more attention to Baxter. She was shocked and upset – she knew that the boys from the Rookery lived in straitened circumstances, but hadn't realised they were subject to beatings.

Once the younger children had practised their letters sufficiently, Rose took them out to the schoolyard for a drill. She put them through their paces then let them play and use the outside privy.

'Why did your father hit you?' she asked Baxter later, having drawn him away from the rest of the class.

'He was angry because I took the end of the b-b-bread,' he stammered as the other children danced in a circle, singing 'Ring-a-ring o' rosies'. 'I di'n't mean to steal it – I was faint with hunger and there was nothin' else.'

24

'It's wrong to steal,' Rose said, but then she felt bad because she didn't know what it was like to be that desperate for food. There was always something – a piece of cake, cheese or bread – in the pantry at Willow Place. Ma insisted that Mrs Dunn should keep plenty of provisions in reserve.

'I know that, miss, but when yer belly feels like it's being gnawed by rats and your legs won't 'old you up no more ...' His voice faded.

It wasn't fair, she thought, that circumstances forced Baxter and his brothers to suffer like this. She had seen their father once or twice, a man with sunken eyes, hollowed cheeks and no teeth, his back bowed with cares. He was usually armed with a bag and a stick with a hook on the end that he used for scraping in the dirt looking for horseshoe nails or digging through the heaps of ash tipped out on to the street for anything to sell.

She wondered what had happened to have brought the family to that. In spite of Arthur's argument that it was sheer misfortune that brought people low, she couldn't help thinking that their own actions must have played a part in it.

Ma rang the bell, calling them back indoors so that the older pupils could take their turn to enjoy the summer sunshine. Rose returned to the classroom and as the day grew hotter, the stench of the tannery and the River Stour grew more intense, until it filled her throat and settled in her chest. She called Baxter up to help her demonstrate simple sums with the abacus, but his heart wasn't in it.

'Since when has five plus four equalled eleven?' she said in exasperation when he failed to get it right for the third time in a row. He could hardly look at her. 'I'm sorry. It isn't one of your better days, is it?'

He shook his head slowly.

'Sit down,' she said. 'Ada, you take a turn.'

They broke off at midday when the pupils left for home. Rose went to check on Minnie while Ma attended to the school accounts. At two, they returned to their lessons.

'You did well today, Rose. Just be wary of offering excessive praise,' Ma reminded her later when they had locked up the school a little earlier than usual for the day and were making their way back home from Riverside. They crossed the road to avoid a puddle that had collected in the gutter as a man drove his cart past them, flicking his whip over his horse's haunches while a cockerel crowed from a basket in the back. They turned the corner and Donald ran ahead, disappearing off to the right into the tan yard while Rose continued with Ma along the street to Willow Place. 'Remember that it must be earned.'

'Yes, Ma, but these were exceptional circumstances. I wanted to cheer Baxter up after I found out that his father had hit him for taking bread.'

'Pa has already had a word with him about that. He says if we trouble him again, he'll take the boys out of school altogether and set them to work.'

'They aren't yet twelve. It's against the law.'

'There is nobody willing to police it,' Ma said as Rose opened the five-barred gate that fronted the pebbled drive leading to the house. 'It's generally understood that poor families can't exist without support from their sons and daughters.'

'I'm scared for him and his brothers,' Rose said.

'I know you are – I am too, but what else can we do, apart from encourage him to remain in education for as long as it takes for him to learn the skills to better himself? We must be thankful that he is still on the register.'

'May I bring some food into school for him tomorrow?' Rose asked, refusing to let the matter rest.

Ma thought for a moment. 'Yes, that's a kind thought. Have a word with Mrs Dunn. Run along now. I'm going to have a lie-down until Pa gets home.'

Rose watched her mother take off her shoes, put on her slippers and go upstairs. She heard the bedroom door close and the floorboards creak as she made her way to the bed.

'Rose,' she heard Arthur whisper to her left. 'Will you give me your opinion?'

She looked across to where he had emerged into the hall from the kitchen.

'You're home early.'

'I know. Pa let me go. I have an appointment with Tabby's father at five.'

'Oh, Arthur!'

'I don't know how it will go,' he said apprehensively. 'Do I look all right?'

He had bathed and trimmed his beard, and dressed in his suit, a white shirt and the shiniest shoes she had ever seen. His hair gleamed, his face glowed from where he'd been steaming his skin with sulphur to rid it of pimples and flesh-worms, and he had a nervous rash at the side of his neck.

'You look very well,' she said, moving forward to straighten his starched collar.

'Thank you,' he said. 'I'd better go. I don't want to be late.'

She wished him luck – not that he needed it, she thought as she closed the front door behind him. She had never seen him looking so handsome.

The evening passed slowly with everyone on tenter-hooks waiting for Arthur to return.

After dinner, Rose and Minnie went up to the room they shared in the attic. Rose knelt on a chair, looking out of the open window and listening to the distant clatter of dishes in the scullery sink as Jane washed up.

'There's no sign of him,' she said, turning to face her sister who was sitting on the edge of the bed, cutting scraps of patterned cotton into hexagons and spreading them across the coverlet.

They both looked up as the door flew open.

'Donald!' Rose exclaimed. 'You know you aren't allowed in here.'

'Oh, don't be so stuffy. Ma and Pa are almost asleep in their chairs in the parlour, and I'm stuck indoors with nothing to do. It's very dull.'

'It serves you right for breaking your curfew last night,' Rose said.

'It wasn't my fault that Joe got hit on the conk with the ball when we were playing cricket. It wouldn't stop bleeding so I went to his ma's to borrow a key to drop down the back of his neck.'

'What for?' Rose asked.

'To stop it, of course. It worked a treat.' He changed the subject. 'Is Arthur back yet?'

'There's no sign of him.'

'Perhaps he hasn't passed muster with Mr Miskin,' Donald said brightly. 'Is that the same patchwork you started making months ago?'

Rose nodded. She and Minnie had begun the patchwork in the winter months, cutting and sewing by the light of an oil lamp, but Minnie had complained that her eyes hurt and they'd put their grand design aside for a while.

Donald grinned. 'You'll never finish it.'

'Of course we will,' Minnie said, sounding indignant.

'I'll eat my hat if you do.' He meant his cloth cap with the japanned cardboard peak.

'Aren't you being a little hasty?' Rose asked. 'You know how Minnie's fingers fly when it comes to sewing.'

'Will you take your hat with salt and pepper?' Minnie asked mischievously.

Donald chuckled. 'I won't need to. It will never happen. What can I do?'

'You can take a turn being lookout.' Rose moved away from the window and Donald rested his elbows on the sill. Minnie handed over the scissors so Rose could carry on with the cutting while she picked up a needle and thread, slipped Ma's silver thimble on to her index finger and began to sew.

'If Arthur brings good news, we will give the patchwork to him and Tabby as a wedding present,' Minnie said, her eyes shining.

'What if Mr Miskin sends him away with a flea in his ear?' Donald asked.

'I don't think he'll do that,' Rose said. 'For one, our Arthur is a good catch – he has prospects. Second, he has been courting Tabby for well over a year, and I can't imagine that her father would have allowed that to continue if he thought he'd make an unsuitable husband. Third, Arthur is in love with her – Mr Miskin can have no doubt on that score.'

'He's on his way. He's at the gate!' Donald exclaimed.

Rose threw down the scissors, Minnie stuck her needle in the pincushion and they chased after their brother down the two flights of stairs to the hall where Ma and Pa had beaten them to the front door.

Arthur was on the step, his brow furrowed and his shoulders slumped. Rose's heart sank. His appointment with the apothecary hadn't gone the way he'd wanted.

'Oh, Arthur,' Ma gasped.

'I'm sorry, son,' Pa said sadly. 'I never thought—'

'I got you all then, didn't I?' Arthur said, breaking into a huge grin. 'Tabby's pa gave me permission to ask for her hand in marriage, and she said yes.'

'Oh,' Ma squealed. 'How wonderful!' She threw her arms around him, making him blush.

'Tabby's waiting at the gate,' he said, extricating himself from Ma's embrace. 'Let me fetch her,' he went on as Pa grasped his hand and pumped it up and down, but there was no need because she was already at the door.

Rose looked up to Miss Miskin – she was not what Ma described as a classical beauty with her mousy hair and slightly sallow skin, but she had lively eyes, an expressive mouth and a womanly figure. She was respectful and quietly spoken – in fact, Rose didn't think she would say boo to a goose. Ma's opinion was that this was a positive attribute, but Pa disagreed.

'Come in, my dear,' Pa said, releasing Arthur's hand. 'Congratulations! I look forward to welcoming you into our family.'

'She will become Mrs Arthur Fortune,' Arthur said, and Pa's face fell.

Rose's brow tightened. What did he mean?

'You are right, of course,' Pa said, growing more cheerful again. 'I always think of you as one of us, by virtue of having brought you up from the age of eight.'

'The name on my birth certificate remains that of my natural parents,' Arthur said.

'You don't have to register a change of name,' Pa said. 'You can take whatever name you like as long as you don't do it with intent to defraud or break the law. There is no reason why Miss Miskin shouldn't become Mrs Arthur Cheevers. In fact, there is no compulsion to marry – it is society that dictates—'

'Oh, don't worry about that now,' Ma said, interrupting. 'Arthur, tell us what happened. What did Tabby's pa say?'

Arthur moved to Miss Miskin's side and took her hand.

'He invited me into his office behind the dispensary, and offered me a brandy. I asked him the question, and blow me down, he said yes. Then he sent me to the parlour where Tabby was waiting. I was dead nervous, all of a quiver, and I could hardly get the words out, but she ... well, you already know what she said.'

'We must call on your parents tomorrow,' Ma said. 'And Arthur, you will need to choose an engagement ring, according to Tabby's preference. Oh, and we must write to Aunt Marjorie, and what about your brother, Bert? We have to invite him. You do have his address?'

'He hasn't been in touch with anyone around here since he left Canterbury. I don't know if he's alive or dead.'

'Well, I'd like to assume the former. It would be lovely if he came for the wedding,' Ma said. 'Your suit, Arthur. It has seen better days ...'

Rose noticed how Pa slid his arm around her waist.

'Let us live one day at a time,' he smiled. 'We will revel in this pleasure for a little while. The arrangements can be made at leisure.'

'But there is so much to do.'

'Agnes, Tabby will want to organise her wedding with her mother. We mustn't interfere.'

'We are thinking of holding the wedding in August,' Arthur said.

'That soon? Is there something you aren't telling us?' Ma asked.

'No, certainly not.' Arthur blushed and Tabby gazed at the bow on the toe of her tiny kid walking shoe.

'Well, you be careful.'

'Leave him alone,' Pa said. 'Come on, my love. It is past nine o'clock.' He lowered his voice to a whisper that everyone could hear. 'Let's go and check them bedsprings.'

Rose wasn't sure what he meant, but felt that it was best not to ask.

On her way upstairs, she gazed at the family pictured in the sepia cabinet card which stood on the chiffonier in the hallway. She recalled the occasion when they had gone dressed in their Sunday best to the photographic studio in the centre of Canterbury, the sign outside it proclaiming, *Making the ordinary extraordinary*.

They'd had to wait for the photographer to set up the sitting to his satisfaction before he returned to the camera and disappeared behind the cloth to take their picture. Each time he was ready, Arthur had moved, fidgeting with his scratchy collar, or Minnie had sneezed, or Ma would have sat back on her chair to find a more comfortable position, or Rose's eyes would have wandered, looking at all the pictures on the panelled walls.

'Oh no, that will not do. It is not aesthetically pleasing,' the photographer kept repeating while Pa constantly looked at his pocket watch, saying, 'We really must get on. I have business to attend to,' when really he hadn't because he'd been up early in the morning to get his work done in advance.

Rose had thought she'd managed to look both sophisticated and alluring, but was disappointed when she'd seen the printed card. Pa looked heroic wearing his medal for saving the drowning men. Ma looked severe while Arthur looked completely nonplussed. Donald was scowling because at the last minute Ma had spat on her lace handkerchief and wiped his face, and Minnie appeared to be about to break into a big grin.

Rose felt a strange sense of yearning. She was looking forward to the wedding, and was joyful for Arthur, but soon he would be gone from Willow Place, and their family would never be quite the same again. One day, they would all have left the nest.

Chapter Three

St Lubbock's Day

The preparations for Arthur and Tabby's wedding continued apace over the next three weeks when Ma closed the school for a short summer break. Miss Miskin asked Rose and Minnie to act as her bridesmaids and Pa offered to buy their outfits for the big day – simple white dresses with short veils.

On the last Sunday in July, the Cheevers family were on their way to church to hear the vicar reading the banns for the third and final time.

'Ma, I wish you had let me stay at home with Minnie.' Rose was wearing her best bonnet and grey silk dress as they walked along Stour Street, past the alleyways and timber-framed houses. A filthy sludge was slowly seeping along the drains and gullies, but the road itself was dry so there was no need for the skirt-lifter that she kept in her pocket.

'Jane is with her. She has a headache from too much sewing late at night – I know you two have been awake all hours trying to get the patchwork finished.'

'Hush,' Rose said quickly, looking towards Arthur who was strolling along with his hands in his pockets, his eyes fixed straight ahead as if he was in a world of his own. 'It's supposed to be a surprise.' Her fingers were sore from trying to complete the patchwork in time for the wedding, and she couldn't see how they would get it done now that Ma had thwarted her plot to stay behind.

'Don't worry, dear. There's no cause for alarm over Minnie. It is just a precaution,' Ma said, taking Rose's arm. Her wedding ring flashed from her finger – she squeezed it on just once a week for their visit to St Mildred's.

'My sister pecks at her food like a bird,' Donald cut in as Pa walked ahead of them. 'She has always been like this – it's a storm in a teacup.'

Rose didn't think so – there were occasions when Minnie was genuinely unwell. It just happened that this wasn't one of them.

'Well, I think we should take her to the seaside for some air,' Pa said over his shoulder. 'It will do us all good.'

Rose's heart leapt. 'We could go on St Lubbock's Day – the tannery will be closed.'

'There'll be no school that day either.' Donald kicked a stone, bouncing it across the pavement.

'May we go by train, Pa?' Rose said.

'Oh, I don't know about that,' Ma said.

'But we must,' Pa said. 'Rose and the twins haven't travelled by rail before. It will be quite an experience. Agnes, where is your sense of adventure?'

'I'm afraid it has escaped me,' Ma said as a gaggle of urchins came pelting along the street.

'Watch yourselves!' Pa bellowed. 'What do you think you're doing, tearing about like wild animals on the Sabbath?'

Four of them raced on past but one stopped.

'Mind your manners. There are ladies present,' Pa said, and the boy took off his cap.

It was Baxter.

34

'M-m-mornin', sir. Mornin', Mrs Cheevers. Good day, Miss Cheevers, an' all,' he stammered before running off after his friends.

They carried on along Church Lane where St Mildred's came into view at the end of a short avenue of lime trees.

'Good morning, Mr and Mrs Cheevers,' an old woman said as they walked past her. She was a local landlady, renowned for her sharp business practices and occasional acts of kindness. Rose never knew quite how to take her.

'The greetings of the hour, Mrs Hamilton,' Pa said cheerily. 'It is unusual to see you here on a Sunday.'

'As you grow older, you find more to thank the Lord for, and start to worry you might not have done enough to deserve your place in Heaven.'

Ma acknowledged Mrs Hamilton briefly as they went on to catch up with the Miskins who were on the way to church as well. Tabby nodded shyly and fell back to be at Arthur's side. Rose felt a pang of – what was it? she wondered. Yearning and a touch of envy? She wished she was walking with her sweetheart, the man she would marry. She smiled to herself. The problem was that she hadn't met him yet.

'Good morning, Mr Miskin,' Pa greeted the apothecary. 'It is another beautiful day.'

'Indeed,' Mr Miskin responded. He was about forty-five years old and had a purple birthmark across one side of his face. His suit trousers were too short, exposing his socks and giving him a rather comical appearance. 'How is business?'

'I have to say that it is excellent. We have just celebrated the delivery of the first batches of hides all the way from Argentina, and they are top notch,' Pa said. 'It will be eighteen months or so until we reap the rewards, but I'm confident that we'll produce leather that's better than ever.'

Mr Miskin nodded and smiled, as well he might, Rose thought, for his daughter's financial security would depend on the success of the tannery once she was married. He changed the subject.

'I've heard much about your recent efforts with the Sanitary Committee. I wish we'd had more progress with the state of the river – I fear more outbreaks of cholera like that of 'sixty-six when all those poor people fell sick and died.'

'I've done my best to rouse the local businessmen from their apathy,' Pa said, and Rose thought of how dead trout had been found floating downstream in a scum of coal tar and the effluent from the tan-pits. 'I don't think Alderman Masters is too worried – the sewage from the barracks makes his plants grow like weeds. He's managed to cultivate all kinds at his exotic nursery.'

'And then there's the issue of the dye works – that needs addressing.'

Rose knew the owner, Mr Beasley. His motto was 'we dye to live while others live to dye'.

'I hope we will soon come to an agreement on the way forward,' Pa said. 'In the meantime, we have a wedding to look forward to.'

'We have received acceptances for most of the invitations that we sent out, according to the list you gave us,' Mrs Miskin cut in. She was tall, like her daughter, but her skin had aged prematurely, her face being criss-crossed with fine lines. 'I'm counting down the days, although I'll be terribly sorry when our dear Tabitha moves out.'

'I have to confess I will be happy when this is all over,' Mr Miskin said with a smile. 'It is the only topic of conversation in the shop. I can't get on with anything.'

'Well, we are almost there. In less than two weeks' time, Tabby and Arthur will be man and wife.' Pa glanced at Rose. 'I wonder who will be next,' he teased.

'What did you mean when you said there was no compulsion to marry, Pa?' Rose asked.

'Oh, I was thinking aloud, that's all. Sometimes I think that people make too much of the institution of marriage.'

'It is the legal recognition of a couple's commitment and obligation to each other,' Mr Miskin said, looking somewhat outraged. 'Not only that, it's for the benefit of the children of that union. You would willingly make bastards of your future grandchildren?'

'Arthur and Miss Miskin have made their decision according to their beliefs. All I'm saying is that it's a shame that society expects everyone to toe the line.'

Hiding her blushes at the rather shocking turn that the conversation had taken, Rose caught up with her mother as she approached the leaning gables and arched windows of St Mildred's. Ma started to tell her and Donald how the stones that made up the walls were mixed with Roman tiles.

'Ma, how many times have you told us this before?' Donald sighed. 'It's Sunday – it's supposed to be a day of rest.'

'You should take every opportunity to improve your mind,' Ma said. 'W. G. Grace isn't merely a cricketer – I've heard that he's studying medicine. And while we're speaking of cricket, is that a ball in your pocket?'

Donald's hand flew to cover it.

'Donald?'

'I must have picked it up by mistake,' he said quickly, when he realised he'd been caught out. He cocked his head and grinned. 'At least I left the bat behind. Don't look at me like that, Ma – I won't practise my bowling down the aisle.'

'Greetings,' said the vicar, shaking Pa's hand at the church door. 'You are one short. Where is Minnie today?'

Ma bowed her head – Rose thought she was in awe of him, which was strange when Ma was normally quite confident in company.

'She is at home, sick,' Pa said lightly.

'Ah, yes. I'm sorry. We will pray for her.' Vicar Holdsworth, wearing his frock coat, waistcoat, white collar and bow tie, took both her hands and held them for what Rose felt was an uncomfortably long time. His grey hair hung in rats' tails over his elephantine ears and his nose was purple and pockmarked. His appearance had used to give Rose nightmares, until she'd been old enough to realise that he was a good man who cared for his flock, doing his best to encourage even the poorest to attend his church, even when they couldn't afford a set of clothes to keep aside for Sundays.

The Cheevers family took their seats in one of the grand oak pews, the ends of which were carved with eagles, while Arthur sat with the Miskins. Vicar Holdsworth read the banns then dwelt for a long while on a sermon about the parable of the loaves and the fishes, relating it to spiritual as well as bodily nourishment, during which Rose heard the rumble of a hungry belly. Donald, who was sitting beside her, gave her a nudge. She looked up at him and he nodded towards Ma with a twinkle in his eye. There was another rumble, louder this time. Donald grinned. Rose bit her lip to suppress a giggle.

'Shh,' Ma whispered. Rose sat up straight and forced herself to concentrate on something else. She gazed around the church, taking in the familiar sights of Sir Francis Head's tomb covered with its black marble slab, and the white wall plaque in memory of William Jackson Esq. who had died from an injury inflicted by an unruly horse. She often wondered what had happened to the horse, and had plenty of time to conjure up all kinds of possibilities.

When Vicar Holdsworth dismissed the congregation, the Cheeverses headed home for a roast dinner. Jane had cooked beef on the clockwork jack in front of the range. Ma and Pa went off to the Dane John for a stroll, Donald disappeared to find Joe, and Arthur walked out with Tabby, leaving Rose and Minnie to get on with the patchwork.

'We should embroider their names and the date of their wedding around the edge,' Minnie said. 'You can do that – your stitches are neater than mine when it comes to lettering.'

'You are better now?' Rose asked, rummaging through the sewing box for the right thread.

'I might have to have a few more headaches in the next couple of weeks if we are to get this finished.' Minnie smiled. 'It's going to be the best present ever.'

Rose gave her a hug as she walked back to her seat beside the window. Her sister could be much craftier than she appeared.

Having made progress with the embroidery in pink, red and blue silks, Rose eventually admitted defeat. 'We'll stop now. It must be time for supper.'

'I wish Pa would buy us a sewing machine. It would be so much quicker,' Minnie said.

'But would it mean as much? We have put our hearts and souls into it.' Rose snipped a long piece of thread from the border she was creating. She folded the material and slipped it under the mattress. 'Come on.'

'I'm not hungry. I'd rather carry on with this.'

'You have to eat or you will be ill. We can't have that. Let's go.'

39

Reluctantly, Minnie put the rest of the patchwork away out of sight, and they went downstairs to join the rest of the family.

Later, Rose plucked up the courage to ask Arthur about Pa and the bedsprings. He chuckled.

'You shouldn't be asking me about what goes on between a husband and wife. What do I know? I'm not yet married.'

'It's clear that you know more than I do,' Rose said, a little hurt that he wouldn't tell. 'How am I to avoid being ruined by men who may or may not be gentlemen if I don't know what that means?'

'Oh Rose, you must speak to Ma about the birds and the bees.'

She nodded, confused. Ma had told her about the dumbledores and wopsies, how to tell the difference and treat the stings of the former with soda and the latter with vinegar, but she wasn't sure how this bore any relation to the question she'd raised. She supposed she would find out one day. In the meantime, there was much to look forward to – the train trip to Whitstable and Arthur's wedding.

The first Monday of August came round quickly. Too excited to sleep, Rose had woken Minnie and they'd been patchworking since dawn when Jane knocked on the bedroom door to tell them breakfast was ready.

'Thank you,' Rose said. 'I wish you could come with us.'

'It's a kind thought, but I'm going to spend a few hours with my family. I'll be back before you, though,' Jane said, and Rose felt a little guilty that she hadn't thought about what the maid did when she wasn't at work. Jane lived in, sleeping on a mattress in the alcove in the kitchen. It wasn't ideal, but Willow Place was creaking at the seams. When Arthur moved out, Rose was going to decline Ma's offer of his old room and ask if Jane could have it instead.

'You'll be down shortly?'

Rose nodded.

'I'll put the eggs on then,' Jane said.

The Cheeverses ate breakfast together, then dispersed to prepare for their day out. Rose found her bonnet where she'd left it crumpled on a chair in the parlour after church.

'Is everyone ready?' she called from the hall. 'Hurry or we'll miss the train.'

Pa was tying his shoelaces as Donald appeared from the kitchen with his bat, ball and stumps which he had collected from the outhouse.

'Do we really need those?' Pa said, looking up as the longcase clock chimed the hour, the brass eagle glinting from the top.

'We'll need something to occupy us,' Donald said.

'It would please your ma no end if you forgot about cricket for just one day.'

Donald opened his mouth to argue, but Pa silenced him with a frown and he put everything back. Minnie and Ma came downstairs. Although Ma denounced the use of the devil's trickery, she had put a layer of cold cream, a dusting of rouge and a light covering of powder on her face. Minnie was wearing a yellow dress, one of Rose's hand-me-downs.

'It's time to go,' Rose said with a sigh of exasperation as Minnie rushed away again to find her shawl. 'I don't know why you need that when the sun is shining – it isn't cold.'

'It might be later,' Minnie replied, returning with a woollen square around her shoulders.

'Don't panic, Rose,' Arthur chuckled as he joined them, running down the steps, still fastening the buttons on his waistcoat. 'You are such a worrier.'

'What time did you get home last night?' she retorted.

'By midnight,' he said, but she knew he was fibbing.

They left Willow Place and made their way by shank's pony along St Peter's, past Tower House and the Guildhall, where a carriage went flying past, the horses' shoes sending sparks up from the slippery tarmacadam. Arthur was carrying two deckchairs while Donald, much to his disgust, was burdened with two parasols and a bag. Pa brought the picnic hamper.

'I can't wait to ride on the train,' Donald kept saying.

'How will we know where to get off?' Minnie asked.

'There is a sign at Whitstable,' Pa said as a gentleman Rose had never met doffed his hat and greeted her father. Pa nodded in return.

They crossed the river at Westgate Towers and headed along St Dunstan's Street, passing a milkmaid who was weighed down by a yoke and two churns, before they took the right-hand turn towards the station.

'I remember my grandfather telling me how there was talk of pulling the towers down way back in – it must have been 1841, when Wombwell's circus came to town,' Pa said.

'Why would they want to do that?' Donald asked.

'To make way for the elephants, but they weren't anywhere near as tall as they had expected. Oh, they were a sight to behold.'

'The best thing I ever saw was Monsieur Blondin walking the tightrope at the barracks with one of the Hussars on his back,' Arthur said and they all looked at him in envy because he was the only member of the family to have watched this feat. 'He could easily have fallen and both of them would have died.'

'I liked the fly man.' Pa had taken Rose and Arthur to the circus where they had seen him walk upside down on a glass ceiling. To this day, Rose still didn't know how he'd done it.

At the station, Pa bought first-class tickets from the ticket office.

'Isn't that a little extravagant?' Ma was wearing a large straw hat with ribbons streaming from the back, all the fashion for a trip to the seaside. 'It's a lot of money.'

'It's fine. It's a special treat,' Pa said. 'Seize the day. Cruel time is fleeing. Soon our family will be reduced from six to five with Arthur's departure. We must make the most of occasions such as these when we are all together. Hold on to my arm, dear wife. I will protect you.'

'We must stand well back to avoid being whisked off on to the rails by the rush of the incoming train,' Ma said nervously.

Pa smiled briefly, making Rose wonder if he was quite himself.

The train arrived without incident and the guard opened the doors, allowing the travellers to board while a young man unloaded punnets of watercress on to the platform.

'This is our carriage, I believe,' Pa said, shepherding his flock to their seats.

The guard slammed the doors and blew his whistle, and with a hiss of steam and a groan of effort, the train pulled out of the station. It rattled along through the outskirts of Canterbury and northwards to Tyler Hill where, with a shrill whistle, it entered a tunnel, plunging the covered carriage into darkness. Rose closed her eyes. She could smell smoke and hear Arthur and Donald laughing out loud.

'I don't like it,' Ma said.

'It is perfectly safe,' Pa shouted. 'The tunnel is only half a mile long.'

Only? Rose thought.

'It holds the weight of Tyler Hill above our heads,' Ma exclaimed. 'How can that be?'

'It is a marvellous feat of engineering,' Pa went on.

'I can see the light at the end,' Arthur said, and Rose opened her eyes again, as they shot out into the bright sunshine.

'I thought we would suffocate to death,' Ma said.

'It is very narrer, I grant you that,' Pa said, wiping a sheen of perspiration from his forehead. 'And not all that tall, no more than twelve foot.'

'I'd like to get out now,' Ma said, shifting in her seat. 'May we walk the rest of the way?'

'It would take far too long, my love,' Pa said gently. 'As soon as we reached Whitstable, it would be time to turn round and walk back.'

Rose tried to brush the black smuts from her dress.

'Don't do that,' Ma scolded. 'You'll make it ten times worse. Oh, Oliver, why did you bring us on this trip?'

Rose gazed out of the window as they travelled on through South Street where the leafy hop bines were climbing the chestnut poles in the hop gardens, and the apples and pears were ripening on the trees in the orchards.

'When are we going to get there?' Minnie asked.

'Very soon,' Pa said. 'It takes but twenty minutes from Canterbury to Whitstable. Arthur, you have got the tickets in your pocket?'

'Yes, Pa.' Arthur had wanted to spend the day with his sweetheart, but she was otherwise engaged with last-minute preparations for the wedding. Her ma was already wielding power over her future son-in-law, deciding that it wasn't appropriate for him to be present at discussions about the contents of Tabby's bottom drawer.

They reached Whitstable and disembarked. As they walked past the engine with its boiler gleaming and breathing steam, Rose was reminded of a picture of a dragon she had once seen in a book. The colourful advertisements for bathing machines and refreshments, and the sharp salt scent of the sea added to her sense that she had stepped into a fairy tale.

Ma put up her parasol and had Rose retie the ribbons on her bonnet before they left the station to walk along the hilltop lawns of Tankerton Slopes. Pa pointed out The Street, a strip of shingle on a clay bank which ran out to sea at right angles to the coast; Tankerton Tower, a castle with a bell tower and lodge; and the windmill on Borstal Hill. Rose turned back to the horizon where the sky met the water. The tide was low and there was a vast expanse of beach at her feet. The sun glinted off the water and glistened off the sand, and a flock of seagulls flew in low above their heads.

'Oliver, are you unwell?' Ma said suddenly.

Rose turned to look at her father and frowned as she noticed a bead of sweat dropping from the end of his nose.

'I have a touch of the ague, that's all,' he said with a shiver. 'I took some tincture of willow bark for it before breakfast this morning. Don't worry – the sea air is making me feel better already.'

'We should have stayed at home,' Ma said.

'How could I be so selfish when I knew how much you were all looking forward to our day out? Really, Agnes, a trip to the seaside is just what the doctor would have ordered.'

'Please may we paddle in the sea?' Minnie asked.

'We can hire a bathing machine so Ma can swim,' Pa said, making a joke as if to prove he was perfectly well.

'Oh no, Oliver,' Ma said. 'I couldn't possibly. You know I have a fear of drowning. And it isn't seemly to be seen without one's clothes in public.'

'You wouldn't be in your birthday suit,' Pa went on.

'Let's hurry,' Rose said, embarrassed at hearing her father talk of nakedness. She couldn't wait to get away and explore the beach.

They crossed the road and joined the other families and couples who were already on the shingle and sand with their chairs and blankets. Ma took some time to choose a spot she was happy with.

'We mustn't risk being left at the mercy of the tide when it turns,' she kept saying.

'We will be perfectly safe here,' Arthur reassured her. 'We will have plenty of warning.'

'Ma, I'm peckish,' Donald said, unfolding the deck-chairs.

'We will eat later,' Ma replied as Pa sat down.

'Can't we have a little something now? We've brought enough food for an army,' Donald asked as Rose and Minnie took off their shoes and stockings. They always had the best shoes in Canterbury, according to Pa who polished them every Sunday and left them in a row inside the front door ready for the rest of the week.

'You heard what your ma said,' Pa said sharply.

It was unusual for him, Rose thought. She wondered if the sea air was actually disagreeing with him instead of having the desired effect.

'Come on, Minnie.' She picked up her parasol, opened it and danced across the beach, twirling it above her head with the twins laughing as they ran alongside her. They left three rows of footprints behind them, among the curly worm casts, cockles and razor shells scattered across the flat sand.

Rose hesitated when she reached the water, letting the almost imperceptible waves lap at her toes before hitching up her skirts and wading in up to her ankles and then her calves. She watched a young woman emerge from a bathing machine into the sea a little further out, her body covered by a shapeless gown. She wished she could swim and splash about in the waves, but she knew that Ma would never allow it.

Minnie soon tired of paddling, and turned her attention to building a sandcastle with a moat with her bare hands and a piece of driftwood. Rose joined her to decorate it with shells and pebbles. As they sat back on their heels to admire their handiwork, Donald placed a dead starfish on the top.

Minnie screamed.

'Hush,' Rose said. 'You are drawing attention to us. Donald, what did you do that for? I think you have deliberately set out to upset your sisters.' But all he did was laugh. 'Sometimes I despair of you,' she went on, but Minnie's face was such a picture that Rose burst out laughing too, and eventually Minnie joined in.

Something caught Rose's eye further up the beach. Arthur was waving at them. She waved back. He began to holler, but she couldn't hear what he was saying.

'We should go and see if everything is all right,' she said. 'Come on, Minnie. And you, Donald.'

They walked back across the sand to find Arthur offering Pa a drink of lemonade.

'Our father isn't well,' he said, looking up as Pa refused it with a shake of his head before he pressed a handkerchief to his mouth and coughed.

'Is that blood?' Ma's eyes were wide with alarm at the sight of the drops of scarlet soaking into the white cloth. 'It is, isn't it? You've burst a blood vessel.'

Pa couldn't deny it.

'It's only a small one,' he muttered.

'You are unwell. You must see a physician,' Ma said.

'I don't think so, not for a scratchy throat and a touch of the ague. I'm not saying that all medical men are quacks, but—'

'Promise me for my peace of mind that you will call Doctor Norris,' Ma interrupted.

'Oh, you are such a nag,' he said lightly, but his words disappeared into another wracking cough. 'This will pass, but I promise if I'm still bad in the morning, I'll send for him. It will pain me to do so, though, considering his charges.'

'You mustn't think about the bill – you can't put a price on your health. Oliver, we should go straight home.'

'Oh Ma, do we have to?' Minnie whined.

'It seems a shame to hurry back when we've only just got here,' Donald added.

'We should go back if that is Pa's wish,' Rose said.

'I don't want to spoil our day,' Pa decided. 'We will make the most of our tickets. Ma and I will retire to the tearoom – I'll feel better when I'm out of the sun. Meet us there at four o'clock.'

'Are you sure?' Ma said, helping Donald pack their belongings and fold the chairs.

'Absolutely.' As Pa stood up, he seemed to lose his balance and totter into Arthur, who grabbed him by the arm and steadied him. 'Thank you, son.'

'What about the picnic?' Donald asked.

'You take the basket,' Ma said. 'Your father seems to have lost his appetite, and to be honest, so have I.'

Rose, Arthur and the twins ate their food on the beach, then walked along the seafront where they bought a pot of winkles from one of the stalls.

'Oh, I don't like the look of those,' Minnie exclaimed, when Donald offered her the contents of a shell on the end of a pin.

'I'm not sure either,' Rose said.

'I dare you,' Donald challenged her. 'Cowardy-custard,' he went on when she refused.

'Don't call me that,' she cried, a little hurt. She wasn't a coward. 'I'll have it.' She took the winkle and ate it, pleasantly surprised by its salty flavour, although not so keen on its texture.

'Another one?' Donald asked.

She declined.

'I'll 'ave them then.' Arthur snatched the pot from Donald's grasp and whisked it out of his reach. They laughed and scuffled until they reached a crowd of people standing on the pavement with their backs to them.

'What's going on?' Minnie asked, and Donald bundled his way through, taking Rose and Minnie with him.

'It's Punch and Judy,' Arthur said from behind them. Rose noticed him searching in his pocket for coins to pay the bottler who was collecting the money from the audience in payment for watching the performance, before she turned her attention to the brightly coloured booth which stood in front of them.

'That's the way to do it!' Mr Punch, a hunchback with a hooked nose, threatened to hurt puppet Judy with a stick. The crowd booed him as he received his comeuppance.

'I don't like it, Rose.' Minnie slipped her hand through her sister's and Rose gave her fingers a reassuring squeeze.

'Don't worry. Nobody is that mean in real life,' she whispered, but she couldn't help thinking of Baxter's pa. There were people like Mr Punch out there – she could only hope that their dear, innocent Minnie never came across one of them.

When the show was over, Arthur checked the pocket watch that Ma and Pa had given him on his twenty-first birthday and pronounced that it was time to meet their parents. They headed over to the tearoom, and Rose was pleased to find that Pa seemed no worse. The family wended their way along Squeeze Gut Alley before reaching the station.

'My feet are killing me,' Ma said, pausing to catch her breath before they got back on the train. 'I can't wait to be home.'

'I feel the same,' Pa said quietly. 'It's been a monsterful day, but I am worn out.'

Rose began to look forward to going to school the next morning and counting down the days until Arthur and Tabby's nuptials. The sun was still shining when they arrived home and it seemed that their family had been favoured above all others, on a pinnacle of happiness.

Chapter Four

The Power of Love

Rose walked up the path to Willow Place with her family, the taste of salt on her lips and the smell of soot in her nostrils. Donald broke away and started running towards the ducklings and their mother who were waddling across the lawn.

Ma called him back. 'You leave God's creatures alone! What are you thinking?'

'I'm sorry, Ma,' Donald said, hanging his head. 'I won't do it again.'

'I'll fetch them some bread,' Rose said.

'Don't you go wasting good food on ducks when they can fend for themselves,' Arthur said.

'I'll use the stale crusts.'

'Oh no, Mrs Dunn will want them for a bread pudding,' Ma said. 'Waste not, want not.'

Pa went on ahead to open the front door. As Rose and the others stepped inside, Jane came rushing through from the parlour, seeming flustered.

'Mr Cheevers, a stranger has called. Although I felt uneasy, he expressed a firm insistence that he was closely acquainted with you and Arthur, so I've taken the liberty of allowing him to wait indoors for you.' She paused for breath. 'I hope I did right.'

'Oh, look what happens when the cat's away. It could be any old beggar or vagabond walking in off the street,' Ma scolded as Arthur brushed past her and disappeared into the parlour. 'Jane, I'm sorry for sounding harsh – I'm a little flustered.'

'I used my initiative. I would have asked, but you were out when he turned up.'

'Oh, Bert,' Rose heard Arthur's voice. 'Is it really you? After all these years? What … Pinch me so I can believe it. Ouch. Not that hard.'

'Bert? Not Bert Fortune? He came!' Ma exclaimed. 'Oh, my dears! Jane, lay another place at the table for dinner tonight.'

'It is only cold meats and potatoes as you requested,' Jane said.

'It doesn't matter. We will open a bottle of wine to celebrate.'

Rose followed Ma and the rest of the family into the parlour where Arthur was embracing another man of very similar appearance to him – apart from being heavier around the jowls, and having a large paunch beneath his colourful silk waistcoat.

'Meet Bert, my brother,' Arthur said, grinning.

'It is wonderful to see you again,' Pa said, taking a seat.

'Mrs Cheevers found me. I don't know how she did it,' Bert smiled. 'She is quite the sleuth.'

Arthur turned to Ma.

'Your aunt and I put our heads together and put an advertisement in the newspapers in the places we thought Bert might be. We knew he'd gone into bricklaying so we made an educated guess.'

'My wife saw the notice. She said, Bert, there's someone looking for you. At first, I worried that it was something to do with the reason I left Can'erbury, but she read it out to me in full and I knew then it was to do with you, Mrs Cheevers.'

'Why didn't you write to me before?' Arthur asked. 'Why haven't you kept in touch?'

'You know why.' Bert looked somewhat embarrassed. 'I never l'arned to do no more than make my mark.'

'You could have sent word somehow.' Arthur paused and cleared his throat. 'You know that our dear mother, Mrs Fortune ...' He glanced towards Ma as if to check how she felt about him talking of their dead mother.

Bert nodded. Rose wasn't sure about him. He was older than Arthur and dressed in clothes that were more about looks than quality. He had an ostentatious gold chain dangling from his pocket, his hair was gleaming, and the ends of his moustache were neatly curled. He was like a man who had suddenly acquired money and didn't know what to do with it.

'I called on Mrs Hamilton – she told me of Ma's passing. How you found her dead in her bed and Mr Cheevers paid for her funeral, then took you in.' He paused to clear his throat. 'I'm very sorry for running away, Arthur. I wish ... oh, what's the use of wishing? You can't turn the clock back.'

'She worked herself into an early grave. She dragged that laundry up and down them stairs, and put it through the mangle outside in rain, ice and snow. And her heart broke with worry for you.' Arthur's voice softened. 'I don't blame you, though, Bert. She wouldn't have wanted us to be at each other's throats. She always thought fondly of you, even after you left.'

'I didn't deserve it.' Bert's voice cracked. 'I was a ruffian and ne'er-do-well.'

'She would have been proud to see her sons now,' Ma said gently. 'Who would have thought it, two trimmin's

boys who have grown into such fine young gentlemen?'
She turned to her daughters. 'Go and get changed.
Quickly.'

The family and their guest reconvened around the
dining-room table a short while later.

'It isn't every day that an old friend turns up at Willow
Place,' Pa said as Arthur poured wine and Jane served
lemonade. 'Bert, tell us how long you are intending to
remain in Canterbury?'

'Until the day after Arthur's wedding. That's why I'm
here. I have a room at the Rose, the hotel opposite the
Corn Exchange.'

'Oh, but you must stay with us,' Pa said.

'Thank you, but I have already made arrangements.'

'So you have made your fortune if you can afford to
stay there?' Arthur asked.

'Not a fortune exactly, but a comfortable living, better
than anything I could have dreamed of. When I left here
– under a cloud, I admit – I had a bit of luck. I talked my
way into an apprenticeship as a bricklayer, went up
through the ranks and now I'm foreman for a building
company.'

'You said you were married.' Arthur sipped at his wine.

'Oh yes, I have a loving wife and four children, two
boys and two girls.'

'You will have to bring them to see us,' Ma said. 'We
would love to meet them.'

'And one day you will. Perhaps you might honour us
with a visit sometime. We have plenty of room for guests.'
Bert continued solemnly, 'I never thought that I'd live in
a house with four bedrooms. Can you believe that, Arthur?
We have four rooms for sleeping in!'

'Do help yourselves to food.' Pa gestured towards the
platter of cold beef and ham, and the bowl of steaming

hot potatoes. 'Oh dear, I'm forgetting my manners. Who will say grace? I am not up to it. I haven't the strength.' His voice wavered, and for the first time Rose was touched by a sense of dread. Pa wasn't right at all.

'I'm dying to meet this young lady of yours,' Bert said, addressing Arthur.

'She is just like any young lady,' Donald sighed. 'They are all the same, only interested in dresses and such.' He stared at Rose and Minnie. 'Ouch,' he exclaimed when Rose kicked him under the table.

'Decorum, Rose,' Pa said. 'And Donald, you must refrain from expressing these ridiculous and unfounded opinions. You know how it upsets your ma and sisters.'

Rose regretted being caught in the act, but as far as she was concerned, Donald had deserved it.

Pa drank a whole glass of lemonade then mopped his brow with a napkin.

'I think you should be in bed, Oliver,' Ma said. 'You look completely done in.'

'You'll be able to spend more time with Bert tomorrow,' Arthur said.

'You're right. If you don't mind, I shall retire early. The sun was too hot for me today, and the soots have got into my lungs.'

Ma reached across the table and touched her husband's forehead with the back of her hand just like Rose remembered her doing to Minnie whenever she'd been unwell. She wondered if they had been looking in the wrong direction, worrying about her sister, not Pa.

'You have a fever. We'll send for the doctor first thing in the morning, if you're no better.'

'Or we can speak to Mr Miskin.' Arthur smiled. 'He'll be able to recommend a cure.'

'Please excuse me,' Pa said, standing up.

'I shall join you,' Ma said. 'Jane, please bring up some mint tea and cold water for his fever.'

'I don't need any fuss. Goodnight, all. God forbid if I'm not well for this wedding.' Pa forced a smile.

Rose didn't think there would be any testing of the bedsprings that night. She couldn't sleep. Minnie was snoring lightly and the window was open to allow the slightest breath of air into the stuffy room at the top of the house. The sound of the young men's voices drifted into her consciousness as she lay beneath a single sheet.

Arthur and Bert were sitting outside on the veranda.

'You should come and join me in London. You can bring Tabby with you.'

'Canterbury is my home. I have everything I've ever wanted or needed here,' Arthur said.

'There is more going on in the Smoke than here. The city is abuzz.'

'I can't just up and go, not after what Mr and Mrs Cheevers have done for me. Pa has taught me how to manage the tannery – I'm his right-hand man.'

'But it doesn't make you a fortune.'

'It's a good business. Leather is always in demand.'

'There's more money in building. There are houses springing up all over the place. You have to see it to believe it. Come and join me, Arthur.'

'I would feel like a traitor. No, I'm happy here. Besides, Tabby wouldn't want to leave her family behind. She was born and bred in Canterbury, like us.'

'What prospects do you have, though?'

'One day, a long way in the future, the tannery will pass to me and Donald.'

'Are you sure about that? Donald is the Cheeverses' son by blood.'

'Pa has never made any secret of his plans. It's a family business. My uncle – Mr Kingsley – is in charge of running the financial side. Pa is the gaffer, and I'm his deputy. Donald helps out in the yard when he isn't at school, or playing cricket.' Rose could hear the smile in Arthur's voice. 'What would I do with that kind of wealth anyway? There are only so many shillin's a man can spend in his lifetime.'

'Are you of sound mind?' Bert laughed. 'You're talking like a lunatic – you can never have enough money. You won't remember how Agnes – Miss Berry-Clay as she was back then – wore the most beautiful clothes and pure-white kid gloves. I remember her as a girl looking down 'er nose at me, and it made me yearn for a fortune so that nobody would ever look at me as if I was worth nothin' again.'

'Life isn't about how much you have in the way of assets. I have riches enough.'

'Where is your ambition?'

'I have none, and I think I will be all the happier for that.'

'Then you are a fool. Oh, don't look at me in that way,' Bert said. 'I've grown cynical. I've been taken advantage of more than once. I've been robbed and beaten and I've worked in return for empty promises. I don't trust no one.'

'Then I'm very sorry for you,' Arthur said.

'We've been brought up different, and that's all there is to it. I admire your loyalty to the Cheeverses, but you're still a Fortune underneath. Promise me you'll consider my offer. Speak with Miss Miskin, and give me your answer after the wedding.'

A few minutes of silence ensued before Bert began to sing. 'Out of the bed I did creep. I searched her pockets … I took the lot and locked me lady in.'

Arthur joined in. 'Now all young men wherever you be, if you meet a pretty girl, you use her free.'

Rose was surprised to hear the humour in their voices as they sung a bawdy song, 'Up to the Rigs of London Town', about a pretty girl at a house of ill-repute, before they moved on to the story of the blue-eyed lover.

'See how them London lights are gleaming through the frost and falling snow,' they sang, the sound of their low voices and haunting pitch of the music tugging at her heartstrings. She was sorry for the young woman whose lover had run away leaving her with their baby and nowhere to stay, but she felt strangely elated too. There was life beyond the tannery, school and the streets of Canterbury. She yearned to experience a little of it for herself, but she was destined to become a teacher and take on the school after Ma, or marry and settle down to run a household and bring up a family like Tabby would after she had wed Arthur later in the week.

For the first time, she wondered if that would be enough. Like Bert, she craved more – not when it came to money because she wanted for nothing in the way of material goods. The trouble was, she didn't yet know what she was looking for.

'Is Pa up and about?' Rose asked Ma the next morning. 'And where is Arthur?'

'He and your father have gone to the yard as usual. Bert returned to the Rose Hotel in the early hours of the morning and Donald should be dressed by now. Didn't you hear me yelling at him to get out of bed?' Ma smiled, but she didn't seem her usual self.

'Is Pa better then? Or are you worrying about the wedding? It's only two days away.'

'What is it with all these questions?' Ma's voice softened. 'Oh, Rose, you are such a sensitive soul. Yes, you're right. I'm a little sad that Arthur is leaving home, even though I know he will be very happy married to Tabby.'

'But we will still see him,' Rose said, recalling the conversation she had overheard the previous night – Arthur would stay on at the tannery, not go to London with Bert.

'It won't be the same, though. Soon he will have his own children to look after.'

Rose gave her mother a hug.

'I don't think your father should have gone to work today. He had a bad night, tossing and turning, and he wouldn't eat this morning. I begged him to stay indoors, but he wouldn't have it. He blames it on the whelks he ate yesterday, but he didn't have any. I wish I'd put my foot down, but you can't tell him what to do.' She changed the subject. 'Where are the twins?'

'I'm here,' Minnie said, running down the stairs with her shoes in her hand. At the same time, there was a loud thud at the front door.

'Donald!' Ma yelled. 'How many times?'

'I'm sorry, Ma,' Donald said as he opened the door. 'I was practising my bowling.'

'Put the ball away. It's time for school.' Ma fingered the back of his collar, then let him go. 'Oh, what are we going to do with you?'

Rose sighed as they left the house. In her opinion, Ma was always too quick to forgive him.

Baxter was waiting, sitting on the wall outside the school, swinging his legs and kicking at the brickwork with his heels. When he saw Rose watching him, he jumped down and stood with his hands in his pockets, his head to one side.

'Good morning, Miss Cheevers,' he said slowly.

'Good morning, Baxter.' She smiled – she would knock him into shape by the end of his time at school if it killed her.

The morning passed pleasantly enough. Rose took the little ones for reading, writing and arithmetic. Ma taught the older ones some geography and science, but after break-time, there was a loud and insistent knocking at the schoolroom door.

'Mrs Cheevers. Mrs Cheevers!' The door flew open to reveal one of the men from the tan yard.

'What is the meaning of this interruption, Mr Hales?' Ma began.

'You must come quickly,' he said, his face etched with panic.

'What is it? What has happened?' Ma touched her throat.

'The gaffer has fallen into a faint – Arthur, Mr Jones and Mr Kingsley have taken him to the house.'

Ma looked wildly towards Rose.

'You will stay here with the children,' she said, her voice quavering, but Rose had no intention of staying.

'Minnie and Donald, you go with Ma while I dismiss the pupils and lock up.'

'Will we come back this afternoon?' Baxter asked when they had left, and Rose was helping the younger children gather their belongings.

'I don't know,' she said.

'Oh?' He looked crestfallen.

'I thought you'd be pleased to have some time off.'

He shook his head.

'Can't I stay and help with anything, miss?' he asked when he had collected up the older pupils' books and put them on Ma's desk for marking.

'I'm sorry, but I have to go now.' Rose hustled him out of the door and turned the key in the lock.

He looked up, shading his eyes. 'I hope Mr Cheevers is better soon.'

'Oh, Baxter, thank you,' she said, touched by his concern. 'I'm sure he'll be fine in a day or two.'

She hurried back to Willow Place, following the sound of shouting. Mrs Dunn and Jane were in the hall watching Arthur, Donald and two of the workmen try to carry her father, who was lying roped to a door, but Pa was too heavy and the staircase too narrow.

'This way,' Arthur gasped, the veins in his neck standing proud from the skin. 'He can go in the dining room instead.'

The men tipped the makeshift stretcher to one side to get it through the doorway and rest it on the table without disturbing Pa. Rose followed Ma and the twins. Normally so capable, Ma didn't seem to know what to do. The sight of her husband lying quite still on his back on the door, his arms flopping over the edge and his face a strange shade of grey, had robbed her of speech.

No one knew what to do so Rose took over. She had no choice.

'Donald, leave that, and fetch Doctor Norris. Run as fast as those legs will carry you. Minnie, get the brandy from the tantalus.'

'Where is the key?' Minnie asked.

'It's on the mantel under the clock. I will fetch sheets and a blanket. Jane, boil up some water. Mrs Dunn, make tea.' Rose returned shortly to give two sheets and a blanket to Arthur.

'Cover him,' she said.

'Thanks, Rose,' he said gruffly. 'It's only a faint and nothing to worry about.'

'I am worried,' she whispered before she excused herself, saying she would look out for the doctor who was just trotting up the drive on his grey cob. He dismounted and tied his horse to the post on the lawn.

'Good morning, Miss Cheevers. I hear that you have an emergency on your hands.' The doctor was a middle-aged man with a fine moustache and horn-rimmed spectacles.

'It's my father.' Rose showed Doctor Norris into the house and he rested his brown leather bag on top of Pa's correspondence on the chiffonier in the hall, as she held out her hands to take his coat and billycock hat. She put them on the stand and followed him as he picked up his bag and went into the dining room. He sent everyone except for Rose and Ma away before listening to Pa's chest with his stethoscope.

'I don't understand,' Ma said as Pa's breathing rattled in his throat. His skin was covered with purple bruises and his body was shaking with cold. 'He was a little under the weather yesterday, that's all. How can this happen so quickly?'

'Mr Cheevers has a fever,' Doctor Norris observed.

'He's going to be all right,' Ma said, her voice taut with anxiety and doubt. 'He will be well again?'

'I cannot say. If I could put your mind at rest, I would, but he is gravely ill.'

Ma's face turned pale and her knees sagged. Rose grabbed at her arm and sat her down on a chair before standing at her side with one hand on her shoulder as Ma rocked back and forth.

'What is it, Doctor Norris?' Rose asked tentatively.

'I believe it to be a rare form of hide-carrier's disease.'

Rose frowned. She'd heard of it before. One of the older men working at the tannery had had a blister on his arm, which had turned to a black scab as though he had been touched by an evil spirit, until gradually it had healed and gone away.

'Mr Cheevers has been in contact with uncured hides at the tannery?'

Rose nodded.

'It is the same as wool-sorter's disease, which seems to be more commonly associated with imported wool rather than that produced in this country.'

'He has brought hides in from Argentina recently,' Rose said, remembering how pleased he and Arthur had been with the new supply of raw material.

'Well, we will never know exactly,' the doctor said. 'What we need to do now is implement treatment, but I have to warn you – the majority of the afflicted do not survive.'

Rose's heart stopped. A pain arced through her chest. This couldn't be happening.

Ma reached up, fumbling for Rose's hand, and her heart began to beat again. She had to be strong for her mother.

'We should not speak of death in his presence,' Ma sobbed.

'He cannot hear us. He is completely insensible and I'm afraid likely to remain so,' Doctor Norris said.

'There must be something you can do,' Rose begged.

'There is very little …'

'Is there any benefit in sending him to hospital?'

'I wouldn't recommend it. There are certain conditions that lend themselves to surgical intervention, but there is nothing to be done with the knife in this case. To be honest, he would be better off at home. The hospital can be a miserable place – they have recently employed a bug catcher to keep the beds clear of insects. And it's always short of money – the last fundraising efforts brought in donations of jam and old newspapers, and rags for bandages, not coins and banknotes to pay for nurses and instruments.'

Rose recoiled at the thought of the squalor and lack of care.

'We will nurse him here then, won't we, Ma?'

Her mother burst into fresh tears before stuffing the corner of her handkerchief into her mouth to stifle her sobs.

'It isn't often that I recommend bloodletting these days, but in this case, there is nothing to lose.' The doctor looked at Rose. 'You will stay, or ask one of the maids to assist? It would be better for your mother to leave the room.'

'I will ask Jane,' Ma said.

'No, I'll do it,' Rose said. How would Pa feel when he woke if they weren't at his side? She still had hope. She glanced towards her mother who was struggling to her feet. 'I'll call you back as soon as it's done.'

'Thank you, dear.' Ma turned and planted a kiss on Pa's cheek. 'I'm praying for you, my love.'

She left the room and Rose was alone with the doctor, Pa and her reservations about the impending treatment, born of her father's lack of confidence in medicine in general.

'Doctor Norris,' she said apprehensively, 'are you absolutely sure this is the right course of action?'

He raised one eyebrow. 'It is the only course. It isn't often that a young lady questions the opinion of a physician of many years' standing. You are right to be cautious, though. Your father is suffering from a febrile pneumonia – bloodletting will strangle the fever and reduce the burning heat of the skin. It will also render the pulse weaker, taking the pressure from the head and heart.' He took a bowl from his bag and an ivory case from his pocket from which he removed a small pointed lancet.

'I have known young ladies who faint upon the sight of blood.'

'I'm not one of them. I'm used to it.' She thought of the blood that stained the cart wheels and the carters' clothes when they brought the hides to the tannery. 'Tell me what to do.'

The doctor drew Pa's arm straight and twisted it slightly so the crook of his elbow was uppermost, revealing the tracery of blue veins against his skin.

'I need you to hold the bowl beneath the arm when I cut the vessel to release the blood,' he said. 'You can do that?'

She nodded. She would do anything for her dear father. All she wanted was for him to be back to his old self. Her hands trembling, she held the bowl.

'Look away if you wish,' Doctor Norris said, but she couldn't. She was transfixed by the way the doctor tapped at the vein, then cut into it with his blade until the blood trickled across Pa's blotchy skin and dripped into the bowl. Pa seemed oblivious.

'That is enough,' the doctor said eventually, checking the pulse at Pa's wrist. 'I will return tomorrow morning first thing to repeat it. In the meantime, you will bathe his face and hands with cool water, and keep the windows open for fresh air, although it is in short supply around here. If he wakes, then offer him some clear broth, nothing more inflammatory than that.'

Pa uttered a low moan. Rose almost jumped out of her skin.

'Is he in pain?' she asked.

The doctor shook his head.

'I will leave you now. Please, give my regards to your mother and let her know that I can be called upon at any time, day or night. I'll see myself out.' He took his leave and made his way out of the room with his bag.

Rose fetched her mother from the kitchen where Mrs Dunn had been feeding her tea and biscuits.

'How is he?' Ma said as she sat down beside Pa and took his hand. She touched his elbow. 'Is this …?'

'It's where the doctor bled him,' Rose said softly. 'He didn't feel a thing.'

'Oh, I wish that he had,' Ma sobbed. 'Oliver, please wake up. You cannot leave us yet. We have so much to do, and so many more happy years ahead of us. Arthur will soon be married. We will have grandchildren.'

'Ma, you don't have to stay with him,' Rose said. 'Let me take some of the burden from you.'

'I will not leave his side. Oh Rose, it is kind of you, but you must remember that I have done this before. When I was a little older than you are now, I nursed my father – the man who adopted me.' Tears rolled down her cheeks. 'His heart gave up on him. He lasted but one night. Oh Oliver, don't you dare leave me.'

Rose could hardly bear to see her mother's distress. She remained with her parents, but at a discreet distance, placing a chair under the window. It was painful to hear Ma talking to her father and to watch her bathe his face and arms, planting kisses on his forehead. There was hope, though, she thought. If the power of love alone could save him, he would be alive and kicking in the morning.

Chapter Five

Ostrich Plumes and Silver Trappings

The house was strangely quiet the next morning, the clock in the hall having stopped. Rose crept downstairs and tiptoed past the dining room where the door was closed to find Jane in the kitchen with her back to her as she took a copper pan from the old pine dresser.

'Have you seen Pa?' Rose asked, wondering if he had managed to get up and go to the tannery for work as usual.

'He's gorn,' Jane muttered.

The doctor had worked a miracle after all, Rose thought.

'Oh Rose ...' The pan fell clattering to the floor and the maid sank to her knees, her shoulders shaking. Slowly, she turned to face her, tears pouring down her cheeks. Rose's heart missed a beat, and then another ...

'I'm sorry,' Jane sobbed. 'The master – he passed during the night. In the early hours.'

Rose ran to the dining room and pushed the door open. Ma was standing at the table bent over her husband, her arms around his neck. Pa was lying still, his eyelids closed with coins, his body shrouded with a white sheet, and his mouth open as if he was about to speak.

Rose hesitated. The silence was truly terrible.

'Oh,' she gasped and burst into tears.

'I don't believe it. This isn't happening,' Ma cried as she straightened and stroked his hair. 'My dearest love, wake up and tell me this is one of your games.'

Rose felt her mother's pain like a knife through her breast.

Ma shook her head. 'I don't understand – it was all so quick. I don't think he ever woke up.'

'Ma? Rose? Jane came to wake me. Tell me it isn't true.' Arthur, still wearing his nightshirt, approached the table, thrusting his fist into his mouth to muffle a howl of grief.

'His soul has flown, taken up to Heaven by the angels,' Rose tried to explain, but it was inexplicable. How could a man who had been in rude health only a day or two before, have succumbed in such a short time? 'The twins. We have to tell them.'

Arthur took a deep breath to recover his wits.

'That can wait until later – I've told Jane not to disturb them just yet,' he said. 'Ma, have you sent for the doctor?'

Ma shook her head. 'What can he do? It is too late.'

'He will need to write a certificate.' Arthur turned back to Rose. 'I'll go and get him. You stay here with Ma.'

Arthur left Willow Place as Mrs Dunn arrived for work.

'Oh my Lord,' she said. 'Who would have thought? Mrs Cheevers, you must sit down and take some brandy.'

Ma refused, shaking her head.

'It just goes to show,' Mrs Dunn kept saying. Rose didn't have the heart to ask her what she meant. It didn't show anything as far as she was concerned except that life was short and should never be taken for granted.

It wasn't long before the twins came running down the stairs. Rose pushed past the housekeeper to try to intercept them before they reached the dining room, but it was too late.

'Ma? Pa?' Donald said, looking past Rose's shoulder as she stood blocking the doorway. 'Is he worse?'

'Oh!' Minnie exclaimed. 'Ma, why are you crying?' She dodged past her sister and went straight to the table. 'Is he sleeping?'

'No, my dears,' Ma said softly as Rose took Donald's hand and led him to join them. 'He has passed.'

'He's dead?' said Donald, frowning. 'He can't be.'

Minnie started to cry. Ma took her into her arms, but nothing could console her. Donald stood stony-faced.

'The doctor is here,' Mrs Dunn said in hushed tones. 'Please, make way for him.'

Doctor Norris approached the table and touched his fingertips to the side of Pa's neck before turning to Ma.

'I'm very sorry for your tragic loss, Mrs Cheevers. Your husband has been taken from you far too young. I will certify the death as being from fulminant fever caused by hide-carrier's disease,' he said quietly.

'Someone will pay for this,' Ma said. 'I should have made him send those hides back. I knew it was a mistake.'

Rose glanced at Arthur who had bowed his head. He shouldn't feel guilty, she thought. No one could have predicted the outcome.

'I should have insisted that we called you out sooner,' Ma wailed.

'It would have made no difference. You mustn't blame yourself.' Doctor Norris turned to Arthur.

'We will look after her,' he said. 'What happens next?'

'I should ask the funeral director to call at Willow Place at the earliest opportunity. I can recommend Randall and Sons – they are professional and respectful.'

'Thank you, Doctor. We're very grateful for your attendance on our beloved—' Arthur broke off and swallowed hard before he could go on, '—father.'.

69

'I will write out the certificate to be presented to the coroner. I don't believe there will be any need for an inquest.'

Mrs Dunn saw Doctor Norris out, and seeing that Ma was in no fit state to do anything, Rose hid the despair she was feeling inside and stepped into her shoes. It was her duty to put on a brave face for her family.

'Arthur, you go and speak to the funeral director,' she said. 'Minnie and Donald, you must fetch the Kingsleys.'

'I can't do anything,' Minnie said mournfully. 'My heart is broken.'

'Your legs aren't, though,' Donald said. 'Come with me. They need to know what's happened – our aunt has lost a brother and Mr Kingsley will need to make arrangements with Arthur for running the business.'

'Thank you, Donald,' Rose said. 'I'll go and write to Aunt Marjorie straight away.'

'She will be here in a day or two ...' Arthur's voice trailed off.

'For the wedding,' Rose whispered. 'Oh Arthur, what will you and Tabby do?'

'I'm more worried about what we'll all do without Pa,' he said, his eyes dark with misery. 'I'll speak to Tabby later. I'm going to order the men to destroy those hides – we can't let this happen to anyone else. And what about the school? We need to let the pupils know that it'll be closed for a few days, at least until after the funeral. I'll put a notice on the door on my way to the undertaker.'

'Mrs Dunn, will you sit with my mother?' Rose asked.

'Of course. I'll look after her.' The housekeeper wiped the tears from her eyes. 'I was very fond of your father. He was a lovely gentleman.'

Rose escaped into Pa's study and sat at his desk. She rested her fingertips on the leather surface and breathed in the faint scent of musk and sweet earth that reminded her of her father.

'How will we be happy without you?' she whispered, her heart breaking into a thousand pieces as she gave in to her grief. 'Dear Pa ...'

Trying to pull herself together, she opened the drawer and selected a piece of paper and an envelope, dipped her pen in the inkwell, and began to write. When fresh tears dropped like rain on to the paper and mingled with the ink, she had to blot them and start again.

Dear Aunt Marjorie, she wrote.

I thought you should know that our dear father passed away during the night. Ma is in no state to write or speak to anyone. Do come quickly if you can.
Your loving Rose

Having addressed and sealed the envelope, she put it aside ready for Donald to post – she couldn't help thinking that it would be good for all of them to keep busy.

There was a stream of callers at the house that day. Mrs Dunn and Jane were like guard dogs, only letting in a selected few: the undertaker, the Kingsleys and Reverend Holdsworth among them.

'It would be wise to postpone the wedding, unless there is some reason why it has to be done in a hurry,' Aunt Temperance said as she sipped brandy in the parlour with Ma, having managed to persuade her to leave Pa's side for a while. Mr Kingsley was there too, topping up his glass from the decanter.

'I wouldn't normally drink during the day, but today is the exception,' he said, noticing how Rose stared at him.

'Please accept my sympathies for your loss. It is a terrible tragedy for us all.'

'I don't know,' Ma said miserably. 'I don't know what to do for the best.' Even though she was an intelligent and educated woman, she had always deferred to their father when it came to important decisions. She seemed completely lost without him.

'I shall be delighted to run the business until young Arthur is ready to return to work,' Mr Kingsley said. 'Well, not exactly delighted in these circumstances,' he went on when his wife gave him a dig in the ribs.

'Arthur has much to attend to here,' Rose said, looking at her brother.

'Mr Randall will be here soon to talk through the funeral arrangements,' he said.

'Ah, the Randalls gave my grandfather a good send-off. Do you remember, Agnes?'

Ma blew into her handkerchief and broke into a fresh burst of sobbing. Rose glared at her aunt. Sometimes she wondered if she had any control over the words that came out of her mouth. Did she have no idea of the offence she caused, or was she deliberately cruel?

'Whatever you decide, a balance should be struck between showing respect and limiting expense.' Aunt Temperance dabbed at the corner of her eye with a hand-kerchief. 'I'm going to miss my darling brother.' She paused for a moment, then continued, 'I expect you will wish to move out of Willow Place now that he is gone, Agnes.'

'Oh no, it's my home. The only way I'll leave here is in a box.'

'Ma, please don't,' Rose begged, her heart aching. They had just lost one parent and she couldn't bear to think of losing another.

'Please, have some respect for your brother's wife,' Mr Kingsley said. 'Dare I venture that you have gone too far?'

'No, you dare not,' Aunt Temperance snapped back. He was under petticoat government for certain. 'It was a perfectly reasonable question.'

'More tea or brandy, anyone?' Arthur asked hastily to change the subject.

'I am drowning in tea,' Ma snapped, 'and I cannot stomach another brandy.'

'I think we should take our leave for now.' Mr Kingsley stood up. 'If there is anything we can help with, don't hesitate to ask. I'll go back to the yard to report the news to the men.'

'I will accompany you, Mr Kingsley,' Aunt Temperance said.

The Kingsleys left as Mr Randall from Randall and Sons arrived at the house. Rose fetched a fresh pot of tea, placing the tray on the low table beside Ma's chair. She poured the tea into fine bone china cups: one with milk and two lumps of sugar for Arthur and one with milk only at the undertaker's request.

Having handed out the cups, she picked up the tray to retreat, but Arthur raised his arm to stay her.

'I'd appreciate it if you remained here with us,' he said quietly. 'Ma needs our support.'

She felt a little nauseous. The spoils of death had made the middle-aged Mr Randall quite the dandy, strutting into their home in his top hat and tails, and with a black cane topped with a silver fox. She thought she could smell the scent of death on the undertaker's weasel-like person, welling up through the dense weave of his suit, but she didn't like to abandon Arthur if he needed her. She put the tray down again and took a seat opposite her mother, who sat immobile, mute and paralysed by grief.

'Ma, would you like to explain to Mr Randall what you require in the way of the funeral arrangements?' Arthur said eventually, but Ma didn't respond. 'Perhaps you will guide us, Mr Randall,' he went on. 'I'm afraid I'm out of my depth.'

'That is exactly what I am here for.' Mr Randall placed his tea untouched on the floor beside his feet. 'I and my father and brothers pride ourselves on our service. I can advise you on every aspect of the process, detail by detail. Nothing is left to chance. You get what you pay for: the privilege of personal attention and years of experience.'

'Ma,' Arthur said gently. 'How much do you think we should spend?'

'What did you say?' Ma looked up, wringing a sodden handkerchief.

'Ah, that is a question I can answer for you, Mrs Cheevers. As a general rule, the expense should be decided according to the wealth and social standing of the person,' Mr Randall said. 'As a businessman of great reputation and renown, Mr Cheevers was looked up to by many.'

'Oh, I don't know,' Ma said, choking on fresh tears.

'He would have wanted a simple ceremony. He wasn't one for making a fuss,' Rose ventured.

'It is important to give a man the kind of send-off that befits his station,' Mr Randall said quickly. 'Due to the nature of dying, one has but one chance to give a beloved family member a right and proper funeral. It would be a travesty and a matter of eternal regret to you in the future, if you should make unreasonable economies at this sensitive time.'

'I wish for him to have the best of everything, no expense spared,' Ma said, her mind apparently made up.

'Are you sure, Ma?' Arthur cut in, giving Rose a glance.

'I shall leave the details to you and Mr Randall. I don't want the bother of it.'

In a way it was a relief that Ma recognised that she was overwhelmed and unable to make rational decisions about the minutiae of the arrangements, such as when the embalming should be done and how many carriages and bearers they would need.

'I would recommend that the horses are dressed in ostrich plumes and black and silver trappings to make a suitable impression,' Mr Randall said.

Rose gazed at Arthur and gave a quick shake of her head. No plumes. No silver. Pa wouldn't have wanted everyone to think the Cheeverses would waste money that could be used for the greater good on fripperies, but Mr Randall was already scribing copious notes.

Ma went on to choose an oak coffin and a headstone from Mr Randall's brochure. Before he left the house, he reminded her that it was usual to place an announcement in the newspaper, and that an arrangement should be made for the reading of Pa's will.

Rose continued with her tasks, choosing invitation cards, decorated with urns and weeping willow, and ringed with black borders, to send out to their friends, family and acquaintances. She asked Minnie and Mrs Dunn to organise clothes suitable for mourning and sent Donald out for black crepe and black ribbon to tie on the door knob to signal that death had entered Willow Place, and to remind visitors to speak softly, not jar the nerves of those who were grieving.

Later, she met with Arthur on the veranda at the back of the house.

'Did you see Tabby?' she asked.

'I've spoken to her and Mr and Mrs Miskin and it's been agreed that the wedding should be postponed for a while. I've seen Bert too and he's returning to London tomorrow rather than stay for the funeral. Rose, you have been wonderful today. I'm very proud to call you my sister. The twins have done well too, and I will tell them so. Life will never be quite the same, but it will go on, and one day, we will be happy again.'

'Even Ma?' she said softly.

'Even Ma,' he echoed.

Her heart was heavy as she wrote a second letter to Aunt Marjorie explaining about the wedding and giving the date of Pa's funeral. When she retired to bed that evening, she and Minnie put the patchwork away, tucking it beneath one of the mattresses.

'I don't think we'll be working on it for a while,' Rose said. 'My heart isn't in it.'

'But it won't be ready,' Minnie said.

'Arthur and Tabby have decided to delay the wedding. We'll have plenty of time to finish it.' Finding it hard to stay strong for her siblings, Rose turned away to hide her tears. With one broken stitch, their patchwork family was unravelling, and Rose sensed that nothing would be the same again.

The day of Pa's funeral dawned grey and wet. The rain, falling like stair rods, hammered against the windows of the parlour, where they had placed his coffin.

'Heaven has never shed so many tears,' Mrs Dunn said when Rose went downstairs, wearing her dress made from midnight-blue muslin, the closest she had to full mourning attire. 'Does Mrs Cheevers need anything?'

'She is dressed, thank you.' She'd persuaded Ma to wash her hair in salted rainwater and rinse it with beer the night before. She had left her looking pale in her dress of black bombazine trimmed with crepe, and a stone of jet in her hair. She glanced at the clock which had been stopped at the exact time that Pa had been pronounced dead, wondering when they would allow its pendulum to start swinging again.

'I had Jane mix up a pomade for the lips. I will ask her to take it up.' Mrs Dunn bustled away, then returned to the hall when the doorbell rang a moment later. 'Look at all these cards,' she exclaimed as she collected them up from the doormat and placed them on the salver. 'Can't any of these people find the courage to engage in conversation with your dear ma? She could do with being taken out of herself. She is making herself ill with grief.' A knock at the door distracted her. Still grumbling under her breath, she walked across to open it.

'Good morning, Miss Treen,' she said. 'Thank goodness you have come. Arthur, Rose and the twins are doing their best, but the mistress is falling apart.'

'That will be all for now, Mrs Dunn.' Rose turned to their guest and relieved her of her stick. 'Aunt Marjorie, come in.'

'Mind your backs,' Donald said, carrying her luggage into the hall and straight on up the stairs to the room Arthur had vacated for her visit.

'How are you, Rose?' Aunt Marjorie asked, removing her bonnet and gloves.

'I'm bearing up, thank you,' she said, summoning the strength to fight the tears that welled up at the sight of their loving aunt.

'How is my dear, dear Agnes?'

'I wish I could say that she was coping. I'm so glad you're here. I think she will respond to you.'

'I will see what I can do. How are the arrangements? I assume that Temperance has been giving you some assistance with those?'

Rose shook her head.

Aunt Marjorie frowned. 'I thought she would have been here, interfering to her heart's content. Never mind. How is the school?'

'It is closed for now.'

'Then it will reopen immediately after the funeral. Agnes must continue with her teaching as soon as possible.'

'I'm not sure she'll want to – she has no enthusiasm for anything.'

'Perhaps she will start to feel better after today,' Aunt Marjorie said, but Rose didn't share her optimism. 'I'm sorry I couldn't be here sooner. When I asked my employers for unpaid leave, they refused my request.'

'How unfair,' Rose said, knowing how close her aunt had been to her father. It was surprising too because she'd always thought of her as being an independent woman who was free to do as she pleased. It seemed that she experienced little or no benefit from spinsterhood.

'I can understand it. I'm in charge of their children, and when I'm not there, they're obliged to enlist one of the maids to look after them, or God forbid, pay attention to them themselves. You may frown, Rose, but there are many parents in this world who have little desire for their children's company. It pains me deeply, but' – Aunt Marjorie forced a small smile – 'it means there is always work for nannies and governesses.'

Soon, more people began to call at the house. Mrs Dunn and Jane took their wet coats and placed a runner in the hallway so that visitors didn't feel they had to remove their footwear. Jane handed out wine, and funeral biscuits with elaborate wrappers from the local bakery, printed with florid poetry, urging people to be wise when ghastly Death had cut down a husband, and to use their hours wisely before the final end. Rose had ordered them according to Ma's wishes, and against her own instincts.

Ma's friend, Evie, arrived with her husband, and the Miskins. The men from the tannery turned up – Rose hardly recognised them in their dark suits. She joined her mother in the parlour where she was sitting at the head of the coffin. Minnie was there too, dressed in white.

'I'm here, Ma,' she said, reaching across to squeeze her hand.

'Thank you, Rose,' she murmured. 'I wasn't expecting so many people.'

'Pa was well-liked,' Rose said, biting back a sob. The grief came in waves. Sometimes she could hold it back, other times she couldn't, but today, she managed to suppress any outward manifestation. She wouldn't break down in front of everyone.

She sat quietly, waiting and listening to the chatter going on around her.

'Have you seen the hearse?' she heard Aunt Temperance saying to Aunt Marjorie as the two aunts, dressed in black, took their seats on the opposite side of the coffin. 'How much is all this going to cost?'

'I'm sure Agnes has spent within her means and according to the depth of affection that she feels for her husband. Perhaps we should do the same, donate towards a marble plaque for the church in recognition of his acts of bravery and charity. Oliver was a remarkable and rather wonderful man. You and Mr Kingsley would contribute?' Aunt Marjorie added.

'If Oliver is to be honoured in that way, it should be bestowed by the dignitaries of the city who can well afford it, not his family.' Aunt Temperance pursed her mouth as if she had tasted a sour plum.

'Will there be food afterwards?' Mr Kingsley asked, having made his way to his wife's side.

'There is wine, tea and biscuits,' Aunt Marjorie replied.

'I thought we would have been burying him with ham,' Mr Kingsley said.

'There is an inn not far from the cemetery.' Aunt Marjorie fiddled with the hem of her glove. 'Refreshment may be taken there, I believe.'

'At one's own expense, I assume,' Temperance said. 'The money being wasted on carriages should have been spent on food for people wishing to pay their respects. What was she thinking of?'

'Nothing but her grief, I believe. Now hush,' Aunt Marjorie warned. 'All animosities should be forgotten at such a time.'

Donald brought more guests to the parlour until there was no room for any more.

'Reverend Holdsworth has arrived,' someone called, but Rose couldn't make her way through the crush to greet him, nor could she hear the words that he spoke over Pa's coffin. It didn't matter, she thought, when there was nothing that could bring him back.

At the end of the service, the mourners began to disperse. Arthur, Donald and the other bearers carried the coffin, decorated with a cross of white flowers on the top. Ma clung to Aunt Marjorie while Minnie clung to Rose as they watched Pa's mortal remains being taken away in a hearse pulled by two fine black horses through the driving rain to the cemetery.

'I should have gone with him to see him put in the ground,' Ma said suddenly.

'No, Agnes. It is unnecessary for ladies to be seen at the graveside,' Aunt Marjorie said in a soothing tone. 'You have said your farewells. It's time to look to the future.'

Was it too soon? Rose wondered. Ma hadn't had much time to get used to her new situation, but perhaps her aunt was worried about the depth of her despair.

'You have made arrangements for the reading of Oliver's will?'

'Arthur has organised it with Mr Bray, the solicitor,' Ma said.

'It's the day after tomorrow,' Rose contributed in case her mother had forgotten.

'Good. I thought it would be in hand – my cousin wasn't the kind of man to leave anything to chance. I'd like to know that all the loose ends have been tied up before I return to Ramsgate. Arthur will set the new date for his wedding soon, and on Monday you can reopen the school.'

'I'm not ready for that,' Ma said quickly. 'I can't face going back to the classroom yet.'

'You will feel better when you get back to your daily routine. Life will start to feel normal again. I'm not saying it will be the same as before. It will just be a new kind of normal.'

'If my Oliver hadn't been snatched away, I wouldn't have had to go through this,' Ma exclaimed. 'What did he do? What have we done to deserve it? It is as if we are being punished for finding happiness together.' She started tugging at strands of her hair, twisting them and pulling them out.

'Agnes, don't do that,' Aunt Marjorie said, taking hold of her hand as Rose imagined she had done when Ma was a child. 'You will end up as bald as a coot.'

'Oh, how could he have done this to me?'

He had no choice in the matter, Rose wanted to say. He hadn't succumbed out of malice.

'I wish I had gone instead,' Ma said, breaking down again. 'I don't know how I will be able to live without him. He was my rock, my refuge, the love of my life … I have nothing left to live for.'

'Oh, don't be silly, child,' Aunt Marjorie said. 'You have your children. Oliver loved all four of them.'

'I loved him more,' she sobbed, the expression of her preference making Rose feel deeply hurt. It was a cruel thing to say even if it was natural for Ma to put thoughts of her beloved husband first at such a time. 'They are a constant painful reminder of his existence.'

'That may be so at the moment, but one day they will be a source of consolation.'

'I will never feel any different,' Ma insisted.

Aunt Marjorie couldn't console her. Like Queen Victoria who had mourned Prince Albert for nearly fifteen years, Rose feared that her mother would grieve for ever.

Chapter Six

The Last Will and Testament

'This occasion is not suitable for the children,' Aunt Marjorie said when they were finishing breakfast in the dining room. 'Surely, Agnes, you aren't going to have the twins accompany you for the reading of their father's will? They can stay at Willow Place with Jane and Mrs Dunn.'

Rose frowned. Mrs Dunn had expressed a wish that she should go to hear her employer's will being read, but it seemed that she was to be disappointed. Rose picked at her ham and eggs. She wasn't hungry. Only Arthur and Donald had eaten everything on their plates. She glanced towards Minnie who was staring into space as she sipped at her tea.

'Rose and Arthur will come with us,' Aunt Marjorie said when Ma didn't respond. 'Rose, you will be a comfort to your mother.'

Rose reached out and touched Ma's hand. Ma turned and shook her head.

'I'm sorry. I can find no comfort in anything at all.'

'It will come,' Aunt Marjorie said. 'Have patience.'

The four of them set out, arriving at eleven at the solicitor's office, Bray and Co., where a clerk showed them into a room with an ornate plaster ceiling and gas-lit sconces.

Inhaling the scent of vanilla, old books and tobacco, Rose settled Ma on a chair at the front of three rows of seats and sat down, she and Arthur flanking their mother, while Aunt Marjorie took her place beside Rose.

Rose caught sight of her reflection in the glass-fronted bookshelves filled with leather-and-gilt-bound legal tomes. She looked weary, she thought. They all did, but today, she was confident that once the will had been read and the last of the formalities gone through, they would be able to start to move on and deal with their sorrow.

'They are expecting quite a crowd,' Arthur whispered in her ear while more people, friends, relations and acquaintances filed in behind them. Aunt Temperance and Mr Kingsley sat beside Aunt Marjorie, and the row behind them began to fill up until there were no more places and latecomers were forced to stand.

'I don't know half of these people,' Rose said quietly.

'They are like vultures,' Aunt Marjorie commented.

'Are you speaking of the solicitors or these new friends of our dear father?' Arthur said.

'New? Oh, I see what you mean,' Rose said.

'It boggles the mind that so many strangers have come to see the show,' Aunt Marjorie said, at which Ma uttered a sob of distress.

'Please, Ma,' Rose said softly, a little embarrassed at her show of sorrow in public. 'Don't be upset. Everyone is watching us.'

Ma turned to her, red-eyed. 'Am I not allowed to be upset? It is all very well not showing your feelings, but in this case, an exception has to be made. I cannot hold in my tears. Oh, my darling ...'

'I don't know why we had to come, Ma,' Rose said, suppressing the despair that was beginning to well up from inside her again. It was upsetting for all of them, and the reading of Pa's will was merely a formality. Her aunt had said so. Ma would receive a jointure and Arthur as the eldest son would inherit the business, and with Oliver's sense of fairness, there would be provision for Rose and the twins. The only real question was whether he had settled the business equally on her two brothers, or made some other arrangement.

'Hush, this must be Mr Bray,' Aunt Marjorie said as a young man in a suit with an oversized wing collar on his shirt entered the room with a file of papers. 'Oh no, it is another of his minions,' she went on as he placed the file on the walnut desk, slid out the captain's chair on its brass castors, flicked off some dust from the seat with a flourish of a handkerchief, and walked off again.

People shifted in their seats as a second man, a gentleman bearing the veneer of wealth in the form of a fine suit and a signet ring, walked in. He took his seat at the desk and removed a pair of gold-rimmed spectacles from the drawer. He placed them on his nose and looked over the top of them at his audience. He cleared his throat with great pomp and ceremony, at which the crowd fell silent.

'Ladies and gentlemen,' he began. 'I regret that we are here together in such sad circumstances. There is not much to say – the gentleman in question kept his bequests brief and to the point.'

There was a general sigh of disappointment as he went on, 'This is the last Will and Testament of Oliver Samuel Cheevers of Willow Place, Canterbury in the County of Kent. I hereby revoke my previous wills and codicils, declaring this to be my last will and testament. I give the estate of Willow Place and the business of Cheevers Tannery, lock, stock, and barrel to ...' he paused '... my loving wife to pass thence to our adopted and natural children.'

Rose sat back in her chair as Mr Bray turned his gaze towards Ma who was frowning.

'However, having made some enquiries to confirm the situation of the recipient of this inheritance, I am required to name the next eligible beneficiary in line as Mrs Temperance Kingsley.'

'How can that be?' Aunt Marjorie exclaimed as a gasp of shock ripped through the crowd. 'Mrs Cheevers – his wife – is right here. This man is talking through his hat.'

Mr Bray shook his head gravely as all kinds of thoughts tumbled through Rose's mind. What did he mean? Was Pa's sister to inherit everything that rightly belonged to them? There had to be some kind of mistake.

'Mr Cheevers died a bachelor. I have to confess that it was unexpected – it was well known and understood that he was a married gentleman, but I had one of my clerks make some enquiries, and there is no record of a marriage having taken place.'

'I don't understand.' Rose looked past Ma at her brother, reading his expression of confusion. What had Pa been thinking of? Ma uttered a cry and tipped forward, clutching her chest.

'We need the smelling salts for your mother. She has fainted.' Marjorie took a silver vinaigrette from her bag and handed it across to Rose, who removed the sponge soaked in hartshorn and ammonia from inside it.

Ma pushed herself up to a sitting position.

'It is going to take more than a breath of hartshorn to restore me to health,' she panted. 'Oh, Oliver, my love, how could you do this to me? To our family? Our children?'

'Mr Bray, there has to be another will, one dated more recently than this one. Please ask one of your clerks to check your files,' Aunt Marjorie said.

'I can assure you that this is his very last will and testament. He didn't make another.'

'Is it possible he went to another solicitor? How about placing an advertisement in the papers?' Arthur said, standing up.

'Then we will have all kinds of ragtag and bobtail telling us they have his will. No, that will not do. I repeat – this is the final expression of Mr Cheevers' wishes. This is his mark – look at the signature.' He ordered a clerk to fetch a magnifying glass so people could check it for themselves, while they sat Ma back in her seat. 'Let us ask the lady herself.'

'I'm sorry, she cannot speak. Please open the window. She needs some air,' Rose said urgently. They all did. She felt quite faint herself.

Mr Bray called his clerk back inside and asked him to usher the crowd out of the office, but they lingered outside, their voices carrying through the open door.

'Well, I never. Well, I never did,' Rose heard them say. 'Who'd 'ave thought it?'

'I always suspected they weren't wed. I never heard the vicar read the banns for 'em, and you know me, I'm a God-fearin' woman who hasn't missed a Sunday since my last littl'un was born many years ago.'

'Could they have got hitched elsewhere?' said another.

'No, they were married over a broomstick,' came a man's voice.

'Maybe they got wed at the cathedral? I always thought it odd that they were regulars at St Mildred's.'

'They live in the parish – why should they go anywhere else?'

''Is sister is a cathedral-goer.'

'Only because she doesn't like to associate with the hoi polloi. She isn't like one of us, and now she'll be even more stuck up. Did you see her? I don't think anything could have wiped the smile off her face.'

The voices drifted away, and Rose took the opportunity to look at her Aunt Temperance who was still sitting in her seat, fanning herself. Mr Kingsley was on his feet and waiting for his wife at the door.

'I hope you will see fit to do the right thing by your brother's family,' Aunt Marjorie said, addressing her. 'It was an oversight. The inheritance is rightfully theirs.'

Aunt Temperance stared at her. 'Who do you think you are to question my dearly departed brother's wishes? It is apparent that he and Agnes were not married, even though they put on a pretence that they were. I don't recall a wedding, do you, Marjorie? We would have been the first to have been invited. Well, you would anyway, seeing how they favour you.'

'It's perfectly plain to me and everyone else that this outcome is not what he intended. Please consider your position. Do you want to be responsible for Oliver's family being put out on the street?'

Rose winced at Aunt Marjorie's blunt words. Surely it wouldn't come to that?

'I will speak with Mr Kingsley,' Aunt Temperance said. 'He will advise on the best way forward.'

'That does little to reassure me, but if that's the best you can come up with for now … Come on, Rose and Arthur. Help your dear mother home,' Aunt Marjorie said.

They half carried, half dragged Ma home along the dirty streets to the sanctuary of Willow Place where she came round for long enough to take a few sips of chicken soup.

'Do you remember what happened at the solicitor's?' Rose asked her as she tucked her up in bed.

'I don't think so, not exactly.' Ma frowned.

'Mr Bray was concerned that he couldn't find the evidence that you and Pa were married,' she began tentatively, not wanting to upset her mother further, but wanting more than anything to solve the mystery of her parents' marital status and secure the inheritance for the family. Ma didn't appear to be listening. She seemed confused and her speech was slurred.

'Oh, Rose, I am so very tired. My arms and legs are like lead weights.'

Rose patted her hand. 'You've been through a lot – you need to rest. We'll talk about it later.'

'You are a good girl.' Ma sank back against her pillows and closed her eyes.

Rose and Aunt Marjorie took it in turns to sit with her until late in the evening. Rose had a strange sense of life being suspended in a moment of time: Ma sleeping; Arthur walking out with Tabby; Donald and Minnie creeping around the house in silence, only half-informed of what had passed at the solicitor's office that morning; and Aunt Marjorie writing a plan of how to proceed, her brow etched with lines of worry.

Rose took the last shift, staying in her mother's room until midnight before touching her cheek and wishing her goodnight.

She thought she heard her mouth the words, 'Goodnight, Rose,' in return. She turned to say more, hoping that her mother would have the strength to talk, but Ma's breathing was slow and regular, and she didn't like to disturb her.

'How is Agnes?' Aunt Marjorie asked when she returned downstairs.

'She is sleeping,' Rose said.

'I wonder if we should call the doctor in the morning. We'll see how she is then. Do you think I should sit with her?'

Rose shook her head. 'There is nothing more that we can do, except give her time to recover. I've left the bell beside her bed so she can ring if she needs anything. Oh, Aunt, what a terrible day.'

'Have a little brandy, my dear.'

'Oh no, I couldn't. I can't bear the smell of it.'

'It will help if you can only get used to it.' Her aunt poured out two half-glasses of Pa's best Armagnac, and handed her one. 'There.'

'Thank you.' Rose took a gulp and coughed as it hit the back of her throat, stinging and burning. 'It's like poison!'

Her aunt smiled. 'It won't hurt you in moderation. Now, sit down – we need to have a talk.'

'Where are the twins? And Arthur? Shouldn't he be here?'

'The twins are in bed, and I doubt we'll see hide nor hair of Romeo until the early hours. I wonder what he will say to Tabby.' Rose sat down on the armchair beside the fire, gazing hopefully at her aunt, the wisest and most learned woman she knew, after Ma. If anyone could save them, Aunt Marjorie could.

'I have to say I'm most surprised that your father didn't arrange his affairs before he passed away. He was usually assiduous in his attention to detail. He can't have intended for his family to be left with nothing.'

'I don't believe that Ma and Pa never married,' Rose said. 'They went by Mr and Mrs Cheevers. We are all called by the surname Cheevers, except for Arthur, who not long ago found out that he is still a Fortune, the name he was born with.'

'It is confusing, I grant you,' Aunt Marjorie said. 'Your parents never wanted to live a lie. Your father was an open, honest and principled man, so when he took your mother into his house, he was prepared to say that they weren't married, but he soon found that other people didn't share his views – there were some who completely cut him off for it. From then on, he decided to hold his tongue and make plans to marry at the earliest opportunity for the sake of your mother's reputation.'

'What happened then? Did he forget, or something?'

'I don't know. Your ma and I have always kept in touch by letter, if not face to face. I can't recall her ever speaking of a wedding.'

'You would have been invited as a witness, surely.'

'I assumed that they'd married quietly. It's possible that they did, and we haven't found the evidence yet.'

'Ma was married before – perhaps she'd had enough of ceremonies,' Rose said.

'Ah, be prepared for another shock.' Aunt Marjorie drew breath and went on, 'Your mother wasn't married when she came to Canterbury.'

Rose felt her forehead tighten.

'I'm afraid you have been misinformed, perhaps intentionally,' Aunt Marjorie said. 'Agnes was working as a governess.'

'I thought – pardon me for interrupting you.'

'It's all right. Do go on.'

'I was under the impression that Ma was brought up in a grand house and had no need to work.'

'A change in circumstance forced her to leave the house outside Faversham. She was incredibly brave, walking out on a secure but potentially unhappy future, to take up employment, teaching two young ladies. Having found favour with the family, it all went wrong for her. It's easy to blame the woman for being weak, but you have to remember that Agnes was brought up with certain expectations. She was intelligent, beautiful and talented. She would have graced any drawing room with her conversation and accomplishments. Oh, I know you think I'm biased because, as I've said before, she is like a daughter to me.

'Anyway, the young gentleman of the family seduced her with a promise of marriage, and you were the result. It changes nothing, Rose. You have always known that you weren't related to Oliver by blood.'

Rose nodded, but her mind was a storm of confusion.

'So Aunt Temperance's teasing about the way I could pass as a baronet's daughter was the truth? She knew?'

'I believe she made some enquiries into your mother's background when she arrived in Canterbury with child. She couldn't prove anything, but she jumped to her own conclusion. She wouldn't let the subject drop, ever hopeful that someone would reveal your true father's name. I've always held my tongue, of course.'

'I was born out of wedlock?' Rose said.

'Which is why Oliver let the story go unchecked. Illegitimacy is still considered a terrible stain on a family's reputation. Which is worse, Rose? To have one's daughter called a bastard and the woman you love denounced a whore? Or let people believe in a more acceptable alternative, that your mother was married and some accident befell her husband, your true father?' Aunt Marjorie poured her another brandy.

She drank it down. It didn't burn so much this time.

'I remember Pa once saying in front of the Miskins that not everyone believed in the institution of marriage,' she said tentatively.

Aunt Marjorie gazed into the bottom of her glass.

'He was a free-thinker in many ways, encouraging your mother to set up the school where others make their wives stay at home, but no, I can't believe that Oliver and Agnes didn't marry out of principle. We will talk to your ma in the morning. She'll be able to confirm that a marriage took place, and tell us where. We can have a copy made of their entry in the register, and take it to Mr Bray. All will be resolved.'

92

Rose hoped it would be as simple as that.

'If it isn't?' she said hesitantly.

'Then we will cross that bridge when we come to it. Now, we must retire and try to get some sleep. We have lots to do in the morning.'

'Aren't you due back in Ramsgate tomorrow?'

'The day after. Don't worry about me. I'm worried about you.'

'I'm fine,' Rose said. 'Pa was my father. The other man – well, he means nothing to me. If I ever met him, I would walk away for how he wronged Ma. In a way, he did her a favour. If she had married him, she would never have met ...' The memory of her father's passing was too raw. She choked back a sob, and Aunt Marjorie finished speaking for her.

'The love of her life,' she murmured. 'You are quite right. I have never seen such joy and happiness in one household as I have seen at Willow Place over the years. You are worn out, Rose. Let us say goodnight, and hope for a better day tomorrow.'

As she retired to bed, feeling numb with exhaustion and a little light-headed from the brandy, she thought she caught the scent of roses wafting across the landing at the top of the stairs. She wondered if Mrs Dunn had asked Jane to refresh the bowl of potpourri with essence because there were no fresh blooms in the garden for the vases. Her candle flickered and died before she reached her room, the unexpected draught adding to her sense of unease. Nothing had felt right since Pa had been taken up to Heaven. How she wished he was here to reassure them that all would be well.

Chapter Seven

The Weeping Willows and Grey Stones of the Westgate

The next morning, Mrs Dunn arrived early for work. Rose heard her shouting at Jane to get up and heat water for the household's ablutions. As it turned out, Aunt Marjorie was already up and about, tending to Ma and making tea. Rose joined her aunt in the kitchen where she was deep in conversation with the housekeeper as Jane bustled about with pitchers and cloths, red-faced at having been caught napping.

'Mrs Cheevers is comfortable,' Aunt Marjorie said. 'She needs encouragement and occupation to take her mind off her loss.'

'It's a terrible thing to lose a husband,' Mrs Dunn said, somewhat disapprovingly, Rose thought. 'She must be allowed to grieve.'

'Unfortunately, she must pull herself together to concentrate on the practical issues that have arisen. You have heard about the will?'

'Of course. It's the talk of—' Mrs Dunn stopped abruptly.

'I was afraid so.'

'Anyway, that's why I'm here before my usual time. Miss Treen, there was another will.'

Aunt Marjorie's jaw dropped slowly. 'Are you sure?'

'Oh yes,' Mrs Dunn said. 'The master made it not long after he saved the carter and his lad from the river. I remember him talking about how the rescue reminded him of his own mortality, and how he needed to make sure his affairs were in order.'

'This will supersedes the other?' Aunt Marjorie said.

'The will that the solicitor read out was dated from the year after I was born.' Rose joined the conversation. Was there hope after all? Was Mrs Dunn's memory of another will able to save them?

'The second will was made when your mother was recovering from the birth of the twins,' Mrs Dunn said.

'Where is it then?' Aunt Marjorie said.

'The master wrote it out himself and asked me and Mr Hales to witness it. We made our mark, he said he would arrange to have it lodged with Mr Bray, and that was the last I saw of it.'

'Mr Bray can't have it in his possession,' Aunt Marjorie said as Rose's heart sank and fresh tears burned her eyes. 'He's been the family's trusted solicitor for many years. It must still be here in the house. If we find it, it is possible that we will not need to prove that Oliver and Agnes were married.'

Rose didn't hesitate. It would be in Pa's desk. She rushed into the study and began to rummage through the paperwork he'd left in a neat pile on the top. There was nothing resembling a legal document there, just notes from the Sanitary Society, a list of names of the poorest children in the neighbourhood whom her parents had been considering for free places at the school, and several sheets about tanning processes in Pa's handwriting. She fell to her knees and pulled the drawers open, searching through them one by one. There were packets of envelopes, and writing paper, a spare bottle of ink, some unopened eau de cologne, pencils and a cravat: personal effects that made her want to cry.

'Oh Pa,' she whispered as she continued her search, aware of Mrs Dunn and Aunt Marjorie standing at the study door, watching her.

'Well?' Aunt Marjorie asked eventually.

Rose shook her head. 'It must be somewhere. He wouldn't have made a new will for no purpose. Perhaps Mr Hales knows where it is. Or Ma,' she went on, standing up and brushing the dust from her skirts. It appeared that neither Jane nor Mrs Dunn had been able to bring themselves to clean Pa's study since he'd passed away. 'I'll go and ask her.'

'I'll come with you,' her aunt said. 'Thank you, Mrs Dunn. You have been most helpful.'

'Well, I can't stand by and let that woman take what rightfully belongs to the mistress,' Rose heard her say as she ran up the stairs to her mother's room.

She found Ma lying in bed, her eyes dull and listless, staring at the ceiling.

'Ma, this is important.' She took a grip of her hand. 'Mrs Dunn says that Pa made another will. When we find it, we will take it to Mr Bray and have the other overturned.'

Her mother didn't respond.

Rose squeezed her fingers. 'Please, Ma. You have to help us.'

'Agnes, you must answer,' Aunt Marjorie said, joining her at the bedside.

'I can't think straight,' Ma muttered.

'Can't or won't?' Aunt Marjorie said sternly, reminding Rose that she was a governess as well as their dear aunt.

'I don't know. All I want is to be back in my Oliver's arms, to hear his voice, to walk at his side.' Ma's body began to shake with grief.

'This really won't do.' Aunt Marjorie raised her voice. 'You have children who need you. Come on, my dear, tell us about the will.'

Rose took a handkerchief from her pocket and dabbed the tears from Ma's cheeks, then held her hand encouragingly.

'I recall Oliver writing a new will naming our adopted and natural sons as beneficiaries with provision for me and our daughters,' Ma whispered. 'I told him to leave it to Mr Bray, but he got in his head that he could simply compose it himself, have it witnessed and lodged at the solicitor's office. I wasn't well at the time – I'd just had the twins and was confined to bed so I don't know exactly what went on. It was' – she sighed deeply – 'a lifetime ago.'

'You're doing well, Ma,' Rose said softly. 'You must have some idea what Pa did with it.'

'No, I'm sorry. I wish I had. I never saw it. I assumed that he'd delivered it to Mr Bray.'

'Or had it delivered,' Rose mused aloud. She wondered if Pa had sent one of the trimmin's boys on that errand. Could the will have been lost on the way? 'Ma, one more thing.'

'Oh, I'm too exhausted for this.' Ma winced. 'I have a pain in my arm and my jaw aches.'

'It's a question you can answer with one word, yes or no. Were you and Pa married?'

'No,' she mouthed.

'Thank you,' Rose said, leaning across and pressing her lips to her mother's forehead. 'We will leave you to rest.' She released her mother's hand and turned to her aunt. 'We have to find that will.'

'I'll write to my employers and ask permission to stay on for a while. They won't like it, but I hope they understand that this is an emergency.'

'Are you sure?' Rose said, worried about her aunt losing her place. At her age and level of infirmity, it would be well nigh impossible to find another position, but she and Arthur needed her to advise them and help them through their current crisis.

'I'm too old for all this,' Aunt Marjorie said, accompanying her down the stairs. 'However, I'll do anything for my dear Agnes and her wonderful family, and if that means turning this house upside down to find this missing will, we'll do it. But first, we will speak to Mr Hales.'

'Should one of us stay with Ma?' Rose asked. 'I've never seen her laid this low.'

'Send the maid to fetch Mr Hales to us. That will save us trudging over to the tannery. My legs are playing up today.'

'You must put your feet up,' Rose exclaimed. 'I'll go and find Mr Hales after breakfast.'

It was quite an interrogation for the poor man, she thought, when Aunt Marjorie requested his presence in the parlour upon his arrival at Willow Place. He'd had to take off his boots at the front door, and his toenails were sticking out through the holes in his woollen socks.

'Do sit down,' Aunt Marjorie said.

His pipe clattered to the floor as he took the chair opposite her while Rose perched on the window seat, hardly able to bear the tension in the air.

'What is this about, Miss Treen?' he asked, picking up the pipe and tucking it in his belt. 'I heard that the missus was sick.'

'She'll soon be on the mend, Mr Hales,' Aunt Marjorie said. 'Now, I have some questions for you. Do you remember witnessing a will for Mr Cheevers about twelve years ago?'

He rubbed his bristly chin, the contact sounding like sandpaper against wood.

'I do recall that occasion. Mrs Dunn and I were present to witness the gaffer's signature.' He frowned. 'I'd 'ave done anythin' for 'im. Anythin',' he repeated emphatically.

'You're very kind,' Aunt Marjorie said.

''E was the best gaffer you could ask for. We all miss 'im on the yard.'

'Please, Mr Hales, let's return to the subject of the will. This is most important. Do you know what happened to the document after you signed it?'

'I wish I could remember.' He rubbed his chin again, more briskly this time, as if he might conjure up a genie to grant him his wish.

'Think, Mr Hales. Think!'

'Can't Mrs Dunn help?'

'The last time she saw it was on the desk in the study. She assumed that Oliver delivered it to Mr Bray's office at a later date.'

'Oh no, that isn't right. I remember now – the gaffer blotted the ink, folded the paper and slipped it into his pocket. Then he took it across to the yard and he was going to give Arthur a ha'penny to take it for him, but Mr Kingsley was there and he said he had some papers to lodge at the solicitor's so he'd do it. For safety's sake, that's what 'e said. It's strange that I can recall his words after all this time when I can hardly remember what I 'ad for my supper last night. For safety's sake.'

'It was kind of him,' Aunt Marjorie said – rather stiffly, it seemed to Rose. 'Thank you, Mr Hales. You may go back to work, but please keep this to yourself. I don't want Agnes to think we've been discussing her business – I fear that it would send her into a relapse.'

Mr Hales stood up. 'I've worked for the gaffer and his grandfather for many years. You can rely on me to hold my tongue,' he said. 'Good morning, Miss Treen. Miss Cheevers.'

When he had gone, Aunt Marjorie asked Rose to fetch the rosewater and sprinkle a little of it across the floor to hide the lingering scent of their visitor's mouldering socks.

'What are we going to do next?' Rose said, returning with the bottle from where it was kept on the scullery shelves. She opened the lid and tipped the bottle, releasing drops of fragrance on to the floor and the chair, then straightened abruptly. 'You don't think Mr Kingsley had something to do with the will's disappearance? Surely not? He's family.'

'He had motive, though.'

'I don't believe he'd stoop to such a thing.'

'He and your father had their differences in the past. When Mr Kingsley married Temperance he expected Oliver, as his brother-in-law, to offer him a partnership in the business. He may well have lost or destroyed the second will – think about what he stood to gain, Rose, and you will see my theory isn't that far-fetched.'

A quiver of fear ran down Rose's spine. She couldn't believe that her uncle could be that wicked.

'So there is nothing to be done? There is no proof. If we ask Mr Kingsley what happened to the will, either he'll deny he had anything to do with it, or he'll blame one of Mr Bray's clerks for mislaying it.'

'All is not lost. Not yet anyway,' Aunt Marjorie said. 'I'll make an appointment to see Mr Bray. There is a ghost's chance that he has this second will somewhere in his files. In the meantime, we must do what we can to restore your mother to her old self.'

For the next couple of weeks, Aunt Marjorie stayed on at Willow Place, and she and Rose did their best to make Ma well again. They took her out for walks through the water meadows and around the Dane John for fresh air and a change of scene, but Ma couldn't put her grief aside even for a minute. Everything from the weeping willows to the grey stones of the Westgate reminded her of Oliver. Ma began to struggle to breathe when she exerted herself, which put paid to their expeditions. It was as though she was losing the will to live.

Why was it that when you had been wakeful all night, dawn came bringing an irresistible desire for sleep? Rose closed her eyes and dreams of happier times came creeping into her mind: a vision of Pa playing bagatelle with them one evening, surreptitiously moving the ivory pegs so that Minnie won, and Donald's brief outburst of fury when he realised he'd been duped; Pa taking her and Arthur right up to the top of the Dane John after the twins were born to look out over Canterbury and the surrounding countryside. Exhausted, she had fallen asleep in his arms as he had carried her home. She remembered feeling safe and loved – until a bloodcurdling scream brought her back to the present.

She sat up abruptly at the sound of a second scream, after which she fell out of bed, feeling as if her heart was about to pummel its way out of her ribcage. She tore down to the next floor to Ma's room where the door was wide open and Jane was just inside holding her hand to her mouth as if trying to keep the screams inside her. There was a jug of water on the floor, a dark stain spreading across the rug. Aunt Marjorie was at Ma's bedside, holding a candle to her face.

'Be quiet, Jane,' she snapped. 'I can't hear myself think.'

'What's wrong? Ma?' Rose pushed past the maid and joined her aunt.

'I'm sorry, my dear,' Aunt Marjorie said, her eyes red, as if she had been crying.

'She is gorn. The mistress is gorn to join the master,' Jane exclaimed.

'It can't be true. She seemed to be getting better,' Rose said, her chest so tight that she could barely breathe.

Aunt Marjorie moved to take the hairbrush from the dressing table and hold its mirrored back to Ma's face. Rose leaned in, anxiously looking for the circle of haze that would prove she was alive after all and Jane had made a terrible mistake.

'Well?' Rose whispered.

Her aunt felt for her mother's wrist and shook her head.

'How can that be?' Rose sank to her knees, holding on to her mother's ice-cold hand. How could they have lost two parents in the space of less than three weeks?

'Jane, go and find Mrs Dunn. Tell her to call the doctor. Rose, you must be brave. Go and find Arthur, and wake the twins. I will stay here.' Aunt Marjorie, for all her ability to hide her emotions, was in tears this time.

How did you break such news to your siblings? Rose went to find Arthur first, but he was already on his way from his bedroom, having been roused by the disturbance.

'What's going on? This racket is enough to wake the dead.'

Rose reached out for his hand in the near darkness.

'I wish that was so. Arthur, it's Ma,' she whispered, her voice breaking. 'She's ...'

'How?' he gasped.

'I don't know. We must call for the doctor. He'll be able to tell us, not that it makes any difference now.' She gazed at her brother – the trail of a tear shone from his cheek, but he dashed it away. 'I'm sorry – you have lost two mothers ...'

Ignoring her, Arthur spun on his heel and walked in the direction of the twins' rooms. 'We must be strong for the twins.'

They knocked on their bedroom doors and called them on to the landing.

'We have bad news,' Rose said, wondering how they had both slept through Jane's screams.

'No?' said Minnie, as if she could read her sister's mind. 'Not Ma as well?'

'This is my fault,' Donald said. 'I did wrong – I wore her out. I was mean to her and Pa, and this is my punishment. I'll never forgive myself, and I'll never play cricket again.'

Numb with shock, Rose made tea for everyone and then the visitors began to call again at Willow Place.

Aunt Temperance came first.

'Mr Kingsley was on his way to the tannery when he met Mrs Dunn, who told him she was on her way to call on the doctor to prevail upon him to visit our dear, dear Agnes. Mr Kingsley in turn sent the trimmin's boy to find me to give me the news.' Aunt Temperance grasped Aunt Marjorie's hands. 'Tell me. Is it really true?'

Aunt Marjorie nodded. 'She is gone, taken up to Heaven to be at her husband's side.'

Aunt Temperance hesitated for just a moment. 'What was it? What carried her off?'

'We will await the doctor's opinion before making wild speculations.'

'It was the shock. I have no doubt. She has been struck down as punishment for the lies she and my brother told, the scandal they hid from their loving family for all these years.'

'This isn't the time for laying blame at anyone's door,' Aunt Marjorie said, her left eye twitching as if she was trying to keep her temper. Rose felt a powerful antipathy towards Aunt Temperance, but she managed to bite her tongue until her aunt excused herself, saying she would call again.

Doctor Norris was the second person to arrive – he certified the cause of death as heart failure. Rose hadn't believed that anyone could die from a broken heart, but the doctor confirmed that the loss of her husband had caused Ma to suffer permanent and fatal injury to that organ on which life depended.

After Doctor Norris left, Reverend Holdsworth turned up. Aunt Marjorie invited him into the parlour with Rose and Arthur while the twins remained with Mrs Dunn and Jane.

'I'm very sorry for your loss, especially for this one being so close to the first.' The vicar rubbed at his earlobes while he spoke. 'We shall pray for the soul of Mrs Cheevers at St Mildred's on Sunday, and ask the Lord to have mercy on the poor children. Suffice to say that God has His reasons for taking them up on the wings of the angels. It is all part of His higher purpose.'

'We thank you for your kindness and consideration,' Aunt Marjorie said, her eyes swollen from crying. 'There is something we need to discuss with you. I would normally not raise the issue until a later date when the initial shock has passed, but it is terribly pressing. I expect you will have heard – there is some difficulty with Mr Cheevers' will. There was a second, more recent will which would have solved the family's difficulties, but it has disappeared.'

The vicar nodded. 'I've heard that his estate has been entailed to his sister, a most unsatisfactory state of affairs.'

'We talked to Agnes before her—' a sob caught in her throat before she continued, '—premature demise, but unsurprisingly she didn't want to speak about it. She was too unwell, and embarrassed perhaps.'

'She was a very private person,' the vicar said.

'All things considered, I don't believe that Agnes and Oliver were married, but we need to be absolutely sure – for their children's sake. I'm clutching at straws, Vicar, but did you marry Oliver Cheevers to Agnes Linnet or Agnes Berry-Clay as she was known then?' Aunt Marjorie asked. It seemed strange to Rose to hear her mother called by an unfamiliar name.

'As far as I'm aware, the couple concerned never entered into the state of holy matrimony. It was quite intentional. When your mother arrived in Canterbury, there was much speculation and gossip about her history. As is common in these cases, interest waned as the next scandal brewed, but when I advised Mr Cheevers to go ahead with a wedding ceremony for just such an eventuality as this, he said he didn't want to set them all off again. He felt that Agnes had been through enough, and they were already living as man and wife by then. In his view – wrongly, in my opinion – they were as good as married.

'He told me they would go elsewhere and marry quietly, but I always suspected that they didn't wed.' A sad smile crossed his face. 'Agnes wore her wedding ring but once a week. I never saw it on her finger except on Sundays.'

'I still can't believe that Oliver, who ran a business and was part of so many charitable organisations, wouldn't have managed his own affairs. You are absolutely sure they were never married?' Aunt Marjorie repeated.

'I have no reason to think that they were,' the vicar confirmed. 'I certainly didn't marry them at St Mildred's.'

'Then we are in the mire as I thought.' Aunt Marjorie was almost in tears. 'They have left their children dependent on the goodwill of their aunt, Oliver's sister. If she should set herself against them, they will be all but destitute.'

'I'm sorry about that, but we must trust that God will forgive the gentleman in question and provide for his orphans,' the vicar said loftily.

'Why did you allow Mr Cheevers to continue to worship at your church, knowing that he was living in sin?' Aunt Marjorie said, asking the question Rose wanted answered.

'Your cousin could be very stubborn – once his mind was made up, there was no changing it. Besides, there are other unmarried couples in this parish who live as husband and wife. It is not as uncommon a situation as you might imagine. Think on this, Miss Treen – it is easier to keep one's flock safe and spiritually secure when the sheep are inside the fold than when they're out of it.'

'I understand that, but I wish you had been more forceful with your sermons on the importance of marriage. Oh, it is done now. It is too late. We must do the best with what we have.' Aunt Marjorie stood slowly, plagued by her aching joints, and the vicar followed suit.

'I shall intrude no longer,' he said. 'Good day, Miss Treen, and Miss ...' he hesitated as though he had forgotten her name, '... Rose.'

Rose winced. She was Miss Cheevers to the vicar, not plain Rose, and then she realised he was unsure how to address her. She felt uncomfortable. Ashamed.

'Destitute? Is it really that bad? Does Ma have nothing of her own?' Rose asked Aunt Marjorie when the vicar had gone, Jane having shown him out.

'I don't think so. She came here to Canterbury many years ago with nothing. She worked at the school on a voluntary basis, so she will have no savings, no nest egg tucked away.'

'Did you ask Mr Kingsley about the missing will?'

'He claims that he never saw it. It wasn't among the papers he took to the solicitor's office. We have to accept his word on it. But I did take the opportunity of asking him to search his conscience as a loving and much-loved uncle, and question the fairness of the terms of Oliver's bequest.' She sighed. 'All we can hope for is that when your Aunt Temperance has had time to think about it, and Mr Kingsley has had the opportunity to put pressure on her, she will change her mind. She must see that she should give up all claim to her brother's estate when there are children involved. She is always most concerned about what society thinks of her – the last thing she would wish for is to lose the respect of her peers by demonstrating a callous disregard for a family's entitlement.

'Because, in spite of that will, you are morally entitled to Oliver's estate. He lived with your mother for over sixteen years as husband and wife. The twins are his children by blood. There can be no question that he ever intended to leave everything he had to that insufferable woman.' Aunt Marjorie shook her head. 'Oh, I know I shouldn't be rude about her, but she's always had ideas above her station. She's driven Mr Kingsley to drink over the years because she's never satisfied with his efforts, but that's enough of the Kingsleys. We have to make sure that you, Arthur, Donald and Minnie are provided for, and we keep the roof over your heads.'

'Are you suggesting we'll have to move out of Willow Place?' Rose glanced around the parlour at the curiosity cabinet, at the curly-haired porcelain doll which had been Minnie's sitting on the child's chair in the corner because Ma had been unable to give it away when Minnie had decided she was too old to play with it, and at the second copy of the family photograph on the wall. It was as if Pa had had a premonition that it would be the last one they would have taken together. It was a shame that he hadn't used that insight to hurry Ma down the aisle at St Mildred's or make sure his most recent will was safely filed, she thought rather bitterly.

'What am I thinking of, entertaining such an idea at this time?' Aunt Marjorie said quickly. 'Let's put these thoughts aside and concentrate on the present.'

It was too late for that, though. In spite of her aunt's reassurances, their future was far from certain.

Chapter Eight

The Best Way Forward

Ma's funeral was a quiet affair compared with Pa's, with only the vicar, Arthur and the Miskins, Rose and the twins, the two aunts, Mr Kingsley, a few of the parents from the school, a couple of workers from the tannery and her friend Evie and husband John in attendance.

This time, they went to the cemetery to say farewell at the graveside. Pa's headstone hadn't arrived from the stonemason's and there was time to ask for Ma's name to be added to save money. 'At least they are side by side,' people kept saying, but it was no consolation when they should have been together still in life.

Holding Minnie's hand throughout the service, Rose turned away when some of the mourners threw handfuls of earth on to the coffin as it lay in the ground, but the words 'ashes to ashes, dust to dust' lingered in her mind as they walked back to Willow Place for a small wake with wine and sandwiches. Aunt Marjorie had invited the vicar to join them, in part to lend his authority to the reading of Ma's will. Would it save them from the Kingsleys? She knew she was clutching at straws, but she had to have hope.

Back at Willow Place, Jane and Mrs Dunn served refreshments to the Reverend Holdsworth, the Cheeverses, Kingsleys and Miskins, while Aunt Marjorie took Pa's chair at the head of the dining-room table. She put on her pince-nez and opened an envelope which she had found with Rose's help in the drawer of Ma's dressing table.

When everyone was settled, Aunt Marjorie spread the paper out in front of her and began to read.

'This is my will made on ...' She seemed to struggle to work out the date. 'In the event of my death all my worldly goods are to pass to Mr Oliver Cheevers, except for the following: the costs of my funeral expenses – to be modest, not ostentatious.' Aunt Marjorie took a gulp of wine to steady herself. 'I leave these specific articles in my memory to the people listed separately.'

'Well, go on. We are in suspense,' Aunt Temperance said.

'To my dear Nanny, the manual of etiquette, which she bought me to replace the one she had given me in the past, and my pair of bronze vases.' Aunt Marjorie had to compose herself again, reminding Rose of her close attachment to her mother. 'The half a sixpence and silver chain to my daughter Rose.' She remembered how the twins used to grab the chain around Ma's neck when they were babies and it would break, and Oliver would take it to the jeweller's to have it repaired. She hadn't worn it much since then, and Rose wondered why something so underwhelming had been so special to her.

'And the point lace that I worked by myself I leave to my daughter Minnie.' It appeared that Ma had had little she could call her own. 'To Donald, I leave the watercolour I made of him when he was three years old. To Arthur, the fine fountain pen given to me on the occasion of my thirtieth birthday.'

'Is that the end of it?' Aunt Temperance said, as Aunt Marjorie fell silent. 'Is that all she had?'

Aunt Marjorie nodded and folded the papers up again. She removed her pince-nez and dabbed away a tear.

'She had nothing except those assets I have mentioned, her clothes and a small sum of money in the bank which will cover today's costs, but you can be sure that she will have riches in Heaven.'

'Amen,' said the vicar, perhaps a little disappointed that Ma had left nothing to the church.

'That is all. Please, enjoy the Cheeverses' hospitality for as long as you wish.' Aunt Marjorie stood up and turned towards Aunt Temperance. 'I need to talk to you and your husband in private. Shall we retire to the parlour? Rose and Arthur will join us.'

'What, now?' Rose said, surprised that her aunt was in such a hurry.

'It is urgent. I want to know that everything is settled before I return to Ramsgate.'

Mr Kingsley picked up the decanter from the tantalus and carried it into the parlour with him. Aunt Temperance appropriated a plate of sandwiches. Arthur, Rose noticed, said goodbye to the Miskins.

'What about us?' Minnie and Donald said together.

'I would be very grateful if you would stay and act as host and hostess for our guests,' Aunt Marjorie said.

'You are treating us like children,' Donald grumbled. 'We are old enough to have a say in our future.'

'Then prove to me that you can behave like a young gentleman, and do as you're told.' Aunt Marjorie pushed the parlour door firmly shut in his face.

Arthur stood leaning against the wall beside the fireplace, his hands in his pockets. Rose sat down on the chaise beside Mr Kingsley. Her aunts took the fireside chairs.

'I have called this meeting to discuss how Rose and the twins are going to manage without the guidance and love of their parents,' Aunt Marjorie said. 'I assume that you will continue with your plans to marry Miss Miskin, Arthur.'

'Yes, of course, when the time is right. She's open to my suggestion that we look after Rose and the twins. It is no hardship, Aunt Marjorie. It is only what Ma and Pa did for me.'

'That is very considerate of you, and quite a sacrifice on Tabby's behalf. However, I was hoping that your aunt and uncle would step in and offer their support.' Aunt Marjorie gazed at the Kingsleys in turn.

'Mr Kingsley and I will play our part in honouring my brother's memory,' Aunt Temperance said. 'Thanks to him, I am now the legal owner of Willow Place and the family business.'

'It was an error on his part,' Aunt Marjorie muttered.

'Who knows what his motives were? We will never find out,' Mr Kingsley said. 'Suffice to say that we will keep to the letter of the law and continue to run the tannery, maximising the profits with Arthur and Donald's assistance. Arthur will take over his father's role as the gaffer while Donald will work in the yard, and continue to learn how the business works.'

'That is reassuring at least,' Aunt Marjorie said.

'We are good and reasonable people,' he said. 'It isn't right that the children should be left with nothing, thanks to the omissions of their parents. It's bad enough that they are orphans, but now we find out that the twins are bastards too.'

'Oh Mr Kingsley, that is too much,' Aunt Marjorie exclaimed as Rose turned her head towards the door on hearing a slight rattle of the handle. She must have been mistaken, she thought.

'It is only to be expected,' Aunt Temperance said. 'Agnes came to Canterbury under a false name and in disgrace.'

'You have always disliked her. I don't understand why when she made your brother so happy.'

'When she first came here as a young girl with you, she was a hoity-toity little thing, all dressed in white and hiding behind your skirts. I had no time for her. She charmed my grandfather – he said it wasn't her fault that she was how she was because she'd been brought up with expectations. When she turned up again later like a bad penny, she was expecting an illegitimate child, created through sin.'

'Temperance, your holier-than-thou attitude is uncalled for.'

'Well, if I'd had expectations of more money than I could ever spend, a grand house and a rich husband, I wouldn't have thrown them all away. Agnes made her bed, and in my opinion, she should have laid down in it, not inveigled her way between my brother's bedsheets.'

Aunt Marjorie flashed Rose a glance and Rose kept her mouth shut, even though her head hurt at Aunt Temperance's insults to her mother's character.

'I agree that Agnes had her faults – everyone does – but she turned into a loving mother who acted on her compassion for the poor. We must put our memories aside for now because there are decisions to be made about the living. Is it possible that the children can stay here at Willow Place under the care of Mrs Dunn and Jane until they are old enough to make their own way in the world?'

'Oh no, Mr Kingsley and I are intending to move in here.'

Somebody gasped – Arthur perhaps. Rose's fists clenched tight. It hadn't occurred to her that they would have to live with the Kingsleys.

'It's quite a commitment, but one I'm prepared to make. There has been little love lost between us over the years, Marjorie, but it's time to bury the hatchet and move on,' Aunt Temperance said. 'I am going to put my heart and soul into bringing up these children as my brother would have wanted. I have never been blessed with a child of my own and this is my chance to be a mother.'

'It's selfless of you, but do you have any concept of what that entails?'

'Mr Kingsley and I have had many discussions in the past on how we would have fed and disciplined them in a different way. We would have sent Donald off to school as soon as he turned eight, for example. Agnes has paraded her children in front of me for many years. Do you know how painful that is when the doctors have confirmed that you are barren?'

Aunt Marjorie nodded. 'I do have some idea.'

'Of course you do. You are not married.'

'There is no need to rub it in.'

'When you are a wife, the first thing everyone asks you is how many children you have. When you say none, they are dumbfounded. Either they slope away as if you are suffering from some contagious affliction, or they tell you all about their perfect sons and daughters, until you can't bear it any longer.'

'This is the first time you've ever confided in me, cousin. I'm glad we are united in our desire to do what's best for the four of them.'

'I have been advised that the best way forward is for Mr Kingsley and I to adopt Rose, Donald and Minnie. It will hide their illegitimacy and give them respectability.'

'Then that is settled at least, but what about Oliver's will? Won't you reconsider?'

'Our minds are unchanged on that matter,' Aunt Temperance said, her voice hardening.

'What about the school? You will secure its future for the sake of the street children as Oliver and Agnes would have wished?'

'Mr Kingsley is going to look at the ledgers to see if it is possible to keep it going. He suspects that the expenditure on the school outweighs the income from the paying pupils, and some changes will need to be made.'

'It sounds as if you have put plenty of thought into this. I'm very grateful that I can return to my dear charges, knowing that all will be well at Willow Place.'

The door handle juddered and twisted and the door opened, banging against the panelled wall behind it.

'How can all be well with this plan of yours? I heard you scheming behind mine and Minnie's backs.' Rose stared at her younger brother who stood in the doorway, his hands gripping tight to the frame, his muscles flexing and the sinews in his neck taut with fury.

'I'm sorry, Donald,' Aunt Marjorie said calmly. 'You shouldn't have been eavesdropping.'

'I'm glad I did! When were you going to mention this to us?' He glared at Aunt Marjorie. 'Why do you all treat me like a child? I'm nearly thirteen.'

'Come with me, Donald,' Arthur said, walking across to him. 'Let's go out and have a game of cricket.'

'I've told you, I don't play any more.' A tear rolled down Donald's cheek and he turned abruptly, walking away with Arthur's hand on his shoulder.

'That one is trouble,' Aunt Temperance said. 'Things will have to change.'

'I'm sure he'll settle down,' Aunt Marjorie said hopefully, making Rose's heart sink to the pit of her stomach at the thought that desperation had brought her sensible aunt to this. She was in cloud cuckoo land if she thought that the Cheeverses and the Kingsleys could live together in harmony. How on earth did she think it would work?

Later the same day, Aunt Marjorie suggested that Rose walk into town with her for a change of scene. On their way, they crossed King's Bridge, passing the half-timbered Weavers' House where they could hear the handlooms working inside making Canterbury silk and Chamberry muslin. Rose eyed the wooden ducking stool which jutted out from the wall above the river.

'If Aunt Temperance was ducked, I am certain she would not drown,' she said, still desperately unhappy about the arrangements for their future with the Kingsleys.

'Don't let her hear you say that,' Aunt Marjorie said. 'I'm glad you didn't go against her today. She is enjoying her new notoriety at the moment. I should let her puff herself up for now – she will soon get over it.'

'I can't bear to hear her speak badly of Ma.'

'Nor I, but the fortunes of you and your siblings depend on her generosity of spirit.'

'If she has any,' Rose interrupted.

'You must treat her with respect and politeness. She knows how much your parents loved you. She won't dishonour her brother's memory or risk ruining her repu-tation by neglecting your welfare. When they adopt you as their own, they are bound to make provision for you in their wills, which means that the tannery will stay in the family and continue to be passed down through your brothers' children and their children's children after that.'

Rose winced. 'I couldn't bring myself to call them Mother and Father.'

'That's fair enough. You can't contemplate it now, but when you've had time to get used to the idea, I think you'll find that it isn't impossible. Rose, promise me you won't be difficult about this. The Kingsleys are your best hope. Do not alienate them.' They walked on past the Hospital of St Thomas the Martyr. 'I wish I could do something – I have a little money saved up for my retirement, but it won't go very far ...'

'I couldn't let you do that. You have done more than enough for us already,' Rose said. 'What about Arthur and Tabby? Couldn't they look after the rest of us?'

'I think your aunt is determined to live at Willow Place – there wouldn't be room for all of you along with a newly married couple.'

'They are going to live in one of the workers' cottages.'

'You would soon hate the sight of each other. You are used to a certain standard of living.'

'I'm sure Arthur wouldn't mind,' Rose said.

'Tabby might, though. She'll want to start her own family with her new husband, not have to run around cooking and cleaning after his brother and sisters.' Aunt Marjorie gave her a hard stare, and added, 'No matter how helpful they might be. No, Rose, that isn't the answer, I'm afraid.

'There is one other person who might be prevailed upon to help you, but I feel uneasy about approaching her. I should explain why. In fact, this is a good opportunity for me to reveal some of the secrets of the past. Remember, though, that anything I say from here on is between you, me and the bedpost.'

Rose nodded.

'You are wearing the half a sixpence?' Aunt Marjorie said.

'It is an odd memento.' Rose pulled it out from beneath her chemise to show her. 'I remember Ma wearing it when the twins were small.'

'It isn't much, I know, but it has a story behind it. I expect Agnes spoke of it many times.'

'She said it was a trinket, that's all. Ma never was one for jewellery – she said it drew unwanted attention to one's person.'

'It is true that the half a sixpence is a love token with little value apart from the strength of the sentiment behind it, but there was a time when Agnes wore the most beautiful and expensive jewels,' Aunt Marjorie said.

'When she was a girl?'

'That's right.'

'And her father employed a French cook and hired a pineapple to impress his friends and neighbours.'

Aunt Marjorie smiled. 'It was to celebrate his son's christening. I will never forget that day. The Monsieur was found drunk in the cellar at Windmarsh Court, the food was a disaster, and the pineapple ... well, it was an interesting botanical specimen, but too precious to be cut into and tasted. There was another party – when your mother turned nineteen, the Berry-Clays, her adoptive parents, decided to celebrate. Agnes wore a scarlet gown and a heavy gold chain with a pendant at her throat. She looked radiant, the most beautiful and elegant young lady I have ever seen.'

'What happened? How did she end up at Willow Place with Pa?'

'Maybe it is a good time to reveal the truth in its entirety. Agnes has gone and she has more than made up for any failings in her character with her love and devotion to my cousin and her children.'

'Failings? My mother was perfect. I will not hear anything said against her.'

'She was a strong, resourceful and intelligent woman, and better than any of us, considering the life she had.'

'Then tell me,' Rose said.

'Your mother was born an innocent child in the Union at Faversham.'

'The poorhouse?' The hairs on the back of Rose's neck stood on end as her aunt nodded.

'She was eight months old when I first met her. It was the hardest thing I've ever done, tearing an infant from its loving mother's arms, and I will never forget it.'

'Why did you do it?'

'The Berry-Clays had employed me as their nanny. It was done out of the purest of motives, to raise Agnes from poverty and ill health, and give her the love of two doting parents, education and the prospect of a brilliant marriage. Consider this, Rose. Which is worse, to grow up without your mother's love, or suffer the consequences of living what is often a very short and disagreeable life in the poorhouse?'

Rose thought for a moment. 'I couldn't say.' She hadn't been able to imagine living without her mother, yet here she was at sixteen, without her.

'I cared for Agnes as though she was my own daughter until she reached the age of nineteen, when, through an unfortunate turn of events, she was compelled to leave Windmarsh Court. Mr Berry-Clay died the day after her birthday, and for various reasons, it was decided that she should be betrothed to the young man she knew as her cousin.

'She didn't love him and he didn't want the responsibility of a wife at that time, his mind being occupied with how he could overcome his father's objections towards his ambition to study medicine. Agnes couldn't bring herself to marry for financial security and not love. She insisted on freeing both of them from their obligations, enlisting me to help her in her plot to leave Windmarsh and obtain a position as a governess under the name Agnes Linnet.'

Rose couldn't believe what she was hearing.

'We did it so she could make use of her education, accomplishments and good manners to teach other young ladies in return for board and a small honorarium. Without it, she would have been out on the streets, vulnerable and scared, because she knew little of life beyond the marsh.'

'How then did she end up on the streets of Canterbury?' Rose asked, remembering what Arthur had told her.

'Do you remember your father's lectures on how to tell if a man is a gentleman?'

She did, she thought with a small smile.

'Agnes was convinced she had met one, the son of the household for whom she worked. Mr Felix Faraday paid her attention, as well he might considering her character and happy disposition. She was naive, though, and flattered when he approached her. As she revealed to me much later, she felt that having been raised in a wealthy household with certain expectations, she was as entitled as any other young lady to welcome his affection for her. He seemed genuine. He offered marriage and made out that his mother approved of the match, or so she was given to understand ...'

Rose bit her lip. 'He was my father, wasn't he, the gentleman of whom you speak?'

'Who was most definitely not a gentleman, but merely the son of a baronet,' Aunt Marjorie said firmly. 'Your mother left the Faradays' household when she was carrying you in her belly, and then she found lodgings with Mrs Hamilton in Canterbury.'

Which was why the old woman had taken an interest in their family, Rose thought.

'Agnes worked as a screever, writing letters and fake-ments. The couple who employed her were on the make and when they were found out – Agnes provided proof of their trickery – they left Canterbury. Agnes had no money to pay her rent, and Mrs Hamilton, being the hard-nosed businesswoman that she is, put her out on the street.

'Oliver found her and took her in when she was at her lowest ebb. In fact, she told me she'd been ready to die when they found her at the foot of the Westgate Towers. In turn, she and Oliver offered Arthur a home, and not long after that you were born. You know the rest. You see, your mother had a strange life, and a tragic end, although I console myself – as you do, I hope – with the thought that she is in the arms of her love.'

Rose nodded as her aunt continued, 'When Agnes left Windmarsh, I regretted that I'd concentrated on preparing her for the rigours of the drawing room, but not the skills for everyday living.'

'Are you lecturing me?' Rose said, half smiling.

'If you're ever in a situation – like now, I suppose – when you have to stand on your own two feet, you'll be thankful that your ma made you study the basics of finance and the value of money. And I will give you this tip to reinforce what your pa has told you – not everyone in the world is of good character. There are those who will think nothing of stealing your money, or tricking you out of it. Be careful whom you trust.'

Give me some credit, Rose thought. Sometimes she felt that her aunt treated her like one of her young charges.

'The half a sixpence. You still haven't told me about that?'

'Oh? So I haven't. I'm getting old, Rose. My memory isn't what it once was. Let me see. From what I've gath-ered, your grandfather gave the half a sixpence to your

121

grandmother, his sweetheart. Under what circumstances, I don't know exactly.

'When Agnes was eighteen, I received some correspondence from Mrs Carter, asking if I could arrange a meeting with her daughter. I knew we would be in terrible trouble if we were found out and I struggled with my conscience over her request for many weeks because she had agreed that she would never contact her daughter again. Mr Berry-Clay had told Agnes that her true mother was dead and I had given him my word that I wouldn't reveal the truth to my charge. Don't look at me like that, Rose. He didn't want to disturb dear Agnes's peace of mind – he had taken her in out of the goodness of his heart.'

Rose felt sorry for her aunt, torn between loyalty to her former employer and her love for Agnes.

'There were a few people who knew about Agnes being born in the Union to an unmarried mother. Mr Berry-Clay trusted them not to reveal her humble origins to all and sundry. Even though he had brought her up to be a respectable young lady, the fact she was illegitimate, if it became widely known, would have tainted her reputation and affected her chance of making a good marriage. I know it's unfair, but that's how it is. Society frowns on the children born out of wedlock.'

'You broke your word. You risked your place at Windmarsh Court,' Rose said.

'Mr Berry-Clay allowed us to accompany him to Faversham. Mrs Berry-Clay wanted Agnes to call on the dressmaker to order new gowns for her birthday. While her father was attending to his business at the brewery, Agnes and I went for a walk down to the creek where I introduced her to her mother who was waiting for us. That was when Mrs Carter gave the half a sixpence to your mother.' She sighed. 'Oh dear. I'd never seen Agnes like that.'

'Like what?'

'She was so shocked and upset that she could hardly bear to look at her mother, let alone speak.'

'Didn't you warn her in advance?'

'You and your ma were very much alike. When Agnes had made up her mind about something, it was almost impossible to change it.'

'Are you saying that I'm pig-headed?'

'I admire the strength of your opinions, but I think you should always be prepared to regulate them when necessary. Anyway, going back to my story ... I didn't want to say or do anything that would raise suspicion on anyone's part. I think if I'd told her where we were going and why, she would have refused. I had to be devious. May the Lord forgive me my sins, but everything I did was for Agnes.' Aunt Marjorie's eyes filled with tears. 'Oh, I miss her.'

'We all do,' Rose said, patting her arm.

'I shouldn't be like this. She was your mother. Oh, if I'd been more circumspect, if I'd followed Mr Berry-Clay's orders ...'

'You mustn't blame yourself. You did what you thought was right.'

'The meeting went badly wrong. It triggered the train of events that ended with Mr Berry-Clay's brother revealing that he had seen us on the wharf with Agnes's mother, which set off her father's collapse and premature death.'

'I'm confused. It's all too much to take in,' Rose said slowly. Poor Ma. What a life she had led. She wished she had talked about it to share the burden. It was no wonder that her heart had given up.

'The half a sixpence is your mother's legacy.'

'And a reminder of such deep sorrows. It seems wrong to keep it.'

'Ah, that's where you're wrong. It is a symbol of a powerful love between two people who were forced apart by circumstances. And it is also a sign of a mother's love. Mrs Carter gave up her child, Agnes, to give her a better life. It wouldn't work out in the way she'd imagined, but she wasn't to know that. Agnes did have a better life – with Oliver and Arthur, you and the twins. The half a sixpence will remind you of your history, and not to repeat the mistakes of the past.'

Rose held the half a sixpence and chain tightly in her hand as they continued walking along St Margaret's, passing the Three Tuns and turning off Castle Street to head for the Dane John.

As well as answering a few questions, her aunt had raised more – like what had happened to force her grandparents apart? Her grandmother was married now, but to whom, if it wasn't to her grandfather?

She opened her palm. The half a coin was set in a silver mount, but the roughened edge where it had been sawn or filed in two was clearly visible. How had the man who was her grandfather done it, and why?

'I wonder what happened to the other half,' she said.

'I wonder,' her aunt echoed.

'Do you think it's still out there? Do you think my grandfather has kept it?'

'If he's still living,' Aunt Marjorie said. 'He'll be an old man by now. Your grandmother is alive and kicking, though, and residing on a farm in the village of Overshill, which is near Selling. I do know that.'

'How come?' Rose looked up.

'I wrote to her to let her know our sad news.'

'I see.'

'I thought she should know that her daughter ... that Agnes had departed this life. I was under the impression

124

that she might consider attending the funeral, but she declined with a short note expressing her sorrow and a wish not to rake up the past. It's sad, but she must have her reasons.'

'I wonder what they are,' Rose said, wishing she could have met her.

'She is married – perhaps she has kept her history from her husband. Oh, I don't know.' Aunt Marjorie sighed. 'I did what I could. Dear Rose, I think that for now we must look forward, not back.'

'Are you absolutely sure that there's no other way?' Rose said, recalling their plight.

'No, I'm afraid there isn't,' Aunt Marjorie cut in. 'You'll be suitably grateful and bow to the Kingsleys' authority, knowing that this situation will not last for ever. You'll be dependent on them until you come of age.'

'That's years away,' Rose exclaimed. 'You know what Aunt Temperance is like – you are being very harsh.'

'Because this is the best chance you, Arthur and the twins have of staying together. The time will fly, I promise.'

Rose wished she could believe her. They continued their walk through the Dane John gardens, looking out from the top of the city wall, before returning to Willow Place. As they strolled up the drive past the ducks, Aunt Marjorie said, 'Be brave. Remember your ma and how she overcame adversity. You are your mother's daughter and you will do the same.'

Chapter Nine

Cod Liver Oil and Malt

Rose put Ma's secrets behind her, preferring to remember her as she was: the warmth of her embrace; her scent of orange flower and rosewater; her laughter when she was jesting with Pa. She kept the half a sixpence around her neck because she had bequeathed it to her personally, mother to daughter.

Aunt Marjorie's luggage was in the hall ready for her departure back to Ramsgate the following morning. Rose and the twins were waiting to wish her farewell as she put on her hat and gloves.

'Do you have to go?' Minnie asked. 'I'll miss you.'

'Unfortunately, my services are required elsewhere. There is no one to look after the children while their parents travel to Italy for a family occasion. Don't worry, I'll come back and check on you as soon as I can.' She embraced each of them before turning to Donald. 'Bring my bags, dear. Goodbye, Minnie. And give my love to Arthur. I assume he is already at work. He is a good boy. Tell him that I expect to receive my invitation with the new date for the wedding very soon.'

'How much did you bring with you?' Donald muttered, struggling with her bags.

'Everything but the scullery sink.' Aunt Marjorie smiled. 'I fear it's too late for me to learn how to travel light.'

Rose stood at the door with her arms wrapped around Minnie's shoulders as they watched their aunt and Donald lagging behind with the bags until they disappeared round the corner at the bottom of the drive. Kissing her sister's hair, Rose released her.

'That's that then,' Minnie sighed. 'What happens now?'

'Donald will go to the tannery as usual when he gets back from the station,' Rose said, wondering how everything could seem so normal and ordinary when everything had changed.

'What about us?'

'That's a very good question. I suppose we should go back to school later.' It was hard to imagine returning to the classroom, knowing it would remind them of Ma's absence. A sudden memory of chalk dust caught in the slant of the sun's rays made her eyelids prick. 'We'll reopen on Monday.'

Minnie bounced on her toes with joy. It was the first time Rose had seen her happy since the day they lost Pa.

'I'm looking forward to seeing my friends again. I've missed them.'

Aunt Marjorie was right, Rose thought as she followed her sister into the kitchen. It was better to keep busy than mope about the house, dwelling on what they had lost. She hoped and prayed that this was the beginning of the road to finding peace and some kind of acceptance of what had happened.

Not long after Donald had returned to Willow Place from the station on his way to the tannery, there was a hammering at the door. Mrs Dunn was already in the kitchen instructing Jane on the order of the day, so Rose went to answer it.

'Oh, it's you,' she said, surprised to find the Kingsleys on the doorstep.

'May we step inside?' Mr Kingsley removed his top hat.

'There's no need to ask permission.' Aunt Temperance pushed past him, an umbrella in one hand and the quivering leaves of a potted aspidistra in the other. She shook the raindrops from her umbrella and dropped it into the hallstand as if she owned the place, which she did, to be fair, Rose had to admit. The fact that it was her right didn't make it feel any better. A little delicacy in front of the twins, who had made their appearance just after the Kingsleys' arrival, would have been kind.

Aunt Temperance removed Ma's parlour fern from the jardinière and put the aspidistra on top instead. 'Take it away. We don't need this any more.' She thrust the potted fern into Rose's hands, a gesture that filled Rose with a sense of impending doom. She had known this was coming, but why did it have to be so soon?

Her aunt turned to Mr Kingsley.

'Send the men in. I will tell them exactly which furniture is to be removed so there are no misunderstandings. Donald, you can assist Mr Kingsley in moving our belongings from the house in Burgate Street. You'll need the barrow from the yard. The smaller items are to be carried covered from prying eyes. I don't want the neighbours knowing what we have and haven't got. And if anything gets scratched or broken, I'll have the culprit tied to the yardarm.'

'My dear, you are too harsh,' Mr Kingsley said.

'We start as we mean to go on, treating them with firmness and authority. Oh, we shall keep that.' Aunt Temperance pointed at the chiffonier. 'I've always coveted it. Rose, find a box and empty it. Go on. Mr Kingsley and I wish to have somewhere to store our bits and pieces. Your parents have no need of it now. Don't throw anything away before I've had a look through to see what we might keep.'

Rose's eyes stung with tears as she went out to the kitchen to put the fern down and ask Mrs Dunn if she knew where she could find a box.

'Oh ducky, what's wrong?' the housekeeper said gently as she carried a bowl of plums across to the table. 'It's the Kingsleys, isn't it? I heard their voices.'

'I need a box so I can clear space for their things.'

'How dare they! What are they thinking?' Mrs Dunn dropped the bowl on to the floor where it shattered, scattering the plums.

'I'm afraid they can do as they wish. This is their home now,' Rose said sadly.

'That's no reason to treat you badly.' Mrs Dunn rushed into the hall to find Aunt Temperance, who was directing the men from the tannery and a local removal company who were moving the furniture. 'Mrs Kingsley, it is a cruel thing that you do, making those girls clear away their dearly departed parents' belongings and precious keepsakes.'

'What business is it of yours?' Aunt Temperance arched one eyebrow. 'Really, Mrs Dunn. You should mind your manners and be grateful that we decided not to bring our own housekeeper with us.' She flashed a glance at Jane who had appeared at the bottom of the stairs with a mop and bucket. 'Or the maids. They were both getting ideas above their station so I sent them on their way. This is a fresh start for Mr Kingsley and me, and we don't need lots of servants when we have the girls here to help out with the chores.'

'I'm sorry if I spoke out of turn, Mrs Kingsley.'

'You must address me as mistress of Willow Place from now on.'

Mrs Dunn bowed her head and backed down. Rose guessed that she couldn't risk losing her place for the sake of her principles.

'What about school, Aunt?' Rose asked.

'We'll talk about that another time. Suffice to say, we need you here this morning and for the rest of the week, but perhaps you will have time to clean and air the premises later today.'

Somewhat reassured by her aunt's words, Rose helped her sister clear out some of their parents' personal effects while the men and Donald moved much of the old furniture out of the house and replaced it with chairs, beds and chests from the Kingsleys' former home.

'It is hard to clear out their clothes,' Minnie sniffed as they stared into Ma's wardrobe. 'I don't want to do it.'

Her chest aching with renewed heartbreak, Rose put her arm around her sister's shoulders and gave her a hug.

'Neither do I, but it has to be done. Waste not, want not. We should keep as much as possible – the dresses can always be altered.' Rose breathed in the faint scent of Ma's perfume as she reached out and swept her hand along the row of garments, hesitating on the practical navy serge that Ma had always worn when she was teaching, and the pale green cotton dress decorated with pink flowers that reminded her of when they had gone to the seaside on the day when Pa had fallen ill, and the grey silk that she had worn for special occasions like her birthday. 'We'll share the shawls and shoes.'

When it came to Pa's clothes, Rose put a jacket aside each for Arthur and Donald, and stowed his heavy winter overcoat under Donald's bed.

When Aunt Temperance decreed that they had done enough in the house for one day, Rose took Ma's key from the hook on the back of the front door, and she and Minnie went to school to open the windows for a while. Having knocked down a few cobwebs from the corners of the classroom, they cleaned the privy and swept the floors.

Minnie counted the slates and workbooks, and wiped the chalk from the blackboard: Ma's last words to her pupils.

'That's better,' Rose said, dashing back tears as she surveyed their handiwork and wondered how many of their pupils would return. She couldn't help feeling that some would have moved to rival establishments and others like Baxter might have found alternative, more lucrative occupations on the streets of Canterbury.

By the end of the day, when they sat down for dinner, Willow Place had changed for ever. Mr Kingsley was head of the table, while Aunt Temperance sat at his right hand. Donald, Arthur, Rose and Minnie took their places, and Jane served boiled ham, parsley sauce, potatoes and carrots.

'Remember to chew each mouthful twenty times,' their aunt said as Donald began to wolf down his dinner. 'It is better for the digestion.'

'My brother's always gobbled his food – it's never done him any harm,' Arthur said.

'We'll have none of that lip,' Aunt Temperance said.

'Manners maketh man,' Mr Kingsley observed, chewing noisily on a piece of fat. 'We will have silence at mealtimes as was the rule at home when I was a boy.'

'It prevents the breaching of other matters of social protocol, such as not talking with one's mouth full,' Aunt Temperance said quickly, aiming this remark at her husband.

Everyone fell silent. Rose pushed her food around her plate, having completely lost her appetite.

'This is just how it should be,' Aunt Temperance said eventually. 'We will live as one happy family.'

Minnie began to cry. Rose reached out for her hand. Mr Kingsley looked at his wife, then cleared his throat and said, 'I'm truly sorry for your loss, my dears, but this is a cross we all have to bear. We must pray that we will live together in harmony.'

'Minnie must make more of an effort to overcome her grief,' Aunt Temperance added. 'Most people lose their parents at one time or another – it's nothing unusual. Life goes on. That's right, isn't it, Mr Kingsley?'

He poured himself a third or fourth glass of wine – Rose had lost count – and Aunt Temperance moved the bottle away from him.

'That sounded rather unkind,' Rose said. 'It's hard for us, Minnie especially.'

'It is much worse for my husband. Imagine becoming a father at his advanced age.'

'He is not our father.' The blood seemed to drain out through Rose's feet.

'He is taking on all the responsibilities of a father; therefore it is only right that you should honour his wish to be known as Pa Kingsley.'

'I will never call him Pa,' Rose said.

'My dear wife, you promised to be gentle with the children, not rush in like a bull in a china shop. Don't worry, Rose. All I hope for is that in the fullness of time, you, Arthur, Donald and Minnie will begin to consider us as your loving parents. We will do things together, share common interests and create memories.' He looked towards the picture of the family on the wall. 'I'll book a sitting with the photographer, and on Sunday we will worship as a family. We will attend St Mildred's, I think.'

'Oh no, that will not do, Mr Kingsley,' Aunt Temperance said.

'It will go some way to prove to our neighbours that we are committed to bringing them up with kindness and according to Christian principles.'

'To this day, I don't know why my brother continued to attend St Mildred's rather than join the great and good of the city at the cathedral.'

'You know why. Oliver preferred to follow in your grandfather's footsteps, associating himself with the common folk of this parish.'

'Of which there are far too many,' Aunt Temperance sighed. 'How I wish we could pick this house up and put it in a more salubrious neighbourhood.'

'Don't judge these people too hastily or you will be considered a snob.' Mr Kingsley belched loudly. 'Excuse me.'

'What are we going to do, Rose?' Minnie sighed when they retired to bed.

'We'll do as Ma and Pa would have wished – we'll make the best of it,' she said. 'I believe Mr Kingsley wants the best for us, but I'm not sure about our aunt.'

On the Sunday, they went to church with their aunt and uncle where they endured a long sermon and the stares of their fellow worshippers. As they walked back home, Aunt Temperance said that they would go to the cathedral the following week for the comfort of the pews and a better class of worshipper. After lunch, Arthur went to walk out with Tabby for the afternoon, leaving Rose and the twins at Willow Place, while their aunt implemented the next part of her regime. Holding a brown bottle and spoon, she lined the three of them up in the hallway.

'Don't look so worried, my dears. This won't kill you.'

'What is it?' Donald asked.

'It's your weekly dose of cod liver oil and malt.'

Rose was aghast. Hadn't they suffered enough?

Her aunt measured out the first dose. 'Eldest first,' she said.

'I'm too old for this,' Rose said.

'You're never too old to look after your health. Come on, open your beak.'

Retching, she took a sip. She couldn't swallow it, nor could she spit it out in front of her aunt, so she had to let the fishy fluid filter between her teeth as Donald took his spoonful, making a great play of spluttering and coughing, clutching his throat.

'Hold your nose, Minnie.' Aunt Temperance poured a third dose, pinched Minnie's nose and forced the spoon between her lips. She turned back to Donald. 'Show me it's gone. I don't trust you.'

He opened his mouth and their aunt nodded her approval. Rose froze, expecting her to ask her to do the same, but she didn't – she turned and stalked back to the kitchen with the bottle and spoon, giving Rose the chance to spit into the aspidistra pot.

'What are you doing?' Donald began to laugh.

'Shh – she'll make me have another dose if she finds out.' Rose wiped her mouth. 'That stuff is disgusting.'

'You must take your medicine, or you'll die.' Minnie burst into tears.

'Oh Minnie, I'm not going to die. Look at me. I'm as fit as a flea.'

'So was Ma, and Pa too,' she sobbed. 'I miss them, and I hate the Kingsleys. Can't you make them go away?'

She couldn't, but she could make sure that they spent as little time with them as possible and to that end she was looking forward to going back to school in the morning. However, their aunt had other plans.

'The school must remain closed,' she said when Rose and Minnie were ready to leave after breakfast. 'You can't possibly run it by yourself. The pupils will find another school.'

134

'They've paid the term's fees in advance – they're owed the education that Ma would have given them.'

'Your mother is dead and the contract broken. What's more, there's no one to teach them.'

'I can do it. It brings in a goodly amount of money,' Rose said, playing on her aunt's greed.

'Hardly. If anything, it's made a loss over the years because your parents gave out free education to the little tykes from the Rookery – a complete waste of time when their characters are fixed by the time they are weaned. Anyway, Mr Kingsley has had a good look at those ledgers and your mother's figures don't add up. Agnes never took an income from her teaching.'

The revelation that the school made no money made Rose begin to doubt herself. She had some idea about balance sheets and termly fees, but Ma hadn't shown her the actual books.

'It seems to me that Jane will need some help around the house from now on, so go and put a note on the door at the school, then come back and work out how you'll apportion the chores.'

'But—'

'That is all I will say on the matter. Run along.'

When Rose reached the school, she found a shadowy figure dressed in tattered rags sheltering from the drizzle in the doorway.

'Baxter?' She lowered the hood of her cloak. 'What are you doing here?'

'I've bin here every morning to see when I can come back to lessons.' He gave her a big grin. 'Miss, I'm glad you're back. I've missed bein' here … I've even missed the readin', like, and the writin' and the 'rithmetic.'

'I don't know how to tell you this, but there is no more school,' she said.

'Why?' he said. 'You are at least as good a teacher as your ma. Better.'

'I'm afraid it's impossible at present. My aunt has expressed a desire that the school should close.'

'What has it got to do with that old bat?'

'Please, this is my aunt you are talking about.'

'I'm sorry, miss. It's just that my blood is boilin' and the words slipped out.'

What did her aunt care about the pupils? As far as she was concerned, those who were wealthy enough could pay to go elsewhere, while the others could continue their education on the streets.

'We'll call this a prize for good attendance,' she said quietly, slipping a coin into his sticky palm. 'Keep this to yourself.'

He thanked her, and went on, 'Will I see you again?'

'Oh, I'm sure of that. Good day, Baxter. Oh, wait a minute. I wonder if we might go on with our lessons somehow? We could meet once a week and continue with the three R's. What do you think?'

'I'd like that, but my pa ... he wouldn't and I don't want to cross him. Thanks, though. Good day, miss.' He ran off into the rain, leaving Rose feeling sore at heart.

Not for the first time, she wondered what her father had been thinking of.

Chapter Ten

Aspidistras and Apple-Pie Beds

The family settled into their new routine over the next few days. Mrs Dunn and Jane adjusted to the different regime and life went on until the middle of September when Aunt Temperance fell out with the housekeeper over their contract with one of the local tradesmen.

One morning Rose was in the kitchen when she overheard them arguing in the hall about the butcher who brought regular deliveries to Willow Place. Aunt Temperance swore he was taking advantage of Mrs Dunn's good nature, providing mutton when she'd requested lamb. She refused to pay his bill and told the housekeeper to cancel his deliveries in future. She went on to grumble about the cost of sending the laundry out and declared it would be more economical for the linens to be washed at the house, at which Mrs Dunn's voice rose to a fury.

'Jane doesn't have time to do any laundering, and you're going to have to have another think if you imagine that I'll be doing your dirty smalls!' Mrs Dunn came marching into the kitchen, her cheeks bright pink as she took off her apron. 'If the Kingsleys want change, they can have it. I'm sorry, Rose, but my temperament isn't compatible with your aunt's. I can't work for her a moment longer. She is driving me to distraction with her demands.'

'Please, don't leave us,' Rose begged. How would they go on without Mrs Dunn, who had been a constant in their lives for so many years? She felt sick at heart.

'It will work out for you – you have your Aunt Marjorie's protection, and Arthur, of course.' Mrs Dunn hung her apron on the hook on the back of the kitchen door.

'How will I manage without you?' Jane joined in.

'Jane, you will do perfectly well – in fact, I think you may well blossom without me.' Forcing a smile, Mrs Dunn turned to Rose. 'If you need any tips for making brawn, you know where I am.' She wiped her hands on a cloth and walked out into the hall to confront Aunt Temperance. Rose followed.

'Mrs Kingsley, I am leaving.'

'Can't you see I'm otherwise engaged, you tiresome woman? I'm expecting Mrs Kinders to call at ten.' Mrs Kinders was one of her acquaintances from the cathedral. 'We'll discuss this later.'

'There is nothing to discuss,' Mrs Dunn said, appraising the situation. 'I promised myself that I wouldn't stay on here when you and Mr Kingsley moved in, but I changed my mind out of loyalty to Mr and Mrs Cheevers and their children. I can't continue any longer – I'm handing in my notice forthwith.'

'You will stay for a full month as agreed in your contract with Agnes,' Aunt Temperance said.

'I shall leave straight away. My mistress is dead and I have no contract with you, so I'm not bound to stay on. I will collect my wages tomorrow, Mrs Kingsley. Good morning to you.'

'Good morning, Mrs Dunn.' Aunt Temperance cast her parting shot as the housekeeper left. 'Just remember that sometimes it's better the devil you know than the one that you don't. Don't just stand there, Rose and Minnie. Those cupboards won't clear themselves.' She turned to the maid who was at the kitchen door, her mouth open. 'Jane, you will step into Mrs Dunn's shoes.'

From then on after Mrs Dunn's departure, Rose and Minnie worked in the house with Jane; Mr Kingsley, Arthur and Donald continued with their duties at the tannery; and their aunt kept up appearances, calling on her acquaintances and inviting them back to Willow Place to show off her home.

One morning in October, Rose was up early. Unable to sleep for Minnie's snoring, she rinsed her face, brushed her hair and cleaned her teeth with tooth powder, made from Ma's recipe of olive oil, salt water and ash, before going downstairs to look for Jane. At first, she couldn't find her. Was she upstairs, fetching the pisspots, or had she gone to the market early? Or – she strained her ears – was that the sound of sobbing?

'Jane?' She made her way to the scullery where she found the maid with her back to her, staring at a huge stack of dirty dishes. 'Is there something wrong?'

The maid turned. 'I'm sorry, miss. I didn't want you to see me like this, but I can't help it. I'm at the end of my tether.'

'Have you slept at all?' Rose asked, noticing the dark rings around her eyes.

'I have had but two hours of sleep because Mrs Kingsley wanted me to get the laundry done by last night.'

'I thought she'd changed her mind about sending it out.'

'No, she's instructed me to do it, along with all the cleaning and baking. I got up early, but as you can see I am way behind like the cow's tail.'

'Let me help. I'll wash the floor and get on with the baking while you get the dishes done.'

'Thank you,' Jane sniffed as Rose reached past her for the mop, and went to give the floor a quick lick and a promise before opening Ma's old book of household management to look for a recipe.

'What are you making?' Yawning, Minnie came to join her a little while later.

'Where have you been?' Rose said, looking down at her sister's muddy feet. 'I thought you were in bed.'

'I've been outside talking to the birds. Cock Robin was singing in the holly bush and Jenny Wren was hopping around by the shed.'

'Take your shoes off, please. I've just scrubbed the floor.' Rose corrected herself. 'Sort of.'

Minnie took off her shoes and slid around the floor in her stockings to remove any trace of her footprints.

'There,' she sang out. 'It's as clean as a whistle.'

'And your stockings will have to go straight in the wash,' Rose said.

'Oh, you're making poor man's pudding.' Minnie's eyes lit up and her hand slid towards the crock of raisins which had been brought all the way from the exotic Ottoman Empire.

'Keep your hands off those.' Rose smiled. 'Fetch me the sugar from the pantry.'

Minnie brought the sugar loaf, and Rose used a hammer and chisel to break it into chunks before cutting it into smaller pieces with the nippers. She placed slices of bread into a bowl and added a layer of raisins, some cinnamon and some orange peel, before pouring a mixture of melted butter, milk and a beaten egg on top with a sprinkling of sugar.

Once she'd put it in the oven to bake, she asked Minnie to keep an eye on the time while she answered the letter from Aunt Marjorie which had arrived the day before. Their aunt had written that she was suffering from pains in her joints, so Rose didn't like to worry her unnecessarily. Instead, she wrote back:

Dear Aunt Marjorie,

Minnie is well. We are becoming accustomed to the new routine. Arthur and Tabby haven't set a new date for their wedding yet.

She paused, unsure what else to say. She thought of describing how Aunt Temperance had made Jane cry by overloading her with work, but decided that that would bring Aunt Marjorie rushing to Willow Place. At dinner on the last evening of her prolonged stay with them, she had looked pale and complained of indigestion as well as her usual aches and pains. Rose wished her aunt could afford a peaceful retirement – she needed a rest, not more strain and stress.

She continued writing.

The Kingsleys have closed the school and let the cottage out. I feel bad about it, but I must respect their wishes. I suppose they feel that they have contributed enough to society by taking on the four of us.

Donald is playing cricket again, and Minnie is sewing. As for me, the days pass quickly in a flurry of cooking and chores, so I have little time to read, but I mustn't grumble. We are happy in our own way.

Your loving Rose

She went out to post it and ran into Miss Miskin on the way back.

'Good morning,' she said brightly, envying Tabby's navy gloves as she unbuttoned the one on her left hand and took it off. 'How are you?'

'I'm well, thank you, but what about you? Arthur has told me what you've been through. I hope you're settling down with your aunt and uncle now. It sounds like it's been a nightmare.'

Rose hesitated, taken aback at Tabby's frank speech.

'I'm sorry. Perhaps I shouldn't have said anything, but I thought that with us soon to be sisters ...'

'Oh, it's fine.' Rose smiled, seeing the flash of gemstones and gold on Tabby's finger. 'Is that the ring?'

Tabby held out her hand so Rose could examine the thin gold band set with three small red garnets.

'It's beautiful.'

'It was a gift from your parents,' Tabby said. 'Oh, I wish I'd had the chance to get to know them better. Your pa was so generous and good-humoured, while your ma was ... well, she was kind and very refined. I always felt welcome at Willow Place.'

Rose couldn't help sensing the unspoken contrast with the Kingsleys' regime. Tabby didn't come to visit them now. Hastily, she changed the subject. 'I hope our bridesmaids' dresses still fit. I'm sure Minnie has grown taller.'

'I expect you'll be next down the aisle, Rose,' Tabby teased. 'There must be a young man who's caught your eye?'

'Oh, not yet.'

'You'll meet someone soon, I'm sure. Being a bridesmaid is meant to be a good way of procuring a husband.'

Rose didn't like the sound of that – the phrase 'procuring a husband' didn't sound terribly romantic when she wanted a gentleman who would fall at her feet and declare his eternal love for her.

'I hope you find someone as wonderful as my Arthur. I know he'll always look after me.'

Rose heard the cathedral bell tolling the hour. 'I'd better be getting back. It's been lovely to see you.'

'You haven't been to church recently,' Tabby said quickly. 'Reverend Holdsworth has been asking after you. I expect you worship elsewhere with your aunt and uncle. I've spoken to Arthur, of course, but he's careful about how much he reveals, not wanting to embarrass his brother and sisters. He's kind in that way – in every way.'

Rose wasn't sure whether she could confide in Tabby or not. Having thought for a moment, she decided there could be no harm in it.

'We haven't been anywhere on a Sunday for a while. My aunt took us to St Mildred's once, and the cathedral twice. Donald didn't mean to, but he had an attack of the hiccoughs and everyone was looking at us.' Rose couldn't help grinning at the memory. Her aunt had expressed her disappointment in the fact that the Archbishop had not made his way from Lambeth Palace to grace them with his presence, and was embarrassed by Donald's behaviour – which hadn't been his fault – and by the Cheeverses' state of dress, which was in her opinion rather too shabby for the hallowed precincts of the cathedral. After that, she told them to stay at home to help Jane and occupy themselves.

'I always wished I'd had brothers,' Tabby said. 'I look forward to seeing you again soon.'

'Very soon, I hope,' Rose responded. As she made her way back to Willow Place, she was lighter of heart than she had been for a while.

The same evening, when they had finished dinner and all of the poor man's pudding had gone, there was a howl of anguish from the hall.

'What has happened to my lovely plant? It is dying!' Holding the aspidistra aloft, Aunt Temperance came marching into the kitchen where the younger Cheeverses tended to congregate around the table, in preference to the parlour. She pulled it out of the pot by its leaves, which had lost their shine and turned brown. 'Ugh. It smells of fish. How strange.' Wrinkling her nose, she flashed a glance at Rose and the twins. 'Do you have anything to say about this?'

'No, Aunt,' Rose said.

'No.' Minnie shook her head for extra emphasis.

'I wonder if it would be worth speaking to Alderman Masters to see if he has any idea what's wrong with it,' Donald said. 'He has green fingers.'

'Oh yes.' Aunt Temperance's hair released a faint puff of white powder. 'What a good idea. Thank you, Donald. I'm very glad of your advice. I think you are growing up at last.'

'You owe me, Rose,' he said when their aunt had left the room again.

'I don't know what you're talking about,' she said archly.

'You know very well – I've seen you spitting in the pot every Sunday while me and Minnie have to suffer.' He chuckled. 'I've a good mind to mention it at dinner-time.'

'You wouldn't.'

'Of course not.' He stood up. 'I'm going to find Joe.'

Rose smiled. Donald also seemed happier than he had been for some time: life was looking up a little. She wondered how long it would last.

Not long, it seemed, because their aunt and uncle's behaviour to Jane was worsening by the day, wearing her down with their nit-picking and bullying. When Mr

Kingsley rolled in late at night, he would rouse the maid from her slumber with requests for strong coffee and Rose wasn't sure what else, but she could hear Jane's yelps of protest from the kitchen as she lay in her bed at the top of the house. Occasionally, her aunt would interrupt them, screaming at her husband for his drunken antics and lack of consideration for her feelings.

One morning after one of these incidents, Rose came into the dining room with Minnie to help Jane clear the plates, and heard her aunt's voice raised in shrill complaint.

'There is no need to speak to me like that, Mr Kingsley!'

Arthur and Donald had excused themselves and Minnie was pushing a piece of buttered toast around her plate. Mr Kingsley was sitting at one end of the table, and Aunt Temperance at the other as if she was Queen Victoria holding court. Rose noted with distaste that her uncle had left his devilled kidneys.

'I will say what needs to be said. The sound of your voice gives me a headache.'

'It's the gin,' Aunt Temperance said. 'I told you not to go out last night.'

'It isn't your place to tell me what to do.'

Rose thought back to Ma and Pa and how she had rarely heard a cross word pass between them.

'You should take a leaf out of Arthur's book and get yourself round to the office early every morning.'

'There's no point when the clerk isn't in until nine. Anyway, I'm not sure I can bear to look at the books today. It's the end of the month and the sales are down – dropped like a stone into the Stour. For the first time in the tannery's history, the losses appear to have wiped out the profits.'

'How can that be?' Aunt Temperance said. 'The figures have to be wrong. It's that new clerk – he can't add up.

I told you it was a mistake to hire him when you had all those other applicants, but when do you ever listen to me?'

'I know his father very well. He came highly recommended.'

'Your judgement is affected when you're in your cups, my dear,' his wife said sarcastically. 'Anyway, what is all this about losses? I trusted you when you said you could run the business with your eyes closed.'

'I know what I'm doing. I've had years of experience with the gaffer, and before that with your grandfather. It will shake down after a while.'

'It better had. You aren't getting any younger and we must feather our nest while we can.' Aunt Temperance turned to Minnie. 'Don't slouch or you'll end up a hunchback. And Rose, wipe that silly expression off your face – it will stay there if the wind changes.'

Rose forced a smile but there was nothing that could change how she felt at having heard their conversation. The tannery would be flourishing if they'd only let Arthur take hold of the reins, she thought angrily. She could see why Pa had refused to take Mr Kingsley on as his business partner in the past.

Mr Kingsley went to his office and Aunt Temperance headed into Canterbury to call on an acquaintance, leaving Minnie and Rose to help Jane make the beds. Rose took the clean sheets from the linen cupboard and carried them into the Kingsleys' bedroom.

'You take the pillowcases off and I'll strip the bed, Minnie,' she said, tearing the sheets off the mattress and piling them on the floor. She unfolded a fresh white undersheet and spread it across the bed, folding and tucking the corners. She took a second one and put that on top, folding it up short.

'You've done that wrong,' Minnie said helpfully, coming across to open it up again.

'No, leave it. It's as I intended.' Rose hadn't been sure that she was going to go through with her plan, but she remembered Mr Kingsley's behaviour the night before and a sense of injustice swelled inside her. What had he been trying to do to poor Jane? She knew it wasn't right, whatever it was. He was a lecherous old man in a position of power imposing himself on a sweet and innocent young woman. 'Fetch me the lavender water.'

Minnie brought the cut-glass bottle over from the dressing table.

'Take the stopper off.' Rose watched her sister fumble with the lid. 'Now tip it out over the sheets. All of it.'

'Our aunt won't like that.' Minnie frowned.

'She isn't supposed to.' Rose smiled, but her bravery was beginning to desert her. It was a childish act, something Donald would have done.

'She'll notice that it's empty.'

'Never mind. Fill it up with water.' Rose plumped the pillows and replaced the woollen blanket and coverlet, swapping her aunt's summer bedding for her winter eiderdown, and putting the coverlet away in the chest at the end of the bed with a few drops of camphor moth-repellent. 'That will do.'

'I don't envy you when she finds out.'

'I don't care.'

'What do you think Mr Kingsley did to Jane last night?' Minnie said, biting her lip. 'I don't like him, Rose.'

'Neither do I, but don't worry. I won't let him lay a finger on you. Come on – we have more beds to change and then I thought we'd go down to the market for the shopping.'

By the end of the day, Rose had forgotten about the bed. It wasn't until ten o'clock when the Kingsleys had retired that the sound of her aunt shouting for Jane reminded her of it. A series of explosive snorts and sneezes followed.

'Rose, this is your fault,' Minnie hissed from where she was lying under her covers. 'What are you going to do now?'

'Face the music, I suppose.' She jumped out of bed and hurried downstairs in her nightgown to the landing where Jane was at the door of the Kingsleys' room, experiencing the full force of her aunt's anger.

'I haven't done nothing,' she was saying as the flame of her candle flickered and trembled in a draught of cold air. 'I don't know what you're talking about, mistress.'

'You have made us an apple-pie bed and now Mr Kingsley has broken his toenail, putting it through my best heavyweight winter sheet, which is torn right through. Jane, you must go. I can't bear to see your face again.'

Rose pushed past the maid. 'It wasn't Jane. It was me.'

'Of course, it wasn't,' her aunt snarled.

'Why would she confess to something she hasn't done?' Mr Kingsley said. Rose could see him in the light of the oil lamp on the dressing table, sitting on the edge of the bed in his gown and nightcap, doubled up with a handkerchief pressed to his nose, and clutching his big toe.

'This is her misguided and rather ridiculous attempt to save Jane's bacon.'

'It's the truth,' Rose insisted.

'You mustn't do this, miss. I've had enough of working here anyway, of being dragged out of bed at all hours to be mauled by a loose-lipped, dribbling drunk.' Jane took off her apron and threw it down on the floor.

'No, you can't,' Rose said. 'Please don't do this. Don't leave on my account.'

Jane turned to her, an expression of pity on her face. 'I'm sorry. I wanted to stay, but I'm completely drained – I can't do this any longer. You'll be all right, miss – you have your brothers to protect you.'

'Go on then, seeing as you've made your mind up.' Aunt Temperance bent down, picked up the apron and threw it at Jane so it landed on her head, covering her face. In a slow, dignified manner, the maid removed it and screwed it up into a ball. 'Pack your belongings and get out of here forthwith.'

'But it's late,' Rose said quickly.

'Never mind. I'll go straight to my mother's – she's only round the corner.' Jane turned and fled downstairs. Rose made to follow her.

'Where are you going?' Aunt Temperance said.

'To help her—'

'Well, don't. Go back to your room. I blame you for this. You're a sly one and I'll be keeping my eye on you in future.'

Rose hesitated, her heart thumping.

'What are you waiting for? I tell you, you're already in a lot of trouble and I'll make your life even more of a misery if you don't do as you're told.'

Her aunt clearly meant every word. Rose retreated upstairs to the attic and ran into Donald on the landing.

'I heard everything.' His teeth flashed in the darkness. 'I thought you were such a goody two-shoes.'

'I've been driven to it. Oh Donald, I feel so guilty – Jane has lost her place because of me.'

'She was looking for another position anyway, if that makes you feel any better. I posted a couple of letters for her – she's applied to several advertisements.'

'I hope she finds somewhere soon. I'll miss her.' Being close in age and spending much time in the house together, they had become friends and allies against the Kingsleys.

Donald chuckled. 'An apple-pie bed. Who'd have thought it? I'm very proud of you.'

'Don't even begin to think that I condone this kind of behaviour. I let my anger get the better of me. I wanted to get my own back on our aunt and uncle, but I didn't think about the consequences.'

'We mustn't give in to their controlling ways. Dear sister, I'm going to look at you in a different light in future.'

She wished him goodnight, already regretting that she hadn't set him a good example. With a twinge of guilt, she wondered what the outcome might be.

'Rose and Minnie, stir yourselves. Your brothers have already gone to work.' In the morning, the bedroom door creaked open on its hinges, and there was Aunt Temperance standing in her floral gown, her hair like a bird's nest and her eyes puffy with sleep. Not Ma, Rose thought sorrowfully, wishing she could turn the clock back. She glanced across at the washstand where Minnie had left the thimble and scissors out. She prayed that her aunt wouldn't notice – she didn't like them patchworking because it took up time when they could have been doing other chores around the house. The patchwork itself was rolled up and tucked under the mattress.

'What are those doing there?' Her aunt's eyes settled on the offending items.

'I forgot to put them away after sewing the buttons back on Mr Kingsley's shirt yesterday,' Rose said, sitting up in bed.

Aunt Temperance appeared satisfied with Rose's explanation, but chided her nonetheless: 'You're late.'

'Where is Jane?' Rose asked, before recalling that, thanks to her, she had gone.

'You know very well. I've told her I won't be giving her a reference. She'll have to go and fish for another place. Anyway, I need somebody to step into her shoes.'

Rose touched her throat. 'Me?'

'Yes, you. Who do you think I mean, the Queen of Sheba? Minnie, get up and make sure you brush your hair and wash behind your ears.'

After preparing breakfast for their uncle, Rose and Minnie ate bread and dripping at the kitchen table before their aunt came in to make sure they weren't slacking.

'Have a look in the scullery,' she said. 'I've never seen so much laundry in my life.'

'You want us to do the laundry?' Rose said, aghast.

'Of course.'

'But I don't know how,' she stammered. 'Ma always sent the laundry out.'

'Your mother was profligate with money. Do you know how much it costs to have one's laundry done?'

Rose shook her head, realising that she had no idea.

'I prefer to have my smalls laundered at home where they don't mix with the dirty linen of others. You must have some idea – you've seen the maid at her chores. Minnie will assist you.'

This was her punishment for the apple-pie bed, Rose thought, and she had no choice but to bow to her Aunt Temperance's demands. Reluctantly, she handed an apron to Minnie, tied one around her waist and rolled up her sleeves before heating up the water. She soaked the sheets and moved the shirts around in the copper with the wash dolly while Minnie scrubbed at the stains with lye soap. Together, they put the wet linen through the mangle and hung it up with wooden pegs on a line which they'd stretched between the poles of the veranda. Rose's arms and back ached, but the physical exertion took her mind off their situation temporarily.

She began to chant a rhyme which Ma had used to say when the twins were born.

'"They that wash on Monday have all the week to dry." Your turn, Minnie.'

'"They that wash on Tuesday ..."' Minnie beat her brow with her fist. 'I can't remember the words.'

'How about, "are not so much awry"?'

'Yes, that's it. "They that wash on Wednesday are not so much to blame."' Minnie grinned as she went on, '"They that wash on Thursday wash for very shame. They that wash on Friday must only wash in need."'

'"And they that wash on Saturday are lazy clods indeed." Do you remember how Ma used to sing "Rockabye Baby"?' Rose smiled at the memory. 'You used to cry when down came the baby, cradle and all.'

'Stop gossiping and get on with what you're supposed to be doing,' Temperance said, appearing at the back door. 'Do I have to stand over you with the whip?'

'I'm sorry,' Rose said quickly.

'I should think so. I want all this dry and folded by tonight, then it can be ironed in the morning.'

Rose was proud of their handiwork. The shirts were bright white and the sheets clean, but when her aunt came to inspect later, she tore the sheets off the line.

'The birds have left their mark. Do it again. Everything in this house needs a proper scrub,' Aunt Temperance went on. 'When you're done, I want all the carpets and rugs dragged out and hung over the line for a thorough beating, but first, go and answer the door. I'm sure I heard the bell.'

Rose was surprised – her aunt's hearing was sharper than hers.

There was a middle-aged man at the door, dressed in a suit and tie, and carrying a briefcase. At first, Rose wondered if he was from the bank and had come to Willow Place instead of the tannery by mistake.

'I'd like to speak to the mistress of the house.'

'May I say who is calling?'

'My business is of a sensitive and personal nature.'

'Oh?' Rose went into the parlour, where her aunt was hovering just inside the door. 'There's a caller who wishes to speak with you. He won't give his name.'

Aunt Temperance checked her appearance in the mirror as she passed through the hall.

'We have no need of any shoe polishes, dusters, or anything else for that matter. Please be on your way.'

'I'm looking for a Miss Agnes Berry-Clay,' the man said. 'She may have married by now, and be known under another name.'

Aunt Temperance raised one eyebrow. 'Who sent you here?'

'I'm not at liberty to reveal that – this is a private investigation. I've been given information that a Miss Agnes Berry-Clay was well acquainted with the owners of a tannery in Canterbury.'

'My name is Mrs Kingsley. I am the proprietor of the tannery across the street. There is no one of that name here.'

'But you have heard of her? Mrs Kingsley, I implore you to think carefully. Do you know of a Miss Agnes Berry-Clay? Or her children, if she has any. This is a matter whereby the lady concerned could be in line to gain considerable financial advantage—'

'This has nothing to do with us.' Her aunt's face had turned white, and Rose wondered what was going on as she turned to her and said, 'This is one of my children. Now, go away.'

'Are you absolutely certain?'

'I have no knowledge of this person.' Aunt Temperance stamped one foot as if to emphasise her point and the man backed down.

'In that case, I will wish you good morning and take my leave,' he said stiffly. 'Good day.'

Aunt Temperance closed the door on his retreating back.

'Why didn't you tell him the truth?' Rose asked.

'Because I don't want strangers poking their noses into our affairs. Your mother is dead and buried.' Rose wished she wouldn't be so blunt – it was painful being reminded of Ma's body lying cold in the grave.

'He said there was money in it.'

'That was a trick. I'm not sure if you can contest a will after an inheritance has already been passed on, but I'm not prepared to risk everything by telling him what he wants to know. I will not let anyone take away what's rightfully mine.'

'I don't see how he could.'

'Someone out there thinks they have found a more recent version of my brother's will. Or they've forged one out of spite. Forget about it, Rose. Go back to work.'

It seemed unlikely that anyone would do such a thing, but then Rose remembered how Aunt Marjorie had told her about her mother faking a letter of application and reference to obtain employment, and she also recalled her aunt's suspicions that Mr Kingsley had had something to do with the disappearance of the will Pa had had witnessed by Mrs Dunn and Mr Hales. She thought of writing to her aunt again, but finally decided to leave it. It would only worry her.

The sisters were still beating rugs after dusk had fallen.

'There you are,' Donald said, joining them outside when he returned from work with Arthur that evening.

'We've been here all day,' Rose said. 'Our aunt is a Tartar.'

'Let me have a go.' Donald took the carpet beater from her hands and began to hit the runner which they'd draped over the washing line. He cursed and swore as puffs of dust exploded from the weave.

'Please mind your language in front of your sisters.' Rose turned to her older brother for support, but he didn't seem to care, standing there with his hands in his pockets. 'Arthur?'

'Donald, that's enough,' Arthur said wearily. 'I'm afraid I have bad news.'

Donald paused and handed the beater back to Rose.

'Tell us,' he said. 'I knew you were hiding something.'

'I knew it was coming, but today it's definite – I'm no longer the gaffer. Mr Kingsley has locked me out of the office.'

'He's what?' Rose exclaimed. 'There must have been some kind of mistake.'

'There's no mistake. He'd been drinking – he keeps a bottle of whisky in his desk. I started a polite discussion, suggesting that I should deal with the complaints from the curriers who buy our leather for finishing. He told me I had no right to be involved with the sales side of things. If I wanted to keep my job, I was to keep my mouth shut and work alongside the other men. He pushed me out of the door and turned the key.'

'He can't do that!'

'Mr Kingsley can do whatever he likes. He has us over a barrel, Rose. He owns the business. He's in charge and there's nothing I can do.' Arthur's fists tightened until they blenched. 'Our aunt is a tyrant. Her husband is a drunkard. Look at you and Minnie – you shouldn't be skivvying for them. It isn't right.'

Rose stared at her brothers. Their clothes were stained and wet from where they had been dragging the butts between the pits.

'I haven't been paid this week,' he went on. 'They say I'm not entitled to anything above a worker's weekly wage minus deductions for my keep. It's a relief that I have no wife to support. They have stitched us up, taken us on for their servants, and purloined everything we owned. I don't know what to do.'

'We will think of something,' Rose said, her heart aching for him. He was no longer the gaffer, his white coat of authority replaced by the stained cowhide apron of one of the workmen. He had fallen back to where he had been before Ma and Pa had adopted him.

'I want you to write to Aunt Marjorie again,' Arthur said. 'She will know what to do.'

'I've said before, she's getting old and frail, and I don't want to worry her. I'd feel guilty if we made her unwell with our troubles. I feel we've imposed on her enough.'

'But I don't want to live like this.' He grasped Rose by the shoulders and gazed into her eyes. 'I can leave all this behind, but you and the twins have nowhere else to go, no other means of support or protection.'

'Oh Arthur, it's a hard life, but we aren't in any physical danger.'

'I'm not so sure.' He frowned.

'You're being overdramatic.'

'While you are too complacent. Our situation is going from bad to worse.'

'The Kingsleys are cruel and mean, but they wouldn't hurt us – they're family.' As Rose said these words, she remembered Baxter and his father. They had been family too, and his pa had thumped him. 'I'm sorry, Arthur – I'm so tired I don't know what to think.'

'I know what I think – they have no affection for any of us,' he said angrily. 'I'm not staying for dinner. I'm going out.'

Rose could guess where he was going, because when he left, he had washed and changed into clean clothes and oiled his hair. She hoped that he and Tabby were going to set a date for the wedding soon – it would give them all something to look forward to.

An hour later, on hearing Arthur's footsteps on the stairs, she put the book she'd been reading down on the kitchen table and followed him to his room. She knocked on the door.

'Arthur, it's me. Please, let me come in.' When her brother didn't answer, she pushed the door open and found him lying face down on his bed, his body convulsing with sobs.

'Leave me alone,' he gasped as she reached out and grasped his shoulder.

'Look at me,' she whispered. 'What's wrong? What's happened with Tabby?'

'I've broken it off with her,' he said, his voice breaking.

'Oh no. Why?'

'Why do you think? I can't possibly go through with this marriage now.'

'You still love each other. Nothing has changed.'

'I will love her for the rest of my life, but everything is different now. How can I provide for a wife and family?'

'People manage. The other men at the yard are married. Look at Mr Jones – he's been at his wife's beck and call for years.' Rose forced a smile. 'Tabby has never struck me as someone for whom money is a priority. She's no gold digger, Arthur.'

'Ah, that is true,' he sighed. 'She is a beautiful soul, an angel without avarice.'

'Her father is quite a different kettle of fish,' Rose observed.

'I don't blame him for wanting the best for his daughter,' Arthur countered.

'Go back to her and tell her you've made a mistake.'

'I can't, because I've done the right thing by her. I have no hope of being the gaffer now that Mr Kingsley is installed as head of the business. My current situation is in the hands of a drunkard who thinks he knows all there is to know about making leather.' Arthur buried his head in his hands. 'Tabby hates me for it, but I've set her free so she can marry somebody else, someone who can give her everything she deserves.'

'What about love? You love each other. Doesn't that count for anything?'

'The only thing that really counts in this life is pounds, shillin's and pence,' Arthur said bitterly. 'Rose, much as I appreciate your concern, I'd be grateful if you'd leave me alone.'

'Yes, of course,' she said quietly, getting up and walking out of the room, her heart broken for a third time at the thought of Arthur's sorrow, and losing a future sister in Tabby. For whom would she and Minnie make the patchwork now?

1876–1877

Chapter Eleven

An Ill Wind Blows Nobody Any Good

Autumn turned to winter and there was no respite from Aunt Temperance's nagging and Mr Kingsley's drunkenness. Rose looked forward to the late evenings when they had finished washing and putting away the dishes. She and Minnie would go upstairs to their room and huddle together in the flickering light of the stubby remains of a candle. Donald would leave the door of his bedroom open and they would talk to each other across the landing. As for Arthur, he would return home late and retire straight to bed. At first, she worried that he was frequenting the inns to drown his sorrows, but he was always stone-cold sober.

Winter passed, then gradually the days lengthened until it was still light when they went to bed, but the hours were filled with work nonetheless. One morning in early July during a summer storm when the winds were whistling between the timbers and lifting parts of the roof, Rose was on her knees, scrubbing the floor in the hall. She had turned seventeen in May, yet she felt about one hundred with her aching muscles and joints, unable to see a future beyond slaving for the Kingsleys. She dunked the brush back into her bucket, picking up more suds on the bristles, and scrubbed harder, wondering what the day would bring.

More of the same, she guessed with a sigh as she heard her aunt's voice from the landing above.

'Hurry along, Minnie.'

'I am hurrying,' Minnie said.

'You have been deliberately going at a snail's pace. I have better things to do than follow you around. If you did things properly in the first place, you wouldn't have to do them again. You are worse than useless.'

'I'm sorry, Aunt.' Rose could sense the fear in her sister's voice. 'This basket is very heavy.'

'Oh, do stop whining. You're giving me an earache.'

'Please let me go at my own pace, I—'

Rose looked up to see a basket of laundry tumbling to the ground, a sheet settling across the floor, and heard Minnie crying out as she came falling against the banisters to the foot of the staircase where she landed with a crack and a thud, her leg twisted beneath her.

Rose leapt to her feet, crying, 'My poor sister! What have you done?'

'She pushed me,' Minnie gasped, her eyes filling with tears as Rose tried to help her move to the bottom step and sit down. 'She shoved me in the back,' she went on, pointing to their aunt who stepped past them and started to inspect the floor tiles.

'You must put your leg straight,' Rose said.

'I can't,' Minnie grimaced. 'It hurts too much.'

Rose glanced at her aunt as she shifted her sister's weight on to the step and took hold of her ankle. Minnie screamed when she pulled her leg forward. The pain was all the worse for knowing that Aunt Temperance had inflicted it.

'Anyone would think the sky had fallen in,' Aunt Temperance said. 'You have only yourself to blame, you clumsy girl.'

162

'You pushed me down the stairs.'

'You tripped on the laundry. I told you to take care with that basket, but would you listen? Stand up, child.'

'I can't,' Minnie moaned, her face pale and her teeth chattering.

'There's no such word. Get up, or I'll whip you.'

'Look at her leg – it's impossible,' Rose said, wrapping her arms around her sister's shoulders. There was no wound, but the lower part of her limb was bent where it should have been straight. 'Please help me get her upstairs to bed, Aunt. I can't manage alone.'

'I can't do anything, not with my lumbago. You'll have to wait for Arthur or Donald.'

'May I go and fetch them?' Rose asked, knowing it would be another hour before Donald returned.

'If you wish. They can make up the time later.'

Rose didn't like to leave her sister alone with their aunt, but she had no choice. She fetched Minnie a blanket, wrapped it around her shoulders, and ran as fast as she could, hindered by the weight of her skirts and petticoats, to the yard where she found Donald tipping a batch of ground bark from the mill into one of the pits.

'Donald, Donald!' She almost fell into his outstretched arms as he caught hold of her before she ran into the pit.

'Rose, what is it?'

'I need your help. Minnie is hurt.' Catching her breath, she went on to explain what had happened. 'Where is Arthur?'

'He is with Mr Kingsley. Rose, they have not stopped arguing today. One of the curriers – Pa's best customer – has complained about the quality of the leather he ordered. He's talking of taking his business elsewhere.'

'Really? That's never happened before.'

'Our uncle thinks he knows best – he's ordered the hides to be removed from the loft before they're ready. He believes that by hurrying the process, we can produce more leather. He's an idiot.'

'Don't say that. We have enough to contend with without you upsetting him. You'll lose your job.'

'I don't care.' Donald bit his lip, his eyes dark with worry as Rose slipped her arm through his and they hurried back to Willow Place.

'How did it happen?' he asked as they reached the door.

'She came down the stairs.' Rose didn't go into detail – she didn't want him confronting their aunt and making things worse – but as it turned out, Aunt Temperance had made herself scarce, leaving the two of them to carry Minnie up the two flights of stairs and put her to bed.

'That looks bad,' Donald observed as Rose made their sister as comfortable as possible. 'Where's the doctor? The old bat has sent for him?'

Rose shook her head. 'You go back to work – there's nothing more you can do here. I'll speak to her.'

'I'll give her a piece of my mind,' he said angrily.

'Don't antagonise her. Let me deal with this. I'll take care of Minnie,' she promised.

'If you're sure.' He leaned in and stroked a stray lock of hair from his twin's cheek. 'I'll be back as soon as I can.'

Rose followed him downstairs, but when she found her aunt in the parlour, her entreaties fell on deaf ears.

'We aren't made of money,' she kept saying. 'Minnie is young and her leg will soon mend.'

Wishing that she could ask Ma for advice, Rose spoke to Arthur when he returned home that evening, but he had no success in persuading his aunt either. He had his own troubles, Rose thought, feeling sorry for him. He hadn't stopped loving Tabby even though he had broken off their engagement, and he was struggling to cope with taking orders from their uncle at the tan yard. Without a stake in the tannery, he had no authority whatsoever over Mr Kingsley.

The next morning, having tried to soothe her sister as she cried and moaned through the small hours, Rose got up, splashed her face with cold water and quickly brushed her hair.

'Don't leave me,' Minnie begged as she stirred in her bed.

'I won't be long. I promise.'

'Don't go.'

As Rose kissed her cheek, Minnie put her arms around her neck and clung on for dear life.

'I'll be back. Trust me.' Having extricated herself from her sister's grip, Rose went downstairs to find her aunt in a mean temper in the kitchen with a pile of dirty plates on the table.

'Where have you been? I expected you down here at six to cook Mr Kingsley's bacon. He's had to go to work on an empty stomach, thanks to you.'

Rose didn't see why Mr Kingsley couldn't make his own breakfast, but she bit her tongue.

'Aunt Temperance, I'm asking you again. Please call the doctor. Minnie is suffering terribly.'

'It serves her right for behaving like a snivelling brat. She was too busy arguing with me to look where she was going and she tripped over those lanky legs of hers. Tell her to get up – she can't lie abed all day when there are some of us working our fingers to the bone.'

'She can't get up.' Rose tried to still the trembling of her lip. 'Her leg is broken.'

Her aunt shrugged.

'What will you tell your friends at the cathedral if she should end up dying from it? Minnie has always been a sickly child.'

'What do you know? You aren't a doctor,' Aunt Temperance sneered.

'A funeral is expensive, as we know to our cost,' Rose went on, finding her courage.

'That's true. When your ma told me how much she'd spent on my brother's send-off, I was horrified. I said to my husband, Mr Kingsley, you are in the wrong trade.' She paused. 'Oh, don't look at me like that with those big blue eyes. Fetch my purse and go and buy the wretch some medicine.'

'Wouldn't the doctor be more appropriate?' Rose dared to ask.

'An apothecary will do. Doctor Norris didn't do your father any good, and I don't want him knowing our business.'

It was better than nothing, Rose decided as she put on her bonnet and shoes while her aunt took a few coins from her purse and counted them out on to the chiffonier.

'Thank you,' she said, taking them before her aunt could change her mind.

She left the house and hurried along the dirty streets, passing the hovels where the windows were stuffed with rags or boarded over to keep out the weather. A young girl was washing the doorstep into one of the houses, a fruitless occupation, Rose thought, when she had to lift her skirts to cross the puddles of filth that lay across the cobbles.

'Rose, is that you? Miss Cheevers?' An elderly woman stepped out from one of the houses, her face half hidden by a parasol trimmed with feathers.

Rose quickened her pace, not having time for an inquisition, and kept walking until she reached the Miskins' apothecary shop. She stopped and looked in through the window at the bottles of colourful potions on the shelves and the advertisement for surgical bandages, elastic stockings and enemas on the hoarding outside.

Would it be indelicate to go inside, considering what had happened between Tabby and Arthur? She thought she heard Pa whispering into her ear, 'Better the devil you know than the one you don't.' She swallowed hard, composed herself and pushed the door open, making the bell ring, and catching the attention of Mr Miskin who was behind the counter, dressed in a white coat.

'How can I help you, miss? Oh, it's you, Rose.' He frowned. 'I didn't expect to see your face again.'

'Perhaps I shouldn't have come,' she said, backing away.

'No, no. Wait! I didn't mean ...' He moved around the counter towards her, stopping in front of a poster for Thierry's Marvellous Balsam.

'I'm sorry for the troubles that have struck your family down. I was angry when Arthur broke off the engagement with my daughter. Any father would have felt the same, but I've had time to reflect on the situation, and although it grieves poor Tabitha deeply, your brother did the right thing in freeing her of any obligation. She will meet a young man with better prospects in future. Now, how can I help?'

'My sister has met with an accident and broken her leg. I'd be very grateful if you could recommend a medicine to numb the pain.'

'Ah, you have come to the right place. The relief of pain is one of our specialities. We have laudanum or extract of willow bark, along with various bandages and splints for comfort.' He frowned. 'Did you say "broken" the leg?'

Rose nodded.

'Have you consulted with a doctor or considered taking the patient to the hospital?'

'We have no money for doctors and hospitals.'

'Of course. Let me see.' He rang the bell on the counter and Tabby appeared from the rear of the shop. She smiled when she saw Rose.

'My dear,' the apothecary said. 'I'm going out the back to the dispensary. Please show Miss Cheevers the range of bandages that we have in stock.'

'Yes, Father.' Tabitha turned away and opened a drawer in the cabinet behind the counter as her father walked away, leaving the two of them alone.

Was it safe to speak openly? Rose hesitated, then the words came out in a torrent.

'I'm sorry. Arthur has been laid terribly low by the loss of our parents and the thought that he had to let you down. He had no intention—' She suppressed a sudden wave of sorrow. 'He still loves you, you know. There has been no one else.'

'I know,' Tabby cut in. Glancing over her shoulder, she went on, 'My father says I should be thankful because bad luck follows Arthur around and I'm better off without him. He says that to lose three parents shows excessive ill fortune. Anyway, he's forbidden me to see him, and I've been crying myself to sleep over it for months because I can't get away, not even for a second. He watches me like a hawk.' She pulled out several different bandages and laid them on the counter. 'Rose, there is still hope. Will you give your brother a message from me?'

'Of course. What shall I say?'

'Tell him I'm prepared to do anything, even run away with him if that's what it will take for us to be married. I could never contemplate marrying anyone else. Arthur has my heart now and for ever.'

168

'This is ...' Rose couldn't describe how joyful she felt about Tabby's romantic declaration, '... wonderful.'

'Promise me you'll tell him. And say that I will be on the bridge on Tuesday evening at six o'clock. My parents are going out.'

Rose nodded as Tabby continued, 'Hush, I can hear my father – he's on his way. Where exactly is the injury you wish to bandage? Is it an open wound, or closed?'

'Oh, it's for Minnie. She's broken her leg, but there is no break in the skin.' She pointed out roughly where it was on her own leg, keeping it covered with her skirts.

'You'll need something to splint it with. I can recommend a ready-made splint and this bandage.' Tabby pointed to the largest one on the counter. 'It is a goodly length and provides much comfort. When you apply it, make it tight, but not so constricting that it stops the flow of blood, or her leg will turn bad and drop off.'

'How much will all this cost?' Rose asked, looking at the brown bottle that Mr Miskin had brought with him.

'How much do you have?' he asked.

She showed him how much she had, counting it out on to the counter.

He gave her a gentle smile.

'Let's call it exactly that amount,' he said, placing her purchases in a paper bag. 'I liked your father. He did much to help people and I'm happy to help you in return. Life must be much harder with both your parents gone.'

'It isn't easy,' she admitted. 'I'm very grateful to you.' She glanced towards Tabby, but she had turned her back and was busying herself, putting the remaining bandages away.

'Tell me. How did Minnie come across her injury?'

'It was an accident,' she said quickly. Too quickly, perhaps, because she noticed the shadow of doubt cross his face. 'She fell down the stairs.'

'She will have to start being more careful in future. Ah, one moment. I have a sample of a new tonic. You look as if you could do with it. Have one teaspoonful daily.' Mr Miskin took another bottle from underneath the counter. 'Go on – it won't poison you.'

She thanked him again and smiled as she slipped the bottle into the bag. She would give it to Minnie to build up her strength.

'Good day, Mr Miskin.'

'Good day,' he said.

On the way back to Willow Place, she found Mrs Hamilton standing in the middle of the street, leaning on her stick. It was too late to divert, Rose realised, her heart sinking at the idea of having to stop and pass the time of day with her.

'Miss Cheevers, how are you?' she said, wrapping her long cream shawl around her shoulders.

'Fair to middling,' Rose said, noticing the old woman's fingerless black gloves and the small crop of white whiskers that sprouted from her chin. She had to be the oldest person she knew – Ma had said she was well into her eighties. 'Are you well, Mrs Hamilton?'

'I've heard that there have been many changes at Willow Place, thanks to the Kingsleys,' Mrs Hamilton said, ignoring her question.

'It's just gossip,' Rose said, not wanting to share how bad things really were.

'You can tell me the truth.'

The hairs on the back of Rose's neck stood on end as Mrs Hamilton's white eyes seemed to stare into her soul, but she wouldn't budge. They would all suffer if Aunt

Temperance thought she had been going round revealing the family's business.

'There is nothing to tell,' she said firmly.

'You are wise to protect your interests by keeping your mouth shut on private matters – besmirching another's good character is not to be done lightly – but the Kingsleys don't deserve anyone's regard over what they've done around here. They have put the tannery workers out of their homes, closed the school so that the likes of Baxter are back on the streets, and who knows what else.'

'I'm sorry, Mrs Hamilton. I have medicine for my sister, and my aunt won't take kindly to me lingering in the street.'

'Medicine? She is unwell?'

'She is a little under the weather.'

'Oh dear. Well, I wish her all the best.'

'Good day,' Rose said, hurrying back home, her heart a little lighter now that she had medicine for Minnie and news that would restore Arthur's spirits.

'You took your time,' Aunt Temperance said when she arrived back at the house. 'Where's my change?'

'There isn't any, I'm afraid.'

'Oh? Let's see what you've wasted my money on.'

Rose followed her aunt into the kitchen where she was made to turn the contents of the bag out on the table. Her aunt's eyes lit up when she saw the bottle of medicine.

'Ah, sleeping drops. They'll come in handy.'

'They are to take Minnie's pain away,' Rose said sharply. Her aunt had no trouble sleeping, especially when she had been on the gin, she thought, watching her take the bottle and slip it into her pocket.

'And a tonic?' Aunt Temperance read the label. 'A weekly dose of cod liver oil and malt is more than adequate for a child's constitution. This is completely unnecessary.'

'It's what the apothecary advised.'

'And this bandage – I will put it aside for an emergency.'

'Let me use it to wrap my sister's leg,' Rose begged. 'And if I could prevail upon you to let me give her a dose of the sleeping drops—'

'She is quiet now.' Her aunt cupped her ear. 'I can't hear a sound, can you?'

Rose shook her head as she continued, 'There are some old rags in the bottom of the linen cupboard – you can use those and the broken stick in the hallstand to splint her leg. I expect her to be up and about tomorrow.'

Rose hesitated, thinking it would be a miracle if Minnie was ever able to walk again.

'Go on then. What are you waiting for?'

'The sleeping drops.'

'Oh no, I will dose her when I deem it necessary.'

Feeling uneasy, Rose went upstairs to splint Minnie's leg, bathe her hands and face and make sure she ate a little food before attending to her chores. While she was dusting the china ladies in the parlour, she heard her aunt calling to her.

'Cloth ears, there is someone at the door.'

Wiping her hands, she headed into the hall and opened the door to find the vicar's wife on the doorstep.

'Good morning, Rose.' Mrs Holdsworth smiled. 'Is your aunt at home?'

'I'll ask her,' Rose said wearily.

'Oh, do come in, Mrs Holdsworth. How kind of you to call.' Aunt Temperance appeared from the parlour and greeted her as though she was her fondest acquaintance. 'Rose, go and make us a fresh pot of tea. Come through to the parlour. To what do we owe this pleasure?'

Rose fetched the tea and poured it, taking her time while the two women made conversation.

'They haven't attended Sunday school or church for many months. It is not for me to offer advice, but my husband is concerned that their spiritual welfare and moral education aren't being adequately addressed. Perhaps you have been taking them to the cathedral instead of St Mildred's every Sunday? That's what the Reverend Holdsworth and I had assumed, until Mrs Hamilton called on us just now.'

'I don't think it is anyone else's business. What did that woman say?'

'Oh, nothing,' the vicar's wife said quickly. 'She mentioned that she had seen Rose out and about, and it reminded me that I hadn't seen any of the children for a while. Mr Cheevers was a much-respected member of our congregation and we've known the family for many years. I'm enquiring after them as a friend of Mr and Mrs Cheevers.'

'I should remind you that they weren't married,' Aunt Temperance said tersely.

'I thought that you might have expressed a little understanding, considering the circumstances. It would be better for Rose and the twins—'

'Better that they weren't stained with the stigma of illegitimacy, you mean?'

'We should treat them with Christian grace and kindness,' Mrs Holdsworth said as Aunt Temperance's teacup rattled in its saucer. 'Are the twins at home?'

She wanted to see them with her own eyes, Rose thought as her aunt quickly made up the excuse that Donald was helping his big brother in the yard while Minnie had retired to bed with the ague.

'Where is the patient? I should really like to see her and offer some words of comfort.'

'Oh no, she mustn't be disturbed.'

173

'On whose authority?' The vicar's wife raised one eyebrow with suspicion.

'Mine, of course. Mr Kingsley and I have taken on these children as our own. We take our responsibilities seriously. It hasn't been easy for me, being unused to sharing my home with anyone except my husband. Only this morning, I sent Rose to Mr Miskin to buy medicine for Minnie. I have given her a dose of sleeping drops and she is sound asleep.'

'Then your desire to leave her in peace is perfectly understandable,' Mrs Holdsworth said. 'Give her my best wishes for a rapid recovery. I will call again soon if I may.'

'"If I may",' Aunt Temperance simpered sarcastically after the vicar's wife had gone. 'No, she may not. How dare she question how I bring up my nephews and nieces! Rose, when you've finished the dusting, get yourself back in the kitchen – Mr Kingsley has requested chicken and ham pie for his dinner.'

'I don't think my sister should be left on her own.'

'It will do her good to be alone for a while to reflect on her behaviour. She has accused me of pushing her down the stairs when she is a victim of her own impulsiveness.'

It seemed that the more her aunt told herself that story, the more she believed it. Realising that arguing with her would make no difference, Rose went back to her duties, preparing a pie for dinner.

She made pastry, sealed the meat, fried some onions and made a gravy, then rolled out the pastry which she'd left to rest. Arranging a layer of pastry in the dish, she blind-baked it with a scattering of dried peas in the bottom then emptied out the peas, placed the pie funnel in the centre and poured the meat and gravy mixture in around it. She rolled out a circle of pastry to place on the top, brushed the edges and crimped them to stick them together before she put it back in the oven until the pastry lid turned a golden brown.

As she put it on the rack to cool, Arthur came indoors from the tannery.

'Something smells good. How's Minnie?'

'She's sleeping.' Rose glanced towards the door to make sure no one else was listening. 'Arthur, I have some better news for you. I've seen Tabby today. She served me when I went to buy medicine.'

'How did she seem?' he said quickly.

'She gave me a message for you. She'll be on the bridge waiting for you at six on Tuesday. She's ready to leave her family and run away with you for love. Isn't that romantic?'

'How can she still have feelings for me after what's happened? It's a miracle.'

'It's no miracle. You're meant for each other.'

'I'll go and speak with her, but Rose,' he went on sadly, 'I can't possibly leave you and the twins, especially now.'

'I can look after Minnie, and Donald can look after himself. Arthur, you have to go. I want you to be happy.'

'No, it's too much for you.' She could see that he was torn: his brother and sisters, or his sweetheart? It was an impossible choice.

When Rose retired to bed that night, she found Minnie sprawled out across the coverlet with her broken leg twisted to one side. She crept into bed beside her, curving her body around her.

'Goodnight,' she whispered, but she was answered by a snore. She gave her sister a nudge, yet she still didn't stir. How much laudanum had Aunt Temperance given her? Rose couldn't sleep for worrying that she was trying to poison her. How could they avoid further grief? She could only come up with one answer: they had to help themselves if they were to have any hope of a better life – but how?

Chapter Twelve

Roly-Poly Pudding and Custard

'It's time you were up, Rose.' Aunt Temperance opened the bedroom door the next morning. 'I need hot water for my wash and the pisspots are overflowing. How is the invalid?'

'She is about the same as yesterday,' Rose said, grimacing.

'I can speak for myself,' Minnie said, holding the bedclothes up to her face.

'You should be out of bed by now,' their aunt said. 'It doesn't do the body any good to laze about.'

'She's broken her leg,' Rose protested. 'She can't possibly walk until it's mended.'

'Well, she can't lie around doing nothing. We aren't made of money.'

Rose couldn't understand how Temperance could make such an assertion when the Kingsleys were living off Pa's legacy. Was Donald right when he said that Mr Kingsley's plan to speed up production of the cured leather was affecting the quality and making the curriers look elsewhere for their supplies?

'Is there a problem with the tannery? Father used to say that leather was always bullish.'

'If you must know, Arthur destroyed the hides from Argentina and cancelled the contract for further deliveries because of what happened to my dear brother, and Mr

Kingsley has so far failed to reinstate the deals your father used to have with the local suppliers. He's doing his best to negotiate, but who knows when they will come to an agreement and deliver enough hides to keep the tannery going? Until then, we expect everyone to contribute to the household – Minnie needs to do her share.'

'How can she work if she can't stand?' Rose argued.

'If she can't manage the chores, then she'll have to go and sit on a street corner, garnering sympathy and small change.'

Minnie's mouth curved into a half-smile. It was a rather unpleasant joke, but a joke all the same.

'I want you to put on some rags while your sister fetches the barrow from the yard to tow you to the Buttermarket.'

Rose's palms grew damp. She couldn't be serious ... could she?

'Pa will be turning in his grave,' she said, unable to hold her tongue.

'What the eye doesn't see, the heart doesn't grieve over. Nobody will recognise her.'

Minnie dragged herself up to a sitting position and glared at their aunt with rebellion in her eyes. 'I can't go. I have no rags.'

'I can soon remedy that.' Aunt Temperance picked up Minnie's skirt, pulled a pair of scissors from her pocket and cut it into pieces.

'What will your friends at the cathedral think of this madness?' Rose said.

'Do you think they care? They are all too busy with their own affairs to notice, and if they do say anything, I'll tell them to mind their own business. As Minnie was foolish enough to throw herself down the stairs, she will suffer the consequences. I challenge any lady or gentleman to resist throwing her a farthing or two at the sight of the misery in those pretty eyes.'

'Please don't. This is unnecessary and unkind.'

'What was unkind was for your parents to die on us, and leave us with four extra mouths to feed and a failing business. If you won't beg, you can sew up your skirt, and then turn your attention to the darning – Mr Kingsley has holes in his socks,' Aunt Temperance said.

'She isn't well,' Rose insisted.

'Her arms are working – needlework doesn't require the use of one's legs. Don't argue with me. If you keep going on like this, I'll make you take your sister out and not come back until you've made at least a shilling.'

Sensing that her aunt was more than ready to carry out her threat, Rose backed down.

'You'll have to do Minnie's share of the chores as well as your own today,' Aunt Temperance said as she left the room.

'Don't worry, I'll be nearby all day.' Rose knelt at the bedside so she could keep her voice low. 'You remember what happened to the aspidistra?'

Minnie nodded, her face streaked with dried tears.

'When our aunt gives you another dose of sleeping drops, try not to swallow them. Wait until she's gone and spit them out – use the pot.'

'Why would I do that when they take the pain away?'

'Because I'm afraid she'll give you too much. Last night you were sleeping like the dead – I couldn't rouse you. Please be careful.'

'I hate that woman.' Minnie's eyes flashed with anger.

'So do I,' Rose said, unable to hide her feelings any longer. 'We have to do something.'

'What can we do? I can't walk – I'm trapped.' Minnie winced as she shifted in the bed. 'What if it doesn't mend? What then?'

'Mr Miskin has said that if you keep your leg in the splint I put on yesterday, it will get better. Of course you'll walk again.' Rose tried to reassure her, although she was far from reassured herself. What would life be like for her sister if she ended up a cripple? She would be completely dependent on her siblings. 'You're going to have to be braver than you've ever been before,' Rose went on gently. 'I'm going downstairs to start on the chores, but I'll be back as often as I can. Remember what I said.'

Minnie nodded as Rose handed her the sewing box.

'I think the pain will lessen if you keep busy,' she said.

During the day, she kept herself occupied with the laundry and making a plan to escape Willow Place and the dreadful Kingsleys. To that end, she met with Arthur and Donald on the upper landing late that night. Arthur stood leaning against the wall looking troubled while Donald practised his bowling moves without the ball.

'What is it, Rose?' he said, pausing partway through a round-arm delivery.

'We have to leave before the Kingsleys do us any further harm. This isn't just about Minnie. Look at how thin we've become because we have to eat bread and porridge while they feast on beef and ham. I think they are trying to starve us to death.'

'And kill us through overwork,' Arthur said, joining the conversation.

'I've been wondering about making our way to Overshill to throw ourselves on the mercy of our grandmother.'

'Your grandmother,' Arthur corrected her, reminding Rose that he wasn't related to her by blood. She wondered how he felt about that. 'Have you written to her to find out if this is possible?' he went on.

Rose shook her head. Although she didn't know Mrs Carter's full address, only that she lived on a farm in the village, she had started on a letter, but even her handwriting had appeared cowed on the page.

'What if they turn you away?'

'I've thought about that,' she said. 'As long as we get away from Canterbury, we'll be out of harm's way. One of us can take care of Minnie while the others look for work. What about Tabby, though? Did you meet with her?'

Arthur nodded. 'I can't say too much, but all is well between us.'

'Oh, that's the best news I've heard in a long time.'

'It doesn't mean we've set a date,' he smiled.

'What are you three whispering about?'

Rose looked up to find Minnie dressed in her nightgown, clinging to the door frame and dragging her foot, her eyes black with pain.

'Hush. You should be in bed.'

'Why do you not include me in your plans?' Minnie said, looking hurt. Rose suppressed a pang of guilt. 'I'm not stupid.'

Donald offered Minnie his arm to lean on.

'Please, trust us,' he said, escorting her back into the bedroom. 'Go back to sleep. Our aunt must not suspect a thing.'

Arthur turned to Rose. 'Pack your things – we'll leave tonight.'

'Not tonight. It's too soon. We aren't prepared.'

'The longer we stay, the more we put ourselves in danger.'

'I know that, but we aren't ready—'

'What is going on up there? Why aren't you asleep?' Rose froze at the sound of her aunt's voice.

'Nothing, Aunt,' Arthur called back. 'I thought I heard my sister cry out, but it must have been a fox outside. I was mistaken.'

'Well, wash your ears out in future,' she shouted.

For a moment, Rose thought that their tormentor was heading up the stairs, but her footsteps faded into the distance.

'They'll try to stop us leaving,' Donald said, re-joining them on the landing.

'We'll leave after dinner this time next week – that way we can travel on full stomachs and in the dark in case the Kingsleys send someone after us,' Rose said. 'Arthur, I will decant some laudanum into the wine. You and Donald must abstain from drinking it, but make sure their glasses are topped up.' It was Arthur's role to pour the wine for their uncle and aunt at mealtimes as if he was some kind of butler.

'How will you get the sleeping drops away from her?' Arthur asked.

'I have that in hand,' Rose said.

'I'll make sure the barrer's clean,' Donald said, 'and I'll see what else I can lay my hands on.'

She didn't censure him. In her opinion, the Kingsleys owed them. 'Just don't draw attention to yourself, or try to bring too much with us – we don't want to be weighed down. And leave the barrow in the yard – don't bring it here or they'll suspect that we are up to something. Don't breathe a word of this to anyone – not to Joe, not to Mr Hales or Mr Jones ...'

'Don't worry. I'll do anything to get us away from here,' Donald said.

'Goodnight then.' Rose waited for her brothers to return to their rooms before joining Minnie who, having exerted herself walking from the bed to the doorway and back, had fallen into a deep sleep. She felt a sense of optimism mixed with dread. Would the Kingsleys find out and thwart their attempt at escape?

On the day they were due to leave Willow Place, Rose went out on her errand to the apothecary where she politely enquired after Tabby.

'She has gone out for the day,' Mr Miskin said. 'Your sister is still suffering from her broken bones? Will you require more bandages?'

'No, thank you. Just the sleeping drops.'

'You know, I wish you wouldn't think badly of me,' he said suddenly, looking over his half-moon spectacles as he gave her a new bottle and took her money. 'Arthur was right to break off the engagement in the circumstances. Like I said to Tabby, it's far better to spend a few weeks or months in misery, than suffer one's whole life in penury. A wedding is like the opening of a bottle of physic. As soon as the mixture is exposed to air – and the bride and groom to the tedium of everyday life – the ingredients start to decay and lose their efficacy. The once potent elixir of love can no longer keep the marriage alive.'

'I don't believe that, Mr Miskin.'

'Perhaps that is why your parents never fell out of love – because they never got hitched. Maybe there is a lesson for us all in that.'

'Mr Miskin? Mr Miskin, stop gassing and get out the back here,' came a woman's voice.

He rolled his eyes heavenwards. 'Yes, dear. I'm just serving a customer. I'll be on my way as soon as I can.'

Hurrying home, Rose took the original bottle of sleeping drops from the dresser in the kitchen, tipped half the contents of the new one into it and topped it up with water. She opened a bottle of wine, poured it into a decanter and added most of the remaining undiluted laudanum to it before replacing the cut-glass stopper. Crossing her fingers, she hoped it would be enough.

Later, she watched her aunt dispensing a dose of sleeping drops for her sister from the dregs left in the new bottle.

'Where is the bottle that you bought today, Rose?' her aunt asked, looking up from where she was sitting on the edge of Minnie's bed. 'This one is nearly out.'

'I've put it away in the dresser.'

'Bring it up next time you come.'

'Yes, Aunt. I came to ask you what I should prepare for dinner.'

'Whatever you can make from the ingredients in the pantry. Mr Kingsley wishes us to make some economies.'

'I'll see what I can do.' The stingy old fool spent money like water on his own pleasures, allowing little for anyone else, even his loyal wife.

'You are turning out to be a conscientious and hard-working maid, Rose.' Her aunt's mouth twisted into a smile as she stared at her through narrowed eyes. 'Perhaps Mr Kingsley and I should promote you to the role of housekeeper. I'm sure that one day you will wish to leave us to get married and have your own family, but we will always need at least one servant, and you suit us so well ... I think we'd find it impossible to let you go.'

Rose suppressed a shiver of fear, wondering if she had done something to arouse her aunt's suspicions.

'Run along now.' Her aunt dismissed her without further comment and Rose breathed a sigh of relief as she headed down to the kitchen to put on her apron and make a chicken stew followed by jam roly-poly pudding and egg custard.

At dinner, Arthur kept the Kingsleys' glasses topped up with wine.

'Aren't you having any?' Aunt Temperance asked him.

'Not tonight, thank you,' he said, touching the decanter to the rim of her glass to catch a drip.

'You know why that is,' Mr Kingsley laughed. 'He was seen with Miss Miskin under the willows last night – he is walking out with her again and he doesn't want to risk the brewer's droop.'

'It's supposed to be a secret,' Arthur said, flushing. 'And Miss Miskin isn't that kind of woman, I'll have you know.'

'Her father doesn't know you have renewed your court-ship then?'

'I don't have to explain myself to you or anyone else,' Arthur said coldly.

'I'll have to have a word in his ear,' Mr Kingsley went on, forgetting the rule about no talking at meal-times.

Rose bit her tongue, glancing at Arthur to warn him to do the same as the clock in the hall struck nine. There was no point in upsetting the apple cart when they would be on the move in a couple of hours' time.

Aunt Temperance yawned, her eyes darkening as the laudanum began to take effect.

'I beg your pardon,' she sighed. 'I've come over sleepy all of a sudden.'

'You have taken more wine than usual,' Mr Kingsley said, smacking his lips together.

'That's because Arthur keeps filling my glass.' For a moment, a cold thrill ran down Rose's spine. Had they been discovered? She thought of their bags, packed and ready under the bed upstairs.

'I shall partake of a little of this magnificent pudding, then retire to bed,' Aunt Temperance went on.

'It is a wonderful dessert,' Mr Kingsley said, his eyes on Rose. Her nerves were jangling. She could hardly eat it with him watching her like that, but she forced herself because she didn't know when their next meal would be.

He cleared his plate, put his spoon down, wiped his mouth and leaned back in Pa's chair, the heavy oak carver worn smooth by years of use. He closed his eyes, his mouth slackened and his jaw dropped. The wine bottle was empty, but his glass was still half full.

'Have you no manners?' Aunt Temperance said shrilly, the sound jerking him from his slumber. 'It isn't polite to fall asleep at the table. You really must set a better example to our dear children.'

Rose sighed inwardly. Why did she insist on keeping up the pretence that they were five years old and she had maternal feelings for them?

'Mr Kingsley, get up this minute.' Aunt Temperance was on her feet, berating her husband and patting him on the cheek. 'How many times do I have to beg you to consider your wife's feelings and put a stop to your drinking? It isn't good for you. You have an old man's nose, bloodshot eyes and stinking breath.'

'I *am* an old man,' he muttered. 'I'm worn out.' He slumped back again.

'You are three sheets to the wind.' Aunt Temperance looked towards Arthur. 'You and Donald must help him up the stairs to bed.'

Rose began to worry that her aunt wasn't going to succumb to the laudanum – maybe she had grown used to it, having partaken of the sleeping drops every day since she'd first brought them back from the apothecary. Luckily, though, her aunt picked up Mr Kingsley's wine glass and drained it herself.

'There, you will not have any more.' She swayed and dropped the glass on the floor, having apparently lost her sense of coordination.

'I'll get on and do the dishes,' Rose said, getting up from the table as was her usual custom.

'Mind you put the plates away this time,' her aunt said, slurring her words. 'I don't want to find them still out in the morning. And I'd like hot water for my wash, not lukewarm.' She yawned again. 'Oh dear, I can hardly keep my eyes open. Goodnight.' She followed Arthur and Donald, who were hauling an insensible Mr Kingsley out of the dining room.

Rose cleared the table, but left the dishes piled up in the sink in one last act of rebellion. As she headed out of the scullery a few minutes later, she ran into Arthur who was at the back door with a carpet bag slung over his shoulder and a pair of boots tied to the handles by the laces.

'What is it?' she whispered. 'You're worrying me.'

'Shh,' he warned as he fiddled with the bolt. 'I've been running this through my head over and over again, and I can only come up with one solution – that I leave for London while you and the twins go to seek refuge with your grandmother.'

'What do you think Ma and Pa would have had to say about this? We must stick together.'

'And I would stay if I could,' he said roughly. 'Look at us. Who would willingly take in four people, four mouths to feed? You and the twins are family. I am a stranger to your grandmother, a cuckoo in the nest.'

'Arthur, we are all the same family,' Rose argued quietly.

'In a way, but I've always felt different. Ma and Pa did their best – and I loved them as they loved me – but I had a mother whom I adored before them.'

'I'm sorry,' Rose began.

'Hush,' he said. 'There is nothing to be sorry about. This is the right thing to do. I wouldn't find work easily. I was born and brought up here in Canterbury. I know nothing of farming.'

'Then we won't go,' she said. 'We won't go anywhere without you.'

'You aren't thinking straight. Listen to me.'

'Arthur, please don't go. I beg you.' She clung to him. 'I can't do this on my own.'

'It won't be for ever.' Gently, he disengaged himself from her. 'Just let me take this one chance of making things better for all of us – you, me, the twins and Tabby.'

'Tabby?'

He nodded. 'She's coming with me.'

'You're eloping?'

'I suppose you can call it that. Anyway, we're going to join Bert in London. I'll send word as soon as I can.' He paused. 'I have a dream and I'm going to make it come true.' He had another go at opening the door.

'The screw for the bolt is on top of the door frame,' Rose whispered. 'I had the foresight to put it there in advance, knowing how our aunt puts it in her pocket when she retires to bed. She has forgotten this evening, which means we have avoided a scene. I've oiled the hinges too so they won't make a sound.'

'Ah, you are much cleverer than me.' Arthur reached up for the screw and twisted it into the bolt. 'Until we meet again, dear sister. Please, say goodbye to the twins for me.'

'Aren't you going to speak to them?'

'No, I can't. I'm sorry. I'm too much of a coward and I don't want them making a scene. Good luck.'

'Take care, Arthur.'

He slid the bolt back, opened the door and slipped out into the darkness, taking part of Rose's heart with him. She wondered if they would ever see him again.

Chapter Thirteen

Overshill

Holding herself together, Rose went upstairs to find Minnie sitting in bed propped up against a pillow, an empty plate beside her.

'You are awake,' she said softly, inwardly thanking Ma for her lessons in keeping one's emotions in check. The tears and accusations over Arthur's departure would come later, when she and the twins were clear of Willow Place, their childhood home filled with precious memories of a time when they had been the happiest family alive.

'I did as you said – I've only taken the tiniest bit of medicine and my head is quite clear, although the pain is terribly bad. Anyway, I've been thinking that I should stay behind with the Kingsleys,' Minnie said quietly.

'That's impossible. I won't let that happen.'

'I'm a burden. I'll only hold you and the others back.'

'That is a kind and thoughtful offer, but I have no intention of leaving you behind and that's my last word on the matter.' Rose dashed a tear from her eye.

'You're crying?'

'It's dust, that's all. Have you packed the patchwork and our sewing box?'

Minnie nodded and pointed to the bag on the bed.

'We're ready then. We'll wait until the clock downstairs strikes midnight, then be on our way.' Rose listened intently for the chimes, and on the last, she picked up their bags – a carpet bag and a portmanteau of her father's which she had found in the shed – and handed Minnie one of Mr Kingsley's fancy walking sticks, which she had taken from the hallstand.

'Where are we going?' Minnie said, thumping her stick against the floor.

Rose put her finger to her lips. 'Shh,' she whispered.

'Sorry,' Minnie whispered back.

'We're going to a place called Overshill, near Selling. It'll be quite a walk, but we'll have the barrow and Donald will drag it along by the handle, and I'll give it a push from the rear if it gets stuck in the mud.'

'I'll walk with the stick,' Minnie said bravely as Donald appeared in the room with another bag and a roll of clothes across his shoulders.

'Where's Arthur?' he asked. 'Isn't he supposed to be here?'

Rose steeled herself as she took Minnie's arm and helped her off the bed. 'He's gone ahead. We thought it was for the best. Come along. We must hurry.' She didn't want to run into anyone, even the knocker-upper with his baton, stick and peashooter. 'Donald, pick up the bags,' she hissed, and the three of them set out down the first flight of stairs. They paused on the next landing to listen to their aunt's soft snores. So far so good.

As they continued down the second flight of stairs with Minnie wincing at every movement of her body, a pewter mug fell from one of the bags and clattered down the steps.

'No, keep going,' Rose whispered when Donald made to retrieve it, afraid that if their aunt woke up, she would beat them half to death.

They struggled through the hall and kitchen to the back door, and Rose pushed it open then helped Minnie across the garden and along the passageway at the side of the house, where they had to force their way past the over-grown laurels in the faint light of a crescent moon, before hurrying down the drive and crossing the street to the yard. Minnie leaned against the wall, breathing hard, while Donald unlocked the gates and nipped into the yard to fetch the barrow. It wasn't an ordinary push barrow, but a more substantial, four-wheeled dog cart with wooden wheels straked with iron, and a handle to pull it along.

Rose lit the wick of the lamp Donald had left hidden in the barrow the day before, and hooked it on the side while Donald loaded it with their bags. Together, they lifted Minnie on top. Rose straightened Minnie's leg as far as she could.

'What have you done with the bandages and splint?' she said, suddenly realising that they were gone, and Minnie was wearing a double layer of stockings instead.

'I took them off – they were too tight.'

'Well, you should have left them alone – they were doing you some good. I should be livid with you after all the trouble I went to.' She placed a blanket over Minnie for warmth.

'I don't need that,' Minnie said abruptly. 'It's the middle of July.'

'You leave it on. You'll soon feel the cold when we get moving, and I don't want you catching your death ...' Rose's voice faded as she thought of Ma and how much she sounded like her.

Donald leaned forward against the handle of the barrow, giving it a good shove. Minnie's cry of protest sent a flock of roosting pigeons rising from a nearby roof, fluttering into the night sky. Donald picked up Minnie's stick and took a top hat from his bag. He made a show of dusting it down and placing it on his head.

'If I were a gentleman, I would—'

'Don't tell me that's … you've stolen Mr Kingsley's hat! He will come and find us for sure.'

'I took what I felt I was owed. They owe us, Rose.'

At first she was annoyed, but then she laughed because he looked both comical and handsome. 'You make a very fine gentleman.'

'I know, and if Pa had been here, I would have gone on to be one.'

She glanced behind him. 'We must keep moving.' She wasn't sure how long the journey would take – it depended on the state of the roads and how they coped with the darkness – but she was more concerned about how the Kingsleys would react when they found them gone.

'I wonder when we will catch up with Arthur. He can take a turn with the barrer,' Donald said when they had been on the move for an hour or so and were clear of Canterbury and Harbledown.

'I'm sorry,' Rose said, suddenly overwhelmed with guilt. 'I have a confession to make.'

'He isn't coming with us?' Donald stopped the barrow again. 'I had an inkling.'

'I wanted him to say goodbye to you, but he … well, he was upset.'

'Where's he gone then?' Minnie said.

'He has eloped with Tabby.'

'He's marrying Miss Miskin after all?' Donald asked. 'That's a turn-up for the books.'

Rose nodded. 'He's planning to stay with Bert and find work in London. He'll come and find us as soon as he can.'

'I wonder what Mr Miskin will think about that.'

'It doesn't matter what he thinks. What about us? How will we manage without Arthur?' Minnie began to cry.

'We're going to stay with our grandmother, if she'll have us, just until we're back on our feet.'

'Who is this woman?' Donald asked. 'What makes you think she'll welcome us with open arms?'

'Mrs Carter is Ma's mother, which makes us her grand-children by blood.'

'Why should she help us, though? She's never taken any interest in us before,' Donald said.

'We have to try – she's our only hope,' Rose explained.

'What about Aunt Marjorie?'

'You know her situation, and she has written to tell me she is unwell. We can't possibly prevail on her to look after us.'

'I see. I hope she recovers soon,' Donald said.

'A body can't recover from old age,' Rose said wistfully.

'That's a terrible shame,' Donald said. 'Oh, I'm starving. Can't we stop for a while?'

Rose agreed and they walked a little way into an orchard where they sat down on a fallen tree and shared the bread, cheese and apples they'd brought with them, but Rose could hardly eat for wondering what they would do if Mrs Carter refused to listen to them, let alone help them.

Having rested, they set off again at dawn, making their way through Dunkirk, a wooded area where the scent of smoke hung in the air. The barrow stopped, its wheel lodged in a rut.

'Put your back into it, Donald,' Rose said.

'I am.' His face turned red with effort.

'Push harder then. What are you? Man or mouse?' Rose gave it an extra shove from behind, sending it bouncing out of the rut and rattling off down the slope with Donald digging his heels in, trying to slow it down.

'You don't know your own strength,' Donald laughed. 'I'm sorry, Minnie.'

'Do it again,' she said, her eyes gleaming with excitement.

'Didn't it hurt your leg?' Rose asked.

'It made me forget about it.' She smiled.

Rose and Donald pushed the barrow together up the next rise. At the top, they stepped aside and gave it a push, letting it speed unhindered down the next slope.

'Where has the road gone?' Donald asked when they were laughing with Minnie at the bottom.

'I don't know.' Rose started to panic when she couldn't find her bearings. Somehow, in their joy at having freed themselves from their aunt's bullying, they'd managed to get lost in the woods where one tree looked very much like another.

'I wish Arthur was here,' Minnie kept saying as they wandered round in circles looking for the road. 'He'd know which way to go.'

'Oh, stop whining,' Rose exclaimed. 'I'm doing my best.'

'As you always do,' Donald said. 'Minnie, you should be grateful for what Rose has done for us.'

'I'm sorry,' Minnie said and Rose fell silent, touched by her brother's support.

The sun was high in the sky and the shadows short when they finally found their way and continued through the deep green lanes of Kent.

'There's a church,' Minnie said, pointing across the fields towards a stone tower surrounded by buildings and trees.

'That must be Overshill,' Rose observed, shading her eyes.

'It isn't far,' Donald said, but it took them all afternoon to get there because one of the wheels fell off the barrow, and it wasn't until a farmer came along in a cart pulled by a big black horse with feathery feet that they had any hope of continuing on their way.

'You look as if you're in a bit of a bind,' he said, pulling up alongside them.

'Our wheel has broke,' Minnie said.

'Ah, allow me to have a look at it. The name's Mr Butt.' He dropped the reins and jumped down.

'We're glad to make your acquaintance,' Rose said, uncertain of him as he inspected the barrow. He was certainly past a chicken in age, and seemed friendly enough with his ruddy complexion and fine white whiskers.

'It isn't broken as such. The fixing that holds the wheel to the axle is missing.' He rubbed at his chin, deep in thought. 'I think it might be your lucky day – I have some wire somewhere.' He rummaged about in the cart while the horse waited patiently with its head down. Eventually, he and Donald managed to reattach the wheel and secure it to the barrow.

'How can we pay you back?' Rose said, thanking him.

'Oh, I won't charge you.' The man smiled as he clambered back on to the cart and picked up the reins. 'We help each other out around here. Good afternoon, ladies and gentleman.'

The horse and cart disappeared into the distance and the three siblings carried on. When they reached the church, they found a young man, a lad who couldn't have been more than a year or two older than Rose, cutting the grass in the graveyard.

'Hello. You aren't from around here,' he said, stopping and walking across to speak to them.

'We're looking for a Mrs Carter who lives on a farm in Overshill,' Rose said.

'You can try Wanstall Farm – you'll find a Mrs Carter there. There's a short cut that way.' He pointed towards a path where the flint wall that bordered the churchyard came to an end. 'Follow it past the pond then turn left on to the main street. Got that?'

She nodded.

'Then you keep going past the Woodsman's Arms and the oast, until you reach the mill when you follow the left fork at the crossroads. You'll pass Toad's Bottom, and then you'll find the farm to your right. What is it you want with the Carters?'

'It's a private matter, but thank you for the directions.'

'It's a pleasure. Good day to you.' He touched his forelock of dark hair, keeping his eyes on her. 'The name is Sam, by the way. Sam White.'

'Well, it's nice to meet you.' He was handsome and had a pleasant manner, she thought, but she soon forgot about him, her mind occupied with more pressing details.

Following the lad's instructions, they reached the main street where they passed a pair of black and white timber-framed buildings – like Willow Place, but smaller – and a village shop attached to a cottage called the Old Forge, in front of which stood a massive chestnut tree. Rose took note of where the butcher's was as they passed a terrace of brick cottages with gardens filled with hollyhocks and roses, before continuing up the hill past the oast with its white-painted cowl, and the mill and adjoining bakehouse.

They took the left fork at the crossroads, taking the barrow along a bumpy track until they came to an unkempt and unloved hovel partly hidden by overgrown bushes and trees.

'What a wreck,' Donald observed.

'Is that the farm?' Minnie asked.

'Of course not. At least, I don't think so ...' Donald walked on, towing the barrow until they reached a brick and tile house a little further on. 'This is it.'

Realising the truth in the saying about it being better to travel hopefully than to arrive, Rose hesitated before she forced the gate open and stepped on to a shingle path that ran across a lawn to a green door with a wrought-iron handle. She knocked but there was no reply.

'There is nobody here,' Donald said in a low voice.

'There has to be. Let's try this way.' She returned down the path and continued along the track to a wooden five-bar gate set in a gap in the wall. A sign written in gold lettering on a black background proclaimed: *Mr S. Carter, Esq., WCF blacksmith and farrier. For all horse doctoring needs: physics and liniments. Quality horses available for sale, broken to ride and drive.*

Looking over the gate into the yard, she noticed a henhouse and woodpile, a gate that appeared to lead out into the fields, and a long timber barn with a horse tied up outside. There was also a granary and stables, and she saw that the house backed on to one side of the yard, with a water pump outside.

Donald began to push the gate open, at which a flock of seven white geese came running at them, holding their wings out and honking furiously. He slammed the gate shut again, and the geese stalked about behind it, as though lying in wait for them. 'What now?'

'I don't know, do I?' Rose noticed a figure appear from a doorway on the far side of the yard. As she grew closer, throwing corn from the pocket of her apron to the hens squabbling at her feet, Rose could see that she was a tall, quite elderly woman – probably in her sixties. Her long wavy hair, dark brown and spun through with silver, was tied back beneath her cap. Her features seemed very familiar and at first Rose wasn't sure why, until she realised that she reminded her of Ma.

The woman was joined by an old man with a bowed back, who stepped out from the timber barn and walked with her to the gate, shooing the geese out of their way.

'Who are you?' he said rather grumpily. 'If you aren't looking to buy a horse, or have one shod, then you'd best be on your way.'

'My name is Rose. This is my brother Donald and my sister Minnie.' She moved the barrow right up to the gate so they could see how pale and ill Minnie was. 'We have walked all the way from Canterbury.'

'And why have you come here?' the man said, frowning.

'Because we are related by blood to Mrs Carter here. You are Mrs Carter?'

'Yes, I am,' the woman said, a sense of wonderment spreading across her face. 'How is this possible after all these years?'

'The girl's giving you a sob story. They're nothing but beggars, hoping to extort money out of you by appealing to your kind nature. Move on, you ragamuffins. You'll find lodgings in the village.'

'Oh Stephen, they are very young.'

'Old enough and ugly enough to look after themselves. How old are you?' he said, addressing Rose.

'Seventeen, sir.'

'There you go then.'

'We have no money,' Rose said, seeing her hopes of help slipping away as Donald suddenly slumped to the ground. On his way down, he caught her eye and winked. She gasped at his cheeky ploy and knelt beside him, patting his face as though to revive him. He uttered a low moan.

'Don't try to move,' she told him. 'You've fainted. Oh dear Lord, give us the strength to carry on to find food and shelter by nightfall. Amen.'

'Amen,' Minnie said helpfully from the barrow.

'We must take pity on them, whoever they are,' Mrs Carter said. 'We can't let them stay out after dark – they'll end up sleeping rough in the woods.'

'Don't let your heart rule your head. The last time you saw your daughter was years ago – twenty at least – and you know how I felt about that. I indulged you then, knowing how much it meant to you and didn't stand in your way. But this time ... Well, we are old.'

'We are only as old as our tongues and a little older than our teeth.' Mrs Carter smiled. 'I remember a time when I had nothing and was desperate. We should at least listen to what Rose has to say.'

Donald slowly sat himself up.

'I have proof of my identity. Let me show you.' Rose fumbled for the half a sixpence at her neck, unfastened the clasp and handed it to her grandmother.

'It is some kind of miracle. It is the very same token that I gave Agnes when she was about to turn nineteen,' she exclaimed, handing it to her husband whose eyes widened like saucers.

'That is the silver chain I made for you, my love. It has the stamp I put on the catch, and the bent link that I made by mistake. It is no trick.' He turned to Rose angrily. 'How did you get hold of it?'

'My ma was called Agnes,' she said.

'Agnes Berry-Clay?' Mrs Carter asked incredulously.

'No, Linnet and then Cheevers, but she was Berry-Clay afore that. She looked much like you.' Rose faltered, feeling the tears gather and spill over. She wiped them away and cleared her throat before going on, 'You know that our mother has passed away. Our aunt wrote to you.'

'And I sent a reply, expressing my condolences. I couldn't bring myself to go to the funeral – it was too late ... Oh dear, this is such a pickle.'

'We are orphans and that is the reason why we have come. Minnie is badly injured and cannot work, so there is only me and Donald here. We have lost our home and are deep in the mire.'

'You are my granddaughter?' Mrs Carter said, as though she was still catching up. 'And these two?'

'My half-brother and half-sister – also your grandchildren.'

'Well I never. Well I never did. In all my years … Mr Carter, look at the state they're in, all skin and bone. I can't have it on my conscience to let them go, and I'd like to get to know my long-lost daughter's children.' She brushed a tear from her eye. 'I never thought I'd get to meet them and here they are on my doorstep. It is fate that has brought them here. Oh, I haven't been this happy and sad all at once before. My poor Agnes. Did I do right by her, or not?'

'Catherine, don't upset yourself over it now – you did what you thought was right at the time,' Mr Carter said. 'You lot had better come indoors,' he added grudgingly. 'Leave the barrow over there.' He pointed towards the henhouse. Rose helped Minnie out and handed her the stick, but her sister couldn't support her weight.

'That's no good, is it?' Mr Carter observed. 'I suppose you'll have to lean on me to help you indoors.'

Rose watched them struggle across the yard and into the house, passing through a corridor into a homely kitchen with a huge table in the middle.

'What happened to your leg?' Mr Carter asked.

'It got broke, sir,' Minnie said, her lip bleeding from where she had bitten it in an attempt to stifle a cry of pain.

'With some force, I think. You sit down on the chair.' He took Minnie's stick and leaned it against the wall in the corner. He placed a second chair in front of her and lifted her leg very carefully so it rested straight. 'You didn't call on a surgeon or a bonesetter? Those bones won't mend if they aren't put straight.'

'We were under the care of our aunt – Pa's sister – and her husband who said there was no money to pay for medical treatment. Minnie's had sleeping drops, and I've tried my best with bandages and a splint, but she took them off because she said they were too tight,' Rose said, sensing that Mr Carter expected her to have done more.

'The upper part of the bone should have been pulled away from the lower with considerable force until the leg was the same length as the other one. I fear it is too late to bring it back to how it was, but I'll have a go at improving matters. We'll arrange to get it done in the morning – these things shouldn't be left.' He looked at her disapprovingly.

Donald was soon completely revived with cheese, fruit cake and tea, and the Carters returned to discussing what they should do with the three of them.

'They can stay tonight, one night only,' Rose heard Mr Carter say gruffly. 'Now, I'm going to turn in. We have an early start in the morning, but I will take some time out to look at the girl's leg. She can't carry on like that. They shoot horses for less.'

Rose frowned.

'Don't listen to him,' Mrs Carter said with a smile. 'We'll talk tomorrow. Rose, Minnie, Donald, I'll show you to your room. It used to belong to my stepdaughter, Jessie. She's grown up and has children of her own now.' A shadow crossed her face – a sad memory perhaps, Rose thought. 'She and your ma were about the same age. Anyway, fetch your bags and get your heads down for the night.'

Somehow they managed to carry Minnie upstairs and Rose made sure she was comfortable while Donald collected their luggage from the barrow. Leaving their clothes on, they lay down on the bed, topped and tailed like a litter of pups. Rose could see the whites of Donald's eyes as they listened to the sound of voices through the door which had swung ajar in a draught.

Mr and Mrs Carter were in the hall, arguing. She could guess what it was about.

'They can go to the Union tomorrow – they will be admitted there.'

'Oh no, over my dead body. I would move Heaven and earth to prevent that.' There was a pause. 'How can you even suggest that, knowing what I went through when I was carrying Agnes?'

'The younger girl is a cripple. Even if I can set her broken bones, there's no guarantee they'll heal straight, or at all for that matter. She is a sickly-looking creature and no use to man or beast.'

'You have a very short memory, Mr Carter. My brother, God rest his soul, broke his head when he had his accident. He was a changed man, and but half of one, but it didn't stop me loving him. The eldest, Rose, has her hands tied when it comes to finding work because she's caring for her sister. I know what that's like.'

'My point exactly, my love. We have our own family, our own children and grandchildren—'

'I understand how you feel, and I agree that it's a burden we could do without, but I can't have it on my conscience to send them on their way until they are back on their feet. They are your brother's grandchildren, his flesh and blood, Stephen.'

'Oh, and don't I know it! I feel like they've opened old wounds by coming here.'

202

So Mrs Carter had married her sweetheart's brother, Rose thought.

'Let's sleep on it,' Mr Carter said, and on hearing someone heading up the stairs, Rose rolled over and closed her eyes. The sheets were clean and the mattress was comfortable, but she couldn't sleep for the hooting owls and whinnying horses, the cacophony of the countryside seeming much more intrusive than the sounds of Canterbury. Everything felt unfamiliar – even the air smelled strange: clean and fresh.

'Rose, are you awake?' Donald hissed when Minnie was fast asleep.

'Yes,' she whispered back.

'We did well – you timed those tears perfectly.'

'They were real,' Rose said, shocked. 'Unlike your faint.'

'That was genius, wasn't it? I reckon that's what made Mr Carter take us in.'

'They haven't decided how long we can stay – I'm worried sick.'

'Don't worry. Arthur will come and find us soon.'

When, though? she wondered. How many years did it take someone to make their fortune?

'I'll look after you and Minnie,' Donald said. 'Whatever happens, I'll find a job, and as soon as I have money in my pocket we'll pay for a doctor to make her well again, if Mr Carter's idea doesn't work. We'll be all right, I promise.'

'I hope so,' Rose murmured. They had escaped Willow Place, but she couldn't help feeling that their trials were only just beginning.

Chapter Fourteen

One to rot
One to grow
One for the pigeons
One for the crow

Rose was woken by the sound of metal hammering against metal. Remembering where she was, she peeked past the curtain, catching sight of a boy outside in the farmyard. He was holding on to a big grey horse while a middle-aged man stood bowed over with its hoof between his knees as he nailed a shoe on to its foot.

Having wished Minnie a good morning, she shook Donald awake and told him to get up, then quickly brushed her hair before walking out on to the landing, afraid they had overslept. She headed downstairs to the kitchen where she found Mrs Carter bringing a basket of eggs indoors, and a maid preparing breakfast: eggs, bread and jam, the sight of which made her mouth water.

'It wouldn't be right to throw them on to the parish, Alice,' Mrs Carter said.

'No, ma'am,' the maid said.

'Or send them on to Faversham to find work in the brickfields. There is plenty of work there, so I've heard, except that it's long and hard, and only for the summer. Ah, there you are, Rose. There's a bucket and water to wash with out there.' She pointed towards the door leading into the corridor. 'Mind you don't splash your feet when you work the pump – my brother used to tease me to death about it.' Her husband appeared in the corridor, taking off his boots. 'Oh, there you are, Stephen. What did she have?'

He beamed broadly. 'A beautiful colt. He's perfect. And Stanley has already put a new shoe on the young man's horse.'

'Who is he?' Mrs Carter said as two more men in their late thirties or early forties followed Mr Carter into the kitchen. She quickly introduced them to Rose as her stepsons, Stanley and Matthew, before returning to the subject of the visiting stranger. 'Didn't you ask him who he was and what business he had in Overshill?'

'I didn't interrogate him as you would have done – he gave me the impression that he wanted to keep himself to himself, but he did mention that he'd hired his mount and ridden this way early from Canterbury to meet with the agent who's selling Churt House.'

'Really? That's interesting. What did you tell him?'

'Not a lot – he didn't ask much.'

'What does he do to afford a place like that?' Mrs Carter said, rather coldly, Rose thought. 'It hasn't been touched in years.'

'Not since the owner died. What was his name?' Stanley – the younger of the brothers – piped up. 'Handley? No, Hadington.'

'The weasley old lawyer who used to fall out with the squire over the boundaries of their estates. That's right,' Matthew said, reaching across the table for a slice of bread. 'You should have remembered him – we used to shoe all his hunters and carriage horses, didn't we, Pa?'

'I sold him a good few animals,' Mr Carter said, his eyes on his wife who turned away and busied herself with slicing more bread. 'He was a good customer and a wicked man, but the less said about that the better.' Mr Carter looked towards Rose. 'What time do you call this?'

'I believe that it's morning, sir,' she said, unsure how to take him. 'I'm sorry I'm late up.'

'It doesn't matter – I'm not surprised that you're exhausted, you poor little mites,' Mrs Carter said.

'They can't be described as little when they're all full grown,' Mr Carter said, the creases at his eyes deepening. He turned to Rose. 'My wife has convinced me that we should give you some support. I can't say I'm happy about it. I was under the impression that we were winding down and our caring days were over.'

'You never stop caring for your children,' Mrs Carter said. 'Look at our Jessie – she's way past thirty and you still worry about her.'

'They can stay, but at the first sign of trouble, they'll be out on their ear-'oles.'

Mrs Carter smiled.

'They can have the cottage at Toad's Bottom for a few weeks,' Mr Carter continued. 'It's in a bit of a state – for various reasons we have rather let it go, but they're lucky to have a roof over their heads at all. And I expect help on the farm and in the house in return. They can pay a small rent, once they've earned a bit of money. There are plenty of chores for the boy: mucking out, repairing the fences and filling the buckets and troughs. It'll be 'op and apple pickin' soon. Rose could turn her hand to that, although we'll probably have more than enough workers with the Irish and Londoners turning up.'

'Minnie can do some sewing and mending when she's well again,' Rose said, concerned for her sister, for whom their journey had been too much. 'I've left her in bed for now.' Minnie had been as white as Mrs Carter's bedsheets.

'First things first,' Mr Carter said. 'We must eat, then set this broken leg.'

'Minnie isn't a horse,' she said, filled with doubt.

'Under all the fur and feather, animals are much like us. We are all made from flesh and bone, heart and lung, muscle and guts. Don't go running down the road to ask Mrs Greenleaf for a cure. She purports to be a wise woman, but she'll only give you an embrocation of juice of toad and a dose of black pepper and gin.' He grinned, revealing his broken and worn brown teeth. 'I would no more rub rotted toad on my own legs, let alone those of my horses.'

Reassured, Rose took food upstairs for Minnie and ate with her before helping her to wash so that she looked respectable. Donald joined them and assisted in carrying Minnie down the stairs and into the parlour, where Mrs Carter opened the curtains to let the daylight in.

They sat Minnie on the chaise and waited for Mr Carter, who turned up with the young lad they'd met at the church the previous day.

'This is Sam who's responsible for the tidiness of the yard and garden.' He moved across to the chaise. 'May I trouble you to lift your skirts, Minnie?' he said.

Rose felt uncomfortable. Mr Carter wasn't a doctor.

'Don't worry,' Mrs Carter said with a smile. 'My husband's head has always been turned by the sight of a well-turned fetlock rather than a shapely ankle. He's treated hundreds of injuries – many people come here to take advantage of his skills.'

'Did you have plenty of rest after you broke your leg?' Mr Carter asked as he examined her.

Rose spoke on her sister's behalf, Minnie having been overcome by shyness.

'She had no choice but to stay in bed, although our aunt did her utmost to make her get up. She even threatened to send her out begging on the street.'

'Really?' Mrs Carter said.

'All she wanted was the house – our home – and the family business. She didn't care about us.'

'You don't think she will come after you?'

'I doubt it.' Rose forced a small smile.

'She would get short shrift if she came to Overshill,' Mrs Carter said. 'What is your opinion, Stephen? Can you fix this poor girl's bones?'

'I'm not sure, but I'll give it a try if Minnie is willing.'

'I'll do anything to not be a burden on my sister for any longer than possible,' she said.

It seemed that Minnie's quiet spirit had satisfied him. He gave her laudanum and brandy for the pain and ordered Donald and Sam stand in position. It was an agonisingly slow process. Rose and Mrs Carter held Minnie's hands while Mr Carter stood behind her and took a strong grasp across her chest, bracing her shoulders as he instructed Sam and Donald to take hold of Minnie's ankle and pull.

'Harder than that, lads. Put your backs into it.'

'But it's going to hurt,' Donald said.

'Unfortunately, we have to be cruel to be kind. Now, are we ready? One, two and three …'

Sam and Donald pulled and Minnie screamed like a banshee. Rose had never heard anything like it.

'Keep the pressure on, that's right,' Mr Carter said. 'Let the muscles stretch.'

Rose felt her hand being slowly crushed between Minnie's fingers.

'Keep going! All right, that will do for a minute. You can rest.' Mr Carter walked round to check on their progress. 'It's a shame it's been left so long. The tissues inside the leg have shrunk and a callus has formed between the ends of the bones. Never mind, we'll keep trying.'

They repeated the stretching five more times until Rose thought she would have no hand left. Donald was red-faced and tearful at Minnie's screaming, while Sam looked petrified.

'I'm afraid we'll have her leg off, sir,' he kept saying.

'That really isn't helping, Sam,' Mrs Carter told him. 'Hold tight, my dear. It won't be much longer.'

'One more time,' Mr Carter said, and Rose had to force herself to stay at her sister's side as she fought against the restraint, tears and sweat mingling down her cheeks.

'You heard what he said,' she whispered. 'Not long now.'

Mr Carter braced himself once more, and Donald and Sam hauled at Minnie's leg with grunts of effort, until suddenly the patient went limp.

'Stop there! She's fainted, but that's quite normal.' Mr Carter moved in closer to examine the result of their efforts as Minnie began to come round. 'That's pretty good – not perfect, but it will do. Now, you lads can go while I bandage this up. Mrs Carter, fetch a bucket of water and the plaster of Paris from the stables – it should be in the cupboard with the physic balls and liniments. Rose, stay with your sister.'

When their grandmother returned, Rose watched Mr Carter wrap Minnie's leg in linen strips rubbed in plaster of Paris, then made wet.

'That'll set hard so the ends of the bones will stay in place until they have knitted together,' he explained. 'The end result won't be perfect, but it will be far better than the present situation.'

'Will she be able to walk and be comfortable?' Rose asked.

'It'll take some time. Minnie's going to have to stay here until this is dry.'

'How long must the plaster stay on?'

'She's young, so a few weeks will do it.'

'*Weeks?*'

'That's how long it takes. If you remove it too soon, the good work is undone.'

'How will you get it off?' Minnie said, looking alarmed.

'We'll have to cut it. Don't worry, I've done it many times before. Don't let the plaster get wet or it will go soggy and fall apart. No baths, no paddling.' He looked at his wife. 'I suggest that you open up the cottage for them for tonight.' He reached for her hand and Rose heard him whisper, 'I'll never forget how you looked after me and the children when Emily passed away, in spite of the pain you must have felt at having had to give up your own child. I owe you this, and more ...'

Rose wrapped Minnie in a blanket and sat with her for a couple of hours before Alice took over so that she could accompany their grandmother to the cottage. Mrs Carter picked up her shawl and stick from the hall, and she and Rose set out to walk down the road from the farmhouse.

'I'm longing to catch up with all your news.' Mrs Carter's voice began to falter as she went on, 'I would like to hear about my dear Agnes, what she was like ... I'm sorry, I should have thought. It's too painful, too raw. Another time.'

'I'd like to talk about her. It upsets me more when people don't mention Ma at all, as if she never existed.'

'I know something of what you're going through. For reasons I will not go into now, I gave up my daughter for adoption. Agnes was taken in by a wealthy family who lived near Faversham. Her father was the owner of one of the breweries there.'

'I have been told some of this story,' Rose said. 'Why didn't you come to Ma's funeral? We thought you would have wanted to pay your respects.'

'I regret that now, but it's too late to do anything about it. It's hard to explain, but when I last saw her to give her the half a sixpence and a chance to ask questions, she didn't say much. She was shocked, I think, to find out that she'd been born so poor and low. She didn't want to know me, and why should she?

'Agnes was wearing white kid gloves, the best – that's what struck me most. The sight of them reassured me that she would be happy and kept in clover for the rest of her life, but I felt miserable, rejected, unwanted and resentful, and I couldn't help thinking that I should have let sleeping dogs lie.' Mrs Carter sighed. 'What about you? You said that Donald and Minnie aren't your full brother and sister.'

'I was told that my father was the son of a baronet, but then Ma met Mr Cheevers, and, well, we thought they were married, but it's been the cause of much grief to us that it turned out they weren't – and had never been – joined in holy matrimony. It meant that Pa's property passed to his sister, Mrs Kingsley, and my brothers lost out.'

'You said "brothers"?'

'Yes, I have an adopted brother, Arthur, who's gone to London to seek work as a bricklayer.'

'I see.'

Rose returned to the subject of her aunt. 'Mrs Kingsley moved into the family home and put us to work. You know the rest – we had to leave.'

'Ah, you have been through the mill, but you'll survive because you are of your grandmother's flesh.' Mrs Carter smiled. 'Let us give you some respite for a while at least.'

They reached the place where the trees had grown in from the woods, casting shadows across a cottage, which was little more than a one-up, one-down hovel adorned with grass which had taken root in the rotten thatch. The porch was propped up with a chestnut pole which appeared to have been appropriated from a nearby hop garden, and patches of damp had crept up the walls.

'I'm afraid that it isn't what you are used to,' Mrs Carter said, but to Rose it didn't matter: it was a palace. 'The gate has been off its hinges since I can remember, and look at those brambles – they need cutting back.'

'I don't want to impose on you and Mr Carter,' Rose said.

'You mustn't worry about it – we aren't poor. Stephen has worked hard all his life and one day I'd like him to retire, but I can't see that happening in the near future – he is too tied up in his work and the horses.'

'You have children and other grandchildren too?'

'I have three stepchildren – I'm Stephen's second wife. There's Matthew and Stanley whom you've met, and Jessie, whose husband is an agricultural merchant in Selling, not far away at all. Then we have two of our own: Thomas who married into the family at Sinderberry Farm, and Prudence who is married to the bailiff.' Mrs Carter smiled. 'I've almost lost count of how many grandchildren there are now.'

She stopped beside the low flint wall that fronted the overgrown garden and exclaimed, 'Oh, this place is full of ghosts.'

'What do you mean?' Rose asked.

'When I was a girl, the Carters lived here – my husband's father and family. There were ten of them at one time. Not now, though,' she said, her voice full of sorrow. 'Most of them are gorn.'

'That's very sad.'

'Well, it comes to us all, I'm afraid. Mind your step.' Rose followed her grandmother through a gap in the garden wall where the stones had fallen away, and along a path overgrown with weeds to the front door. Mrs Carter pushed it open. 'There's no key – I'll ask one of the men to fix the lock.'

Standing beside her grandmother, Rose peered into the darkness beyond, her eyes taking time to adjust to the light. Mrs Carter walked inside across the damp earthen floor, turned to the window and opened the shutter, letting the sunlight in.

'There, it isn't as bad as I thought it would be,' she said. 'Have a look upstairs.'

Rose trod carefully up the staircase, which opened on to a tiny landing with a door into the bedroom. The floor-boards creaked and bowed under her feet, and the shutters dropped off as she tried to open them.

'The windows need a good clean. We'll go and fetch a broom, and dustpan and brush, and some vinegar and carbolic. You'll need at least one saucepan, spoons and a knife. And I'll let you have a little tea, and some potatoes, mutton and onions to start you off,' Mrs Carter said. 'What do you know about running a household?'

'A little. I know that one should not stretch one's legs beyond the end of the coverlet – that's what Pa used to say. We had a housekeeper at Willow Place and a maid until our aunt moved in with us, then Minnie and I did the cooking and cleaning under her instruction.'

'Oh Rose, you are quite right about living within your means. Have you any money at all?'

'We have a few shillings,' she said. 'Enough to buy bread.'

'That should tide you over until your brother is paid his wages. You will find work during the summer, so make hay while the sun shines because it's harder to come by in the winter months.'

'You have saved our lives,' Rose said. 'I'll never be able to thank you enough.'

Mrs Carter smiled. 'Old Pa Carter – Stephen's father – used to grow fruit and veg on the ground here. It needs some digging over and a few barrows of well-rotted horse manure added to it. There's plenty in the heap at the farm – you can get Donald to fetch it. I'll let you have some of the seeds I kept from last year to sow, and one of the men will bring you a few pullets from the market in Faversham. When they're ready, we can let you have a piglet to fatten.'

'I'd like that. We didn't have a pig or hens in Canterbury.'

'You can use the whole pig, except for the squeak. It's very economical to keep if you feed him on scraps and acorns. What else can I say? Oh, there is firewood – you can clear the old trees in the corner. Don't go taking logs from the woods – they aren't yours to burn. Check the chimney isn't blocked before you light a fire – I expect it'll need sweeping by now.'

Rose returned to the farm with her grandmother, who handed her a basket of basic provisions and two jars of jam. Donald was allowed to leave his duties in the yard to wheel Minnie and their belongings, along with a broom and some cleaning materials, in the barrow to the cottage.

'When shall I come back, Mrs Carter?' Donald asked.

'My husband expects you at six in the morning. Rose, I can find plenty of chores for you in the house in return for remuneration in kind.'

'We're really very grateful,' Rose said. 'We'll see you tomorrow.'

They spent the rest of the day making Toad's Bottom cottage their own. They had a table, a bench and a fireplace with a stove downstairs, and a mattress, double bedstead and chest upstairs. Rose put the photograph of the family on the mantelpiece, then looked out of the window and saw Donald solving the problem with the gate by taking it off its remaining hinge and leaning it against the wall to one side.

'That will have to be put back on,' she called as she ran down to join him. 'The hens will escape.'

'Hens?'

'Yes, we will have hens. And a goat, perhaps. And a great fat pig. Oh, this will be the making of us,' she said, laughing for the first time in a long while. 'If we work hard, and scrimp and save, we'll be set up for life.'

'There's a long way to go,' Donald said. 'Don't get your hopes up – it all seems too good to be true.'

'Maybe you shouldn't look a gift horse in the mouth.'

'You are looking through a rose-tinted lorgnette, Lady Rose,' Donald teased.

Rose made a pirouette, coming to an abrupt stop and almost overbalancing as her shoe got stuck in the mud in the streamlet alongside the fallen wall.

'Oh, what a godforsaken place!' she exclaimed, leaving her shoe behind.

'You've changed your tune.' Donald grinned as he leaned down and picked it up from the mud.

'I can't wear that now.'

'You'll have to hop back to the house then. Here.' Donald held out his arm and helped her to the doorstep. 'I'll find some newspaper to dry your shoe overnight, just like Pa used to. I wish he was here, and Ma, and Arthur.'

'We all do,' Rose said, biting her lip. 'Come on. Let's keep busy. We need firewood, flint and kindling. And water.' She set her brother to do the sweeping while she dusted the cobwebs and washed the windows. She and Donald turned the mattress on the double bedstead and found an old blanket in the cupboard over the stairs.

There was no coal cellar as there had been at Willow Place. The rusty door latches had small plates fitted over the keyholes to keep out the dirt and there was an old muslin nailed across the front window to stop the soot obscuring the light. There were ants, beetles and spiders, marching up through the gaps between the floorboards upstairs, dangling down from the ceilings and scuttling across the walls. The timbers were half eaten by woodworm and rot, but Rose refused to let anything dampen her spirits.

'First things first. Mrs Carter said the chimney is likely to be blocked.' Rose remembered how Pa had had the chimneys swept every year. She was afraid of the smoke if they should light their fire, having had a fear of coughs since Pa's demise. 'We can use the broom handle.'

'It won't be long enough,' Donald said.

'We'll tie a stick to the end. That should do it.'

After a while, Donald managed to clear the chimney, the soots, feathers and twigs falling down and spilling across the floor. Rose sighed. They would have to start cleaning all over again, but who cared when they were free of the Kingsleys and Minnie had a chance of walking? That was all that mattered.

Chapter Fifteen

Work for Idle Hands

Within two weeks, Minnie was suffering from a lack of fresh air and activity, confined to the cottage with her plastered leg and some sewing that their grandmother had given her to do. Donald was hungry and exhausted from working on the farm, unused to such heavy physical labour, while Rose was struggling with taking on the role of a parent to the twins and looking after a rather recalcitrant house. She had never known anything like it.

When it rained, they had to put a metal bucket which they'd found in the garden to catch the drips in the bedroom, and fight a constant battle with the creepy crawlies that seemed determined to gain entrance. During a dry spell, the front door would shrink and not shut properly.

On their third Sunday in Overshill, Rose closed the downstairs window and looked down at her brother snoring lightly on the spare horsehair mattress which Mrs Carter had brought round on a cart a few days before. Smiling ruefully, she wished she could be more like him, lying there without a care in the world, but it would be different later when he realised how little they had in the way of food.

Donald had been paid, but only two shillings on account of his lack of experience and stamina, and even though

Rose had been frugal, they had just three eggs, half a loaf of bread, ham, lemonade, beer and the remains of a pot of jam left. There wasn't much keeping the wolf from the door, but Rose didn't like to ask Mrs Carter for more because she didn't want to cause trouble between her and Mr Carter.

She woke Donald and told him to wash behind his ears and change into his Sunday best.

'I don't see why we have to go to church,' he grumbled. 'We haven't got Ma and Pa breathing down our necks now.' A shadow of regret crossed his eyes. He didn't mean to be grumpy, she thought. He was having a hard time dealing with the loss of their parents too. He just showed his grief in a different way.

'I want to demonstrate that we're respectable members of the community. People are suspicious of us.'

'Rose, you don't have to keep up appearances like Aunt Temperance.'

'We're going to say our prayers. We will thank the Lord for our good fortune in finding a place to stay.'

'What about Minnie?'

'She'll stay here. I don't want everyone gawping at her because of her leg, and anyway Mr Carter has said she mustn't leave the house until it's mended.'

Leaving Minnie to sit in a chair looking out on the birds in the garden, Rose and Donald went to church for the first time in a long while. They walked up the steps into the churchyard, past the yews and gravestones, before entering the building through the dark oak door and shuffling into the row of seats right at the back of the Church of Our Lady, behind the pews. Rose knelt to pray for the souls of her parents, for Arthur and Tabby, and for the Carters for taking them in, but as she whispered her final amen, she became aware of the gossips murmuring behind their backs.

'I 'aven't sin them around here before.'

'They say they're Mrs Carter's long-lost grandchildren from Canterbury, but I don't know how that can be.'

'In this village, you are never more than a foot from a Carter,' somebody else said. 'There are even more of them now – not Carters by name – but their flesh and blood all the same.'

'They turned up on the doorstep of Wanstall Farm.'

'The sister is crippled, so I hear.'

'I don't think we'll ever know the half of it.'

'It's a shame. They've been given the cottage at Toad's Bottom when there are local people who've had their eye on that.'

'It's falling down, has been for years. You'd have thought they'd have put them up in the farmhouse. Old Carter isn't short of a shillin' or two.'

'It's a terrible thing to be orphaned at any age. Is there no other family?'

Trying to ignore them, Rose looked up at the stone pillars and soaring arches above her head. The stone bosses where the ribs met caught her eye. There was a nun's face, a rose and a green man with a beard of leaves and a kindly expression that made her feel a little better. She wished they were back at St Mildred's, where they were always welcome. Here in Overshill, she was painfully aware that they were outsiders.

The organist began to play from behind a carved wooden screen, and the vicar – an elderly gentleman with his grey hair brushed forward on to his forehead and cheeks – stepped up to the lectern in his cassock, surplice and stole.

As the service went on, Rose felt the weight of Donald's head gradually pressing on her shoulder, surprised that the growling of her empty belly didn't wake him. She was starving, and it didn't help that the vicar, who had an unfortunate lisp and a tendency to stumble over his words, had decided to dwell on the parable of the Great Banquet.

Eventually, the service came to an end, and they returned to the cottage.

'What shall we do now?' Rose looked at the sorry state of the garden, comparing it with the ones they'd seen on the way back from church. If only they had their own fruit trees and a vegetable patch, instead of a half-cleared expanse of mud and brambles. She and Donald had been taking turns to dig over the soil, turning up the stones and flints and tossing them aside, but it would be a while before they could plant anything.

'We could take Minnie out in the barrer,' Donald said.

Rose didn't argue. If they kept busy, they wouldn't have their minds on their empty stomachs. She went indoors and changed out of her Sunday best into a hessian skirt and cotton blouse.

'Where are we going?' Minnie asked when Rose joined her downstairs and Donald told her of their plan for the afternoon.

'Do you remember how Ma used to take us on nature walks when we were younger? I thought we'd go and explore the countryside around Overshill.' Donald helped his sister off the mattress. Rose handed over her shawl and stick, a lump in her throat as she remembered long walks through the water meadows where the cattle grazed beside the Stour, and how Ma would show them the water voles and damselflies among the yellow flag iris.

'There's no need for us to go out and look for insects – I've seen them all this morning: ants; greenbottles; spiders. Ugh.' Minnie grimaced.

Rose smiled again. 'Do you remember how we had to find bugs and look at them with the magnifying glass, and how Donald got stung on the nose by a wopsie?'

'It wasn't funny,' he said.

'Oh, it was,' she countered as they walked outside to the barrow which they'd left under the window. 'Your nose swelled up until you looked like Mr Kingsley coming back from the tavern.'

Rose took Minnie by her arms and Donald lifted her legs to get her into the barrow, where she perched on some straw with a pillow under her plaster cast.

'We should take some wittles,' Donald said.

'I wish you'd speak properly,' Rose scolded. 'You're becoming quite the country boy.'

'Boy?' he spluttered.

'Man, I mean,' she said, realising she had hurt his pride. 'I'll see what we've got.' She found the bottle of lemonade, some bread and a little ham which she had to cut the fat from because it had gone over and smelled bad. There was precious little left for their supper. She packed the provisions into a basket, carried it outside and gave it to Minnie to look after, before letting Donald take charge of the barrow.

'Ouch,' Minnie cried out as they set off.

'Are you sure you don't want to stay here?' Rose said.

'There's no way I'm letting you go off again without me. Waiting for your leg to mend is very dull.'

A dog trotted past, the look on its face reminding Rose of Arthur's expression when he'd been on his way to call on his sweetheart. She wouldn't dwell on his absence, she resolved, following Donald into the woods where the woodcutters' saws had fallen silent for the Sabbath. At least she, Donald and Minnie had each other.

'It's very bumpy,' Minnie said through gritted teeth as they made their way along a path between the chestnut trees with their glossy leaves and spiky green fruits.

'This isn't wise,' Rose fretted. 'Mr Carter was most insistent that Minnie should rest. All this bouncing about will break her bones again.'

'She'll be all right,' Donald said. 'Anyway, it isn't far.'

A while later, they were still walking and Rose began to feel light-headed.

'Donald, this feels more like a wild goose chase than a nature walk to me.'

'It's further than I thought, but don't worry, my dear sisters. We'll be there soon.' Donald pushed and pulled the barrow to force it out of a rut, then turned along the narrow lane that ran through the top of the village. At the same time, a man on horseback rode towards them, moving to one side to let them pass.

'Thank you, sir,' Rose said, frowning at her brother for his lack of manners.

'That looks like hard work,' the man observed, bringing his big grey horse to a halt.

Rose found her eyes drawn to him, a young man in his late twenties or early thirties with clean-cut features and a square jaw, who spoke with an unfamiliar, exotic accent. He doffed his hat, revealing a mop of honey-blond hair.

'I wonder if you can help me,' he said. 'I don't know this area well, and I'm looking for the road that takes me back to Selling.'

'You're heading in the right direction,' Rose said. 'Keep going until you reach a crossroads and turn right so that you're heading north.'

'Thank you,' he said. 'I wish you all a good day.' Kicking his horse forward, he passed them at some speed, his mount shying away from the barrow and propelling him out of the saddle and up its neck.

'Who was that?' Minnie asked as the rider regained his seat and the horse's hooves clattered away down the lane.

'I don't know,' Rose said, turning to face her sister once she'd seen the stranger disappear safely around the corner at the bottom of the hill. 'Have you seen him around here before, Donald?'

Donald shook his head as he stopped in a gateway.

'I thought he looked rather handsome,' Minnie said.

'I didn't notice,' Rose said, blushing.

'You're fibbing,' Minnie laughed. 'You couldn't keep your eyes off him.'

'I wanted to make sure he didn't part company from his horse. I thought he was going to fall off,' Rose protested.

'Oh, do stop jabbering and open the gate,' Donald said impatiently.

Rose reached out for the rusting iron catch, but it didn't feel right.

'Whose land is this?' she asked.

'Oh, don't worry about that.'

'I think we might be trespassing.'

'The man who owns the estate is dead, and the house is empty. There's a couple of old servants living in the lodge beside the stables, that's all, and I reckon they're half blind and deaf. I've already seen how the land lies.'

'Are you sure?' Rose said doubtfully.

'Trust me,' Donald said.

She lifted the catch and pushed the rickety gate open, sending a flock of sparrows flying out from the hazels and making her jump out of her skin.

Donald laughed, and shoved the barrow into the field.

'We can't be seen from the house. I've been this way before. Sam showed me – he knows everything there is to know about living in the country.'

A lark sang from the clear blue sky above their heads and Rose began to relax a little.

Donald turned the barrow around and let it start to run down the hill and pick up speed. He ran alongside while Minnie screamed in protest, but gradually the barrow slowed to a stop where the ground levelled out at the bottom of the slope. Donald pushed it through a gap in the bushes and lowered it down a small drop on to a pebbled beach next to a stream where they were hidden by the blackthorn and brambles.

'You see, you made it in one piece.' His eyes twinkled with amusement as he turned Minnie to face the water. 'And we're quite safe from prying eyes,' he added, glancing at Rose as he stripped off his shirt and kicked off his shoes.

'You aren't going in the water? No, I forbid it,' she said, noticing how his ribs were visible and his calves were skin and bone, a stark reminder of their predicament.

'You can't stop me. Pa larn'd me how to swim.'

Ma had instilled a fear of water in her – her mother had seen Pa rescue Arthur from the River Stour as a small boy when he had almost drowned. Pa had taught Donald to swim, but not the girls.

'It really isn't wise.'

'It's only up to your waist at its deepest. Come on, Rose. I'm going to show you how to tickle trout.'

'I'd like to go for a paddle,' Minnie said.

'Well, you can't – you know what Mr Carter said about getting your plaster wet.'

'It's so tempting,' she went on wistfully.

'I know, but there's no point in spoiling it now. You'll be able to paddle as much as you like when the plaster comes off.' Rose was dreading it – she couldn't see how Mr Carter could remove it without taking Minnie's leg off as well. 'Donald, we should go.'

'I've told you, there's nobody here. I can't see any harm in taking a chance if it means we fill our bellies tonight.' He handed Rose a sack from the barrow. 'Minnie, you be lookout.'

Rose thought for a moment. She was hungry. Desperate. They all were. She remembered Baxter and the way he had described his hunger as like rats gnawing at his body. She understood now.

It was wrong, but if the fish were there for the taking … once wouldn't hurt, would it? She uttered a silent prayer for forgiveness for what she was about to do as she slipped off her shoes and followed Donald into the river. The gravel scraped the arches of her feet as she waded along behind him, working upstream and keeping to the far bank where the branches of the overhanging trees and bushes trailed across the surface of the water.

Donald stopped suddenly and raised his finger to his lips.

'There,' he whispered as she peered past his shoulder.

'Where?' She couldn't see anything except for a few fronds of weed against the freckled riverbed.

'You have to get your eye in. Just there.' He pointed. 'You can just make out the edge of its fin.' He knelt on one knee and reached under the water. 'You start at the tail, and tickle it with your finger all the way along the belly until you reach the head, when you can' – he paused before continuing – 'grab it by the gills, like this.'

He wrenched a silver fish from the river with a splash, sending sparkling droplets of water flying across Rose's line of vision. He laid his catch on the bank and hit it on the head with a stone.

'Where's the bag? Quickly. We want to try for another one before they sense something's amiss.'

Rose held the sack open and Donald dropped the fish inside. She twisted the top closed, her heart beating fast. It was exciting, exhilarating. For the first time in a long while, she felt alive.

'You have a go this time.'

'Oh, I couldn't,' she said.

'Chicken.' Donald grinned and Rose couldn't help grinning back. She would show him, she thought, thrusting the bag into his hand before walking along the stream with her dress flowing behind her in the current and her eyes staring into the water, hunting for fish. At first she wasn't sure whether she was seeing stones or prey, but then she made out the shadow of a trout against the riverbed.

She knelt down carefully, feeling her belly tighten against the cool flow of the water. She reached out her hand for the tail and missed, and the fish shot upstream.

'Try again,' Donald said. 'Go in slower this time.'

'What makes you such an expert?'

'Ah, that would be telling.'

'Tell me then.'

'It was Arthur.'

'Arthur?'

'He says every young man worth his salt should know how to tickle a trout. Oh, I miss him.'

'So do I.' Rose tried again, and this time, she felt the cool, slippery smoothness of the fish's tail and its belly and then, with her heart in her mouth, she grabbed it tight at the head and pulled it from the water.

'It's a big one,' Donald said. 'Hold on tight. It'll fight you.'

It struggled fiercely for its life, and part of her felt sorry for it when she laid it on the bank as Donald had done with the first fish. He stunned it for her.

'There, it's done,' he said as she stared down at the dead eyes and gleaming skin before he slid it into the bag and waded back across the river, holding her hand. They crossed the pebbles to the barrow where he gave the bag to Minnie.

'Well done,' she said, clasping her hands together with delight. 'What a catch! Now all you have to do is chase down some taters to go with them.'

'Tuck that under your skirts,' Donald said cheerfully to Minnie. 'If anyone asks, don't admit to anything on pain of death. Let's go before we are found out.'

'But you said—' Rose began as a sudden cracking sound echoed around their ears. 'Run!' she exclaimed, but it was too late because a man was almost upon them, a smoking pistol in his hand. He was an elderly but wiry figure, dressed in a torn smock with his trouser-legs tied at the ankles with string.

'Don't shoot,' Minnie said, trembling as Rose and Donald moved to either side of the barrow. 'We're out for a nature walk, that's all.'

'Oh, it's you, the orphans.' The man moved closer. 'What exactly is the *nature* of your walk?' Rose didn't like the way his hands shook, an infirmity of age no doubt, but it was unnerving to see it when the finger of one of those hands was on the trigger of a pistol. He turned to Minnie. 'Lift your skirts, young lady.'

'I will not,' she said, flushing. 'That is most improper of you to ask.'

'It isn't when you're clearly up to no good – we have a lot of poachers trying their luck on the estate. I tell you, I won't have it. Lift your skirts or I'll do it for you!'

'Minnie, you don't have to do that,' Donald said, but Minnie gave him a look and eased her petticoat to her knees. 'Will that do, mister?'

'I'm not convinced. By all rights, I could ask you to turn out that barrow, but I can see that you are an invalid ...'

'We took a wrong turn,' Rose said. 'The gate was open and we didn't think there would be any harm in extending our Sunday afternoon walk. It's a hot day so when we saw the river we couldn't resist ...'

The man lowered his pistol. 'I'll let it go this time, but if I find you here in the future, I'll call for the constable.'

'Thank you, sir,' Rose said, breathing a sigh of relief. 'You'll see neither hide nor hair of us again.'

'That was a lucky escape,' Minnie said, bursting out laughing as Rose steered the barrow home with Donald. 'Oh, that was funny. The look on that man's face! I don't know how I didn't give it away. All I could think was that I was sitting on the fish.'

'I don't know why you are in such a rush, Rose,' Donald said.

'I just want to get away from there. If the truth be told, I feel ashamed of what we did. I mean, I'm glad we have food for the table, but it wasn't ours to take. We stole it.'

'It will taste all the better for that, you'll see,' Donald said.

He was right. The fish was delicious baked in a pan over the fire and eaten with bread and a swig of beer.

'We have disposed of the evidence,' Donald said, chuckling as he took the bones out to the midden at the end of the garden. 'I hope that puts your mind at rest, Rose.'

'You must promise me you won't go tickling trout again. I thought that man was going to kill us.' With a shudder, she recalled the glint of his pistol and his shaking hands.

'I'm not stupid. I won't go back to the same place in a hurry.'

'You mustn't go at all. I hope he doesn't squeal on us to Mr Carter.'

'You're beginning to sound like Ma.'

'Do I have to tell you what will happen if you get caught?' she went on.

He shook his head. 'You think I'm some dozy clodpole, but I'm not. I won't get caught, I promise. You really must start trusting me.'

Rose mopped up the last of the fish with a hunk of bread, all too aware that promising not to get caught wasn't the same as promising not to step out of line in the future.

Another day passed, and on the Tuesday morning after their trout-tickling adventure, Mrs Carter called at Toad's Bottom.

'I thought you'd like to come over to the farm. Minnie can sit and watch while we pick the soft fruit and make jam. This time next year, you'll have some of your own to use in preserves. Has Donald dug that bed for the canes yet? Old Pa Carter used to have great success with his raspberries.'

'We'd like that. Thank you, Mrs Carter,' Rose said.

'Oh, that's enough of that. Call me Grandma, like the others do.'

'Yes, Grandma,' she said, smiling. It was going to take her a while to get used to having a grandmother when she'd spent so many years without one.

They helped Minnie into the barrow and Rose towed it along the track where the wild flowers were in bloom in the hedgerow: ragged robin; clover and cranesbill, untouched by the scythe.

'We'll go through the yard, Rose,' Mrs Carter said, opening the gate for her.

They passed Donald who was helping Matthew in the forge, pumping the bellows to fire up the furnace, and wiping the sweat from his brow as the coals turned orange. Rose parked the barrow alongside the pump as the cockerel crowed from the roof of the pigsty and the geese honked to be let out of the barn.

'Put your arm around my shoulder,' she said to her sister.

'No, I can manage by myself.' Minnie took her stick, which Mr Carter had modified and made into a crutch for her, and climbed awkwardly out of the barrow before the three of them headed into the house and joined the maid in the kitchen.

'Have you had any breakfast?' Mrs Carter asked.

Rose glanced at Minnie. 'A little, thank you.'

'The crust of the bread,' Minnie said and Rose shot her a look.

'That won't keep body and soul together.' Mrs Carter sent the maid to the pantry to find a meat pie and cake.

'Donald has already had his fill,' the maid said, returning with half a pie. 'The cake is all gone.'

'He's a young man with a good appetite,' Mrs Carter said fondly. 'We'd better get baking this morning. Alice, you start on the cakes with Minnie, while Rose and I pick the fruit. There are blackcurrants, raspberries and rhubarb. Mr Carter loves a rhubarb crumble.'

She handed Rose a trug made from chestnut and willow held together with copper nails, and they went out into the garden. Rose's grandmother showed her how to select the tender, pink-veined stems of rhubarb, then snip bunches of fragrant blackcurrants from the bushes, and pick gooseberries without being caught by the spikes on the branches. It was warm work in the sunshine as they made their way along the rows of plants, and the dumbledores buzzed lazily among the leafy branches of the medlar, reminding Rose of home.

'This is ideal weather for picking,' Mrs Carter said. 'Did you grow any fruit at all in Canterbury?'

'We didn't. The garden was very small, much smaller than this, and one of the men from the tannery looked after it.'

'I expect your ma kept house for you all, didn't she?'

'Oh no, she left that to our housekeeper. Ma was a teacher – she ran a school.'

'I see. Your grandfather and I used to attend the same school in the village here. I remember reading to him ...' Mrs Carter reached into a bush and plucked out a gooseberry, a faraway look in her eyes. 'My husband doesn't like me to talk of him – the thought of days gone by fills him with sorrow, but I think of them from time to time. Matty was on watch at the top of the church tower one night, but the other men who were supposed to be watching with him hadn't turned up. I read him a chapter about sheep from a farming book – he was surprising in that way, a poor country lad with a thirst for knowledge.

'Anyway,' she went on, 'it was a memorable night. A gang of men came through Overshill and attacked the farm, setting the rick and stables on fire. Matty raised the alarm, and all our neighbours came running to help put the fire out. No one was hurt and the flames didn't reach the house – we had a lucky escape.'

'Matty was my grandfather?' Rose said.

'Oh yes, and he was quite a character. As a boy, he was a cheeky ruffian who delighted in playing tricks on me, then he grew into a handsome young man. You wouldn't believe it now, but there was an occasion when the Carter brothers got into a fight over me. You see, Stephen was a little in love with me even back then, but I chose his brother. Listen to me, rambling on …'

'It's fine,' Rose said, transfixed by her grandmother's tale. 'Do go on.'

'Matty and I were about to be married when Jervis – the eldest Carter boy – went off to join Sir William Courtenay.'

'Who was he?'

'Ah, we thought he was the Messiah at first. He gave the impression of being a good man with his preaching and his promises of riches for the poor, but he turned out to be a liar and imposter. He had a gaggle of followers who ranged the countryside with him, trying to persuade others to join them in rising up and overthrowing the wealthy farmers and landowners.

'There was a battle over at Bossenden, not far from here, and to cut a long story short, Matty and Jervis were charged with murder, convicted and sentenced to transportation for life.' She couldn't disguise her venom. 'I hate Jervis for what he did to us.'

'My grandfather was a murderer?' Rose said, shocked.

'Oh no, he wouldn't have hurt a hair on anyone's head. He was wrongfully convicted of a crime he didn't commit – he attempted to stop Jervis, who was a hot-headed thug at the best of times, from firing his gun, and when it was too late, he tried to stem the flow of blood from the victim's wounds. The evidence against him was too compelling to overthrow – he was arrested with blood on his hands.' Mrs Carter sighed deeply before changing the subject. 'Let's go back indoors – we have more than enough for crumble and jam.'

In the kitchen, she asked Rose to rinse the dust from the jars and wipe them dry, while Minnie stripped the blackcurrants from their stalks with a fork into a big brass preserving pan. The maid added sugar and water, placed the pan on the range and gradually brought it to the boil, continuously stirring it with a wooden spoon, and skimming the scum from the top.

'I've done the jars,' Rose said.

Her grandmother picked one up and held it against the light from the window.

'No, that won't do. It must be perfect or the contents will spoil.'

Rose washed and dried the jars again.

'That's better. Next, you and Minnie can shape papers an inch and a half larger than the tops of the jars. When we're ready, we'll brush them with beaten egg white – when you've tied them on, they'll dry out and form a tight seal.'

They stayed at the farm all day, sieving the boiled fruits through muslin to make jellies, or pouring them straight into the jars to make jams. To make the lids for them, Rose placed a paper on the top of each jar. She tied a piece of string around the top of the first one, and Minnie pressed her finger on to the first throw of the knot while she threw the second. She pulled the ends tight, trapping Minnie's finger.

'Ouch,' she said.

'You'll have to move out of the way quicker,' Rose smiled. 'Next one.'

Later on, when she was back at the cottage sitting by the ashes of the fire in the kitchen as she patched Donald's jerkin in the light of a flickering stub of candle, Rose mulled over her conversation with Mrs Carter. Her grandmother must have been with child when Matty Carter had left England's shores, she thought, putting two and two together. The needle slipped as she stitched, causing her to prick herself. She made a knot, snipped the thread and sucked the blood from her finger. That's why there had been so much trouble for the family: for Mrs Carter, for Agnes and now for her and her siblings. She would never succumb to a man's advances before marriage, especially now that she'd suffered the consequences.

Chapter Sixteen

The Gentleman Who Pays the Rent

As time went by, Rose began to feel a sense of tranquillity, living in Overshill away from the Kingsleys and the busy streets of Canterbury. She worked hard in the cottage, making it a home and looking after Minnie, while helping her grandmother in the house, but no matter how many hours she put in and no matter how much extra Donald did on the farm, they never seemed to have enough food on the table. She wished she could ask for more, but Mr Carter had made it clear that she shouldn't.

Towards the end of August, the jellies and jams that Mrs Carter had given her for helping pick the fruit had gone. She'd also run up a small amount of credit at the bakehouse, and couldn't see any way of paying it back. The garden was almost bare, apart from a row of winter cabbages, which wouldn't be ready until February or March, and the hens Mrs Carter had promised them hadn't yet materialised.

On a sunny day at the beginning of September when she was taking a quarter of an hour away from her chores in the farmhouse to spend time with her sister, Rose walked in from the garden where she'd been checking on the old coop that Donald and Sam had repaired together.

'What on earth are you doing?' Rose laughed when she saw her sister in the kitchen with a range of sharp implements lined up on the table: the knife that Mr Carter had sharpened at the forge, a knitting needle and a skewer.

'I have an itch.' Minnie grimaced as she poked a twig of hazel inside her plaster cast. 'And I'm trying to find something to scratch it with. This stick' – she pulled it back out again – 'is too bendy and the knife too big. And I tried tying one knitting needle to another, but they came apart and one is stuck down by my ankle. Oh, Rose, I'm fed up with this. It's been more than six weeks. Surely the bones are mended by now?'

'I'll talk to Mr Carter,' she said – finding the opportunity much sooner than she expected because a few minutes later he arrived at the cottage door, shoving Donald roughly along in front of him.

'I've just found this one helping himself to Mrs Carter's beans,' he said, his eyes flashing with anger.

'I did not,' Donald said. 'I never.'

'Turn out your pockets – go on.'

Donald fished around in his jacket and, like a conjuror, pulled out a handful of green beans, a potato and three onions.

'You have very deep pockets, boy,' Mr Carter said. 'Proper poacher's pockets. Don't tell me you found them just lying around because I know you haven't.'

'Donald, how could you?' Rose exclaimed.

'He needs a damned good hiding if you ask me.' Donald squirmed as Mr Carter tweaked his ear. 'He's got to learn to keep his hands off other people's property. This is his last chance. If he does it again, he'll be straight in front of the vicar – he's also our local magistrate – and he'll decide his punishment according to the law of the land.'

'He won't do it again,' Rose said quickly. 'I'll make sure of it, I promise.'

'We'll see about that,' Mr Carter said. 'Good day, young ladies.'

When he'd gone, Rose turned to her brother.

'Donald, if you ever do something like that again, I swear you will stew in your own juice.'

'Why are you so cross with me?' He had tears in his eyes. 'You said we had nothing for dinner. Minnie needs food – we all do, to keep body and soul together. Look at me.' He lifted his shirt and pinched the spare flesh on his belly.

There was no fat on his bones, but that didn't make it right.

'You can't go around pilfering from the farm,' Rose told him, 'especially when the Carters have been so good to us. We need to make more money.'

'How? I've been asking around, and there's nothing else out there. I wish Arthur had let me go to London with him. I'd have found work there. We should all go. There's nothing keeping us here in Overshill.'

'We aren't going anywhere until Minnie's better. Mr Carter has had great success so far with mending her leg. I'm not prepared to ruin her progress by uprooting her to London. It could so easily be out of the frying pan and into the fire.'

'You've become very dull. Where's your sense of adventure?'

'I'm responsible for you two – I have to be sensible.'

'Rose, you were going to ask Mr Carter about getting this blimmin' cast off,' Minnie interrupted. 'I'm going to die from this itch.'

'How could I? It wasn't a good time, thanks to Donald.'

She felt like dropping everything and walking out. It was all too much. She turned to her brother with tears pricking at her eyelids. 'I do everything I can for you and this is how you thank me. How can I face the Carters, knowing what you did?'

'Oh, I'm sorry. Rose, I don't know what we'd do without you.' Donald stepped towards her and gave her a hug. 'I'll speak to Mr Carter about Minnie and I'll grovel to him to make sure I keep my job at the farm.'

'Thank you,' she said, moving back. She used to believe that people like Baxter's father held their fate in their own hands, but that belief had turned out to be wrong. She hated the fact that her brother had stolen from the Carters, but she could understand why he did it. She glanced towards the table where Mr Carter had left Donald's haul. At least one positive thing had come out of it – they'd have a good supper tonight.

The next morning, Donald had already left for the farm when there was a knock at the door.

'I wonder who that is.' Minnie stopped sweeping the floor and leaned against the besom she'd made from twigs tied together, while Rose went to answer the door.

'Grandma?' she said, fearful of being read the riot act about the missing beans.

'Hello, my dears. I've brought you a gift. May I come in?'

'Yes, of course.' Rose held the door open and Mrs Carter stepped inside with Sam following, a wicker basket in his arms. 'Morning, Sam.'

He grinned. 'You're going to love this.'

'Come on through, lad,' Mrs Carter said. 'Wipe your boots on the mat. Minnie, let us through to the garden.'

The four of them went out the back and walked along the shingle path to the coop in the far corner as the contents of Sam's basket squawked and clucked.

'We have hens,' Minnie exclaimed. 'Thank you, Grandma.'

Rose smiled, thinking of the eggs they would have.

'Rose, open the coop. Sam, put the basket inside and let them out,' Mrs Carter said. 'Go on. What are you waiting for?' she added when Rose slid the plank of wood across and Sam stood stock-still, gazing at her. Blushing, she stepped aside.

'Stop giving my granddaughter the eye,' Mrs Carter said lightly, as Sam put the basket on the floor of the coop. He untied the string holding the lid down and opened the basket to reveal three bright-eyed brown hens that bobbed their heads up and down, surveying their new home.

'You'll have to lift them out of there.' Mrs Carter turned to Rose and Minnie. 'What do you think, girls?'

'This is the best thing that's happened to us for a very long time,' Rose said.

'I love them,' Minnie said as Sam picked them out of the basket one by one and placed them on the floor. They cawed and clucked as they explored the coop. One pecked and scratched at the earth, looking for food.

'How much do we owe you?' Rose asked.

'I told you – they're a present from me and Mr Carter. It won't take them long to settle if you give them a little corn or mash. Mind the foxes – let them out in the morning and bring them in at night. Sam, you go on back to the farm. I'll be along later. Rose, are you going to ask me to stop for a while so I can take the weight off my old feet?'

'Of course. Come on in.'

'I'm going to stay and watch the hens,' Minnie said, and they left her at the coop and went inside to talk for a while.

'I'm sorry about what Donald did yesterday,' Rose began.

'Oh, it wasn't your fault. You know, you look worn out. Are you well?'

'I'm a little tired, that's all.'

'It isn't surprising. You have a lot on your plate. I remember what it's like to care for someone day in, day out, to watch their every move and make sure they don't get into any trouble.'

'Oh, Minnie's a good girl. She knows not to overdo it with the chores, or her leg won't mend.'

'My brother John – he was such a funny and handsome lad.' Mrs Carter sat down on the bench. 'I miss him as he was before the accident, and after. He died in his sleep at the age of forty-two, unmarried, childless ...'

It was clear that her grandmother wanted to tell her what happened even though it was causing her some distress. She went on, 'Thomas Rook, my ...' there was a slight hesitation before she continued, '... pa was tenant back then. He was a progressive farmer, keen to make improvements to raise yields and make life easier for the labourers. He bought a horse-powered threshing machine—'

'Excuse me for interrupting, but what is that for exactly?'

'You are a townie, not a country girl. I forget.' Deep creases formed at the corners of her eyes as she smiled. 'It was a monstrous beast made from metal and wood, for separating the grain from the stalks, and a sight to be seen. John was on the top, feeding the barley into it, when his smock got caught. He fell and broke his head.' Mrs Carter shuddered.

'He came off much worse than Minnie in some respects. He could shuffle about all lopsided, but he was no longer himself. He was happy in his own way, but he couldn't be trusted. Given the chance, he would eat the larder bare, and he couldn't dress himself or tie his laces. It was awful time-consuming watching him, and there were times when I wished I could walk away.'

'I'm sorry,' Rose murmured. 'How must your pa have felt?'

'Guilty through and through. He smashed up the machine in a temper, and we never did have another. You might think these are tough times, but they were a hundred times worse back then.' With a small smile of resignation, she moved on to the subject Rose had been dreading. 'I understand why your brother filched those beans of mine. It doesn't make it acceptable, mind you, but Mr Carter and I have forgiven him on this occasion. I had to put in a good word with my husband about the way Donald's been working on the garden so you can grow your own next year, but I can't help noticing that precious little of the muck heap has gone.'

Rose wished she could persuade him to dig harder.

'Stephen's given him his punishment: whitewashing the stables. He'll be home late tonight. Oh, and my husband will be calling on you this evening to take that cast off Minnie's leg. Donald told him she was suffering with an itch, which reminded him that it was time to check on the outcome of the bone-setting.'

'She'll be over the moon,' Rose said, trying to get a word in edgewise as her grandmother continued with scarcely a breath.

'Would you be able to help Alice with the baking today? She is overwhelmed with work.'

Rose nodded.

'And don't worry about the rent this week. It can wait.'

'I don't know how to thank you.'

'You don't have to.' Mrs Carter smiled. 'We're family. And Mr Carter understands that too.'

Rose worked in the kitchen at the farm all day, then later that evening, Mr Carter came round to the cottage with a large saw.

'You are going to cut my leg off?' Minnie said worriedly, sitting on the bench with her leg outstretched.

'I hope not.' He grinned. 'You'll be quite safe if you sit very still. Rose, you must steady her leg – hold the cast at her ankle.'

She felt a little faint as she watched him saw slowly through the plaster bandage and gradually rip it apart, sending up small clouds of fine white powder and revealing the lost knitting needle.

'Well, is it healed?' Minnie asked.

Having torn the cast right off, Mr Carter examined her leg.

'The ends of the bones have formed a good, strong callus, but the muscles will take some time to recover. It isn't quite straight and this leg is slightly shorter than the other, but you'll be able to get around on it without too much pain. It's better than I expected.'

'Can I go out and about now?'

'Yes, you'll need to do plenty of walking up and down hill: the more the better.'

'Will I be able to work?'

'As long as you don't tire yourself out. You can continue with your mending and join in with the 'op picking when it starts.'

'This is a miracle,' Rose said, suppressing her impulse to throw her arms around Mr Carter's neck in gratitude, but he changed the subject, apparently accustomed to successful outcomes.

'How are the hens? You have shut them in?'

Rose nodded. 'We're hoping for eggs very soon.'

'You might find they take a few days to settle in and start to lay. What are you having for supper tonight? I reckon your brother's going to be a mite peckish by the time he comes home.'

'Oh, I don't know. Some ham and bread, perhaps.' She had saved the onions from Donald's pocket the day before.

'That doesn't sound like much.'

'It's enough,' she said, not wishing to impose on the Carters any further, but when Donald returned from the farm in the dark that evening, covered in whitewash and smelling of horse, he brought one of the pies she had baked with Alice.

'You haven't been up to your usual tricks?' Rose said suspiciously.

'Mr Carter made me bring it.' He placed it on the table. 'It's still warm.'

They feasted on mutton and potato pie, and looked forward to better days now that Minnie could contribute more to the household and Donald had served his punishment.

They joined in with the hop picking, then the apple harvest after that. According to their grandmother, some of the trees had been grubbed out to make way for grazing for Stephen's beloved horses, but when Rose stood in the orchard gazing at the early morning mist, the fairy rings in the wet grass, and the branches laden with fruit, she felt there were still more than enough trees on the farm.

She turned to her sister, who'd had no breakfast because the hens had grown lazy about laying eggs as the days shortened.

'Let's get started.' Rose walked across to collect a basket from where they were piled up on a cart. 'We'll pick together. It will make the time go quicker.'

The hop pickers from London and some of the Irish had stayed on in Overshill, making the harvest a sociable occasion. Sam was there too. He took his place beside them and showed Rose how to pick.

'You take hold of the apple like so,' he demonstrated. 'Give it a twist and when it's ripe, it breaks cleanly off the tree.'

'Thank you for that,' she said, a little sarcastically. 'I have picked apples before.'

'When?' Minnie said.

'Oh, a couple of times,' Rose responded, wishing she hadn't mentioned it. She had once or twice, while out walking, been unable to resist taking an apple and putting it in her pocket to eat later. It was wrong, she knew, but she had never seen so many apples ... and she hadn't been caught, and nobody had missed them.

She and Minnie picked from the lower branches while Sam climbed a ladder up to the higher ones. After a while, he returned to Rose's side, his presence making her feel uncomfortable.

'Rose, are you avoiding me?' he said in a low voice.

'I don't mean to be rude, but everyone is looking at us. It's awkward.'

'Let them. I don't care. You're a lovely person, Rose, and I was wondering if you'd walk out with me sometime.'

'I'm sorry. It's a lovely thought, but no, not on this occasion.' She was flattered, but she wasn't sure about him. Would he make a good match? Her doubts were soon confirmed when she caught sight of him larking around behind the hedge with one of the Irish girls later the same day. She felt both offended and relieved – if he was that free with his affections, then she didn't have to feel guilty for rejecting him.

After a week of picking from dawn to dusk, Donald continued working for Matthew Carter in the forge, Minnie took in more mending and an order for making up aprons for the family who ran the bakehouse, while Rose returned to helping her grandmother in the farmhouse. The morning after the apple harvest, Mrs Carter met her in the yard.

'There's no time for dawdling today, Rose. We have to put the apples in store so they'll keep until after Christmas, but before that we're going to move the pig and her piglets to the orchard to clear up the windfalls. This is Margaret.' Rose followed her grandmother to the pigsty. 'I give our sows the same name so as not to cause confusion.'

'But I *am* confused.' Rose frowned.

Mrs Carter chuckled. 'We only keep one at a time. Stephen doesn't like pigs – he says they scare the horses. Anyway,' she leaned in and scratched behind the sow's ear, 'it all started when I was a girl. Ma Rook's name was Margaret.'

'Your mother?' Rose said.

'That's right, except she wasn't my ma.'

'Oh?' What else could she say?

'She was my grandmother. It turned out that the person I had thought was my sister, Ivy, was actually my mother.'

'My parents gave me the name of Rose Agnes Ivy Catherine.'

'Ah, you are Agnes after your mother, Catherine after me, and Ivy after your great-grandmother.'

Rose touched the corner of her eye, recognising how Ma had kept the memories of her forebears alive through her.

'I can't help noticing how Sam takes an interest in you.' Mrs Carter opened the gate into the sty and let the sow out, her piglets scampering along behind her.

'He doesn't any more – he asked me to walk out with him and I turned him down, not being sure if he was a gentleman and if I liked him enough. He got one of the

Irish girls to dry his tears – if he shed any, that is – the very same day.'

Mrs Carter smiled wryly as she picked up a wooden board and directed the sow down towards the gate into the orchard, the piglets following her in single file, snorting and snuffling as they went.

'I can safely assume there'll be no wedding bells then?'

Rose laughed. 'Definitely not.'

'I'm not saying you should rush into wedlock, but there are advantages in being married, especially if it's to a young man who works hard to bring home the bacon. Someone will come along, but in the meantime, you can have one of the piglets to rear instead. I'd suggest that we keep him here at the farm with the others – they can make a terrible mess, rooting about in a small garden. You can collect acorns and bring any scraps you have to feed him.'

'I've never looked after a pig.'

'Then there's all the more reason for him to stay here and grow fat.'

'Thank you, Grandma.' Watching the sow and her piglets investigating their new surroundings and crunching on the windfalls, she felt a little more secure at the thought that they might one day have a gentleman who could pay the rent.

1878

Chapter Seventeen

Mighty Oaks from Little Acorns Grow

They collected buckets of acorns to feed the pigs in what little spare time they had, and Minnie took up patchworking again. They managed to make ends meet, but it was a hard life. When Rose looked back, she realised that Ma and Pa had had it easy.

In the winter, they were always cold – Rose would wear her coat and two layers of black wool stockings indoors as the water in the bucket they put out to catch the drips turned to ice, and her fingers became swollen and itchy with chilblains.

But there were compensations: ham served with home-grown winter cabbage from the garden; the sight of the woods in spring, carpeted with windflowers; finding frogs and wiggleheads in the stream; planting potatoes in the freshly dug beds; watching Donald and Sam playing cricket with the other village lads.

By early summer, they had been living in Overshill for nearly a year. The weather was unusually warm and dry, and the farmers were complaining that the barley wasn't growing as it should. The June drop of immature fruits was more than usual, leaving fewer apples on the trees, but the beans, carrots, beetroot and potatoes that Rose had planted in spring were flourishing. The hens were happily laying at least four eggs each and every week, and the pig was growing fat.

Rose had received word from Aunt Marjorie that she would pay them a visit, and she was expected in a couple of days. All it would take to complete her happiness would be for Arthur to walk in through the door with news from London, and for Donald, who was now four-teen and old enough to know better, to stay out of trouble.

For the first time in a while, she let herself dare to believe that they would be all right.

'I feel as if I might melt, Pig,' she said cheerfully. He was the second pig they'd had and Mrs Carter had let them rear him at home this time. He was in the sty that she and Donald had built, rooting about in the mud-pit he'd made. They hadn't given him a proper name because she felt that would make it much harder when it came to the day when he would be turned into pork chops and sausages. She filled his trough with water then returned indoors, shooing the hens away from the back door where they cawed and clucked in the expectation of a handful of corn from her apron pocket.

'Go away, ladies,' she said, smiling. 'The last time you came indoors, you made a terrible mess, and I'm about to clean the floor.'

Wanting the cottage to look perfect for Aunt Marjorie's visit, she swept the dust into the pan and tipped it out before picking up the mop from the outside privy where she'd left it. She made to knock down the spider that was dangling from the ceiling, then changed her mind. Live and let live, she thought. She walked back indoors and mopped the floor until a loud knocking interrupted her. Looking up, she noticed the figure of a young man silhouetted against the doorway where she'd propped the door open.

'Arthur?' she murmured, but her mind was playing tricks on her. The realisation that it was a stranger standing there, not her brother, stilled the rapid beating of her heart. She glanced down to see if he was carrying any bags – he had none, which meant he wasn't one of the higglers who sometimes stopped by trying to sell her items she didn't need. Who was he? And what did she look like? Her hair was adrift and her cheeks hot from her exertions. Her apron was grubby and her feet were bare.

'Good afternoon, sir.' She leaned the mop against the table and stepped towards him. 'I think you've taken a wrong turn.'

'Good day to you, miss.' He touched the peak of his cap, then, as if suddenly brought to his senses, doffed it and bowed his head. 'I swear the heat has made me forget my manners,' he said with a smile before a flicker of recognition crossed his eyes. 'Do I know you from somewhere? Have we met?'

'We have,' she said, remembering how they had bumped into him when he was riding his horse and they were out on their walk. She blushed, recalling how they had nearly been caught poaching trout that day from the Churt estate.

'My horse wasn't too keen on your barrow,' he said, grinning. 'He almost unseated me.'

He seemed rough and ready, well-dressed yet not a gentleman.

'You aren't from around here, are you?' she said tentatively.

'Ah no. I wasn't before, but I suppose you could say that I am now. I'm sorry, you must be wondering why I'm here.'

'To be truthful, yes. Not many people find their way down here unless they're calling at the farm.' She was embarrassed: although she was proud of what she had achieved, she still couldn't repair the roof, or fix the porch.

'Actually, I was wondering if you'd be so kind as to let me have some water for my dog. It's a hot day and I've walked further than I expected. There's no water in the stream – it's all dried up.' He mopped the sheen of perspiration from his brow.

'Oh?' She couldn't see a dog.

'He's waiting at the gate,' he said.

She looked out to see a liver and white spaniel slavering and panting.

'He'll have heatstroke,' she said. 'Bring him into the shade. Quickly. I'll fetch water.'

'Thank you. You are most kind.'

It was what anyone would do. She hated to see an animal suffer, she thought, pouring fresh cold water into a pie dish as he whistled for his dog.

'I'm much obliged,' he said, offering it to the dog.

'Would you like a drink too?' she asked. 'The water is clean – it comes straight from the well.'

'That would be most acceptable, thank you.'

She offered him a glass and watched him drink it straight down before he wiped his mouth with the back of his hand. 'What can I give you in return? A half-crown for your trouble?'

He must have been touched by the sun. Since when had water come with a price?

'It isn't necessary, sir. I did it out of kindness, not from expectation of a reward.'

'Let's not have any of this "Sir" nonsense.' He smiled. 'My name is Freddie.'

She frowned, unsure of his desire for familiarity.

'Mr ...?' she said.

'Mr Freddie Wild. And you are?' His eyes latched on to the silver chain around her neck, making her feel uneasy. Her fingers automatically rose to cover the half a sixpence.

'Miss Rose Cheevers,' she said, deciding to change the subject to relieve the tension that had arisen between her and the stranger.

'If your dog is ever sick, Mr Carter at the farm does some horse doctoring. He looks after other animals as well.'

'I've just had the – I can't call it a pleasure, of meeting with Mr Stephen Carter for a second time. On the first occasion, my horse cast a shoe and I led him to Wanstall Farm to have it replaced. This time, I came to introduce myself as a new neighbour and resident of Overshill, but he gave me short shrift.'

'You have recently moved then?' Rose surmised.

'Not yet. I've signed the deeds for Churt House.'

'You've bought it?'

'Yes, after many months of negotiation. I'll be moving in very soon. When you met me out riding last summer, I was exploring the area so I could be certain it's where I wanted to settle down.' He paused then went on, 'Are you here alone?'

'That's a most impertinent question,' she said. 'Suffice to say, I live with my brother and sister.'

'I'm sorry if I've overstepped the mark with what is only natural curiosity on my part,' he said. 'I find the English obsession with social niceties somewhat frustrating. Forgive me – I'm used to speaking bluntly, not beating around the bush.'

'Oh?' Rose wasn't sure how to respond as he fixed her gaze with his lively blue-green eyes.

'For example, I could be polite and say what a wonderfully quaint place this is, but that would be untruthful and therefore insincere because it seems to be falling down around your ears. Do you see what I mean?' He gazed at her earnestly and she nodded, even though she wasn't sure if she did or not.

'Were you expecting someone? It seemed from your reaction ...'

'I thought at first that you might be my brother, Arthur. He's living in London, as far as I know.'

'You have an older brother?' he enquired.

'I think of him as my brother – I was brought up with him, although he is not related to me by blood.' She wondered if she had said too much. She wasn't sure if it was wise to reveal one's business to a complete stranger.

'I'd best be on my way. Thank you again. Good afternoon, Miss Cheevers. I hope that we'll become better acquainted in future.' He turned and whistled for his dog, who dragged himself up and ambled along at his heels as he made his way back down the garden path.

She wasn't sure how she felt about that. His presence had made her restless.

'Who was that?' Minnie said, returning from the farm where she'd spent the morning helping Alice with the laundry. Although her leg had mended and the muscles had strengthened, she still walked in a way that reminded Rose of the puppets' jerky movements in the booth at the seaside Punch and Judy show. Her aunt had ruined her sister's life – Minnie could work, but who would choose to marry a cripple?

'Oh, just a gentleman asking for water for his dog.'

'How strange.'

'Not really. The stream has dried up and he was some way from home.'

'Where's home?'

'He says he's bought Churt House. Oh Minnie, no more questions. I'm only interested in getting everything ready for our aunt's visit.'

'Anyone would think the Queen was gracing us with her presence.' Minnie smiled.

'I thought we'd give up our bed for her – she isn't used to sharing.'

'That's a good idea. You know, I can't wait to see her. It's been such a long time.'

They continued with the preparations until Donald arrived back, hot and perspiring. He went straight out the back of the cottage, stripped off his shirt and poured a bucket of water over his head.

'That's better,' he said as Rose handed him a cloth to dry himself. 'What's for supper?'

'Chicken stew with carrots and onions.'

He wrinkled his nose. She knew what he meant – onions were cheap and plentiful, but that didn't improve their flavour.

'A stranger called on Rose today.' Minnie joined them, her apron splashed with stock where she'd been stirring the pot.

'He came to ask for water for his dog,' Rose said. 'He's moving into Churt House.'

'I saw him at the farm, the same gentleman whom we met while we were out walking,' Donald said. 'He seemed all right, but something he said ruffled Mr Carter's feathers. I don't know what it was, but he told him not to set foot on his land again.'

'How odd. He seemed very pleasant to me.'

'I wonder where he's come from and how he can afford a place like that,' Donald said. 'He must be rolling in it.'

'I'm sure we'll soon find out – you can't keep anything secret in Overshill,' Rose said lightly. 'Which leads me on to something I heard the other day …'

'What was that?' Donald folded his arms, so she knew there was something in what Mrs Greenleaf had said when she'd met her at the counter in the village shop.

'There's talk of a gang of youths running amok in the woods and fields with dogs. I don't want to find out you're caught up in it. The squire has said his men have been told to shoot poachers on sight. Donald, I don't want you to get hurt … or worse.'

'Oh, nothing will happen. You do exaggerate.'

'You will be careful to keep out of trouble?'

'Of course I will. Who do you think I am?' he said rather crossly.

'I'm worried that you will get into a scrape because of your friendships with the other lads.' Having heard her grandmother's story of Sir William Courtenay and Bossenden, she knew all too well how a person's character could be ruined by their association with the wrong 'uns.

'I'm not stupid. We don't get up to much, and if we did, we wouldn't get caught.' There was a smirk on his face and she wished she had Ma's air of authority.

'The rabbits you brought back the other day?' she queried.

'The ones you were more than happy to take off me for the pot? I told you, I just happened upon them.'

'The truth, Donald! I want to hear it from you. I won't tell anyone.'

'Why the interrogation? You keep saying you don't want to end up looking like an onion. Tell me, where would we be without a few little extras? You've done it yourself, pocketed an apple or two now and again.'

'I know.' She would always feel guilty about that.

'I'm always hungry and I'm fed up with living hand to mouth while others have more than enough to live on. Look at the squire and Mr Carter.'

'Mr Carter earned his fortune by hard work,' Rose said. 'Don't you dare speak badly of him when he and Grandma have gone out of their way to look after us.'

Donald took a small leather pouch from his pocket.

'What is that?' Rose said.

'Baccy,' he answered, cutting a piece from the block and popping it into the bowl of a cutty pipe.

'You've taken up smoking? Donald, you are fourteen years old.'

'So?'

'Who gave it to you? Who encouraged you in this?'

'Sam got it for me. Everyone smokes. There's no harm in it.'

'You know how Ma disapproved. She said you might as well throw your money on the fire and burn it. It's an ungentlemanly and dirty habit. What will Mr Carter say?'

'Oh, I wouldn't do it at work. I'm not that stupid.' He lit the tobacco, put his lips around the end of the pipe and drew in his cheeks.

'Ugh, that stuff stinks. Take it outside.' When he exhaled a series of smoke rings, she added, 'Donald, I insist.'

'Arthur should have let me go with him to London. I'd have done better there,' he grumbled as he swaggered outside.

Rose noticed that he didn't say that he would have been able to send money back to help his sisters. He was selfish, she thought, and although she loved him, she didn't always like him very much.

A couple of days later, Mr Carter lent Donald a pony and trap from the farm to fetch Aunt Marjorie from where the coach dropped her off on the turnpike road. It seemed to Rose that she had walked in from another life, bringing along memories of Ma and Pa and Willow Place, but it was the happiest of reunions.

'We began to wonder if we would ever see you again,' Rose said, greeting her. 'Come in.'

'Can I smell brawn?' Aunt Marjorie's nose twitched as she went inside the cottage.

'The butcher sold us a pig's head and Grandma lent us a pan big enough to cook it in.'

'How marvellous. You all look very well, my dears, but Minnie, you still have a limp.'

'I'm grateful to be able to walk,' Minnie said. 'Mr Carter mended my bones.'

'I'm very sorry that you had to suffer at your aunt's hands. She is a wicked woman. Did you report her actions to the police?'

Rose shook her head. 'What good do you think that would have done? Who would they have believed?'

'It's their job to look into crimes such as these.'

'Well, it's too late now.'

'I wish you had come to me. Why didn't you?'

'We couldn't possibly impose on you. You are ...' Rose paused, noticing the hurt in her aunt's expression.

'I am old. That's what you're saying?'

'No, not exactly.'

'Well, I am. I have lost three teeth since I last saw you – from the ones at the back, fortunately – and I have gained more wrinkles, but it doesn't mean I'm ready to be put out to grass.'

'I'm sorry. Aunt Marjorie, you have enough to cope with without worrying about us. All is well. We did the right thing in coming here. We don't have much, but we have hens and a pig, and a place to grow our own vegetables and fruit. Donald has work on the farm, while Minnie and

I do what we can. I wonder if you'd like to call on our grandmother while you're in Overshill?'

'Has she expressed an interest in meeting me?'

'No, she hasn't. I just thought—'

'I won't then,' Aunt Marjorie cut in. 'It would be wrong to disturb her without an invitation. What about Arthur? Have you heard from him?'

Rose shook her head sadly. 'I'm afraid not. I hope he and Tabby are well and happy.'

'He has not sent you money?'

'Not yet,' she said.

'I trust that he will one day.' Aunt Marjorie looked older and frailer than before, and Rose wondered how she found the energy to run around after small children. 'Shall we eat? I've had a long journey on an empty stomach.'

As always, she declared the brawn to be the best she'd ever tasted.

'Are there any handsome young men in the village, Rose?'

She shook her head.

'Sam White still has a fancy for you,' Donald said, grinning. 'He isn't walking out with anybody now. I reckon he'll ask you again one day.'

'Tell him not to bother because I would turn him down for a second time,' Rose said.

'That's right, my dear. Don't marry unless it's for love or at least two thousand a year.' Aunt Marjorie turned to Donald. 'You'll have no trouble finding love. You've grown into a fine young man, looking after your sisters like this.'

If only she knew, Rose thought, as Donald gave her a wink.

The three of them were a family now, keeping their own secrets between them.

Chapter Eighteen

Don't Look a Gift Horse in the Mouth

One afternoon not long after Aunt Marjorie's visit, Rose was on her way to deliver a saucepan that Matthew Carter had repaired for Mrs Greenleaf, who called herself the wise woman of the village, dispensing advice, herbal remedies, and some said casting spells for a fee. One of the farm boys could have gone in her stead, but Rose had jumped at the chance to earn another penny or two, running errands for the Carters.

She hurried along towards the row of cottages that stood opposite the village shop and the chestnut tree, looking for number two.

'Miss Cheevers,' she heard someone call.

'Mr Wild,' she said, a little embarrassed at the way he hastened across the road to her, drawing the attention of the passers-by, including one of the regulars at the Woodsman's Arms and Mrs White, Sam's mother.

'How lovely to see you again,' he said, his eyes twinkling with humour as his gaze settled on the saucepan in her hand. 'Do you make a habit of carrying cooking implements around the village?'

'Oh no. I'm running an errand for the Carters. Anything for a little extra money.' She shut her mouth quickly, wishing she hadn't said that, and hoping that he hadn't noticed. 'My brother and I work at Wanstall Farm in return for the cottage at Toad's Bottom and just enough to make ends meet.' She changed the subject, sure that Mr Wild could have no idea what it was like to struggle from day to day to put food on the table. 'How are you finding Overshill? Have you moved into Churt House yet?'

'I took possession of the keys this morning, intending to stay there for the first time tonight. The rooms smell musty with damp and it's so empty that your footsteps echo around the place.' He sighed. 'It's going to take a long time to make it feel like home. I'd better let you go on your way, much as I enjoy talking to you. Good afternoon.'

'G-good afternoon,' she stammered, feeling unnerved by their meeting. There was something about Mr Wild that intrigued her.

She tried to put all thoughts of him aside during the next few days, but she was reminded by the frequent gossip that came via visitors to the farm. Mr Wild had moved some furniture into his house. He'd had a new carriage delivered from a renowned carriage-maker in London. He'd travelled to Romney to purchase a flock of sheep. He was causing quite a stir.

But one afternoon, something happened to put him right out of her mind. Rose was thinning out the carrots in the garden at the cottage, pulling them up by their feathery tops, when Minnie came limping along the path as fast as she could with a packet in her hand.

'This has just arrived – it's addressed to you. I think it must be from Arthur.'

Rose almost snatched it from her. She held it up to the sunlight and examined the handwriting. It was a masculine hand, but she wasn't sure that she recognised it.

'It isn't from Aunt Marjorie,' she confirmed, trying to suppress the butterflies in her stomach as she tore it open. 'Oh!' she said as she took out three banknotes and a purse of coins wrapped in paper. 'There's no note. Let me check the postmark.' It was smudged and unreadable. 'It has to be from Arthur!'

'Of course it is,' Minnie said, smiling. 'I knew he wouldn't let us down.'

Rose could hardly believe her eyes as she counted the money. The butterflies began to dance with joy inside her. 'I wish I could give him the biggest hug. If only he knew what a difference this will make to our lives! Why hasn't he sent his address so we can write back?'

'Do you think he doesn't want to be found?' Minnie asked.

Rose refrained from giving her sister her theory about why Arthur hadn't been in touch before – because he'd felt like an outsider as the adopted son.

'Perhaps he wishes to surprise us by turning up out of the blue in the near future. Our dear brother ...'

'I've never seen so much money.'

'We must put it somewhere safe.'

'Where?'

'Let me think about it.' Rose felt rather mean, keeping the hiding place secret from her sister, but she didn't want her to let on where it was to Donald, in case he decided to waste it on baccy and beer for his friends. She'd already earmarked some of it for paying off their debts at the bakehouse and the village shop, and some for treats: some sweets; a leg of lamb; half a pound of raisins for baking. She tucked it into her blouse and carried on with the gardening for another hour before she was disturbed for a second time.

'It's Freddie. Mr Wild, I mean, is here,' Minnie said, emerging from the cottage with her thimble still on her thumb.

'What can he want this time?' Rose said, surprised.

'He calls here rather often,' Minnie said snidely.

'This is only the second time – you are exaggerating. He is older than me by at least ten years – I'm sure there's nothing in it,' Rose said, although since his first visit, she had occasionally, in the dead of night and in the quiet moments of the day, wished that there was. She'd been struck by his manner and handsome appearance, but was he a gentleman? He wasn't in the conventional sense of the word. 'Go back to whatever you were doing, Minnie. There's no need for you to listen in to our conversation.'

'I'm sewing at the table. How can I not overhear when I'll be in the same room? And why are you blushing?'

'That's enough of your teasing. Send Mr Wild out here.' Rose glanced at the dirt engrained in her fingernails, and the smattering of freckles on her arms, then wondered why she was being so vain as to hope that he had any interest in her.

'Good afternoon, Miss Cheevers. Have I caught you at a bad time?' Mr Wild strode along the garden path, took off his hat and smiled, his hair glinting like gold in the sun.

'No, it's fine. Was there something you needed?'

'Actually, I was wondering if you might be able to help me. Would you happen to know of a suitable candidate for housekeeper at Churt House? She would need to be honest, hard-working and neat in appearance.'

Rose shook her head. 'We don't know many people around here. You'd be better off asking Mrs Carter. She knows everyone – she's lived here for most of her life.'

'I'm asking you,' he said.

'Well, I'll let you know if I hear of anyone, Mr Wild.'

'Oh Rose, when I said I'm asking you, I mean that I'm asking you.' He grinned, showing his even white teeth.

'Me?'

'You're honest?'

'Well, yes. On the whole.'

'And you are hard-working and neat in appearance. You've made the cottage into a home for your brother and sister.'

'But I have little experience and Churt House is very grand.'

'It is, but it wouldn't be beyond your capabilities.'

Her cheeks burned. He had chosen her, but why? 'If you are doing this out of charity, then I can't accept.'

'It isn't that,' he said quickly. 'It's simple. I need a house-keeper and I thought of you.'

'I wouldn't know where to start when it comes to managing the maids. Will you have maids?'

'Yes, and a cook, butler and footmen – whatever's needed to run an English country house. You said the other day that you were working at Wanstall Farm – will Mrs Carter object to you handing in your notice? Is that why you hesitate? Out of loyalty?'

'I don't think she would mind me taking up a new position. She has a maid already and there isn't really enough work in the house for the two of us. If I should accept the offer of becoming your housekeeper, won't your staff feel that I'm stepping on their toes?' She remembered the man with the gun down by the river as they carried their precious haul of trout under Minnie's skirts in the barrow many months ago. 'You still have a caretaker looking after the house and estate?'

'It isn't a problem. The Toveys are moving to Somerset to be closer to their daughters. They were due to stay until

Michaelmas, but I've said I will let them go before then, if I've found a replacement. By the way, I've heard that your sister takes in mending.'

'She sews on buttons, darns socks and makes a good seam.'

'I have a few items that need repair. Do you think she'd be interested?'

'Yes, I'm sure she'd appreciate the extra work,' Rose said. They all would. It was money coming in, after all.

'Thank you. I'll get it sent down to you.'

They fell silent, unsure what else to say to each other. She wondered if she should offer him a drink, but it didn't feel right, inviting a stranger into the house. She had her reputation to think of.

'Will you give me your answer today?' he said eventually.

'I need a little time,' she said. 'I hope you don't mind.'

'Not at all. I expect you'll want to discuss it with your family. It would be a live-in position with a wage and rent-free accommodation – they can come with you. I thought I'd have one of the cottages done out for you – I mean, for my housekeeper, whomsoever that turns out to be.' He smiled. 'I must take my leave. Good day, Rose.'

After he'd gone, she took a walk to the village shop, then returned to tell the twins of her good fortune over a suppertime feast of sausages, potatoes and ale.

'It's all very well Arthur sending this money, but I wish he'd come to see us,' Donald said.

'So do I. The patchwork's ready,' Minnie said. 'I'd like to give it to him and Tabby.'

'I'm sure we'll see him again soon,' Rose said, 'but in the meantime, Mr Wild has offered me a place as his housekeeper. What do you think of that?'

'I never imagined you'd end up as a housekeeper,' Donald said. 'What do you know about keeping house anyway?'

She glared at him and he laughed. He was teasing.

'I have to admit I'm a little daunted by the idea of supervising the other servants.'

'What about me and Donald?' Minnie asked.

'He's offering accommodation for all three of us. Don't worry – I wouldn't leave you behind. I haven't given him my answer yet because I wanted to know how you felt about it too.'

'I wouldn't be too hasty,' Donald said. 'It all seems very suspicious to me. Mr Wild doesn't need to have anything mended – he can buy new clothes every day of the week. And why has he asked you, when he could choose anyone as housekeeper, somebody with experience of running a large establishment? Rose, he is a wealthy man.'

'I hadn't really thought about it,' she said, suddenly doubting herself again. 'Do you have any idea what line of business he's in?'

'He told someone in the Woodsman's Arms that he'd made his money from sheep farming and wool.'

It didn't sound like a very romantic way to make one's fortune, Rose thought. 'What else have you heard about him?'

'I thought you didn't listen to gossip?' Donald grinned.

'Is he married?'

'No. There's no Mrs Wild.'

'Is he engaged then?'

'Not for want of trying by the mothers of the young ladies of Overshill.' Donald scraped his plate clean. 'He's said to be quite a catch, but although it's early days, no one's managed to wind him in yet. He'll be snapped up soon enough by some society lady, I expect.'

'What do you think Grandma will think of this?' Minnie said.

'I don't know, but I'm going to find out.' If she should accept the position and give up the cottage, would Mrs Carter be upset or relieved? Rose wasn't sure.

She took advantage of a moment the following day when she was helping her grandmother sort through the linen cupboard upstairs in the farmhouse, dividing the contents into piles to keep, mend or use for rags.

'I had a little windfall yesterday.' Rose held one end of a sheet while her grandmother held the other, shaking it out and pulling it smooth before folding it neatly and placing it on top of the 'keep' pile. 'Arthur sent some money from London as he promised.'

'That's good news. I hope you've put it in a safe place. No, don't tell me,' she smiled. 'Just remember that everyone keeps their savings under their mattress.' Rose made a mental note to find a better hiding place for it as her grandmother went on, 'Don't broadcast your good fortune to the rest of the village.'

She thanked her for her advice.

'Now, you can put the sheets back in the cupboard – the ones with holes on the top shelf and the ones in use on the next two down.'

Rose did as she was asked.

'Next, pick up the rag pile and bring it downstairs – we'll put them beside the medicine cabinet in the tack room. Stephen uses them for bandages and poultices, and for mopping up.'

Laden with old sheets, Rose followed her grandmother down the stairs and outside into the yard where Matthew Carter was applying a hot shoe to a horse's hoof, sending up a plume of sulphurous smoke as Donald held on to the horse's head. They crossed the cobbles to the tack room, a dark room without windows where Rose could make out the shadows of the saddles, bridles and harnesses on the walls.

'I wonder if I could ask your advice,' she said, as her grandmother cleared a quantity of leatherwork from the top of a cupboard.

'Put the rags there – that'll do,' she said. 'How can I help? What is it?'

'The new owner of Churt House – Mr Wild – has asked me to be his housekeeper.' Rose put the linen down. 'I wanted to know what you think. I don't want to offend you or put you in a bind by accepting his offer if you need me here at the farm, but I'm aware that there isn't really enough work here for both Minnie, me and Alice.'

'That's very thoughtful of you. What is Mr Wild going to pay you?'

'A good wage and a rent-free cottage.'

'So you would give up Toad's Bottom?'

She nodded.

'I assume that Donald will still work for Mr Carter, only we'd have to find somebody else if he gave it up.'

'Oh yes, he would carry on here at the farm.'

'It's a wonderful opportunity for you to better your prospects, and you'll only be up the road. I would accept, if I were you.'

'I wouldn't be so hasty.' Mr Carter's voice made Rose jump. She turned to find him in the doorway with the sun streaming past him. 'You don't know anything about that man.'

'Neither do you to make such a judgement,' Mrs Carter countered.

'I know more than enough,' he said sullenly. 'What are you two lurking about in here for anyway?'

'We've brought you some more rags. Don't come back indoors until you're feeling more cheerful.' As Mrs Carter walked out past him, she gave him a peck on the cheek. He gave her a long-suffering smile in return.

'If you stop fighting, it means you've stopped caring, Rose,' her grandmother said as they returned to the house. 'Don't listen to my husband. He's taken against Mr Wild for some reason, known only to himself. You tell him you'll take the job. And don't spend all of your brother's money at once.'

Rose wasn't sure if Mr Wild would be at home when she called on him on the Monday morning, but she had errands to do in the village so she decided she'd take the chance after she'd done her shopping and been to the bakehouse. Having put on her bonnet, she picked up her basket and walked into Overshill where she stopped to buy a marrow from a boy who was selling them outside a garden gate, before walking up to the mill to buy bread. The door of the bakehouse was propped open and she could hear voices inside. She stopped and listened.

'I don't understand why the Carters took them in – I wouldn't trust the boy as far as I could throw him.'

Donald? she thought. What had he been up to this time?

'Mrs Carter is their grandmother, Mrs Greenleaf. She's kind to everyone.'

'Well, he's bad through and through.'

'Don't you remember Stephen Carter's brothers? Jervis was worse than young Donald – he was a thieving, murdering thug. As for Matty, when he was convicted of playing his part in the killing of that constable, some said he were innocent, others that he deserved what was coming to him.'

'Don't let Stephen Carter hear you say that – he won't have anything said against his younger brother.'

Matty? They were talking about her grandfather, and she felt a fresh pang of sorrow at never having met him.

'I've taken to locking my doors of an evening, just in case.'

Rose became aware of someone moving up beside her. She turned.

'Mr Wild,' she said. 'I was just coming to see you at the house.'

'Miss Cheevers, what a pleasure it is to run into you.' He cocked his head towards the door. 'Ignore them. They have nothing better to do than spread gossip and rumour. Shall we give them something to talk about?'

'What do you mean?' she said, smiling.

He held out his arm.

'Thank you, sir,' she said, taking it and stepping inside with her head held high.

'Ah, look who it is,' the woman she recognised as Mrs Greenleaf said. 'Talk of the devil.' She stopped abruptly, her eyes almost popping out of her head. 'Mr Wild? How lovely to meet you at last. We've heard so much about you.'

'So many stories, no doubt,' he said, being charming. He turned to Rose and gave her an enchanting smile. 'What do you want to buy?'

She had clean forgot.

'Two loaves, please,' she stammered, 'and I'd like to settle my bill in full as well.'

The baker's son fetched the ledger from behind the counter and checked the amount she owed against her name.

'It's quite a lot.' His voice sounded excessively loud and shrill.

'I thought so – I'm afraid that it slipped my mind last month, but I've remembered it now. Please – very quietly – tell me how much it is.'

He told her in a whisper, and she counted out her shillings and pence as she handed them over.

'Walk with me, Rose,' Mr Wild said as they left the bakehouse together.

'You are supposed to call me Miss Cheevers,' she said.

'By convention. I had hoped we were well enough acquainted for me to call you by your first name.'

'If I am to be your housekeeper, you must respect convention. It would be wrong – overly familiar – to address me as anything but Miss Cheevers. And in fact, I believe it is the custom in a grand English house to address one's housekeeper as Mrs Cheevers, even though she isn't married.' She remembered Mrs Dunn.

'It's hard to remember all these strange customs.' He chuckled. 'Miss Cheevers, may I relieve you of your basket? Temporarily,' he added when she hesitated. 'There are people around here who suspect me of being a criminal or a fake, but I can assure you that my intentions are entirely honourable. I wish to carry your purchases as far as the crossroads – if you can bear my company ...'

'Of course, Mr Wild. Thank you.' She handed over the basket, their fingers touching fleetingly.

'It's Freddie.'

'It would be wrong to address you as such when you are to become my employer – if the offer still stands.'

'You have decided?'

She nodded shyly. He had this way of making her feel awkward, gauche.

'You've made me very happy. I shall travel lighter of heart, knowing that you will join me at Churt House on my return.'

'What do you mean, your return?'

'I'm going away for a while.'

'How long for?' she asked tentatively.

'Eight to ten months, maybe more.'

'That long?' She wasn't sure if she'd managed to disguise her distress. She felt unreasonably disappointed at his unexpected announcement. 'I had thought you would wish to establish yourself at your new residence. Or perhaps you don't intend to live there?'

'I have business interests to attend to. I would stay here in Overshill if I could. I find that it has much to recommend it, more than I could ever have imagined.'

They stopped at the crossroads. 'Will I see you before you leave?'

'I'm leaving for Southampton in the morning, then taking the steamship to New York.' He hesitated, gazing into her eyes. 'You will be all right until I come back? You have money to pay your rent on the cottage? I'm sorry, it's none of my business.' He handed her the basket. 'Goodbye, Miss Cheevers.'

'I wish you a safe journey and successful trip,' she said. 'Good day, Mr Wild.'

Deeply regretting that she couldn't start at Churt House straight away, she turned and walked back to the cottage, watching the swallows darting through the sky, catching insects to feed their chicks. Even though she hardly knew Freddie, she was going to miss him, as well as the chance of a steady income. Luckily, they had the rest of Arthur's money to tide them over for a while, although she bitterly regretted going on such a spend-up at the beginning.

1879

Chapter Nineteen

Let the Punishment Fit the Crime

'I'm home. Is all well?' Rose called as she hung her summer bonnet on the hook in the wall at the bottom of the stairs. She'd just returned from doing some chores for their grandmother at the farmhouse. It was the middle of May and she'd turned nineteen, almost without noticing. She was still waiting for Mr Wild to return from his travels and each time she walked past the end of the drive leading to Churt House, she had a spring in her step, thinking ahead to when she would be housekeeper.

Minnie appeared, her figure silhouetted against the doorway leading to the back garden.

'I hope you've kept yourself busy,' Rose said, walking towards her.

'I've finished the mending that Mrs Greenleaf wanted. I don't know why she doesn't do it herself.'

'It's because she's as blind as a bat – according to Donald, anyway. It is one of those afflictions which comes with advancing age. Did you collect the eggs and feed the hens?'

Minnie looked down at her shoes. 'I'm sorry. I forgot,' she mumbled.

'Oh, go on. Go and do it now.'

Minnie turned away and picked up the basket from the windowsill. Just as Rose sat down on the bench and began to untie her bootlaces, she was disturbed by a hammering at the door. She rushed to open it, finding one of the younger village boys on the doorstep. She didn't know his name, but she'd seen him out scaring the birds from the fields and herding a lively goat and her kids through Overshill.

'Miss Cheevers, come quickly!' he cried.

'Why? What's happened?' She pulled her shawl around her shoulders.

'It's Donald.'

'Has he been hurt?'

'No, miss. He's bin caught thievin'.'

Her heart plummeted. 'Why? What? Where is he?'

'Mr Carter's got hold of 'im,' he said. 'Have you got a penny for a poor messenger boy who's put himself out to come and find you?'

She felt in her pockets, but they were empty, so she tipped the contents of the jug on the mantel out on the table, finding a feather, a cherry stone and a coin which she handed to the boy.

'Thank you, miss.' His eyes gleamed. 'I'll show you the way.'

'Wait a minute.' She ran out to the back garden where her sister was scattering handfuls of corn for the hens.

'I have to go out. I won't be long.'

'But you've only just come in. I'll come with you.'

'No, you wait here.' She didn't want to worry her yet – she would find out soon enough. 'I haven't time for questions. Make a start on the vegetables – there's a cauliflower and some carrots.'

Rose hurried into the village with the boy.

'Can you tell me what happened?' she said, trying to catch her breath.

'Oh no,' he said quickly. 'I wa'n't nowhere near the scene of the crime. My ma's brought me up to be as honest as the day is long.'

Rose was disturbed by what she felt was an accusation. She had tried to be a good sister and mother to Donald.

They stopped where a crowd was assembled at the chestnut tree outside the village shop.

'Ah, there you are, Rose.' Mr Carter showed her through to where Donald was tied by the wrists to the ring in the tree. 'You have found your brother in a bit of a pickle, I'm afraid.'

'What's he gone and done this time?'

'I ha'n't done nothin'.' His face was white, but the set of his chin remained defiant.

'You were caught red-handed,' Mr Carter said. 'Mrs Greenleaf here saw him at her window with a cherry pie half in his mouth and a meat one stuffed in his pocket.'

'I spent all morning baking.' The victim of the crime, an elderly woman who lived alone, was trembling and crying. 'When I saw 'im at the window – well, he frightened the life out of me.'

Rose frowned. Mrs Greenleaf obviously had sharper vision than Donald had previously claimed.

'It isn't right,' someone else said. 'How can we sleep soundly in our beds at night when there are scoundrels like him roaming the village? We warned you there'd be trouble, bringing strangers into our midst. I put the blame on you fair and square, Mr Carter.'

'They are my wife's family,' he said somewhat snappily. 'They needed a roof over their heads. What was I supposed to do? Send them on their way, a penniless young woman with a crippled sister and a numskull for a brother – for it turns out he is a numskull with no respect for anyone else's property. I've been let down, and right now, I could cheerfully wring his neck for what he's done.'

Not if she got her hands on him first, Rose thought, her cheeks burning with shame.

'What are you going to do with him?' she said, afraid that the baying crowd were about to take Donald's punishment into their own hands, and give him a good hiding.

'The constable will be here soon,' Mr Carter said. 'Mrs Greenleaf, it is up to you to decide if you wish to press charges.'

Rose could hardly breathe. This wasn't a petty crime. It was larceny. If Mrs Greenleaf pursued her complaint, Donald could end up in prison. Her hands clenched with sudden anger. What had he thought he was doing? How many times had she told him?

'In my 'umble opinion, he should be l'arned his lesson,' Mrs Greenleaf said. 'Send the boy for the vicar. He'll be in the vestry.'

Frowning, Rose wondered what she meant. Were they to pray for Donald's soul? But then she recalled how Mr Carter had once told her that the Reverend Browning was also their local magistrate.

'Please, not that,' she said quickly. 'Mrs Greenleaf, he'll work for you for nothing, until he's paid his dues, and I'll bake pies to replace the ones you've lost.'

'Oh no, that won't do at all. I wouldn't want the likes of him anywhere near me. He needs to be corrected so he can see he's done wrong, then he can be reformed and come back into society.'

'There are reasons why he did it,' Rose said, desperate to keep her brother away from the courts.

'There are no reasons, just excuses,' Mr Carter said sharply. 'I have to agree with you, Mrs Greenleaf. I've done all I can for that boy and his sisters.' He turned and looked along the street in the direction of the Woodsman's Arms where a young man was walking towards them, stumbling now and then as if he was in his cups. 'Ah, here is the constable.'

Mr Carter and Mrs Greenleaf stepped across the road to have a private discussion with him while Rose went to speak to her brother.

'How could you?' she said coldly. 'How could you do this to yourself, to us? What would Ma and Pa have thought? And Aunt Marjorie? And Arthur?'

'I'm sorry, I'm truly sorry,' he sobbed. 'It were for nothing too. I saw them pies on the windowsill cooling down. And I could smell 'em as I moved closer, and my fingers twitched ... I was drooling for 'em ...'

'Why didn't you walk away when you knew they weren't yours?'

'Sometimes, I have these pains in my belly so bad I can't think straight.'

She recognised that frantic, gnawing hunger, but she couldn't excuse his response. She wasn't sure how she felt. Sympathetic? Angry?

'I was bringing the rest back for you and Minnie. Rose, what will happen to me?' he asked, his voice wavering.

'I don't know.' Donald had been selfish and taken advantage of an old woman, but she blamed herself – she had let him run too wild.

Five minutes later, the vicar arrived, dressed in his dog collar and with his shirtsleeves rolled up.

'You sent for me, Mr Carter?' He surveyed the crowd. 'It's time you good people went home. I'm sure you have better things to do.'

The crowd began to disperse, a handful of them retiring to the Woodsman's Arms to discuss the day's turn of events over a tankard of ale.

'You can tell these men to let me go now, Vicar.' To those who didn't know him, Donald sounded confident, but behind all the bluster, he was scared. He'd thought he would get away with it.

279

'You aren't going anywhere, my lad,' Mr Carter said.

'He will be. He's going to Canterbury Gaol where he'll be placed on remand until he comes to trial.' The constable glanced towards Mr Carter, his eyebrows raised in question. 'That is the usual procedure unless—'

'I won't intervene this time,' Mr Carter cut in.

'Please, I beg you to have mercy,' Rose said, as the sun burned the back of her neck. 'He's only a boy – young, foolish and hungry.'

'He's old enough to know better. I turned a blind eye before – for your sake, not his. I can't do it again. He promised me, and he broke his word. Take him away. I can't stand the sight of him.'

'Ah, let's not be too hasty,' the vicar lisped. 'How old are you, Donald?'

'Fifteen, sir.'

'Plenty old enough to be treated as a man,' Mr Carter said.

'He's still a juvenile in the eyes of the law, though,' the vicar pointed out.

'What would you recommend then?' Mr Carter asked.

'I want him locked up,' Mrs Greenleaf joined in.

'He'll be placed under house arrest – I'll take him to the vicarage where he'll remain overnight under lock and key. This appears to be a straightforward case with witnesses.' The vicar turned to Mrs Greenleaf.

'I saw him, the thieving rascal. And Mrs Cole, my neighbour, can vouch for him having the pie in his pocket. Search him, Constable.'

'There is no need – I can see the crumbs,' the constable said.

'Then there is little question of his guilt.' The vicar sighed and rolled his eyes towards the sky. 'It is a sorrow to me when my sermons fall on deaf ears. Never mind. Constable, if you will take witness statements now before time erases important details from the complainant's mind …' He thought for a moment. 'I can discharge the accused, but this is a serious charge. Theft is an indictable offence, and I could, of course, commit him to be tried at the Quarter Sessions, but he is not quite sixteen and minor larcenies of juveniles may be tried summarily, even though the offence itself remains indictable. So, I will send for the magistrate, Mr Lunt from Selling, and meet tomorrow at the vicarage to settle this sorry affair. Bring your statements and witnesses, Constable, and I will see you then.'

Rose pressed her hand to her mouth as the constable untied Donald from the tree and led him off, still protesting his innocence while the crumbs of pastry fell from the front of his jerkin.

'Please, let him come home with me. You know where we are – you can come and fetch him tomorrow.' Rose tightened her shawl around her shoulders as Mrs Greenleaf turned her back, and Mr Carter picked up his stick and walked in the direction of Wanstall Farm without a word.

How could she ever face their neighbours again? And Mr Wild? The shame was almost unbearable, making her scurry away like a rat on its belly.

'Rose, what has happened?' Minnie pulled herself up from the bench when Rose arrived back at the cottage, slipping off her shawl as the front door scraped closed behind her. 'Where have you been?'

'I wasn't that long, was I?' Rose said, wondering how to break the news to Donald's twin.

'It seemed like for ever. Well, what is it?' She shrank back. 'Your silence is scaring me.'

'It's Donald,' Rose began.

Minnie's reaction was more muted than she'd expected. In fact, she tried to console Rose with a boiled egg and toast.

'I'm sad to think of our brother spending the night under lock and key, but you mustn't blame yourself. It was his fault.'

'I must bear some of the responsibility,' Rose sighed. 'I haven't been firm enough with him. It was easier to back down than confront him over his escapades.'

The next morning at the appointed time, she left Minnie at home doing her sewing and went off to the vicarage, but on her way up the lane, Sam waylaid her.

'Good morning,' he said.

'Hardly,' she said glumly.

'Morning, then. I can guess what brings you here.'

'I'm sure everyone has heard about Donald by now. I'm on my way to offer him my support in any way that I can.'

'Even though he's as guilty as sin?'

'I know what he's accused of. I wasn't there, so I can't say exactly what happened.'

'I hope it goes right,' he said.

Rose thanked him.

'We should meet later,' he blurted out. 'Perhaps we could sit up at yours.'

'I beg your pardon?'

'Oh Rose, let's stop pretending. You're a very fine woman, and in spite of what happened with the apple picking last year, I'm still fond of you and I reckon you're sweet on me. I don't see what's to stop us having a kiss and a cuddle.'

'Why are you talking of this now when I have other things on my mind?' She gazed at him, at the look of rejection in his eyes. She had hurt his feelings, but then he hadn't shown her much respect when he'd gone off with the Irish girl. 'I'm sorry. Let's leave this for today.'

'Tomorrow then?' he said, but it was more of a statement than a question.

'Tomorrow,' she agreed reluctantly, but if they did end up spending the evening together, she would make sure Minnie or Donald sat up with them. Could they be right for each other? She wished she had someone to advise her, but in the meantime, she had her brother to worry about.

'I'll be thinking of you more than usual today,' Sam said before touching the peak of his cap and walking on towards the farm, his jacket slung over his shoulder.

Rose continued into the village.

Reverend Browning had turned one of the rooms in the vicarage into a mock court with a table across the far end under the window, and chairs set out in two rows like the pews in the church. To one side of the table, there was a pair of wingback chairs in which the constable was sitting alongside the prisoner.

Poor Donald. Rose's heart went out to him. He looked more like a boy than a young man with his head bowed, and his eyes darting from person to person. When he caught sight of Rose, standing waiting with Mr and Mrs Carter, the vicar's wife, Mrs Greenleaf and several other villagers, he gave her a brief smile.

'Please be seated,' the vicar lisped when he and the other magistrate had taken their places at the table. 'Allow me to introduce you to Mr Lunt, the magistrate for Selling, whom I called to the bench today, in order to deliver a verdict and pass sentence if necessary on the prisoner who stands before us, according to the evidence from the witnesses and statements gathered.'

The constable gave Donald a nudge, and he stood up, trembling.

'The prisoner – Donald Cheevers of Toad's Bottom Cottage, Overshill – stands charged of the following offence: that on the twelfth day of May 1879 in the county of Kent, he did feloniously steal two pies, the property of

Mrs Greenleaf. I call on the prosecution to state their full name and occupation for the record.'

'I am Mrs Greenleaf, widow and wise woman of this parish.'

'Explain to the court the events of the day concerned.'

She told them how she had found Donald with the pies.

'I sent for the constable, who tied him up because he seemed to be at risk of making his escape,' she went on.

Mr Lunt asked a few questions then let her sit down again before he called the constable to give his account. He was well known for his acquaintance with the Woodsman's Arms and Rose wondered, as he stood and faced the magistrates, how much weight could be given to his testimony.

'How did you respond to Mrs Greenleaf's complaint? How much of the stolen goods did you recover?'

'The boy came to fetch me, and I attended the scene of the alleged crime straight away. The window of the cottage was open. The accused was with Mr Carter. I spoke with Mrs Greenleaf, then I recovered a whole pie from one pocket of the prisoner's coat, and some crumbs on his face and hands.'

The prosecution called another witness who gave a history of Donald's misdemeanours.

'He's done it before. He's well known around our way, but folks turn a blind eye, seeing he's an orphan and all that.'

'I have no more questions,' Mr Lunt said. 'I've read the witness statements and it seems clear that there is no confusion in the events which took place. I see no need to call further witnesses. Is there anyone to speak in this young man's defence?' There wasn't, so the magistrate went on to address the prisoner.

'You have pleaded guilty. Do you have anything to say?'

'Nothing, sir.'

Mr Lunt rubbed at his chin as he thought for a moment.

'Reverend Browning, there is nothing to discuss. The evidence is straightforward and compelling, is it not?'

The vicar nodded. 'I feel that society should be delivered from the prisoner's malpractices for some time. There is no doubt of the defendant's guilt.'

Mr Lunt turned to the prisoner. 'Donald Cheevers, the Bench awards you six months' hard labour, followed by eighteen months' imprisonment.'

Rose gasped. She'd guessed he wouldn't get off lightly, but not that he would receive two years in gaol. She looked towards Donald who gazed back at her, trying not to cry. She began to feel a little faint and then the room went dark and silent, until she woke to the flapping of a fan in her face and the acrid smell of salts in her nostrils.

'Oh, what a to-do.' Her grandmother was at her side, and the vicar's wife in front of her.

'Two years of hard bed, hard board and hard labour for a common thief,' Mr Carter said, joining them.

'This is too harsh a sentence,' she heard her grandmother say. 'He is a boy.'

'He's fifteen, old enough to be responsible for his actions,' Mr Carter said.

'I remember how my pa let Matty – your brother – off for filching onions when he was a boy, out of compassion for your family, Stephen. The situation is similar. It isn't right to send Donald to prison where there will be hardened criminals to learn from, for a petty theft. He was hungry.'

'What kind of excuse is that? We have done everything to make sure he and his sisters had food in their bellies. Listen, my dear, I can forgive a mistake, and find some compassion in my heart for a crime born of desperation. This is different. Donald is a wanton boy, lazy, irresponsible and weak-minded.'

'Every man is illuminated by the divine light, but it takes time for him to see the error of his ways.' Mr Carter paused to clear his throat. 'I look back at my brothers. If only someone had taken Jervis in hand and forced him to reflect on his actions, he might not have gone on to do what he did. He and Matty broke Ma's heart.'

'She was on her way out already,' Mrs Carter said gently.

'These people have brought shame and embarrassment to our door. I feel they have let us down, just like my brothers did. I've fought hard to build my reputation and my business, and I will not have my standing in Overshill damaged by the thoughtless actions of this young felon and his sisters.'

Rose winced.

'It's Donald, not my granddaughters who have done wrong.'

'They will all be tarred with the same brush.'

'Oh Stephen, you are weary. Let us leave this conversation for now. You were awake all last night, worrying. You'll feel better when you've had some rest.'

'Let's go home.'

'After I have spoken to Rose, who looks like a rabbit caught by lamplight.'

'I wish to speak with my brother,' Rose said, starting to recover her wits.

'He has forfeited all rights to his freedom,' Mr Lunt said gloomily.

'You may have five minutes with the prisoner,' the vicar said. 'In the meantime, we'll arrange for the boy to be delivered to Canterbury at the earliest opportunity.'

Rose slipped away to join Donald who was sitting slumped in his chair.

'I'm sorry,' she said. 'I can't believe they've done that – it isn't right. How I wish I'd been stricter with you.'

'I should have taken more notice. I never thought it would come to this. I'm scared, Rose. What will they do to me?'

'You will serve your sentence – it is but two years and the time will fly by.'

'I wish I'd never done it. I wish I'd never set eyes on them pies.'

'We'll visit. I promise.'

He slumped down further. 'I've done my sisters a terrible wrong – how will you manage to pay the rent without my wage? Oh my Lord, you will starve without me.'

'We will cope,' Rose said, relieved that he wasn't so selfish as to forget any consideration for her and Minnie. 'We have a little of Arthur's money left.'

'You will have your place as Mr Wild's housekeeper as soon as he comes back from his travels. In the meantime . . .'

She squeezed his shoulder. 'We will get through this,' she said before walking away, weighted down with care like a cat in a sack of stones, waiting to be drowned.

She heard her grandmother calling after her, and Mr Carter telling his wife to let her go as she hurried back through the village to the cottage where Minnie was waiting.

'How is he? Oh, you've been crying.'

'So has Donald – it is terrible to see him like that. He's being sent to Canterbury Gaol for two years.'

'Two years!' Minnie echoed miserably. 'What will we do without him?'

'What we have always done. We will manage.'

Getting by wasn't going to be easy, though. The following morning, Rose heard Minnie screaming in the garden and ran out to find her sister staring at the empty coop, a few feathers drifting across the ground in front of her.

'Someone has taken the hens. I thought it was a fox, but no, I heard someone running and the hens squawking, and I couldn't chase after them.'

Rose's heart sank. How could things get any worse?

'We should go and warn our grandmother at the farm that there are thieves about.'

'They have their geese to guard the yard, but yes, you're right, we should let them know.' Rose dressed quickly and they ran down the lane and into the yard, where the birds had been shut out in the orchard.

Sam looked up from where he was hammering nails into the barn roof, and waved.

She waved back.

'What do you want?' Mr Carter said, approaching them.

'Someone has stolen our hens,' Rose said.

'You should have kept a closer watch on them,' he said gruffly.

'They took them while we were abed,' Minnie said, looking hurt at his accusation that she would neglect them. They weren't merely a source of eggs – they were fond of them.

'Where is Grandma?' Minnie went on, perhaps hoping to garner some sympathy from her.

'She's sick,' Mr Carter said. 'Your brother's shenanigans have worn her nerves to shreds. Now, go away and leave us alone. I can't stand to see your faces!'

'Please let us see her,' Rose begged. 'Perhaps we can do something to help?'

'Alice is taking care of her,' he said, as the maid appeared on the back doorstep behind him.

'We don't want the likes of you around here.' Alice threw a bucket of suds across the pathway, splashing Rose's feet. 'Sometimes we forget that my mistress is advancing in years. She doesn't need all this worry at her time of life.'

'That's enough, Alice,' Mr Carter said. 'Rose and Minnie, just go away. The doctor's said that my wife has a weakness in her heart, and has ordered her to rest. She is the love of my life. She *is* my life, and if I should lose her through this, I'll never forgive you or that brother of yours. She put her faith in you ...' He dashed away a tear. 'I wish we'd never set eyes on you.'

Rose took Minnie's hand and turned away, her heart pounding. She'd never had any intention of causing any harm.

As they walked back to the cottage, she thought of Ma and how she'd died from a broken heart, and how she'd blame herself if the same should happen to dear Mrs Carter because of the strain of coping with the extra burden of her long-lost grandchildren. How could they stay in Overshill now?

'We will take a few days to settle things here then pack up and go,' she decided.

'Are you sure?'

'It's for the best. We are not liked here.'

'What about Mr Wild? If we stayed in Overshill, you'd have work at Churt House.'

'He's gone away on business. Who knows how long he will be? We can't afford to sit and wait for his return, and besides, when he hears of our fall from grace, he will make some excuse and change his mind.'

'I don't think Freddie would look at it in that way. He isn't like the rest of them,' Minnie said.

'My brother is a common criminal. A housekeeper's character has to be beyond reproach. What's more, Mr Wild is recently established in the village – he won't help his reputation by employing me. Look at how they all hate us.'

'Our grandmother loves us still,' Minnie said.

'That's true – she thinks the best of people. I don't like to be the source of disagreement between her and Mr Carter. They deserve a quiet life.'

'I shall miss her,' Minnie went on. 'Why don't you write to Aunt Marjorie?'

'You know why – she is old and unwell.' And if she was being honest with herself, Rose felt deeply ashamed about what Donald had done. She couldn't bear to tell their dear aunt of how he had let them all down.

'What about Arthur? How will he know where we are?' Minnie asked.

'I don't know.' Where was Arthur when they needed him? It appeared that he didn't want them to find him just yet.

'We could go to London?'

'Do you realise how big London is? We'd never find him, not in a month of Sundays.'

'There might be work for us there.'

'I don't think London would suit us. Some people have said that there is work to be had in Faversham. We should go where we are more certain of making a living, and we wouldn't be too far away from Donald. I should like to visit him soon.'

'Will we say goodbye to Grandma?' Minnie's eyes glistened.

'No, we'll slip away quietly. I don't think we'll be missed, not fondly anyway.' She would let Sam know that they were planning to move away from Overshill, and wondered about leaving word for Freddie. She felt bad about running away. He had treated her with respect, as an equal. They had both been outsiders and united by that – but why should he care what became of them?

Chapter Twenty

Like a Flea on a Dog

Rose wasn't sure if she was doing the right thing. Mixed emotions churned inside her as she approached Westgate Towers towing the barrow, with Minnie limping alongside her carrying a small posy of flowers that she'd picked from the hedgerows along the way. She'd sent a letter to the prison to arrange the visit in advance, but it was short notice and she suspected that the bureaucracy involved might mean that they couldn't see Donald on this occasion.

'Look out,' she warned as a cart loaded with milk churns rattled past, rather too close for comfort. 'I'd forgotten what Canterbury was like.'

'It's very smelly.' Minnie wrinkled her nose, and just as Rose began to fear that she was going to start complaining about their lot, her eyes lit up at the sight of a sweet shop on the corner of the street.

'Please, Rose.' Minnie stopped in front of the window with its mouth-watering display of treats.

'We should save our money,' Rose murmured, hating to let her sister down.

'We don't have to buy many, only a quarter, or two ounces,' Minnie begged.

'Oh, go on.' Rose gave her a threepenny bit. 'Give me back the change.'

'Thank you.' Minnie rushed into the shop and emerged some time later with a paper bag in her hand, and grinning from ear to ear.

'What took you so long?' Rose smiled back.

'There were too many to choose from ...' Minnie offered her a sweet. Rose took one then Minnie did the same before handing her the bag to look after. 'I can't trust myself not to eat them all at once.'

Rose walked on to the prison, her breath fresh with mint. The austere façade of Canterbury Gaol was marked with a stone reading *House of Correction*, and the name of the architect George Byfield.

'You must stay and guard the barrow,' she told Minnie, parking it beside the iron railings made to look like wooden rods and axe heads.

'I want to see Donald!' Minnie's eyes flashed mutinously. 'Can't we leave the barrow somewhere? What about Mrs Hamilton, or one of the men at the tannery?'

'I don't want to run into the Kingsleys.'

'Mr Kingsley will be in his office.'

'I'd really rather not go there.'

'What about one of the street boys? Baxter would do it for a penny – if we can find him.'

They went walking through the familiar places of their childhood, until they reached the Rookery and asked the gaggle of children who were playing hoops in the middle of the dirt if they knew where Baxter was, in return for sweets.

'You're in luck,' one of the girls said. ''E's got a job at the tannery.'

Which meant they would have to risk confronting the Kingsleys after all, Rose thought to herself.

'Thank you.' She handed over a few mint drops then slipped the bag back in her pocket. 'Come on, Minnie, we must keep going. Do you want to ride in the barrow?'

'No, I'll keep walking.' She leaned on her stick and made off towards the tannery, limping along with her head down.

When they turned up the street towards Willow Place, Rose felt her pulse beat a little faster. The gate was closed across the drive and there were ducks on the lawn, but their old home had been painted: the oak framework stained black and the walls freshly whitewashed. The leaded windows shone in the sunshine, the laurels had been cut and there was a pram in the shade of the crab-apple tree.

'Oh dear, I hope our aunt hasn't been allowed to adopt a baby,' Rose said as she caught up with Minnie, but her sister's attention was on the sign beside the gateway into the tan yard. It read: *Milsom Bros. Tanners, purveyors of fine leather ...*

'Look, Rose. What's happened to the Kingsleys?'

'They've gone?' She couldn't quite believe it. 'Where? Why?'

'This isn't a place for two young ladies,' a workman said, opening up the gate to allow a carter out of the yard. 'Oh, Miss Cheevers? Is that you?'

'Mr Jones,' Rose said.

He smiled. 'I didn't recognise you at first, my dears. I'm afraid you'll find this place much altered. Your aunt and uncle sold up some three months ago. The business wasn't doing too well with your father and Arthur gone, and Mr Milsom, a Canterbury man, and his brothers, made them an offer they felt they couldn't refuse.' Mr Jones shook his head. 'Mr Kingsley weren't a businessman, just a fly-by-night, and Mrs Kingsley encouraged it. Oh, I shouldn't speak badly of them in front of you, but they brought the tannery to its knees. A couple of the men were laid off before the Milsoms took over.'

He hooked the gate back against the wall, and pulled his pipe from his belt.

'I'm very sorry about that,' Rose said, knowing her father would never have let it happen.

'I'm glad to see you. We've all been wondering how you were. It's like you disappeared into thin air.'

'I know. We had to leave Canterbury in a hurry.' As a few of the other workmen stepped up to see what the stir was, Rose didn't like to go on to explain that they were on the run again, thanks to Donald.

'We've come to see—' Minnie began.

'To pay our respects to Mr and Mrs Cheevers,' Rose interrupted quickly, not wanting everyone to know their business. When would Minnie ever learn?

'It's you, miss!' came a cry of delight. 'It's me, Baxter.' Hastening across to them, he whipped off his cap in greeting.

She smiled. 'You are well?'

'I'm errand boy for Mr Milsom senior – I get to work on the yard and in the office, wherever I'm needed.'

'And depending on the weather,' Mr Jones remarked. 'You are always in the office when it's raining.'

'Can you blame me, sir?' Baxter said cheekily.

'I suppose not. You're a smart boy and you'll do well for yourself, if you don't keep talking back.'

'Are you back in Canterbury for good?' Baxter asked.

'We're paying a short visit, that's all. I wondered if I might ask you to look after our barrow for a couple of hours while we attend to some personal matters – in return for a penny, of course.'

'Isn't that our old barrer ...?' Mr Jones stopped abruptly.

'It belonged to the Kingsleys,' Rose said, hoping that nobody was going to try to take it back. 'Minnie struggles with her walking – we keep it with us so she can rest when she needs to.'

'Is that why you keep the kettle hanging from the side?' Baxter said. 'For making tea when you stop? You appear to have brought everything but the kitchen sink with you.'

'We're between lodgings,' Rose said smoothly, surprising herself with her capacity for telling white lies.

'I'll keep an eye on it, but it must be worth more than a penny to watch all of that. How about thruppence?'

Rose couldn't help chuckling. 'Tuppence and that's my final offer.'

'Tuppence, it is.' Solemnly, Baxter reached out and shook her hand. 'Have a lovely day, ladies.'

'He's just the same,' Minnie said as they set off for the gaol.

In spite of the authorities claiming they had not yet received Rose's letter of application for a visit, they managed to sweet-talk the warder in charge and persuade him to let them see Donald. Another man with a bunch of keys jangling on his belt took them through to a small, windowless room with a table and chairs, where they sat and waited until he reappeared with their brother.

'Donald?' She hardly recognised him in his prison clothes at first – he looked worn out.

'Sit!' barked the warder.

Donald shuffled forward and took a seat opposite his sisters. He reached across the table to take Minnie's hand, but the warder's truncheon came down hard against the back of his fingers, making him recoil.

'How did you manage to come and see me?' he asked. 'Who's looking after the hens?'

'I'm afraid they've gone. It's a long story and we don't have much time. How are you anyway?'

Minnie bit her lip, trying not to cry. 'What are they doing to you?'

'It isn't that bad in here. We have gruel every day – oats, onions, lard and pepper and salt, and goodness knows what else. The water tastes like it's come straight out of the river. Some of the prisoners have had belly-rot really bad, and the bread has stones in it that fair break your teeth.' He showed them a chip out of his upper molar.

'You look just as handsome as before, but you are very dirty,' Rose said with a rueful smile.

'Are you lonely?' Minnie fretted.

'Hardly. There are about one hundred and fifty prisoners – I am one of many, like a flea on a dog. I'm on a ward with several others my own age and several younger. I've taken the youngest boy who's ten under my wing. It isn't as bad in here as you think. It's bearable.'

He was putting on a brave face, Rose thought. He'd been in gaol for merely a week – he had a very long way to go.

'We've missed you,' Minnie said.

'I've missed you too. I'm sorry for what I've done, and I can't believe you're here after what I put you through. I didn't think you'd want to see me again.'

'Of course we do, you clodpole,' Rose said.

'What do you do all day?' Minnie asked.

'There's plenty to keep us occupied – there are four treadmills for hard labour and a crank mill for grinding corn. Some pick oakum and others are allowed to work in the garden to grow vegetables. There's even a man who does shoemaking, but there's no talking unless a guard speaks to you.'

'What about you, though?' Minnie said.

'I get to go on the treadmill eight hours at a time, walking up the height of a mountain – it's awful tiring when you are on it, all you are thinking of is keeping it turning, and how your legs ache. But don't worry about me!' His eyes flashed fiercely. 'I got myself into this pickle and I'll take my punishment. I tell you, though, if I ever get out of here, I'll never do it again. I'll die of hunger rather than take what isn't mine.'

'Do you promise that solemnly, hand on heart?' Rose said.

He nodded, and placed his hand on his heart. 'I promise.'

'We'll be back to visit as often as we can,' Minnie said.

'I think I shall die here,' he said, suddenly mournful.

'I will not let that happen. I would swap with you,' Minnie said sharply.

'It's kind of you, but it wouldn't be allowed.' Donald turned to Rose. 'You haven't told me what really brings you here from Overshill. I'm not stupid – I can tell something isn't right.'

'We've come to let you know that we're going to put down roots elsewhere when we've found work. The word is that Faversham is pleasant enough.'

'Faversham? You're moving because of me?'

Rose didn't deny it.

'I thought you were braver than that,' he went on.

'It isn't just the gossips – they're bad enough, but I can't possibly take up my place as housekeeper at Churt House now.'

'I see … the Cheeverses are not to be trusted. How can I ever make this up to you? I've been such a fool. Ma would kill me if she knew.'

'What's more, this has made our grandmother ill. Mr Carter blames us for her state of health. I thought it best to get away – I couldn't have her death on my conscience.'

He buried his head in his hands. 'I've ruined your lives as well as mine.'

'No, you haven't. We will start again. You will join us when you're let out. What's done is done, water under the bridge,' Rose said sadly. 'We will get through this and one day we'll be reunited with you and Arthur—'

'And live happily ever after?' he finished for her.

'That's right. We have to believe that.'

'Visiting's over,' the warder said.

It was with many tears that they left Donald behind and made their way back outside into the bright sunshine to collect the barrow. Rose quashed a yearning to visit their parents' graves – Ma and Pa would have understood her reasons for not making the diversion to the cemetery. For the time being, her priority was to look after the living, not pay her respects to the dead.

'We are going in the right direction?' Minnie said after they had been walking for a while.

Rose sighed. It didn't really matter as long as they were putting some distance between them and Overshill, but she knew they were heading towards her intended destination when they came across a waymark for Faversham and the tall crown spire of St Mary of Charity rose into the sky ahead of them.

'What will we do for money? Where will we live?'

'I don't know yet,' Rose said sharply. 'There will be work in Faversham, and failing that, there's always the poorhouse.'

'No,' Minnie cried, making Rose wish that she hadn't been so brutal.

'I'm sorry for snapping at you. I'm a little weary. Let's say that I wouldn't choose to go there, but if it means the difference between living and dying, we will choose the former.'

They kept walking until they reached the outskirts of the town, following the Ospringe Road and passing the Union, Ma's birthplace with its view of the gravel pits. Rose crossed the street to avoid it, in case its shadows could trap them and pull them in.

'I've heard about those places,' Minnie said. 'They're worse than the Rookery where Baxter lives.'

'We would have food and a roof over our heads.' And live among the lunatics and the sick, Rose mused, keeping her thoughts to herself. 'We won't need to go there – we'll soon find work and lodgings.' Had she done the right thing, dragging Minnie away from Overshill when she had no character reference or suitable clothing to apply for employment? She had thought she could turn her hand to teaching, but no one would look at her twice when they noticed the stains and rips on her dress. Touching the half a sixpence at her throat, she prayed for guidance. What would Ma have done?

'Two bundles a penny, sweet violets!'

'Any milk here! Fresh cheese and cream!' came the calls of the street-sellers in the market.

Rose hadn't been to Faversham before, although she felt some affinity for the town when she spotted one of the breweries. According to the signage, it was owned by the Berry-Clays, the name reminding her of her mother's former association with them. She wondered if she had run along the same streets as a girl.

'Are you all right, Rose?' Minnie reached out and touched her shoulder.

'I was just thinking of Ma.' She changed the subject. 'We must find somewhere to stop for the night.'

Minnie tripped, crying out as she fell on one knee. Rose heaved her back on to her feet and ordered her to get into the barrow.

'I can't do that – it's too much for you,' Minnie protested, but it didn't take a lot to persuade her. Once she was sitting on top of their possessions, Rose dragged the barrow along the street, wondering where they should stop for the night. She felt nervous about asking for a room at the inn. It was busy, there were carriages flying in and out of the stableyard, and people everywhere. She had no idea what it would cost and was too scared to enquire.

'Shall we sleep in the barrow?' Minnie suggested. 'We have plenty of blankets.'

'That isn't such a bad idea,' Rose said, turning the barrow round and heading back out of Faversham.

Eventually, they reached the gravel pits where they found a dip in the ground, hidden from prying eyes by the shadow of a dense hedge. Minnie soon fell asleep while Rose lay looking up at the night sky, listening to the scuffling of badgers in their sett, and the shrill shriek of a fox. She thought of Arthur in the smog, and Donald locked away in gaol, and Mr Wild. What must he think of her letting him down like this, or was she being naive even thinking he'd notice? Her heart ached as the stars twinkled in the blackness above her. She missed Overshill, and worried about their dear grandmother, but she felt Freddie's absence even more. She doubted she would ever see him again, and that's what hurt her the most.

Chapter Twenty-One

Up the Creek

'Minnie, it's time to get up.' Rose unfolded her limbs and stretched before shaking her sister's shoulder the next morning. 'We have much to do today.'

'Oh, do we have to?' she groaned.

'If we aren't to starve, yes. Come on.'

Minnie sat up and gazed groggily around her.

'Where are we? Oh, I remember.'

'Today we find work, or beg for sanctuary at the Union.' Rose shuddered at the thought of falling so low, but she couldn't let Minnie starve on the streets. If there was anything she could do to keep them out of there, she would do it. She thought of the women she'd seen on the wharf, wearing flimsy clothes and too much of the devil's trickery on their lips and cheeks, and changed her mind. She would do almost anything, but not that.

She took the leather bottle out of the bottom of the barrow, undid the stopple and drank the warm, brackish water. Once she'd offered it to Minnie, she used the rest to wash their hands and faces, thinking longingly of ham, bread and hot milky tea.

'Do I look respectable?' she asked Minnie, nibbling on a piece of the cake they'd brought with them.

'Almost,' she said. 'Let me brush your hair.'

When they were ready, they set out for Faversham again, knocking on doors on the way, looking for work, but there was nothing for a woman who had no fixed abode or reference as to the quality of her character. After the seventh or eighth rejection, Rose began to see that it was hopeless. She had to think of an alternative. Perhaps she could find work at an inn? They must need cooks, servers and chambermaids.

She went into the Ship Hotel and asked to speak to the landlord, who sent one of his minions to dismiss her as quickly as possible.

'There's nothing for the likes of you here,' the young man said, staring at her.

'The likes of me ...?' Her voice faded as she realised what he meant.

'There'll be work at one of the brickfields, I expect,' he said more kindly. 'Try Kingsfield. Ask for Abel – he's one of the gaffers.' He gave her brief directions to the place.

'Thank you, sir,' she said.

'Hurry along,' he added.

She didn't hesitate. She knew when she wasn't welcome.

'Well?' Minnie said, when Rose returned to where she had left her with the barrow, outside a nearby shop.

'Nothing.' She shrugged.

'We aren't having much luck, are we? We should've prayed harder in church.'

'Maybe. Anyway, it's no use standing around. We must make our way to Kingsfield to see if there's any work there.'

'What kind of work?'

'I'm not sure exactly. We'll have to see.'

The sun was high in the sky when they entered the gateway to the brickfield, a stark expanse of earth stripped

302

bare of grass and trees, where several gangs of men were working among stacks of burning bricks.

A hot gust of air blew up a cloud of orange dust. Rose could feel it tickling at her throat and sticking to her forehead. She could smell rot and ash, and hear a regular tap-tapping sound, and the cries of the gulls overhead.

'This is truly horrid.' Minnie coughed. 'We can't possibly stay here.'

'We have to endure it,' Rose said, feeling bad-tempered and a little faint with the heat.

'I wish we'd stayed in Overshill, or even in Canterbury.' Rose couldn't restrain herself.

'You lazy, ungrateful toerag! You've had me and Donald running around after you for months while your leg mended. Now that you're well, you could at least show some gratitude. I'm doing my best.'

'I'm sorry, Rose.' Minnie's lip quivered and her eyes filled with tears. 'I am grateful. You've stuck by me through thick and thin. I'll work anywhere … it's just that this place looks like hell on earth.'

'I know and I'm sorry too. I shouldn't have yelled at you.' If it wasn't for Donald they wouldn't be here, she thought bitterly. 'We have to put our fears to one side and take what we're offered.' Reaching for Minnie's hand, she recalled Aunt Marjorie's tale of Ma's bravery when she was forced to leave home. Their mother had been completely alone.

Nearby, a man was loading a stack of bricks on to the back of a cart drawn by a sorry-looking nag of a horse, nothing like the ones that Mr Carter sold from the farm. Another dusty man hawked and spat at their feet as he headed towards a pile of bricks that he was in the process of dismantling.

'Excuse me, sir,' Rose said. 'I've been told to have a word with Abel.'

He stopped and raised one eyebrow. 'What do you want with him?'

'I've heard he has need of more workers.'

'Maybe. He's down there somewhere.' He pointed towards the wharf. 'Mind your step as you go. What's with the barrer?'

'We are moving into new lodgings today, not that it's any of your business,' Rose said quickly. 'Thank you anyway.' With Minnie trailing along behind her, holding her shawl across her face, she towed the barrow across the bumpy ground until they reached a crowd of women and children who were hard at work, sifting dirt. Beyond them was a wharf where a flat-bottomed Thames barge sat in the grey sludge of the creek. Further out into the water was a second barge with its rust-red flax sails unfurled.

A middle-aged man with a baccy tin tied to his belt approached, a smoking cutty pipe between his lips.

'You look like you've taken a wrong turn,' he said, smiling.

'Are you Abel?' Rose asked.

He gazed at her quizzically. 'Who wants to know?'

'My name's Rose.' She shrank back, uncertain of him. Was he in any way a gentleman? 'We're looking for paid occupation, and came here because we were under the impression there was work to be had.'

'Well, there's some truth in that. The streets of Faversham aren't paved with gold, but there are bricks to be made, and the season is short due to the weather.' He paused and chewed on the end of his pipe, ruminating for a moment. He had an accent that was more Essex than Kent, and his skin and clothing were the colour of brick dust. 'Have you sifted dirt before?'

'No, I can't say that I have, but—'

'I haven't any work today, but come back tomorrow morning at six o'clock sharp.'

'I'm not too proud to tell you that we're desperate,' Rose said, her heart sinking. How long would they have to wait without a wage coming in?

'I'm sorry, but there's nothing I can do,' Abel said.

'I don't know how to make bricks,' Minnie said, stepping up beside her.

'Oh, you won't get into one of the gangs.' Abel laughed. 'You'll be with the other women, sifting the dust that comes off the barges from London. The larger pieces – the breeze – get caught by the mesh and we use the ashes that fall through to mix with the clay to cure the bricks. You're paid for the number of baskets of dirt that you sift. It isn't for everyone – some can't get used to the filth. The gangs come back every summer, but the women … they don't stay long. I can't promise anything, but I expect something will come up over the next few days.'

Rose and Minnie returned four mornings running, sleeping in the barrow and eking out the little money they had, buying tea and food from the costermongers at the market. On the fifth day they were hired.

'You're persistent, I'll give you that. I thought you'd have given up by now,' Abel said. 'Let's see – you'll need aprons and sieves. I'll rent them out to you and you can pay me back with interest at the end of the week. I'll dock it from your wages.'

'What rate of interest will you apply?' Rose asked, convinced now that Abel wasn't a gentleman. He was scruffy, dirty and rude, and she wasn't sure that she could trust him.

'That's a very smart question. How about fifteen per cent?'

She swallowed hard. 'That's too much. We'll never pay it off at that rate.'

'Perhaps it is a little high. I'll reduce it by one per cent out of the goodness of my heart. What do you think?'

'It's still too much.'

'Oh, come on. You won't find a better deal, and besides, you can't work without the tools of the trade.'

It was a reasonable argument, but you could hardly call it a trade, Rose thought.

'The aprons are over there.' Squinting, he pointed to a makeshift table, an old door supported on broken bricks. 'Take it or leave it. It's up to you.'

'I'll take it, thank you,' she said, upset at having been forced into a corner. She thought briefly of Baxter and how poverty had robbed him of the opportunity of making choices.

'You'll need one long apron and one of the shorter, thicker ones each, then go and join the rest of them. They'll show you what to do.'

She glanced towards her sister, who nodded and limped towards the table as though she had the weight of the world on her shoulders. Rose picked up the first heavy leather apron from the pile and placed it around her waist, belting it up. She helped Minnie with hers before picking up a second, smaller and thicker apron which she laced up tightly on top of the first. The leather ran smooth beneath her fingers and she felt a lump catch in her throat, remembering the tannery and the cured hides that Pa had been so proud of. If there had been any justice in the world, Arthur and Donald would still be there, continuing his legacy.

'Keep your chin up, Minnie.' Rose forced a smile. 'We'll soon have money for a room. There'll be no more sleeping in the barrow.'

Minnie grinned back. 'We'll be able to live in a mansion.'

'That's wishful thinking, but it's good to have a dream, something to hold on to.'

Abel gave them each a heavy iron sieve before they joined the other women who were sitting in a semi-circle around a heap of refuse. Unsure of where to take her place, Rose moved to one end and sat down, her legs crossed under her skirt and aprons. She patted the ground beside her. Minnie sat down too, but she struggled to make herself comfortable, having to keep her mended leg straight, which made Rose wonder how long she would be able to work before her old aches and pains returned.

'What do we do now?' Minnie said.

'Watch the others,' Rose whispered back, trying not to make a spectacle of themselves, but that was impossible. She felt several sets of eyes on her as the other workers stared, their faces covered with scarves and rags to stop the dust getting into their mouths and noses.

Her nearest neighbour, who sat with her arms exposed to the elements, knocked her sieve against her padded apron, the contact between iron and leather making the hollow drumming sound that Rose had noticed when they first arrived at the brickfield.

One of the cheerful urchins swept up the piles of fine dust that fell through the women's sieves and collected it into baskets, a separate one for each worker. When a basket had been completely filled, two girls dragged it to the set of scales that stood alongside the table. Abel weighed the basket, checked its tag and recorded the weight in his ledger, and the girls moved it aside where it remained until one of Abel's gang members collected it and took it away.

Copying the other women, Rose picked up her sieve. A boy of Minnie's age shovelled refuse into it, and she began to knock it against her apron, sending some of the dust spilling out through the mesh. The smell was revolting, and she was almost sick when she spotted some rotten orange peel and a piece of bone left in what Abel had called the breeze. She couldn't stop retching.

'This reminds me of the tannery,' Minnie said, apparently feeling more at home than her sister. 'We'll get used to it.'

'I hope so.'

The women in their coarse cotton gowns and battered black bonnets didn't speak at first, but after a while their curiosity began to get the better of them.

'Where have you sprung from?' one asked, removing her grubby scarf from across her mouth.

'Canterbury,' Rose said, at which Minnie glanced up with a frown.

'What's yer name?'

'Rose, and this is my sister, Minnie.'

'She won't last a day here. She isn't strong enough. Look at her.' The woman was young, Rose thought, only a few years older than she was. Her complexion was as brown as a berry from the sun, her hands were coarsened from manual labour and her arms were all sinew and muscle. Her hair fell in tangles from beneath her bonnet, a coppery colour dulled by a coating of dust. 'My name's Flo. This is Hope, my friend. Them over there' – she pointed to two boys of about five and seven – 'they're my sons.'

'Shouldn't they be at school?' Rose said.

'School?' Flo laughed. 'Not while Abel pays them a penny or two here and there for sweeping up and fetching and carrying.'

'It can't be good for them, being brought up in the dust and the dirt.' Rose spluttered as the wind swept the ash into her face.

'Who are you to come and tell me how to bring up my children when you have none of your own?'

'I'm sorry. I didn't mean to offend you.'

'What's Abel doing hiring the likes of you anyway? There's barely enough work to go round as it is,' Flo's friend said harshly. Rose didn't take to her – she had a sly glint in her narrowed eyes, and her knuckles were scraped as if she enjoyed a good fight.

'We came back four days running,' she said. 'The gaffer said there was someone who'd gone away sick.'

'Yes, the poor angel. She's been taken into the Union. I fear that the only way she'll come out again is in the parish coffin.' Flo seemed to wipe away a tear. 'Isn't there work to be 'ad in Can'erbury?'

Rose shook her head.

'It's the same wherever you go. There isn't enough to go round.' Hope gave her a hard stare. 'It's not paid well – they treat us like the dirt we sift. I barely earn enough to keep me out of the poorhouse.'

'Oh, don't listen to that one,' Flo said. 'She kept out of the poorhouse all last winter and the one before.'

'Oi, keep at it,' Abel shouted.

Rose noticed how Minnie winced at the sound. She had become a mouse, thanks to her aunt's cruelty, and Rose wished she could find a way to help her rebuild her confidence.

As the morning passed, her fingers began to grow stiff and her wrists sore. The sun grew hotter, its rays warming the earth and sucking the stench of London's waste into the air.

At noon, a barge drifted into the wharf-side on the high tide and the children went running down to the creek, laughing and waving, to greet it.

'That's the next lot,' Flo said. 'We can thank the Lord that we'll never run out of dust.'

Rose continued sifting with half an eye on the men and boys who unloaded the refuse from London before loading the barge with bricks for the return journey. She wondered if any of them would end up in the hands of Arthur and Bert. The thought that it wasn't impossible raised her spirits.

'I do this for my boys, nobody else,' Flo said. 'If it weren't for them, I'd 'ave thrown myself in the creek many years ago.'

'Serves you right for picking a bad 'un,' Hope said.

'Speak for yourself. Look at you. I know he beats you black and blue.'

'He don't. Not any more. I've told him. I won't 'ave it.'

'You should kick him out,' Flo said. 'What a pair we are. Are you married, Rose?'

'No,' she said.

'Have you ever been kissed?' Hope said with a sly smile. 'You must have been by now, a pretty one like you.'

She kept her mouth shut. She wasn't sure she could trust them with her business yet. She yearned to share the burden of her secrets, but she couldn't risk letting slip a word about Donald's conviction and whereabouts. It would wreck what they had achieved so far. She glanced towards her sister.

'The cat's got her tongue. She's got something to hide, if you ask me,' Hope said, revealing her stained teeth.

'Oh, leave her alone,' Flo said. 'She'll soon start talking when she's used to us.'

'Are you all right?' she heard Minnie murmur.

Rose nodded. She wasn't looking for friendship, just the means to survive.

The pile of waste kept growing and the dust coated everything, inside and out.

She began to see how the brickfield worked. The gangs dug out the red earth and chalk, and mixed them together with the sifted ash. They made bricks from the yellowish mixture and stacked them in clamps beneath which they lit kindling. The ash in the bricks burned and baked them, and when they were done, they were left to cool before they were loaded on to the barges, ready to be used for the great railway bridge at Greenwich, and the expansion of London.

'Where are you living, Rose?' Flo asked at the end of the day when the brickfield fell silent, the knocking stopped and the last of several barges that had come in that day slipped silently along the creek to the estuary.

'Oh, not far away,' Rose said, giving Minnie a warning glance, but it was too late.

'We ran away from home and now we are sleeping in our barrow.'

Minnie couldn't lie to save her life, Rose thought. She had once thought it a virtue, but now it seemed like a vice.

'A barrow?' Hope chuckled. 'Hey, Flo, the snooty one 'ere – I thought she was lady of the manor, but it turns out she's lady of the barrer. Oh, don't look at me like that, Rose. A barrer? That's tickled me half to death.'

In spite of her embarrassment, Rose smiled.

'You're one of us now and we're goin' to help you,' Flo said. 'It isn't right that you and your crippled sister sleep in a barrer, so I'm goin' to 'ave a word with my landlord about a room – it's a new house near Abbeyfield.'

Rose thought quickly. 'It will have to wait until I have my wages.'

'He'll accept a deposit in the form of any valuables you might have.'

'I have nothing of any worth.' They had left Overshill almost empty-handed.

'Well, don't worry about that now – I'll let you know what 'e says. What were you running away from?' Flo said.

311

'There's no need to be shy – you're one of us now, no longer a virgin as such,' Hope joined in. 'We're all running away from something … or someone.'

Rose told them a little of the truth, that they had been orphaned and forced to live with their aunt who had pushed Minnie down the stairs.

'It's a shame about 'er limp. She's a very pretty girl,' Hope said. 'It was lucky she didn't land on her 'ead.'

'Keep your sister close by,' Flo said. 'There are men around here who would pay a tidy sum for her company, if you get my meaning.'

'You aren't suggesting that—' Rose exclaimed.

'Oh no, I'm saying that you should take precautions.' Flo lowered her voice. 'She seems a little simple – I fear she could be easily led astray and taken advantage of. Rose, you're frowning. You do know what I'm talking about?'

'I'm afraid that I do.' She blushed. She didn't know exactly what happened between a man and a woman – Arthur never had enlightened her about the bedsprings – but she understood how easily a young woman – Ma, for example – could be ruined by a liaison out of wedlock. She assumed that their mother had had a choice, but Rose was quite sure that Flo was referring to a situation where Minnie wouldn't be allowed to say no.

Rose couldn't bear the thought of anyone hurting her sister again. In spite of their occasional differences, she needed her. Without her, she would lie down, close her eyes and hope to die.

That evening when they were back at the barrow under the hedge with the blankets draped over the top, Minnie sewed two handkerchiefs together by moonlight.

'That's for you to stop the dust getting up your nose.'

'Thank you,' Rose said, touched by her sister's kindness. 'As soon as we can, we'll find something better, I promise.'

Minnie looked at her. Rose knew what she was thinking. Don't make promises you can't keep.

What would they do at the end of the summer when the evenings drew in and the weather was no good for brickmaking? She thought of the times when she had sneaked stale bread out for the ducks, how Ma had warned her to waste not, want not. What would she give to have plenty, with enough spare for a bread pudding, succulent with raisins in the centre, crispy on the outside, and packed with mixed spice? All she could taste now, though, was waste and brick dust.

Chapter Twenty-Two

Gentleman or Rogue?

The next day it was raining. The dust was set and wouldn't sift through the holes. The kindling wouldn't light under the clamps, and a fierce easterly wind blew across the brickfields. Rose prayed that the rain would stop and the sun would break through the clouds, but it continued to pour down, turning the brickfield to a clay sludge that stuck to her boots and dragged down the hem of her skirts.

Having waited until their clothes were sodden, the men and the women gave up and set off home.

'I expect the gaffer and 'is men will be on the booze later,' Flo said, but Rose didn't care. What about their money? She couldn't afford to lose a single day's income.

'You get good days and bad days, Rose,' she went on. 'You need the money? Well, we all do. When I miss a day or two on the brickfield, I go hungry so my boys can have full bellies. It's a hard life, but when it gets terrible bad, you can do as Hope does and go down the wharf. You can earn a few pennies there.'

Rose felt her stomach turn with disgust.

'I've not tried it yet, but she says it i'n't so bad now she has some regular fellows.'

'You wouldn't do it.'

'I would if it was the only way I could feed my boys.'

'Where is their pa?' Rose asked.

'He's missing, lost at sea.' A tear trickled down Flo's cheek, mingling with the rain.

'I'm sorry. I didn't mean to upset you.'

''E's bin gone three summers, but there you go.' She shrugged. 'What can I do about it except pray that 'e's at peace in Davy Jones's Locker?'

'I haven't heard of that,' Rose said, frowning.

'It's another name for the bottom of the sea.'

Rose shivered. It would be a cold, dark place, filled with monsters and strangling fronds of weed, but she couldn't help wondering if it would be a kinder place than the brickfields of Faversham.

'I've spoken to my landlord, old Poddy,' Flo went on. 'I'm lodging near Abbeyfield, and there's a small room in the attic if you'd like it, but you'll have to decide soon, or it'll be snapped up.'

'Well, thank you. If it's still available next week, we'll take it.'

'Rose,' Minnie nudged her. 'Can't we take it now? Everything in the barrow is soaked through.'

'We can't until we've been paid.'

'Suit yourself,' Flo said.

'I really am grateful – I'm not just saying it. I don't want you to feel offended ...' She bit her lip. 'You have a heart of gold, thinking of me and Minnie like this.'

'It's all right, ducks. I understand. Just bear it in mind. It i'n't much fun being homeless. People say there's virtue in looking at the stars at night, but most of the time there's too much cloud to see 'em. And the fresh air is supposed to be good for you, except that when you're sleeping near the water, you can't help breathing in the foul vapours. Only the other day, they found a mother and her littl'un along the bank over there' – she pointed along the creek – 'dead as doornails. They looked like they were sleeping,

315

but they were gorn into the hands of the Lord. Someone sent for the coffin from the Union and had 'em buried in a paupers' grave.'

'Why didn't the mother seek help from the poorhouse?' Rose asked. 'What a terrible thing to have happened to an innocent child.'

'At first we thought they was murdered, but the doctor said no, they expired from the bad air getting into their chests,' Flo explained. 'People who knew her said the mother was a lunatic – she'd been directed to the Union, but she didn't get there. I reckon it would 'ave bin her salvation.'

Rose wondered if she'd been too addled to find her way, or if she'd made the choice to die beside the creek rather than suffer the shame of accepting the hospitality of the poorhouse. What would she have done in that situation? Her grandmother had chosen the latter, and Rose was grateful for that, because if she hadn't, she might well not have been born.

The rain stopped and the sun crept out from behind the clouds as they made their way back to the barrow. Rose pulled the oilcloth from over the top and spread it out on the bushes to dry.

'As soon as we're paid, we'll rent a room, I promise,' she said, feeling a little more cheerful as steam began to rise from the rest of the blankets and clothes she'd put out. 'Minnie, pick some of that mint over there. I have a fancy for some tea.' She lit a small fire, warmed the water they'd carried back from the pump in the town, and made tea with fresh leaves of wild mint.

'This must be what heaven is like,' Minnie said, lying back in the barrow and looking up at the sky as they ate bread and jam.

'I hope so.'

'I think it must be a place where the sun is always shining,' Minnie smiled.

The next day, the sun came out again, and they went back to work at Kingsfield. Abel paid their wages and extended Rose's credit for another week, so she had just enough for the rent on the room in Flo's lodging-house.

'You're lucky – I've had another family interested in the place,' Flo's landlord said, showing them up three flights of stairs to the attic. It was hot, there was no fireplace and the privy was at the end of the garden, but it would do, Rose thought. Beggars couldn't be choosers.

'How much is it?' she asked.

Old Poddy named a price. 'I can't go any lower.'

'Are you sure you won't take a shilling less, half a shilling?'

'You're wasting my time,' he said crossly.

'It's a high price to pay, but we'll take it, thank you. I'm sorry if I've caused you offence, but' – she smiled – 'I had to try.'

'I know you did, but I have to make a living too,' he said, holding out his hand for payment.

Rose gave him almost all of her money in return for the key before she and Minnie went to fetch the barrow from where they had left it among the bushes near the gravel pits.

On their way back, they bought leftovers – cheese, bread and broken biscuits – from the stalls at knock-down prices because it was the end of the day. At the house, they parked the barrow at the rear where the privy stank and a big fat pig terrorised them, chasing them around the garden before they unpacked their belongings and carried them up the stairs.

Rose opened the window to air the room and made the bed while Minnie prepared a meal from their purchases.

'I've cut the cheese into the thinnest slices possible,' she said, chuckling. 'Don't you think that looks like a dinner fit for Queen Victoria herself?'

'It looks … wonderful.' Rose sat on the edge of the bed and they shared the meagre offering, pretending it was boiled beef in gravy, the scent of which was drifting up through the house from another room.

'Let's leave our clothes on,' Minnie whispered when they were getting ready for bed.

Rose forced a smile. 'We'll pretend we are wearing our best silk nightgowns.'

'And this is our grand house – just like Churt House in Overshill.'

'I think that might be a stretch of the imagination too far.'

They prayed for their dearly departed parents, and for their brothers, and Aunt Marjorie, and then huddled together on the lumpy mattress with another person's smell on the pillows and their stains on the coverlet. It was painful to recall how comfortable they had been at Willow Place and how far they had fallen.

The next morning, they ate cold porridge flavoured with a sprinkling of sugar, from three days before.

'Eat, Rose,' Minnie urged her, handing her the spoon. 'You must eat. That's what you've been telling me.'

She had no appetite. She picked up a spoonful and let it slide back into the bowl. Arthur could have used it as mortar for his bricklaying, she thought.

'You have it.' She pushed the bowl towards her sister. 'Your need is greater than mine.'

'You are wasting away.'

Rose looked at her arms. It was true. She was all skin and bone.

'You're pining for someone,' Minnie went on.

'I beg your pardon,' Rose said, glancing up.

'I wonder who that could be ...'

'I'm not missing anyone in particular. I'm sorry I let Sam down and I'm a little ashamed that I haven't thought of him since.' She'd wanted to tell him face to face that they were leaving Overshill, but when she'd called at his house, his ma had told her that he'd gone out for the evening.

'I was thinking about Freddie, not Sam.'

'We'll have less of that kind of talk, thank you. I worry about Donald, and miss living at the cottage, that's all.'

'I think you'd do better if it wasn't for me holding you back.'

'You must never say that again. I've done what anyone would have done. None of this is your fault.'

Minnie returned to the subject of the state of Rose's heart. 'You were happy when Mr Wild came to call on us.'

'He was good company, but he didn't mean anything in particular by visiting us when he was passing.'

'You mean it suits you to think that his attentions towards you were nothing special?' Minnie leaned her hands on the table. 'He offered you a place at Churt House.'

'Yes, a situation, paid employment. He didn't ask me to walk out with him, nothing like that.'

'Perhaps he would have done if you'd given him a chance.'

'He is a gentleman of great means as far as we know. He can have absolutely no interest in me – he will marry someone of the same standing as him.' Rose wasn't entirely convinced that this was likely. He had neither title nor place in English society, and people were suspicious of him. She did feel sore about Freddie, though. That night, she shed a silent tear over what might have been.

As the summer passed, their hands grew rough and calloused as they continued to work in the dust and dirt. On a Friday three months later, Rose and Minnie joined the line of women and children waiting to be paid as usual. Abel sat at the table on the brickfield, doling out their money according to the notes in the ledger in front of him, now and again brushing the paper with his hand so he could read what he had written through the dust. Another man, his second-in-command whom they knew as Stamp, stood at his shoulder, looking out for trouble.

Minnie shuffled forward in the queue. Abel counted some coins into her hand. She tucked them into the pocket of her skirt and stepped aside to wait for Rose.

Abel looked at Rose as he dropped her money, one shilling at a time, on to her outstretched palm.

'Is that it?' she said, looking at the sorry amount. It wasn't much of a return for a week's grafting.

'Let me see,' – he ran his finger across one line in the ledger – 'it's what you're due minus deductions. Unfortunately, you're experiencing diminishing returns with the rise in the rate of interest.' He tipped his head to one side, looking sly. 'Didn't I mention that before?'

'No, you didn't. Sir, this isn't right. I've been paying you back.'

'Not quickly enough, I'm afraid. That's the trouble with taking advantage of credit when it's offered.'

She was caught in a trap, she realised. Abel had never had any intention of letting her pay off her debt. She was devastated.

'Please, I beg you to keep to your word and let me pay according to our original agreement.'

'We never said anything about fixing the interest rate,' he said. 'Come on, miss, I've been good to you, giving you work and lending you money.'

'I'm very grateful, but I was caught between the devil and the deep blue sea at the time.' She thought quickly, calculating how much she'd need for the rent on Monday. There wasn't enough. She could ask him for more, but that would mean even less pay next week. She and Minnie were in a precarious state and she didn't know what to do.

'Are we done? Only there are others waiting.' He jumped in, taking advantage of her hesitation. 'You wish to borrow more to tide you over ...'

She nodded. She had rent to pay. Rent day wasn't called Black Monday for nothing.

'I have a suggestion,' he said in a low voice, and seeing his eyes turn greedily to her sister, Rose began to tremble.

'No, not that,' she said sharply.

Abel shrugged. 'It's up to you. I'll 'ave her one day, though.'

Blushing with shame, Rose turned away and joined Minnie.

'What was the gaffer talking about?' she asked.

'Oh, nothing ...' Rose changed her mind. What was the point in hiding their predicament? 'We are short of money to pay the rent and I don't know what to do.'

'We'll manage,' Minnie put her arm through hers. 'We always do.'

They walked back to the house in Abbeyfield that evening as the sun set. There was a nip in the air presaging autumn. Soon the brickfields would close down for the winter, then where would they go?

'You will be careful in your dealings with the gaffer, won't you?' Rose said as they went up the narrow stairs to their room.

'Why do you say that? I like him – he's been kind to us. He gave me extra today. Look.' Minnie pulled the coins out of her pocket. 'An extra shilling. The other day when we were waiting for the dirt to come off the barge, he showed me a cat – she's made a nest for her kittens under one of the upturned boats, the broken one down the far end of the wharf where the mud starts.'

'You didn't say.'

'I didn't like to. I know you don't think much of him, but the kittens – they were so pretty, all black and white, like they're made of patchwork.' Minnie gazed at her. 'I didn't do anything wrong.'

'I'm sure you didn't, but I don't trust that man. He is conniving and wicked. Minnie, do you remember what Pa used to say about gentlemen? Abel isn't one and I'm afraid that he intends to do you harm.'

'Oh Rose, you have gone mad,' Minnie sighed. 'He wouldn't dream of hurting me. He's nothing like our aunt.'

'Just promise me you won't go anywhere else with him, no matter what story he gives you.'

'The kittens are real. They aren't a story. Come with me and see them for yourself. Please … then you'll know I'm telling the truth about Abel.'

'I don't doubt that there are kittens. It's the gaffer I'm worried about.' Rose noticed how Minnie set her mouth in a stubborn straight line before she responded.

'Abel's told me he'll help us if we get into trouble paying the rent. He's a good man. He looks after us.'

Trying to change Minnie's opinion of the gaffer was hopeless, Rose realised, because she'd already been taken in by his lies. There was only one thing for it – she wouldn't let Minnie out of her sight.

Life continued at Kingsfield through the end of August and into September. Any hope they'd had that they would be able to visit Donald again had to be put aside for now in the struggle for survival. The work was dirty, dusty and poorly paid, and they could only just make ends meet, what with Minnie struggling to sieve the dust from dawn to dusk, and Rose trying to meet the repayments of Abel's loan, which she'd been forced into at the beginning, and was now turning out to be a noose around her neck. No matter what she did, she never had enough money to cover the interest in full, and the amount outstanding was rising slowly and steadily every week. She'd made a mistake in accepting his terms.

The worst thing about the brickfield, though, was that she couldn't get herself clean. When she returned to their lodgings, exhausted at the end of the day, there was only cold water from the pump and a tiny, ever-diminishing piece of soap that they'd brought with them from the cottage to wash with. She did her best with their under-clothes, washing them and hanging them on the bedposts, not wanting to expose the patches and frayed hems to their fellow tenants. She still had her pride. If she lost that, she'd have lost everything.

Minnie was beginning to look unwell, her eyes sinking back in their sockets, her skin growing paler and her feet breaking out in sores. It wouldn't be long before there came a point when Rose couldn't cover the rent for the room to keep her sister safe and warm at night. She thought of writing to Arthur to beg for help, but she had no forwarding address.

Another week came and went. The days were beginning to shorten and the nights to draw in, a reminder that the season was coming to an end and their situation would only get worse.

On the Friday morning, Rose woke with Minnie snoring beside her as usual.

'Minnie,' she whispered, reaching out and gently shaking her shoulder. 'It's time to get up.'

'Do we have to?' she mumbled before raising her head and going on more cheerfully, 'Can't we wait until our maid knocks on the door, bringing hot chocolate and roasted pheasant?'

Rose smiled, in spite of her worries. 'Come on, stir your stumps.'

After eating a sweet plum and a bite of stale bread, they walked to Kingsfield. On the way, Rose glanced up at the speckled gulls that were crying from the roofs of the buildings.

'They're waiting for their ma and pa to bring them fish,' Minnie said wistfully.

Rose turned at the sound of Flo's voice as they continued along the street.

'Morning! Look at you two scurrying ahead,' she said, sending her boys in front of her. 'You didn't wait for us.'

'I thought you'd already left,' Rose said, and they hurried together through the gate under an enormous pale blue sky as the last of the mist cleared, leaving streaks of pink while the sun peered above the horizon, turning the dirty expanse of the brickfield to gold.

Minnie dropped back to chatter to a couple of the younger women who had found their way to the brick-fields not long after their own arrival: two friends who had drifted into Faversham when they had been unable to find casual work on the farms.

'Minnie, stop gossiping,' Rose called. 'It's time we got started.'

'Don't nag, Rose,' Minnie called back. 'I'll be with you soon enough.'

Rose decided not to take her to task in front of everyone for the way she'd answered her back – it could wait until later.

With the mud sticking to her boots and the scent of the sea and dirt sharp in her nostrils, Rose took her place. One of Flo's boys – Trouble, they called him – shovelled dirt into her sieve and she got to work.

Knock, knock, knock. The damp from the early autumnal mist made the sifting a little slow to start with, but she soon got into the rhythm. She was stronger now, although her arms still ached by the end of the day. Minnie found it more of a trial than she did.

She glanced along the semi-circle. Where was Minnie? Still talking, she thought resentfully. Had she forgotten how badly they needed the money? Rose hadn't talked too much of her concerns about losing the room because she hadn't wanted to upset her sister, but Minnie must have realised how dire their circumstances were as they'd been existing on porridge, bread and cheese, plums and water for two weeks.

She caught sight of the two young women at the end of the row, and frowned. No Minnie. Her pulse tapped against her temple, fast and insistent. Where was she? She dropped the sieve at her feet and jumped up. Where was the gaffer?

A sensation of dread slipped down the back of her neck like a cold key. How many times had she told Minnie to keep in plain sight?

'What's up, ducks?' Flo reached for Rose's arm to pull herself up.

'Have you seen my sister? Please tell me you've seen her.' She was panicking now. 'He's taken her,' she added, looking round wildly. The gang were standing about, smoking and drinking tea. In the distance, another group of men were labouring, pulling down a stack of cured bricks and carting them to the wharf.

'What are you talking about?' Hope exclaimed.

'Abel. He's got my sister!'

'Hey, calm yourself. You're making too much of it. You know how 'e treats her special. He's like a father figure, taking her to see how them kittens 'ave grown,' Hope said.

'It's all right, Rose,' Flo said. 'He had some fish trimmin's for them this morning. That's where they've gone.'

Reluctantly, Rose sat down again, looking and listening for her sister.

'They should be back by now,' she said, thinking she could smell the stench of rotten fish in the air. 'Something's wrong.'

'The gaffer's an 'ard master, but I can't imagine that 'e'd do any 'arm to our dear Minnie.'

'He would. He told me he would have her one day,' Rose exclaimed.

'Why didn't you say somethin'?'

'I warned Minnie to watch out for him, but I couldn't bring myself to speak of it to anyone else – not even you, Flo – because of the shame I felt at the way he spoke about my sister. This is all my fault!'

'Of course it isn't. You 'aven't done nothin' wrong.'

'I'm going to look for her.'

'I'll come with you,' Flo said.

'Don't worry,' Rose said, aware that her friend could ill afford to pause in her toil.

'You can say what you like, but I'm with you.' Flo got up again, and together they headed down to the wharf. 'Watch out,' she warned, pulling Rose out of the way of one of the men who was struggling towards a barge with a pallet of bricks on his back.

'Do you know where these kittens are?' Rose wished she'd taken more interest in Minnie's enthusiasm for them. If she had gone with her to see them, there would have been no reason for her to accompany Abel.

'That way, I think, where the boat's turned over.' Flo pointed past the oyster bawleys as a gull screamed, except it wasn't a bird … it was the heart-rending cry of a human being. A girl.

'Minnie,' Rose screamed back. 'Where are you?'

'They're over there somewhere.'

Rose and Flo set off at a run, passing the warehouses and following the bank until they reached the path where the boat's hull stuck up from the reeds. Behind it, they found Abel fastening his trousers and three paces beyond him, Minnie standing in the mud, her dress torn and her pale breast exposed.

'What have you done to her?' Rose cried.

'Nothin' that she didn't ask for,' the gaffer said.

Rose turned to Minnie. 'Has he hurt you? Oh Lord above, he's had his way with you!'

'No, he hasn't.' Minnie kept shaking her head and repeatedly clutching at her bodice, trying to pull it up to protect what was left of her modesty. 'We were only kissing, that's all.' She looked at Abel. 'That's right, isn't it? Just a little peck on the lips. And I said he could do it,' she went on fiercely.

'Why is your dress torn then?'

'It was the cat – she gave me a scratch for feeding her kittens. Abel kindly looked at my wounds. Rose, he was being a gentleman.'

Rose almost laughed out loud. 'A gentleman! He is a cad to bring you here under false pretences and expose you to ruination, because no matter what you say, your actions speak louder than words.' She turned to the gaffer. 'You will be judged for this.'

'Oh, listen to you,' Abel said, meeting her eye. 'Your sister's told you what happened.'

'I think you must marry her now,' Rose said, refusing to be cowed.

He laughed. 'Marry? I have a wife, four daughters and a babe in arms back at home.'

This revelation shocked Rose to the core, and it must have shown on her face because Abel continued, 'Life is tough and short, and you have to get the most out of it that you can.' He glanced back at Minnie. 'Take notice of your sister – no harm's been done.'

'Just leave her alone in future! If I see you anywhere near her ...'

'You'll what?' he said, grinning now. 'Don't worry your little head about it. I won't be going near her again.'

Minnie uttered a sharp cry. 'Abel, what are you saying?'

'There'll be no more kittens and walks by the creek.' His voice was gentle, as if he did have some affection for her. 'Here, let's cover you up.' He picked up her shawl, which was lying in a puddle, wrung the water out and placed it around Minnie's shoulders. 'There you are.' He scowled at Rose. 'Nothing happened! Sisters, eh!'

Rolling his eyes, Abel strolled away back towards the wharf. Rose watched him retreating, filled with hate. How dare he hurt her innocent sister! She was only a child. Her ire rose like bile in her throat as she recalled her aunt's treatment of Minnie, and now this. All she wanted to do was hurt him back, punch and bite and kick ...

She felt Flo's hand on her shoulder, keeping her from running after him.

'It will do no good,' she murmured. 'You can't win – 'e's the gaffer and he's like the king rat who can do what 'e likes down here in 'is kingdom of filth and brick dust. If you go after 'im, he'll 'ave you off the site in a second. Look after your sister.'

'We're leaving,' Rose said firmly.

'You can't do that. You'll end up at the Union.'

'I don't care. I really don't care any more. Anything has to be better than this.'

'I'm sorry, Rose. I thought you had more sense.'

'I can't bear the idea of watching that man walking up and down, giving his orders, and all the time thinking of what he's done to my sister.' *And how he demeans me whenever he hands out our wages, and reminds me of my folly in accepting his loan*, she wanted to add, but didn't. He had planned this. He had set it up from the start. 'He says he won't touch her again, but I don't trust him.' She paused and reached out for Minnie's hand. 'Come with me. We're going home.'

'I'm not going anywhere.' Minnie wrenched her hand away, spitting like a cat in a fury. 'Why couldn't you have left us alone?'

'You will come with me, or I'll leave you here and never return,' Rose cried. 'You can stay, mired in the mud and filth you're making of your reputation by lowering yourself to associate with that man – a married man, I must point out.'

Minnie let out a sob.

'Or you can walk with me, with your head held high, back to our lodgings where we will take stock.' The words 'take stock' reminded her of Ma – it was something she would have said.

'You would leave me behind? Disown your own sister? After all we've been through?'

'It's your choice.' Trembling, Rose waited, gazing out across the flat grey expanse of the estuary where a barge's red sails hove to and started to head up the creek. What was Minnie's answer going to be? The barge moved closer and it was almost upon them when she felt her sister's fingers tangling with hers. She didn't look at her. She merely squeezed her hand tight and started trudging back along the path, following Flo past the warehouses to the wharf where the brick-makers and bargemen stopped their work to stand and stare.

She led Minnie to where Abel had lit a fire to burn some of the rubbish, took off their aprons and dropped them into the flames. The gaffer shouted and cursed, and came running to pick them up, beating out the smoke that had risen from the leather.

'You're a pair of ignoramuses,' he growled. 'Sod off. I never want to see you again.'

'The feeling is mutual,' Rose said, her heart thundering in her chest. She turned and walked away with Minnie, as he aimed a volley of unrepeatable epithets after them. When they reached the street, she let her sister have a piece of her mind.

'What did you think you were doing? What would Ma and Pa have thought of you? Didn't it cross your mind that I'd be worried sick, finding you gone missing?'

Without Abel to prompt her, Minnie's fight seemed to have gone out of her.

'Rose, I'm sorry.' She burst into tears. 'I don't mind him – he's been kind to me. I didn't necessarily like him in the way he wanted me to, but he said he'd give me a shilling if I … I thought if I closed my eyes …'

'For a shilling? You would value your life that cheaply? You could have been strangled and left for dead!'

'I know how it is. A shilling is better than nothing when Black Monday's almost upon us.'

'I'm sorry too. I didn't realise ...' Wracked with guilt, Rose stopped and put her arm around her sister's back, pulling her close and stroking her hair. She felt the familiar shape of her bones under her shawl, and saw the fresh red bruises on her arms. 'He didn't actually force himself upon you?'

'No. All we had was a kiss and a cuddle ...'

'That's a relief then.' They didn't have to worry that she was with child, at least, Rose thought, but she decided to check with Flo later, just to be sure. 'Promise me you'll never go off with anyone again.'

Minnie nodded. 'What are we going to do?'

'We have three days to work that out. We'll think of something.'

She blamed herself – she knew how some of the men stared and made comments about them, but generally, they'd been respectful, and she'd felt able to relax in the company of the other women. Having been shocked out of her youthful complacency by Baxter's treatment by his desperate father, she had thought she'd been perfectly aware of the dangers on the streets and how to handle them, but it turned out she had been wrong. She harked back to life at Willow Place with Ma and Pa and how they had protected them. She didn't think she would ever feel truly safe again.

Chapter Twenty-Three

As the Crow Flies

Back at their lodgings, Rose lay down on the bed, filled with regret and worry, and thinking she would never sleep again but, exhausted by the morning's events, she eventually dozed off. Later, she felt a hand on her shoulder.

'What's the time?' she said, stirring.

'About five o'clock. I've brought you tea and cold beef,' Minnie said in the quietest, most contrite of whispers.

Rose sat up, rubbing sleep from her eyes. 'How did you manage that when you promised not to leave my sight?'

'I'm sorry.'

'It's no use apologising.'

'I only slipped out to the market to see what I could pick up cheap.'

'How could you after what happened this morning? You're as bad as Donald.' Rose frowned, her mind filled with doubt. What had Minnie been up to? Where had she found the money for food?

'I took a shilling from your purse and a few pence from the little bit I've been saving to buy thread to put towards the patchwork. Please don't be cross with me,' Minnie said, as though reading Rose's mind. She sat on the edge of the bed and handed her a cup of hot milky tea. 'I'm trying to make up for—'

332

'Thank you,' Rose interrupted. The cup was crazed with cracks and the contents smelled odd, as if the milk might have been off.

'Can you find it in your heart to forgive me?'

'Of course I can.' She sipped at the tea, watching Minnie arrange slices of cold beef on two bread rolls, one each. She was starving.

As she ate, she thought of Arthur, wondering where he was and how they could ever begin to find him. He would help them. He'd helped them before. She thought of Mr Wild and her missed opportunity to work for him, and then of Donald, but that only roused her to anger again, because if he hadn't stolen Mrs Greenleaf's pies, Minnie wouldn't have dreamt of selling herself to anyone, let alone a cur like Abel.

'We have to find work,' she said.

'Where? What can we do? Look at us in our rags. Who will take us on looking like this?' Minnie paused, her eyes downcast. 'I wish we were back at Willow Place when all we had to do was get up in the morning and go to school with Ma. I didn't like the lessons – I felt stupid because I had to sit with the littl'uns, but' – she brightened as though she was back to her normal self – 'I loved skipping and playing hoops and British Bulldog at break-times.'

'Perhaps we could consider selling the patchwork. That would bring in a little cash to tide us over. We'd have to change the inscription, or trim it off.'

'Oh no,' Minnie's eyes filled with tears. 'It belongs rightfully to Arthur and Tabby.'

'We could make another one. I know it wouldn't be the same, but—'

'We can't afford to buy any more scraps.' Leaving her food untouched, Minnie went to the window and looked out, her fingers gripping the edge of the sill. 'We're trapped.'

They were indeed caught, caged by poverty, Rose thought, as a lassitude spread through her limbs.

Minnie took a turn to sleep on the bed. Every so often, she shivered and shouted out. Rose touched her forehead – the heat of Minnie's body seemed to ooze from the pores of her skin. Was she suffering from a chill, or succumbing to the vapours that rose from the creek? Was it something Abel had done to her? Or was it – she pulled the top of her blouse aside – to do with the cat? There were scratches, red raw, raised and angry across her chest and collarbone.

Rose ran down to see if Flo was back from the brickfield, hoping she would have some idea of what was wrong with Minnie. To her relief, she was in her room with her boys.

'What is it?' Flo said, running upstairs with her to the attic.

'It's my sister – she's ill and I don't know what to do.'

'So she is.' Flo knelt at the bedside. 'Minnie, dear, can you hear me? It's me, Flo.'

'I can hear you. There's no need to shout in my ear like that,' Minnie muttered.

'That's a good girl. Tell me where you feel poorly.'

'My throat,' Minnie said with a small gasp.

'Lie still then. Rose, she needs beer – a good dark stout, followed by some beef broth and an inhalation of Friar's Balsam. Don't worry.' Flo fumbled in her pocket for her purse and pulled out a few coins, forcing them into Rose's hands. 'You can pay me back later.'

'I don't know how to thank you. I don't know when I'll be able to find the money.'

'It's all right. I have a little put by, so it can wait. I trust you to do the right thing by me.' She smiled. 'Go on. Fetch what you need. I'll sit with her until you get back.'

Rose walked swiftly into town and bought according to her friend's instructions. When she returned, she poured a little stout for Minnie to drink.

'Ugh, that's horrid,' she said. 'I don't like it.'

'You have to have some – it'll give you some of your strength back,' Flo said sternly. 'You'll soon get used to the taste.' To prove it, she took a big swig from the bottle, then wiped her mouth with the back of her hand before handing the bottle to Rose. 'You look as though you could do with some of it too. It's a very fine porter. Now, what about this broth?'

'I have a portion of cold beef tea,' Rose said, but her sister refused to take it, rolling over and closing her eyes. Flo sipped at it instead, while they watched over Minnie.

'Flo,' Rose whispered when she thought her sister was asleep, 'I wonder if you can tell me something. Actually, I'm ashamed at having to ask, but with my mother dead, I've no idea …'

'Go on, spit it out.'

'It's about the birds and the bees, and what happened to Minnie today.'

'Oh, that.' She cocked one eyebrow and tucked a greasy lock of hair behind her ear. 'Dear, innocent Rose, who's never been kissed.'

'I'm worried because Minnie said nothing passed between her and the gaffer, but could she … is there any way she could be with child?'

Flo chuckled. 'Well, let's see. If she were telling the truth, then no, it's impossible, but if she were lying, then yes.'

'I don't think she'd lie,' Rose said, uncertain.

'I might if I were her. There are lots of reasons why, the main one being that she doesn't want to upset you. What the eye doesn't see, the heart don't grieve over, and all that.'

'I suppose so, but I don't like to think that she can't tell me.'

'I shouldn't worry. If 'e did have his way with her' – Rose winced at Flo's frank way of putting it – 'then nobody but 'im and the girl will know.'

'Unless she is with child. What then?'

'You cross that bridge if you come to it. It isn't inevitable, and there are things that can be done. There are wise women in the villages around here who can help.'

Rose thought of Mrs Greenleaf at Overshill and shook her head, praying that it wouldn't come to that. Moving across to the bed, she touched her sister's brow – the fever had subsided, at least for now. Poor Minnie was too simple a soul to lie – she was being silly, not believing her story.

'I should get some sleep while you can,' Flo said.

'Thank you,' Rose said, grateful for her presence.

'Don't think anything of it. You'd have done the same for me if it had been one of my boys who'd got 'imself into trouble.'

It crossed Rose's mind to ask Flo if she could help her with the rent, but she decided against it. It wasn't fair when she had little enough already. It seemed that by Monday, the Union would be their only hope.

When Flo had gone, she slipped under the sheet alongside her sister and closed her eyes.

She woke twice in the night to attend to Minnie, who drank a little water and used the pot rather than dragging herself downstairs and out to the privy. After that, Rose fell back into bed and sank into a deep sleep, only to be woken in the morning as dawn broke by Flo shouting through the keyhole.

'There's a gentleman and 'is servant asking for you! They're waiting downstairs. Old Poddy won't let them in.'

'I don't know any gentlemen,' Rose said, getting up. With a glance back at Minnie, who stirred and raised her head from the pillow, she opened the door.

'They have two fine white horses, and another one with them.' Flo rushed in and pulled down the blanket that Rose had hung across the window. 'Look at them – they're a sight for sore eyes.'

They were indeed, Rose thought, staring at the two steeds that could have come straight out of a fairy tale, and another brown one which looked a little sunken in the back.

'The gentleman is a handsome fellow. You never told us you were so well connected.'

'We aren't.' Rose's heart beat a little faster.

'It's Arthur,' she heard Minnie say from behind her. Had Arthur come to find them at last?

'He has never sat on a horse in his life. What did you say to him, Flo?'

'I told him – in return for a tidy sum, I will admit – that you are indeed lodging here. He wishes to speak with you. What are you waiting for, Rose? This could be your salvation.'

She glanced at Minnie, who could hardly contain herself.

'We are saved,' she kept saying.

'We don't know that for certain. If it's Arthur, then yes, but if it's anyone else …'

'Who else can it be?'

'He says his name is Freddie,' Flo said.

'No!' Rose couldn't believe it. How could she bear to have him see her like this, brought so low on the brick-fields of Faversham, her hands rough and her clothes stained and stinking? Why would Mr Wild come for them?

'I told you he was fond of you,' Minnie said.

'There must be more to it than that,' Rose said as a fight broke out on the stairs.

'Unhand me, man, or I won't be responsible for my actions!'

'Mr Wild!' Rose exclaimed as he appeared in the doorway. 'Please, we aren't respectable.'

'I'll avert my eyes, I promise,' he said. 'Grab your clothes, pack your belongings and come with me. Now! That scoundrel, the Irishman and a couple of his men, are outside wanting their money. Do as I say and we can be away.'

Flo stuffed their possessions into Pa's old suitcase while Rose dressed, then found Minnie's clothes for her. She paused, noticing the bruise on Freddie's face for the first time. 'What happened?'

'I got thumped – my fault. Come on. Come back to Overshill with me.'

'We can't. It's extraordinarily kind of you to come and find us, but we are strangers to you.'

'Hardly,' he smiled. 'You gave me your word that you'd take up your place as my housekeeper when I returned from my travels. Lo and behold, by the time I got back, you'd vanished.'

'You must have heard what my brother did by now,' she said quietly. 'There are other, more suitably qualified candidates for the position.'

'I don't care about your brother, Rose. It's a good thing I turned up here when I did. You aren't safe and you're almost dead on your feet.' He moved close to her. 'I will brook no argument.'

'Where will we live?'

'You will stay with me, of course.'

'I have no wish to be beholden to you.'

'You have accepted help before,' he said softly.

She flushed. How did he know?

'The money you assumed was from your brother ...'

Light dawned. 'It was you? You didn't care to enlighten me when I went on about how wonderful Arthur was.'

'I have more than enough to spare – it was a mere drop in the ocean.'

'I wouldn't have accepted it if I'd known it was from you,' she said. 'It is the principle of it.'

'I think you are too deep in the mire to worry about principles,' he retorted.

'Oh, I shall worry about Arthur now.'

'When we've got you and Minnie back safely, we'll look for him. I have contacts in London.'

She turned to fasten the ribbon on Minnie's bonnet, but her sister stumbled and fell into her arms. Freddie dived forward and took her weight.

'She is ill?'

'Yes,' Rose admitted.

'All the more reason not to hang around here any longer. She needs a doctor. Let me carry her down the stairs.'

'Rose, you bring the suitcase and I'll bring the rest,' Flo said, and they struggled down the wooden steps to the bottom of the stairs, where old Poddy was waiting.

'Good riddance, I reckon,' he said. 'I can't be doing with this aggravation.'

Outside, Abel and his men were in an altercation with two others, while Freddie's servant – Rose wasn't sure who he was as she didn't recognise him – held on to the horses.

'You will ride back,' Freddie said.

'We don't know how,' Rose said.

'You can learn. It is the fashion for a lady to ride side-saddle, but today you will ride astride with me.' Freddie's manservant strapped their luggage to the brown horse before vaulting into the saddle of one of the white horses. Freddie lifted Minnie up behind him.

'Put your arms around Jack's waist and hang on,' he said firmly. He mounted his horse and held out his hand. Reluctantly, Rose took it, shocked by the strength in his fingers as he pulled her up, helping her to spring, in spite of the weight of her skirts, into the saddle behind him.

'Let me at them – those whores owe me!' Abel shouted from where he was being restrained by two men on the other side of the street.

'Ignore him,' Freddie muttered. 'Hold on tight, Rose.'

Closing her eyes, she reached for his waist and grabbed on to his jacket.

'Goodbye,' she heard Flo call after them, as Freddie spurred his horse forward, the sudden lurch throwing her against his back. She thrust her arms around his waist and held on for dear life as they headed through the streets with Abel bellowing all kinds of threats and epithets after them.

'I'm so sorry, Mr Wild,' Rose tried to say, but her breath wouldn't come fast enough for her to form the words.

'What a load of ruffians!' Freddie exclaimed as he slowed his horse to a steady trot.

Holding her arms around his warm body and breathing in his scent, Rose turned to check on Minnie who was almost asleep, resting her head against the servant's shoulder. Every so often the third horse would put its ears back and kick out as though it resented its burden.

'Do you think those men will follow us?' Rose asked.

'They've got better things to do than chase us back to Overshill,' Freddie said. 'We must push on, though – Minnie needs to see a doctor as soon as possible. Are you all right there? You're almost squeezing the life out of me.'

'Oh, I'm sorry,' she said, trying to relax her grip.

'Don't be – I find it strangely comforting.'

Rose allowed herself a small smile on hearing the humour in his voice, but if the truth be told, she was scared for her sister.

'How long do you think it will take to get to Overshill?' she asked as they followed the road towards Canterbury before turning off towards Selling.

'Not long – it isn't far as the crow flies,' he said, but it seemed like an age, riding past the woods and orchards, and the hop gardens where the last of the hops were being picked. In the distance Rose heard the whistle of a steam engine on the London to Dover line, reminding her of the family's fateful trip to Whitstable. Glad that Freddie couldn't see her crying, she clung on tighter, more for comfort than necessity, for the horse's pace had settled to a gentle walk.

Eventually, they took the lane to Overshill and rode up the long drive across the rising parkland to Churt House.

The horses' hooves clattered across the cobbles as Freddie took them into the stableyard. He jumped down and helped Rose from the horse's back before lifting Minnie from the other steed to allow his man to dismount. Together, the two men put Minnie's arms across their shoulders and carried her into the rear entrance of the house. Rose followed them along a gloomy corridor to what appeared to be the servants' hall, where Freddie and his man stopped.

'Rose, please fetch Mrs Causton,' Freddie said. 'I expect she's in the kitchen at the end of the corridor with Cook.'

'Yes, of course.' She hurried along to the next door and pushed it open to find three women engaged in various tasks in a kitchen at least four times the size of the one at Wanstall Farm.

'Mrs Causton?' Rose said.

The oldest of the three, a middle-aged lady with tightly curled dark hair and wearing a sober grey dress, looked up from a recipe book. 'That's me.'

'Mr Wild has asked me to fetch you.'

Mrs Causton addressed the cook, who was dressed in uniform: a white starched cap and apron over a black dress. 'Put some extra vegetables in the pot. Mr Wild appears to have guests.' She turned to the maid, a slender girl of about seventeen. 'Mary, come with me.'

'Yes, Mrs Causton,' the maid said, tucking a stray lock of her chestnut hair back under her cap.

Rose hurried back with Mrs Causton and the maid following behind her.

'Oh, who is this?' Mrs Causton exclaimed when she saw Minnie. 'She's sick.'

'This is Miss Minnie Cheevers and I'd like a bed made ready for her upstairs – she can share a room with her sister,' Freddie said.

'I don't think we have a suitable room, Mr Wild.'

'There's one three doors from mine. There are two beds and a washstand – we can soon find a dressing table.'

'I suppose it will have to do,' Mrs Causton said rather stiffly, before sending the maid off to find linen and pillows.

'I need someone to fetch the doctor,' Freddie said. 'Rose, could I prevail upon you to take my man's place? Jack, you can take a fresh horse and ride out from here – I believe the nearest physician is in Selling.'

Rose swapped places with Jack, taking Minnie's weight and helping to support her on their way back along the corridor. They came to a dark oak staircase and struggled up two floors to a landing, where Freddie paused for breath.

'You're doing well – you must be very strong,' he said. 'It's this way.' He pushed a door open and they entered a bedroom where Mrs Causton and the maid were already plumping pillows and straightening blankets on the beds. They stepped aside to let Rose and Freddie make Minnie comfortable on the bed closest to the window.

Rose stroked her sister's hand, but all she could do was roll her eyes and moan.

'Please, can I have some water?' she said. 'She's terribly hot.'

'I'll get it,' Freddie said, disappearing.

'I think we should light the fire to banish the damp,' Mrs Causton said. 'Mary, fetch some wood and matches. I wish we'd known about this in advance so we could have been prepared.'

'I'm sorry to be a nuisance,' Rose said.

'I shouldn't grumble, I suppose. You and your sister look as though you've been through the mill.'

As the maid and Mrs Causton continued with lighting the fire and dusting the surfaces, Freddie returned with a tray of water, tea, bread, cheese and cake.

'Thank you, but I don't think Minnie's up to eating anything,' Rose said.

'It's for you as well. You need to keep your strength up.' Freddie turned to Mrs Causton and the maid. 'That will be all for now.'

'Of course, Mr Wild,' Mrs Causton said, collecting up the dusters and box of spare matches. 'How many can we expect for dinner?'

'I'm not sure yet, but I'll let you know as soon as I can,' he said.

'I'll stay here with Minnie,' Rose said. 'I'm not going to let her out of my sight.'

Freddie excused himself, coming back with the doctor about an hour later. He stood in the doorway with his eyes averted.

'What is the history?' the doctor asked Rose, having introduced himself and examined the patient. 'When did she first show these symptoms?'

She explained that Minnie had fallen ill the day before, withholding the information about the episode with Abel, not wanting to besmirch her sister's reputation in front of Freddie. There was no need for him to know the sordid details.

'Will she get better? I need to know,' she said, her voice quavering. 'I've suffered much loss – I don't think I could bear any more.'

'I must be guarded in my prognosis as one never knows which way these cases will go. Your sister has a fever along with signs of nervous exhaustion and melancholia.'

'Will you bleed her?' Rose asked, remembering her father's futile treatment.

'Not on this occasion. I'll prescribe a tonic to be given four times a day with chicken broth, along with regular wrapping of the arms and legs with bandages soaked in cold water to drag the fever from the vital organs.'

'How will I get her to take the tonic when she's barely conscious?'

'You'll need to sit her up and pour it gently into the mouth, a little at a time. She's sleepy, not completely coma-tose.'

Rose thanked him.

'I'll return in the morning,' the doctor said, taking his leave. Freddie accompanied him downstairs, leaving Rose to carry out the doctor's instructions, aided by Mary who delivered cold water, cloths and chicken broth.

'The master told me what to bring,' she said. 'How is the patient?'

Rose's courage suddenly deserted her and she burst into tears.

344

'There, there,' the maid said, walking across to gently pat her on the back. 'Let's see what we can do. I nursed my sister back to health when she had scarlet fever – it was a miracle that she survived. We lost three others.'

'I'm sorry to hear that.' It was hardly reassuring, Rose thought, but she was grateful for Mary's presence.

That night, she couldn't sleep, getting up frequently to wrap Minnie's arms and legs with freshly cooled bandages to bring her temperature down. By morning, when the sky began to lighten through a gap between the heavy brocade curtains and the smell of toast and boiled bacon drifted up the stairs, Minnie stirred and opened her eyes.

'Where are we?' she muttered.

'Mr Wild rescued us from Faversham – we're back in Overshill.'

'Why? What happened?'

'Hush now. You need to rest.' Feeling weak with relief, Rose let Mary in when she knocked at the door, bringing coffee, buttered toast and scrambled eggs.

'The doctor's downstairs talking to the master. He'll be up to see her soon, not that she'll need him by the looks of her, miss.' She placed the tray on the washstand. 'I'd better make myself scarce. Mrs Causton don't like me gossiping.'

Mary left and the doctor turned up five minutes later, pronouncing Minnie's health much improved, the best news Rose could have wished for. He advised her to continue with the tonic and broth before riding away from the house to his next call.

Rose ate breakfast, rinsed her hands and face, and dragged their luggage, which had appeared outside the bedroom door during the night, into the room. She rummaged through their belongings, looking for a dress that was marginally cleaner than the one she'd worn for the ride back to Overshill. As she fastened the last button on the bodice of her brown cotton gown, trying to ignore the stains down the front, and the musky smell that emanated from the cloth, she heard a knock on the door.

'Come in,' she said, looking up. 'Good morning.'

'I hear that your sister is going to be all right,' Freddie said.

'Yes, thanks to you.' She shrank back a little, embarrassed by her appearance, although he gave no hint that he had noticed how grubby her clothes were. 'I'm sorry, but I haven't got the means to pay the doctor's bill at present.'

'Don't worry about it. I'll settle it.'

'I can't let you do that. It's very generous of you, but—'

'Let's not argue about this now. You'll wake your sister.'

He had a point, Rose thought.

'Why don't you come out on to the landing? Leave the door open so you can watch Minnie, while we sit and talk for a while.' He pulled up two chairs just outside the bedroom door and offered one to Rose.

'You know why we went to Faversham?' she said quietly as she sat down.

He nodded. 'Your brother is locked up in Canterbury Gaol. There were plenty of people who were keen to enlighten me as to his whereabouts when I came back from my travels to find the cottage at Toad's Bottom empty. I sent my man to ask Donald where you were – that's how I found you.'

'How was he?' Rose interrupted.

'Fed up, frustrated and worn out, as you'd expect. It isn't right, locking these young lads up in the expectation they will learn to behave. I prefer the idea of reformatory schools, but never mind that. Back to you and Minnie. Why on earth did you run away?'

'Where do I start? The villagers hated us, we'd let the Carters down, and I was too ashamed to stay. I couldn't afford the rent on the cottage without Donald's wages, and I knew I'd lost my place here. Who would take a convicted criminal's sister to look after their house?'

'We come from different worlds, Rose. You are nothing like your brother, and I would never have considered changing my mind over you being my housekeeper for this. I thought you were made of sterner stuff, perfectly able to withstand those tiresome people who have nothing better to do than pass an opinion on everyone else's business. The finger-pointing would soon have passed. There must be another reason why you took your sister away from the relative safety of Overshill.'

'I didn't mean to put her in danger. I did my best – I found work and lodgings.'

'Yet, I found you in quite a predicament with men chasing you for repayment of your debts, and Minnie looking very unwell.'

'You don't understand. When Donald went to gaol, the Carters' maid told us that our grandmother was ill. Mr Carter was worried about her heart and blamed us. I couldn't have her death on my conscience, so we fled.'

'She wouldn't have died because of what Donald had done,' Freddie said, somewhat scathingly. 'It wouldn't have been your fault if she had. And she's perfectly well, by the way. I've seen her since I've been back. Oh, she looks a little older, I grant you, but she's alive and kicking.'

'It wasn't very long ago that I lost my mother. Her heart broke when she heard the solicitor reading our father's will, and two weeks later she died from heart failure, having given up the will to live.' Rose trembled at the

347

memory of seeing Ma lifeless in her bed. 'I didn't want that to happen to Mrs Carter. I couldn't be responsible for her dying from a broken heart.'

She was aware of Freddie's hand reaching towards hers, then moving back again.

'I apologise for jumping to conclusions,' he said softly. 'I didn't realise that you'd lost your mother in that way. I can see now why you'd worry about Mrs Carter. Rose, I wish I'd been here.'

'Can you forgive me for running away without leaving word for you?'

He nodded. 'I spoke to the Carters to ask if they knew where you'd gone and for what reason.'

'Mr Carter didn't want me to associate with you in any way,' Rose said. 'I really don't know why.'

'I'll explain sometime. Not now, though.' Freddie changed the subject, a smile playing on his lips. 'Promise me you won't go running off again, at least not without telling me.'

'I promise,' she said, feeling chastened. 'I'm sorry for putting you out like this.'

'Forget it – it's in the past. You're welcome to stay here for as long as you wish.'

'In what capacity, though? When do I take on my role as your housekeeper?'

His eyes sparkled. 'Imagine my surprise when I came back to find my housekeeper in waiting gone! I've employed Mrs Causton through an agency.'

'Oh dear.' She dug her fingernails into the palm of her hand, burying her disappointment.

'You must stay. It's the least that—' he stopped abruptly. 'Your sister will take some time to recuperate. Wait until she's fully recovered before you start worrying about where you will go.'

'I can't sit around doing nothing in return for our board and lodging.'

'I see.' His brow furrowed. 'I'm sure I can find you some occupation. I need someone with an eye for detail to assist with decorating and furnishing the house, the main rooms first.'

'I don't think I'm qualified to do that. I've never taken any interest in wallpapers and paint.'

'You seem to be able to turn your hand to almost anything.' He chuckled. 'Look at you: you can clean, cook, turn a house into a home and even make bricks.'

'Oh no, I sifted the dirt for ashes to mix with the clay for the men to make the bricks.' She felt ashamed at how far she had fallen. 'When I lived in Canterbury, my mother ran a school for fee-paying pupils and poor children. I was a pupil teacher there. Teaching – that's what I'm good at.'

'Let me see if I can change your mind.'

'How can I give my opinion on colours and curtains when I don't know what your preferences are?'

He stood up. 'Come with me and I'll show you the rest of the house, if Minnie doesn't need you?'

'She's sleeping, but I don't want her to wake up and find herself alone,' Rose said, caught up in Freddie's enthusiasm.

'Mary can sit with her. I'll send for her.'

'But what about the other servants?'

'What about them?'

'They'll talk.'

'You are my advisor, Rose. There's nothing inappropriate about your position in this house. You should stop worrying about what other people think.'

She smiled, reassured. It was a hard habit to break.

'Come with me,' he repeated. 'There's so much I want to show you.'

'It's such a large house,' she said. 'Where does one start?'

'At the bottom?' He cocked one eyebrow. 'At the top? Oh, I don't know. What does it matter?'

Soon, they were laughing as they moved swiftly from room to room, pulling the covers off the furniture the previous owner had left behind, and opening curtains.

'This place is too big, too grand. I don't know why I settled on it.'

'Why did you then?' Rose said, wondering if he was a little mad.

'I could say it was for the magnificent views of Kent, or the beauty of the grounds, or its convenient situation, but it was none of those things.' He paused before going on, 'I could see its potential – there's plenty of space for a family.'

'More than enough for several families,' Rose pointed out, thinking of the cottage at Toad's Bottom, as she stopped in the doorway into the next room, a dark library filled with shadows and musty old books.

'I'm not a believer in evil spirits, but I don't like this room,' she said as a shiver ran down her spine.

'There's a draught coming down the chimney, that's all. Apparently Mr Hadington spent much of his time here, especially towards the end.' Freddie slipped his arm around her back. 'Don't worry. There are no ghosts here, just a huge number of volumes on English law, and I think we can dispose of those.'

'We should replace the books with ones you'd like to read,' she said, turning away and putting some space between herself and her host. The contact, although intended to be a gesture of reassurance, had made her heart beat faster.

'I'll let you suggest some suitable titles to fill the shelves. I'm not much of a one for reading,' Freddie said, and they continued up to the next floor where there were several bedrooms and dressing rooms, along with a larger room at the end of one corridor.

'This will make a good nursery one day,' Freddie said.

'You speak as though you're set on having children,' Rose said softly, her heart almost breaking as she pictured him with a wife at his side, an infant in her arms and another hiding behind her skirts. 'I expect you will soon bring your sweetheart to Overshill?' She shrank back at the sight of his quizzical expression. She had overstepped the mark in pursuing that train of thought. 'All I meant was that you'll soon be thinking of marriage, if you aren't wed already.'

'You mean that a man of my age should be planning to settle down? I'm in no hurry.' He smiled. 'What do you think of my idea to let in more light on this floor by installing an extra set of windows on the rear landing?'

'Can you do that?' she asked, grateful to him for changing the subject.

'With you at my side, overseeing the works, I can do anything.'

'You have too much faith in me,' she said.

'You don't believe me? We'll see, shall we?' His voice was gentle. 'You're a strong woman to have survived the ordeal you've been through, Rose. I have great admiration for your strength of character.'

She didn't know how to respond. With a flush of embarrassment creeping up her neck, she turned at the sound of the maid's voice as she walked up behind them.

'Mr Wild, there's a Mrs Carter to see the Miss Cheeverses. I've asked her to wait in the hall.'

'Thank you, Mary,' Freddie said. 'Rose, you'd better go and find out what she wants.'

Reluctant to leave Freddie's company and apprehensive about what her grandmother was going to say, she went downstairs to face her. Mrs Carter was resting on a chair with her bonnet on her knees and a stick in one hand. When she saw Rose, she struggled to her feet.

'When I heard from Mrs Greenleaf, who'd seen Mr Wild and the horses going by, that you were back and Minnie was ill, I had to come. How is she?'

'She's making a good recovery – I'll show you.' Rose reached out to take her grandmother's arm and led her slowly up the stairs. 'How are you?'

'Much better for knowing you're both safe. Why did you run away like that and without a word? It's caused me much grief.'

'I'm sorry. Mr Carter said that we were making you ill, what with Donald going to prison, and I couldn't help remembering how Ma went so quickly. I never meant—'

'I know. He's a silly old fool for saying that to you when he knows better. To give him his due he did send two of the lads after you, but they only got as far as the outskirts of Canterbury before giving up. Oh, never mind that now.' She patted Rose's hand. 'It's in the past.'

Rose walked her along the corridor to the bedroom and opened the door. Her grandmother rushed over to Minnie's bedside and took both her hands.

'My dear, you appear to be in better health than I expected.'

Minnie sat up, beaming from ear to ear, her traumas on the brickfield apparently forgotten. 'I'm glad to see you, Grandma. I've missed you.'

Rose choked back a tear at the sight of her sister and grandmother together, talking about the farm, how the Carters had hatched more geese and reared more piglets, and how – in spite of his thieving – they missed Donald and his cheeky smile. Having spent an hour with them, Mrs Carter bade them farewell.

'I won't stop any longer – I've never liked this house. I came to Mrs Hadington's wake and found it very dark, dirty and cold,' she told Rose as they walked downstairs together. 'It's strange how life goes around and comes around. I can trust you to keep a secret?'

'Yes, of course.'

'The previous owner of the house – I can hardly speak his name.'

'Mr Hadington?'

'He was my father by blood.' Rose bit her lip as her grandmother continued, 'My parents, the Rooks, were my grandparents. Ivy, their daughter, was a maid here when he had his way with her against her will. When they found out she was with child, the Rooks decided to pass me off as their own, but I found out the truth later – through Matty Carter, in fact. Promise you'll say nothing.'

'Cross my heart and hope to die,' Rose said. What a tangled web, she thought.

'Will you be staying for long?'

'I'm not sure of our plans just yet. It's too soon.'

'If you want to come back to the cottage, it's there waiting for you. All you have to do is ask. Oh, I almost forgot! I have a letter addressed to you. It arrived at the farm last Tuesday.' She handed Rose an envelope from her pocket.

As soon as her grandmother had gone, Rose opened the letter.

Dear Rose, she read.

> *I am frantic with worry, having not heard from you for the past few months. Please let me know you are safe.*
>   *Yours truly,*
>   *Aunt Marjorie*

She begged some paper, a pen and ink from Freddie, and wrote straight back.

Dear Aunt Marjorie,

First of all, let me say how sorry I am for not letting you know of our recent trials which caused us to leave Overshill. I thought it was for the best, but on hearing of your distress and worry, I realise I was remiss in not notifying you. There is so much to tell that I can't possibly write it all down in a letter. Suffice to say for the present, Minnie and I are staying with a Mr Freddie Wild at Churt House in Overshill. I must allay any concern you might have for our reputations by saying that he is a gentleman. I don't know how long we will be at this address, but I trust that any mail you send here will be redirected if necessary.

Dear Minnie has been unwell, but she's on the mend now.

I hesitate to write to you of Donald, who is being held at Canterbury Gaol for stealing pies. He is not due for release until May 1881, a matter of great sorrow for his sisters, as you can imagine.

I trust that you are well,
Yours as ever,
Rose

In spite of Rose's suggestion that she should go, Freddie sent Jack to post the letter.

'Thank you,' Rose said. 'You've been incredibly kind to us, Freddie.'

'It's a pleasure,' he said, his hands in his pockets and his dog at his side as they stood in the corridor leading to the servants' hall.

'I was wondering if you would mind me asking my grandmother to sit with Minnie while I go to Faversham one day soon,' she said.

'I thought that was the last place on earth you'd wish to return to, but I expect you want to visit your friend.'

'I didn't have time to say a proper goodbye and I'd like to find her before work stops on the brickfields for the winter.'

'How are you thinking of getting there?' Freddie asked.

'By shank's pony, of course. I like to walk.'

'Oh, we can't have that. No, I'll take you there, if it's acceptable to you ...'

'It's very generous of you, but I don't know.' Was it right for her to travel without a chaperone? She trusted Freddie, but she could imagine what the neighbours and Aunt Marjorie would have to say about it.

'You'll be quite safe,' he said, his lips quirking into a smile. 'Mrs Causton will come with us – she has some errands to run in town.'

'Then I accept, if it's no trouble.'

'I wouldn't have suggested it if it was. There's no need to bother Mrs Carter – one of the maids will look after Minnie. We'll go tomorrow.'

Rose wondered what she could take with her as a gift for Flo and her boys. In the end she begged Cook for some cake and plum jam, and put them in a basket.

The next morning, she travelled in the carriage with Freddie and Mrs Causton, whom they dropped off at the market near the Guildhall before driving on to Kingsfield. Rose felt increasingly anxious as they grew closer to the place that held such unhappy memories for her.

'Don't worry about the Irishman,' Freddie said as though reading her mind. 'Let me deal with him.' He passed her a small purse.

'What's this for?' she asked, feeling its considerable weight in her hands.

'For you to give to your friend. She's a good woman.'

'Are you sure? Don't you want to give it to her yourself?'

'I think she'll be happier to accept it if we say it's from you and Minnie, rather than me,' he said. 'It would hurt her pride to think I was offering her charity.'

Rose didn't argue any further, knowing that Flo and her boys were always short of money. It would be her friend who would be disadvantaged if she let her pride take over. The contents of the purse could be the difference between them staying out, or being forced to enter the poorhouse for the winter. She placed the purse in her basket along with the cake and jam as the carriage pulled up alongside the brickfield. Freddie opened the door and helped her out.

The stench of London's refuse hit her nostrils, and the sound of the knock, knock, knock of leather against leather took her straight back to when Minnie had gone missing with the gaffer. Where was he?

'Take my arm,' Freddie said. 'We'll walk together.'

She slipped her hand through the crook of his elbow and they walked across Kingsfield towards the wharf where the women were sifting dust.

'What do you want?' a man said, walking up to them.

'We are here to speak with Flo,' Rose said, refusing to be cowed.

'Oh, 'er. She's over there as usual.' He pointed towards the figure in the centre of the semi-circle of workers.

'Where is the gaffer? The Irishman?' Freddie asked.

'He got into a fight outside the Ship a couple of days ago. He suffered a heavy blow to the head which cracked his skull. Killed him outright, it did. It was a terrible shock to us all, but I can't say he didn't deserve it. He was a wily one, always looking out for himself.' He shook his head. 'I pity his poor wife back home. Anyway, I'm the gaffer now if anyone's asking.'

Leaving Freddie to continue talking, Rose ran down to the women and tapped Flo on the shoulder. She turned abruptly.

'It's you,' she exclaimed, throwing down her sieve and struggling to her feet. 'I didn't think I'd see you again.' Rose leaned towards her and kissed her dusty cheek.

'I wanted to thank you for everything you did for us,' Rose said, a tear in her eye. 'I don't know what Minnie and I would have done without you. Here,' – she thrust the basket into Flo's arms – 'this is for you and the boys.'

Flo looked into the basket.

'Nobody's ever given me anything before,' she said, starting to cry.

Rose gave her a clean handkerchief from her pocket. Flo wiped her eyes then tried to hand it back to her. 'Keep it,' she said, smiling gently. 'You'd better get back to work. The new gaffer's watching.' They wished each other all the luck in the world, and Rose returned across the brick-field to the carriage with Freddie, happy that between them they had given Flo and her boys financial security through the lean months at least.

Later the same evening, Rose sat with Minnie and pondered how the day had gone. She had already decided that she wouldn't tell her sister of Abel's passing, not wanting to upset her. She guessed that Flo's future was mapped out – next summer and the one after that she would be back at Kingsfield, sifting dust. Rose was left wondering what she and Minnie would do, and where they would go when Minnie was fully restored to health. The questions plagued her mind for the rest of the day, and later when she was gazing out of the window at the sun sinking behind the horizon, she felt her heart sinking too, because she had no answers. She'd lost the place that would have been hers, if it hadn't been for Donald. Had her decision to run away played a part as well? How could Freddie rely on someone who fled whenever trouble struck? She'd had her reasons – sound ones – for leaving Overshill, but now she felt rather a fool.

Chapter Twenty-Four

A Full Sixpence

Within a week, Rose had heard back from Aunt Marjorie.

Dear Rose and Minnie too,

*I am very relieved to hear you're safe. I have been worried
sick since I heard back from your grandmother that you
had left Overshill without leaving a forwarding address.
I am most disappointed and distressed to hear of Donald's
transgressions. He was a naughty boy from the start, but
I never thought he would stoop to thieving. Perhaps I am
judging him unfairly. I shouldn't dwell on my disappointment in him.*

*I wish you had let me know of your trials. You know I
would have done everything in my power to help you.*

*I look forward to visiting you and your family as soon
as I am released from my duties. Due to ill health and not
being as young as I was, I am relinquishing my place with
the Richardsons and looking to find a modest house where
I might live out the rest of my days in peaceful occupation.*

Your ever loving aunt,
Marjorie

Rose wished she could help her, but what could she do?
She was dependent on Freddie for everything, and occu-

pied with looking after Minnie, whose health continued to improve over the next month. She and her sister dined in their room, and once or twice in the servants' hall. It was an odd establishment, she thought, finding the distinction between master and servant much blurred, even compared with the way her parents had treated the servants at Willow Place.

Freddie dropped by to see them now and again, passing the time of day and talking of his progress with improving the Churt estate. He gave Rose various tasks to keep her occupied and satisfy her desire to make herself useful, including supervising the team of painters and decorators he'd brought in to start on the main rooms in the house and gradually obliterate all trace of the wicked Mr Hadington.

One day in October, Rose was looking out of the drawing-room window when she saw a carriage arriving at the house, bringing a flurry of helpers to unload what turned out to be a delivery of trunks, bags and boxes. Freddie directed them to carry everything into the house.

'Look at this.' She turned to Minnie, who was sitting perched on a chair that they'd covered with a linen cloth to protect it from the decorators' paint. There were two men on ladders, preparing the ornate plaster ceiling for the first coat, and another one measuring up for new wallpaper.

'I wonder what's in those boxes,' Minnie said, walking across to the window. 'Our Mr Wild is very nice, but he's a bit of a mystery, isn't he?'

'I suppose he is,' Rose agreed. She still didn't know much about him, and wondered if she ever would. 'What are you going to do today, Minnie?'

She shrugged. 'I thought I might go for a walk to see Grandma.'

'Oh, I'll come with you.'

'You're needed here. Don't worry, I won't do anything silly. You have to trust me.'

'I know, but it's difficult after what happened.'

'I'll go straight to the farm, and straight back, I promise.' Minnie gazed at her. 'Cross my heart and hope to die. Please, Rose.'

Was it safe? Rose wondered. Could she rely on her to keep her word?

'Go on then, but don't let me down.'

'Thank you.' Minnie flung her arms around her neck, half strangling her with joy. 'I'll be back by twelve.'

Rose watched the carriage depart, and Minnie limping down the drive. She wished she could feel that light of heart, but she was beginning to wonder how much longer they could stay now that her sister was well again.

'Could I have a word?'

Detecting the scent of the outdoors and fresh soap, she turned to find Freddie standing behind her. He had a liveliness about the eyes, wide shoulders and a well-kept beard. He wore quality clothes, moleskin trousers and crisp white cotton shirts. If she could change a single thing about him – well, there was nothing that could be altered to make an ounce of improvement.

'Is this about the order for the wallpaper?' she asked. There had been a mix-up the day before when extra lengths of blue patterned paper had been delivered instead of the pale grey she had requested.

'No, it has nothing to do with the house. I'd be grateful if you'd come along to the dining room. I'd like to speak with you in private.'

She'd loved the time she and Minnie had spent at Churt House with Freddie. She'd always known that it was too good to last ...

'That sounds ominous,' she said apprehensively.

'Not at all,' he smiled.

She followed him along the landing to the dining room next door where the carpet had been rolled up and stood on its end in one corner, the furniture moved to one side in preparation for the refurbishment. There was a silver tray with a coffee set and plates, and a covered platter on the table.

'Take a seat,' he said, pulling one out for her. 'Let me pour you some hot chocolate or coffee. I wasn't sure which you preferred so I ordered both, along with some pastries.'

'Hot chocolate, please.' She watched him pour it out. He handed her a plate so she could choose between the apricot and almond pastries, and she wondered if he'd arranged this occasion to soften the blow when he gave her and Minnie their marching orders.

'I noticed that you had a delivery today,' she said, trying to make conversation.

'That was the rest of my belongings that I had shipped from abroad. Please humour me for a moment.'

He took a purse from his jacket pocket and opened it up. He pulled out what looked like a coin and held it out. 'Look at this.'

Rose stared at it: a half a sixpence, much like the one she was wearing, but darker and more tarnished.

'This is some kind of trick. You've seen the half a sixpence around my neck and you've gone out to have another one made.'

'Why on earth would I do that?'

'I honestly don't know.' A pulse throbbed at her throat. Whatever this was, it felt like a moment of great importance, a turning point.

'It is a match. Put them together and you'll see that they are two halves of the same coin.'

'No! This can't be. You are playing some kind of game.'

'Really, this isn't a game, and I can only prove that it isn't by comparing these pieces side by side. Rose, will you remove the silver chain from your neck so we can do so?'

She stared at him and he gazed back intently, without guile.

'There is something I haven't been telling you.' He took a deep breath. 'I believe that we have something in common.'

She couldn't see how she and Freddie could have any association, apart from the one they already had, but he seemed so genuine, almost desperate and a little sorrowful, that she gave in. She reached her hands to the back of her neck and unfastened the clasp, letting the chain slip into her palm before placing it on the table with the half a sixpence still attached. Freddie put his half a coin against it, touching it with his fingertip until the two halves were snugly side by side, perfectly matched.

'I don't believe it.' Rose felt faint with surprise.

'Neither do I,' he breathed. 'Oh, this is wonderful. I've been looking for Agnes and now I've found you, my guardian's granddaughter.'

'What does this mean?' she said. 'I don't understand how this is possible.'

'I arrived in England in April the year before last. I disembarked in Southampton, whence I made the journey to London to meet with my banker and lawyer, and pursue my mission to find the person who was deeply loved by my most generous and loving guardian, the most remarkable man who ever walked this earth,' he said, his voice growing husky.

'You are a long way from home?' Rose ventured.

'Home is half a world away in Tasmania, Van Diemen's Land, whatever you prefer to call it.'

She could picture it on the globe that used to be in the dining room at Willow Place.

'Anyway, I came here looking for some real estate, a place where I could make a home and farm a few sheep and the like. I was a shepherd once. Matty – Mr Carter, my guardian – told me a lot about Overshill, the village where he was born and brought up.'

'Mr Matty Carter was my grandfather, my mother's father …'

Freddie nodded. 'When I called at Wanstall Farm, a man came to the door – my guardian's full brother, Stephen Carter. It was a shock, the similarity. I thought I was seeing a ghost. I asked him about Churt House, thinking I'd tease out the information from him. I would reveal my identity and fondness for his brother soon enough.

'However, Mr Carter couldn't hide his dislike of the previous owner of Churt House who had died a couple of years previous. He said he didn't understand why the good died young, and a miserable old lawyer who inflicted lasting harm on young innocent girls and swindled people of their life savings, and charged over the odds for his services, should live well into his nineties.

'Anyway, I respect Mr Carter. He's a man made good, but his hatred of Mr Hadington felt almost personal and I thought to do a little more digging, but I didn't get very far. When I hinted of the past and my association with his brother, he gave me short shrift, and sent me away with a flea in my ear. I know why – he didn't want to upset his wife with talk of Matty. He said he didn't want to make her ill with it, that it was dead and buried. He didn't want to upset himself with memories of the past, and what's more when I mentioned that my guardian wished me to give some of his legacy to Mrs Carter, he said there was no way they would accept the money. He made me promise not to let her know of my association with Agnes's father.'

'Mr Carter had good reason to hate Mr Hadington,' Rose said. 'I will tell you if you promise me it will go no further.'

'You can trust me to keep your confidence, Rose. What is it?'

'I have it on good authority that he took advantage of a young woman by the name of Ivy Rook when she was a maid here. I believe she was very young when he forced himself on her. Anyway, she left Churt House because she was with child – that child became my grandmother, Mrs Carter.'

'That is a surprise to me. Matty never mentioned it. Not that it matters now.' Freddie smiled briefly. 'Perhaps Mr Hadington's longevity was a punishment for his actions – he died alone and miserable, according to Mr Tovey.'

Rose couldn't help hoping so.

'How did you find the Carters?' she said, changing the subject slightly. 'There must be thousands of them. It's such a common name.'

'Matty gave me all the information he had. He'd made one last attempt to find his daughter by sending an agent to Overshill where he'd lived as a boy. The agent found Catherine Carter at Wanstall Farm. She gave him the name of a Miss Treen of Windmarsh Court near Faversham.'

'Miss Treen? Not Miss Marjorie Treen?'

Freddie nodded. 'Apparently, she was the former nanny of her daughter whom she had adopted out. Matty was shocked to hear that she had been parted from her mother. He couldn't understand it, although he blamed himself for putting his dear ones in the situation where he had abandoned them.'

'I know Miss Treen well,' Rose told him. 'She was Ma's governess and my pa's cousin once removed. I call her Aunt, and she's been part of my family since before I was born. I've had a letter from her only recently.'

'Miss Treen had left Windmarsh Court by the time the agent made his investigations,' Freddie continued, 'but a maid recalled that she'd had relatives at one of the tanneries in Canterbury. The agent disappeared without trace, and we'd reached a dead end, by which time Matty was dangerously ill. It wasn't until I travelled over here that I tried again, sending a second man to the tanneries.'

Rose remembered the man who had called at Willow Place looking for Miss Agnes Berry-Clay, and how Aunt Temperance had dismissed him, thinking he had news of a more recent version of Pa's will.

'What did your man find out?' she asked.

He shrugged. 'He thought he'd come close to finding my guardian's granddaughter, but the woman at the house insisted that she knew nothing of it, and that the children who lived there were her own. Although others told him otherwise, he wasn't able to pursue it further at that time. You are most definitely Agnes's daughter?'

Rose nodded.

'I see. It's good to find out the truth at last.'

'Didn't the Carters at the farm tell you about me, and my brother and sister?' Rose said.

'I decided to keep my mission to myself. Originally, the agent found out that Mrs Carter had no idea where Agnes was, so there was no reason for me to think that she had suddenly discovered her whereabouts since his visit. Nobody had seemed that interested in her – why should they be when she had been born illegitimate?' He stopped abruptly. 'I apologise – I'm talking of your mother.

'If I hadn't stopped at the cottage for water, I might never have known who you were. It was only because I spotted you wearing the half a sixpence that I realised there could be a connection between you and the Carters. I did a little research at the Woodsman's Arms over a pint of ale and discovered you were Catherine's granddaughter.'

'I imagine you would have found out eventually,' she said. 'You know how they like to talk.'

'That's true.'

'What happened to my grandfather?'

'He died two years ago at the age of sixty after a long and hard life. I promised him on his deathbed that I would find his daughter and let her know that he had ...' he paused before continuing '... loved her before she was born, always and for ever. Those were his very words.'

Rose couldn't speak.

'I'm sorry if I've upset you. My guardian was like a father to me.'

'Did my grandfather ever marry?'

Freddie shook his head. 'He said Catherine was the only woman for him. He couldn't bring himself to love anyone else. He did once try to renew his association with her. He sent a letter, telling her he had received a pardon, and asking her to travel to Tasmania with their child, but he didn't hear anything by return. He waited for years, smoking his pipe of an evening as he watched the sun set. At the end, he said that if they weren't to be reunited here on earth, they would be in Heaven. I don't know how that works.

'If you ask me, Catherine had taken him at his word. When he was convicted, he asked her to break their engagement, leaving her free to take another as her husband. I suspect that by the time she read his letter, she was already married to Stephen.'

'It's very sad,' Rose said. 'Was my grandfather unhappy then?'

'He was content, being someone who found joy in the smallest of things. He was kind too. He took me in when my mother, well, she couldn't keep me. She left me on his doorstep, knowing he'd look after me after my father – a convict, transported for stealing a few shillings – made an attempt to escape the colony by sea and disappeared. No one ever knew what became of him. So you see, we have both led unconventional lives, and had to overcome prejudice and loss.'

'What does this mean for us?' Rose asked, bemused by the turn that events had taken. 'You have deceived me all this time, letting me think that you had a high opinion of me, making out that I would be a good housekeeper, and wanting to protect me from the gossips when we were in the bakehouse ... and coming to rescue us from the brickfield. I thought ... Oh, I've been so vain and shallow, imagining you liked me for myself. Now I find that you did everything out of obligation and duty to your guardian, my grandfather ...'

'I'm sorry, Rose. I didn't mean to upset you or hurt your feelings.'

'Why didn't you tell me the truth the first time we met? I remember how your eyes lingered on the half a sixpence ... this is such a shock.'

'I wanted to explain, but I had to be careful because I knew very little about you and your situation. Before my guardian passed away, he asked me to look for Agnes, your mother, so I could pass his wealth to her. Failing that, I was to find her descendants and allocate his money to them, according to my discretion.

'It is a matter of the deepest regret that I didn't have everything arranged before I set off for my most recent business trip. If I'd been more trusting, you and Minnie wouldn't have been exposed to the rigours of the brick-field.'

'What's different now?' she asked.

'I've got to know you. Matty didn't want his hard-earned assets going to someone who would fritter them away. I didn't know if you'd be able to handle the sudden change in your fortune. I thought if I gave you enough money to tide you over, then it would buy me time.'

'Why offer me the place as housekeeper?'

'I thought I could keep you safe: you, your brother and sister. Unfortunately, the house wasn't ready, and events rather overtook us.'

'I'm not sure how I feel, having learned that you have deceived me.'

'You've clearly inherited many of my guardian's traits: intelligence, application and a strong will.'

'It is no use trying to flatter me,' she said. 'It won't wash.'

'Your stubborn streak and refusal to let people help you through the bad times might not be considered a positive attribute.' Freddie poured more coffee into his cup and sat back, watching the steam rise. 'You must decide for yourself. You're a wealthy, independent woman in your own right.' He paused before continuing, 'Of course, it will take me a while to organise the transfer of your share of the money – you might as well stay here until then.'

'How long?' Rose asked, her heart thudding in her chest so loudly she thought he'd be able to hear it.

'About three months, which would work well for me if you're happy to continue with overseeing the decoration of the house. It would be a shame for you not to finish

369

what you've started, and miss out on seeing the end result. What do you think?'

'I'm not going to make any hasty decisions,' she said, sipping at her hot chocolate.

'I hope you don't rush away. I was depending on you to keep an eye on the place while I'm away on business. I leave in three weeks' time.'

She did owe him a debt, she thought.

'It wouldn't be too onerous, I think.'

'How long will you be away for this time?'

'About a month.'

'You are a busy man.'

'It's quite a challenge, emigrating and continuing to look after one's business interests at the same time. I will be back though, Rose.' He lowered his voice. 'Whatever you decide, I'd like to maintain our friendship, if that is agreeable to you.'

'Yes, I think so.' She gazed at him. Of course she wished to keep in touch with him. 'This is almost too much to take in.'

'You'll need to talk to Minnie.'

Rose knew what her sister would say: stay because they'd found some happiness in the brief time they'd been living at Churt House.

'You haven't asked how much he left to you. You are too polite. I know I'd want to know ...'

'Well, I suppose I should have some understanding,' she began.

He mentioned a sum, an amount beyond her wildest dreams, and she gasped.

He grinned. 'He was a very wealthy man.'

'What will I do with it?' She began to panic. It was wonderful that she and her siblings would never want for anything, but it was too much.

'Whatever you see fit,' he said with a smile. 'It's your money. I can't tell you what to do with it.'

'I'd like to set up a trust for the education of the street children of Canterbury, and make sure that my aunt has a home and the comforts that she deserves for her retirement.'

'You have stunned me into silence,' Freddie said.

'If you thought I would rush out to buy dresses and shoes, you don't know me at all.'

'I didn't mean it like that. If I'd suffered like you and your sister, my first thought would have been to buy comforts for myself, not give to others.' He tipped his head to one side. 'You're a remarkable young lady.'

'Tell me more about my grandfather, and how he made his fortune,' she said, blushing at his compliment.

'Your grandfather used to say that money meant nothing unless you had someone to share it with. I didn't always think that way. When I was younger, I was obsessed with finding gold. I'd seen my mother struggle, and I didn't want that for myself, so I went panning for riches. I remember the excitement and rush of anticipation I felt each time I dunked the pan in the water, rinsed the stones and gravel, and stared until I went boss-eyed, looking for that elusive sign of gold. There were false alarms: a stone glistening in the sun; a light-coloured fleck of sand.'

'Someone said that you'd made your fortune rearing sheep and selling wool.'

'It's more complicated than that. Your grandfather was, as he used to say, l'arned about sheep farming by Catherine's father, Mr Rook. He took the Carters under his wing in return for a favour done by old Pa Carter who rescued him from drowning as a small boy in Ghost Hole pond, the one by the church. When Matty arrived in Tasmania, he made himself useful, working as a convict on an estate. Gradually, he managed to make his way up, and then, when he was freed, he bought some land through a friend of his. He reared sheep – he was good at picking the best rams and most prolific ewes, and made quite a success of it.

'Anyway, there was a creek on his land and we were there one day, taking shelter among the trees from the sun, when we started wondering if there could be something in it. We had a go at panning, and after several weeks, we found a sliver of gold. We kept it under our hats so to speak, so as not to have everyone taking advantage of our prospects.'

'What happened to the sheep?' she asked.

'Oh, they were fine – we had a pair of dogs to keep them in check, and took on a trustworthy boy to watch them until lambing time when we drove them back to the home farm.' Freddie smiled. 'In the evenings, we'd sit around the fire and sing. Your grandfather was a great singer. He played accordion and fiddle and used to tell me of the time when he was in the choir at the church in Overshill and the vicar sacked the whole lot of them for drunkenness, and offences against music.

'I find it ironic that his family had nothing when he was a boy, yet when he received his freedom in Tasmania, he made more money than he ever needed. He had bonds and investments, and gold in the bank, but all he wished for was to be back home in Overshill in the arms of his sweetheart.'

Rose couldn't hold back her tears.

'I'm sorry.' Freddie offered her his handkerchief.

'Thank you,' she said, wiping her eyes.

'Would you like a brandy? I believe that helps in times such as these.'

'No, Mr Wild. I need to keep a clear head.'

'Rose, I'll ask you once more – let's not have any more "Mr Wild". Call me Freddie.'

'All right,' she said. 'Thank you, Freddie.'

'Can you find it in your heart to forgive me for keeping this from you?'

She nodded and he smiled with apparent relief. She could forgive him anything.

'I expect you want to go and tell your sister the good news,' he said.

'I wish I was in a position to tell my brothers too,' she said. 'I've told you about Arthur, my stepbrother – I was brought up with him when Ma and Pa took him in after his mother died. He's called Arthur Fortune.'

'You can write to him.'

'If I only knew where he was. He went to London, intending to marry his sweetheart, Tabby, and find work in the building trade. I don't know his address.' She smiled ruefully. 'I would go and search for him ...'

'Then you would be looking for a needle in a haystack. I can make some enquiries next time I'm there.'

She thanked him again. 'I can't believe what a coincidence this is,' she said. 'It seems impossible.'

'I prefer to think of it in a different way. It isn't fate or destiny that brought me to you – it's the result of my investigations, based on the information that Matty gave me throughout the years. I could have given up the search, but I didn't, because I'm not that kind of man.'

It was true, Rose thought, gazing fondly at him. Not only was Freddie Wild a gentleman and her grandfather's ward, he was her hero.

Chapter Twenty-Five

The Truth Will Out

Before he went away, Freddie gave Rose a modest advance on the money she would expect to receive in January, which meant she could purchase new dresses for her and Minnie to replace the ones they'd worn out during their time on the brickfield. In addition, she ordered supplies for Minnie to finish the patchwork for Arthur and Tabby, and start on a second one. She helped her with it, finding it useful to fill the passing hours as the trees began to lose their leaves and the nights drew in.

She found other occupations, walking into the village to take the air and run the odd errand for Cook and Mrs Causton, but there wasn't much for her to do as most of the supplies for the house were delivered by the respective tradesmen, and the number of household servants had swelled to include a butler, two footmen, four maids, a gamekeeper to replace Mr Tovey, and a gardener and his boys.

On one of her expeditions, she went into the village shop to buy a box of pins for Minnie's sewing. Her heart sank when she saw Mrs Greenleaf at the counter before her, talking to the shopkeeper. The old woman turned, gave her a glare of contempt and returned to her conversation.

'We don't want the likes of that around here. Why did Mr Wild bother to go and drag her and her sister back to Overshill? He is a strange man indeed.'

'Because he has more kindness in the tip of his little finger than you have in your entire heart, Mrs Greenleaf,' Rose said tersely, bringing her up short. 'That's all I will say on the matter.'

She bought the pins and left, running into Sam who was working in the graveyard, cutting back the brambles.

'I heard you were back,' he said, looking a little sheepish when she stopped to speak to him. 'You're staying at the Hadingtons' old place.'

'I'm sorry I didn't see you before Minnie and I left Overshill,' she said, uncertain how to proceed. 'I called on your mother.'

'But I wasn't there,' he finished for her. 'I'm sorry too – I should have told you that I was walking out with somebody else, a girl from Selling. I didn't think you'd be all that upset though, considering you didn't seem that keen on me …'

'It doesn't matter.' She realised she hadn't had any feelings for him, not like the affection she felt for Freddie. Sam was a young lad, rather dull and predictable, while Freddie was a man, thoughtful and well travelled, never boring.

Minnie was pleased. 'You couldn't have meant that much to him,' she said on her return.

Work continued on the refurbishment of the house, but in spite of the hustle and bustle, the time seemed to pass very slowly until Freddie returned from his business trip.

Rose and Minnie were sewing in their room upstairs when he knocked on the door.

'Are you in there?'

'Come in,' Rose called back, her heart missing a beat at the sound of his voice.

'Am I interrupting anything?' He pushed the door open.

'Not at all,' Rose said, getting up. Lightly tanned and with his hair longer, she thought he looked more handsome than ever.

'I have something to show you two young ladies. Come down to the servants' hall.'

'Hurry, Minnie. What are you waiting for?' Rose said impatiently as he rushed away again, his feet thundering off down the stairs.

'Let me find my stick,' she said. 'I feel a little unsteady on my feet.'

'That's because you've spent too long indoors, staring at those tiny stitches of yours.' She'd offered to go out walking with her that morning, but Minnie had declined because it had been raining. 'Minnie, are you all right?' Rose glanced from her sister's delicate, almost translucent complexion to her breasts and belly, which had grown fuller since they'd left Faversham. She'd assumed that Minnie was merely acquiring the curves of womanhood, but now she wasn't so sure.

She waited for her to limp out on to the landing and close the door behind them, before making their way to the servants' hall where everyone was standing around the table. Freddie was sitting at the head with a pineapple on a platter in front of him. Rose recognised it from the pictures in one of the books Ma had used to teach from, but the maids and the gardener's boys were all agog at the sight of it.

Freddie glanced up and caught her eye, giving her a secret smile.

'I thought I'd canvass everyone's opinion to see if we should try growing these at Churt House,' he said, slicing the crown of spiky leaves from the top and cutting into the fruit. He carefully divided the yellow flesh into rings, cut them into segments and passed them round. 'I have a fancy for eating our own pineapples.'

'Really? It's far too cold for them in winter,' Jack said.

'Others have grown them in this country with great success. I'm sure we can do it too, if we build a pinery and provide them with heat.' Freddie looked towards the gardener. 'What do you think?'

'We're busy putting the garden to bed for the winter,' he said grumpily.

'That's all right. I'll roll my sleeves up and help out. I'd never ask anyone to do anything I wouldn't do myself.'

'What is required for this project?' the gardener asked.

'Enough men to dig out three trenches four foot deep and forty foot long, then a carpenter to build a wooden frame over the top, and a glazier to cover it with glass panels. We'll need horse manure and milled oak bark. Mixed with water, those ingredients will ferment slowly, releasing heat and providing the plants with constant warmth, mimicking a tropical climate.'

The thought of the oak bark reminded Rose of the tannery and how Pa would have it stirred into the water in the pits to tan the hides.

'What do you think, Rose?' Freddie said, standing up and moving round to her. 'Do you approve of this plan?'

'Well, yes,' she said shyly, the taste of pineapple, like sweetened rosewater and wine, still on her tongue.

Minnie found it amusing.

'He's doing everything he can to impress you,' she said when they returned to their room from dining with the servants that evening, Freddie having retired early to bed because he was weary from his travels.

377

'Don't say that,' Rose said rather sharply, because she was feeling sore. Freddie wasn't the kind of man who went around taking advantage of women. If he had wished to seduce her, she thought regretfully, he would have done so by now, and it was too late anyway because it appeared that Minnie had scuppered their chances of a peaceful and contented way of life.

Rose lit the lamp and stoked the fire in the grate, then turned to her sister who had bounced on to her bed.

'I'm going to have to get changed under the covers,' Minnie said, her teeth chattering.

'We need to have a little talk first,' Rose said, sitting down alongside her. 'I'm not going to beat around the bush. Is it at all possible that the gaffer did more than kiss you? Did he disrobe and ...?' She was afraid that her sister knew more about the topic of their conversation than she did.

Minnie nodded. 'He told me not to tell you what we did.'

Rose swore out loud.

'Rose!' Minnie exclaimed.

'I'm sorry, but he's an evil, wicked, manipulative, nasty—'

'I liked him,' Minnie cut in angrily.

'He made you like him. He is to blame for this, not you.' Rose refrained from revealing how Flo had told her of Abel's death. 'Minnie, listen to me. Don't be alarmed, but I think you're with child.'

'Oh dear.' Minnie leaned back against her pillow, which was one shade paler than her complexion.

Not having the heart to be cross with her, Rose reached out and tucked a lock of her sister's hair back behind her ear. It was too late. In a few months' time, Minnie would be a mother. How were they going to deal with that? At least they had money to support them this time. They could move on and settle in another county where nobody knew them, but that would mean leaving Overshill, and the Carters, and worst of all, Freddie. She would never confess it to him, but she had grown to love him, heart and soul.

The following morning, Rose looked out of the window of the dining room where the decorators were positioning the new furniture according to her instructions. The mid-November sunshine had turned the moon into a pale skeleton of itself in the clear blue sky while Freddie was knee-deep in a trench which ran across the kitchen garden. Brandishing a spade, he wore his shirtsleeves rolled up and buttons undone in spite of the cold. Jack and one of the gardener's boys were digging with him. Feeling guilty for spying, she stepped back when Freddie glanced up at the window.

As soon as she could, she fled to find peace and time to think in the library, a place of calm since she and Freddie had had it redecorated and replaced Mr Hadington's books with the titles that she'd remembered on the shelves at Willow Place, along with many others. She sat down on the window seat with the sun streaming in through the glass, and a book in her hand. She found herself flicking through the pages without reading a word.

'Rose?' She looked up to find Freddie standing in front of her, fastening the buttons on his shirt. 'I thought I might find you here. What do you think of our handiwork so far?' He cleared his throat. 'I saw you watching … Oh, I have embarrassed you, perhaps.'

She smiled ruefully.

'Now that you're here, I can speak with you on a rather delicate matter,' she began.

'What is it? You can speak to me about anything.'

'It's Minnie.'

'Is she sick?'

She shook her head.

He smiled. 'She's with child. I knew it.'

'How did you know?' she said, confused.

'I can tell these things. When women are in the family way, they have this look about them. She is blooming.'

'I don't want to put you in an awkward situation, so I'll look for somewhere she can go and have the baby in secret,' Rose said.

'What for, when she can stay here?'

'There's no way she can remain here at Churt House. My sister's actions, intended or not, have brought shame on us, on me too because it was my fault. I didn't protect her. I failed to keep her close.'

Freddie took a seat right beside her and sat looking at her, his head slightly to one side, a small smile on his lips.

'It isn't a laughing matter,' she said, annoyed that he didn't seem to be taking her seriously. 'My sister's carrying the bastard child of a married man, a ruffian at that. It makes no difference that he's dead. We'll be ostracised in the village as we were when we first arrived in Overshill on the run from Canterbury, and you'll be the subject of gossip and suspicion.'

'For goodness' sake, I'm not worried about that. They can say what they like. This is my home, my domain, and I choose who lives and works here. It's none of their business.' He waved a hand. 'You worry too much about what other people think.'

'This is England, not Tasmania. I think you must have lived in a very different society.'

'You come across bigots wherever you go, but this country seems to be a particular haven for the petty-minded. I would never let a child suffer because of the circumstances in which he or she was conceived. If your grandfather – dear Matty – had judged my poor mother, I would not have ended up where I am today. A child is a gift, a blessing, but I understand there is some stigma attached to—'

'It ruins lives, that of the mother and child,' Rose interrupted.

'Yes, and it's a pity that the man doesn't receive his fair portion of opprobrium.'

'That's true,' she said bitterly. 'You never hear of a man being forced into the poorhouse and having his infant torn from his arms.'

'You have experience of this?'

'My mother … and grandmother, Mrs Carter. Well, you know the rest.'

'It was different. Matty loved your grandmother. He had no intention of abandoning his child.'

'That's all well and good, but—'

'No buts. No doubts. I wish for you and Minnie to stay here as you are, and that's my last word. You will speak to the other servants and remind them that there will be no whispering on the stairs or chattering in the scullery.' His eyes flashed with humour. 'I've heard you keeping them in order. You're much more assertive than you seem.' He grew serious again. 'You will need to call the doctor for her?'

'Not at the moment,' she said. 'She seems very well.'

'If she ever has need of medical attention, you must send for one immediately … and send me the bill afterwards. Have you got that?'

'Yes, thank you, but I'll pay you back as soon as I receive my money.' Before she had come into the room she'd thought she'd never smile again, but he'd reassured her, and now she wanted to throw her arms around his neck and hug him in return.

'Will you sit with me for a while after dinner tonight? I have a fancy for some company. We can dress it up as a meeting about household matters, if you're worried about being spoken of behind your back.'

She hesitated, her neck flushing with heat.

'Of course, I'll understand if you decide you need to attend to Minnie, or you have other plans ...'

'No, I'd like to ...' she stammered, unsure what he was really asking for.

'I'll see you at dinner then.'

'I look forward to it,' she said softly.

Having changed into her favourite new dress with its pale cream brocade bodice, flared sleeves and burgundy skirt, Rose went downstairs with Minnie to the dining room for six o'clock, finding Freddie waiting to greet them at the door.

'A very good evening to my two favourite young ladies. You look beautiful tonight. Quite breathtaking, Rose,' he added as her sister went straight to the table.

Minnie was subdued at first, but she soon cheered up with Freddie telling them all about his adventures, while they told him about everything that had happened at Churt House while he'd been away: how the turkeys he'd ordered from Norfolk had settled into their new home; how one of the biggest chestnut trees in the park had had to be cut down when struck right through the middle by lightning; how Rice, the butler, had shouted at the footman when he'd spilled the gravy.

'It's time you thought about retiring to bed, Minnie,' Rose said, when they had finished their meal.

'Oh, I thought I'd stay down for a while longer,' Minnie said.

'What about the patchwork? You've almost completed the second one?'

'Ah, I still have the lettering to add – the date and names, like we did for Arthur and Tabby.' Minnie glanced from Rose to Freddie and back, her eyes sparkling with humour. Rose made to give her a nudge with her toe under the table. 'Ouch!' Minnie said deliberately, even though she had barely made contact. 'What did you do that for?'

'My foot slipped,' Rose said, blushing. 'I'm sorry, Freddie. We have forgotten our manners.'

He chuckled. 'I forgive you. Minnie, you'd better get on with that embroidery.'

'I had,' she said, and Rose couldn't help wondering if they'd been plotting something together. 'I'll wish you goodnight.' Minnie got up and kissed Rose, and then Freddie on the cheek, before leaving them alone together.

'You wished to speak with me,' Rose said to break the awkward silence between them.

'Shall we go and sit in the parlour where it's warmer and more comfortable?' His smile made her heart somersault. 'I picked up a few sweet chestnuts in the park today – do you like them roasted?'

'I do. I used to buy them from a barrow as a treat when we lived in Canterbury.'

They retreated to the parlour and Freddie offered her a chair in front of the fire. He pulled up a second chair and placed it beside her, then picked up a bowl of sweet chestnuts from the side table. Sitting down, he took a knife from his pocket and began to score their skins. Then he put them in a long-handled skillet drilled through with holes, placed a lid on top and held it over the fire, leaning forward in his chair.

Rose watching him staring into the flickering flames.

'I should have told you the truth about my guardian before,' he began.

'I know – you've already explained. There's no need to speak of it again,' she said gently.

'I wanted to prove to myself that you weren't a gold digger, a woman after my money, but then I realised I was being a cad for even thinking of testing your character. I didn't need to. I saw how you cared for your sister, how you treated the servants and how you respected your grandmother. Rose, I feel quite ashamed of my behaviour. Matty would have given me a good telling-off over it.'

He gave the chestnuts a good shake in the skillet as their sweet scent began to fill the room.

'And now I may have to beg for your forgiveness a second time, if the subject I wish to touch on offends you.'

'What is it?' she asked.

He cleared his throat and turned to face her. 'I believe that you once had an association with one of the farmhands, Sam. He is closer to you in age than I am ... Oh, it's none of my business.'

'But you wish to know if I have any romantic attachment to anyone?' she said. Freddie was bold and fearless, not afraid to speak his mind on all matters, every single one except the one that really counted. He was shy that way. 'No, I haven't. Sam did pay me some attention, and I did agree to walk out with him, even though I knew we weren't right for each other. He didn't make my heart miss a beat like ...' her voice trailed off as she stopped herself adding, *like you do*. 'He's walking out with a different young lady now, and I wish him all the best for the future.'

Her face grew warm as Freddie gazed into her eyes. 'Do you think you will marry one day?'

She tilted her head to one side. 'If somebody – the right person – should ask me, I should certainly consider it,' she said in challenge.

He took a deep breath, his cheeks high with colour.

'Sweet Rose, you have bewitched me with your beauty and good sense. I never intended to fall in love with you … In fact, I didn't think I would fall in love again …'

'You have been in love before?' she said sadly.

He nodded. 'She didn't love me back.' His tone was harsh.

'You still have feelings for her?' She straightened. She would not be second best. She would only be with him for love, just as Ma and Pa had been together, albeit with their decision not to get married.

'I felt no anger towards her, only at myself for letting her deceive me. She was a mistress of lies.'

The smell of burning stung her eyes. 'The chestnuts are on fire,' she said, pointing to the skillet where smoke was emerging from around the lid.

'Oh dear.' Freddie gave them another good shake.

'What did this lady do to you?'

'She told me that she returned my sentiments in full measure. I promised her marriage and a happy and contented life, but I discovered not long after my declaration that she was in love with someone else, and intending to continue their liaison while married to me. When she met me, she thought she'd found gold.'

'I'm sorry,' Rose said.

'I don't require your pity. I had a lucky escape. If I'd married her, I'd never have travelled to England. I'd never have met you, Rose.'

'I've never been in love before,' she said, meaning before she'd met Freddie.

'Oh? Feelings can grow,' he said hopefully.

Rose looked at him, really looked at him, her face burning.

'You mean, you're asking about my feelings for you?'

He nodded. 'I hope you aren't offended by my declaration, and you don't think me presumptuous. I've tried to be patient. I've given you time, but I can't keep quiet any longer. I am in suspense. Do you think there is any way that one day you could love me in return? I know it's a lot to expect, and this has come as a shock to you ...'

'It isn't much of a surprise,' she said softly, as the chestnuts began to pop. 'Minnie has always said you have shown an unusual interest in me.'

'In a good way, I hope,' he said with a wry smile.

'Oh, of course. She's very fond of you. We both are.'

'For me, it was love at first sight, but I fear that to my dishonour I didn't offer you the full truth. I am a coward – I had been open before and had my heart broken. Since then, I've learned that there are times when you have to take a risk and this is one of them.'

Was he about to propose? she thought, her breast filled with a mixture of joy, despair and panic. It was what she wanted, but she couldn't let him go on without revealing her secret, one that could jeopardise her chance of making a good marriage.

'I need to say something,' she said quickly.

He frowned. 'Why do you always assume I'm doing things for you out of respect for your grandfather? I'm not. This time, I'm doing it for you, for us. I love you. I've loved you since I first set eyes on you.'

'Let me speak,' she said. 'There is something that could alter your intentions, if not your feelings towards me.'

'There is nothing—'

'Listen to me. It's important.'

'Well, go on,' he said impatiently. 'I know about Minnie and her child. What is it?'

'You know much of my family's history, but not perhaps that my parents, Ma and Pa Cheevers, were never married, and that my father by blood was the son of a baronet.' She stared at him as a shadow of doubt or confusion crossed his eyes. She'd done it now, wrecked her chances by speaking the truth, but she couldn't have it on her conscience to keep it from him. Her heart broke as she watched him stand up, take the skillet from the fire and place it on the stone hearth in front of the brass firedogs.

After a pause, he turned and fell on to one knee in front of her.

'It doesn't matter to me where you came from. As you know, I didn't have the most auspicious start to life. What's important is the here and now, and the future, not the past.' He took her hands and clasped them in his. 'Rose,' he said, looking into her eyes, 'you are my star. You guide my every move. Everything I do is for you.'

Her heart was beating in her throat as he went on, 'Will you do me the honour of becoming my wife?'

She felt his fingers tremble as he held her hands.

'Yes,' she whispered. 'Yes, I'll marry you.'

'My dearest Rose ...' He smiled, his teeth gleaming in the dimly lit room. 'May I kiss you?'

'I think you should ...'

He leaned in towards her and pressed his lips gently against her mouth.

'Again?' he murmured, his voice filled with heat and passion.

Smiling as she felt his arms around her waist, she responded, 'As many times as you wish ...'

Minnie burst into tears of joy when Rose and Freddie told her of their engagement at breakfast the following day.

'I knew it,' she cried. 'I knew it all along. When will you be married?'

'As soon as possible,' Freddie said lightly. 'I'm not going to give your sister time to change her mind.'

'She won't,' Minnie said, getting up from the table. 'Wait here a moment. I have something for you.'

'Not now,' Rose said. 'Your eggs will get cold.' But it was too late. Minnie limped out of the dining room, returning a few minutes later, holding something behind her back.

'This is my gift to you and Freddie. I hope you like it.' With a grin and a flourish, she unfurled the patchwork she'd been making. 'I'll have to add the date of the wedding, and have it made up into a quilt for you.'

'It's beautiful.' The pattern of pink, green and cream cottons blurred in front of Rose's eyes.

'Thank you, my dear sister,' Freddie said, jumping up from his seat. 'I hope it won't be very long before I can call you "sister-in-law".'

He and Minnie folded the patchwork together.

'Keep it safe until we've set the date,' he said.

'It will have to be on a Wednesday,' Minnie said.

'Why is that?' Freddie asked.

'There's a rhyme that Ma told me when Arthur and Tabby were planning their wedding. "Monday for health, Tuesday for wealth, Wednesday's the best of all. Thursday brings crosses, and Friday losses, and Saturday no luck at all."'

'I'm surprised you remember that,' Rose said, wishing that Ma and Pa had been around to share their good fortune.

'Then a Wednesday it will be,' Freddie said. 'We don't want any bad luck.'

'You don't believe—' Rose stopped when Freddie winked at her. He wasn't superstitious – he was humouring Minnie, and she loved him for it.

Rose called at Wanstall Farm to invite her grandmother to their impending nuptials. She found her in the farmyard, feeding the hens and geese. Mr Carter offered his congratulations and returned to negotiating the sale of a pair of carriage horses to a client.

'My husband took against Mr Wild when he first turned up in Overshill,' Mrs Carter said. 'He couldn't make him out, not being one of us, and I've since learned that he gave him the cold shoulder when he revealed his connection with our family. Do you know of it? Only I'm not sure if it's my place to say.'

Rose nodded.

'Stephen didn't mention it at first, thinking to protect me from the sorrows of the past, but he's never been any good at keeping secrets, and one day he let slip that Mr Wild had come to look for Agnes. Finding my long-lost grandchildren has been a great delight to me, and hearing of my daughter has been painful and a joy at the same time. And now I am touched beyond measure that dear Matty never forgot our child, even when he was far away from home. I trust that you have received your share of his inheritance?'

'It's being settled at the moment,' Rose said. Freddie had agreed to her proposal that she allocated a share of the money to Minnie, and some to Donald to be held in trust until his twenty-fifth birthday. She knew he wouldn't like it, but she needed to be sure he wouldn't throw it away.

'Then your future is secure. That is a great comfort to me, as it must be to you.' Mrs Carter paused before continuing, 'Tell me. There's no delicate way of putting this, but is our Minnie in the family way?'

'She is. There's no point in trying to hide it. Soon it will be obvious to everyone.'

'You will encourage her to keep the child?' A tear glistened at the corner of her grandmother's eye. 'It would be a tragedy to separate them.'

'Don't worry. It's already been decided that Minnie and the baby will remain at Churt House.'

'Mr Wild is a good man,' Mrs Carter said.

'I know – I'm the luckiest woman alive. Now, I must get back. I've got lots to do – the wedding is in a few weeks. You will join us?'

'Nothing will stop me,' she smiled.

They married quietly on a Wednesday one month later in the Church of Our Lady in front of a small group of well-wishers, including Aunt Marjorie and some of the servants from the house. The Reverend Browning officiated, Minnie was bridesmaid, and Mrs Carter and Jack were witnesses.

Wearing a pale blue dress, stole and veil, Rose walked down the aisle with Minnie at her side, to join her beloved Freddie who couldn't contain his excitement, beaming from ear to ear, as they said their vows and he placed the ring on her finger.

'You may kiss the bride,' the vicar lisped.

'Was there ever a more beautiful couple?' Aunt Marjorie sobbed loudly as Rose and Freddie headed into the chapel to sign the register, and when they returned outside into the bright winter sunshine, she showered them liberally with rice.

Freddie was still picking the grains from his coat as he and Rose walked arm in arm back to Churt House a little behind the others, who appeared to be in a hurry to get out of the cold and partake of the wedding breakfast.

'This is the best day of my life, Mrs Wild,' he declared.

'And mine.' She couldn't stop smiling and her cheeks ached.

'I plan to travel again next spring: March and April. I wish to settle my business interests in a way that someone else can manage them on my behalf.'

'Oh?' Her spirits fell. She'd known he'd go away from time to time, but she hated the idea of it. 'I'll miss you terribly.'

'I thought you'd come with me. I believe it's customary for a husband and wife to accompany each other on their journey through life.'

'Really? Freddie, that's a wonderful idea. Of course I'll come with you. I don't want to waste a minute of our time together.'

'That's one thing settled then,' he said, and they continued to walk towards the house.

'It's been an honour to meet the woman whom you call Aunt. She's quite a character. Steely, I think, and very old-fashioned, but with the kindest of hearts. I saw her talking to Minnie and asking her about the expected month of her confinement. She wasn't judging her. All she asked was to have the chance to hold the infant in her arms one day.'

'I wondered if we might prevail on Aunt Marjorie to act as Minnie's companion while we're away, and to help Minnie out in the nursery. She's had many years' experience of nannying,' Rose suggested.

'It would be a way of supporting her in her retirement,' Freddie said.

'She's looking old and weary, and she's been complaining that her knees are giving her gyp ever since she arrived last week.'

'We have more than enough space – she can have her own quarters on the same level as the nursery so she doesn't have to keep struggling up and down the stairs. I'd noticed that she finds it hard to get around. Tell her she can move in as soon as she wishes.'

'Are you sure?'

'I'll do anything to make you happy, Rose. I have no family ...'

'You do – you're part of mine now,' she said, then added ruefully, thinking of Donald, 'For better or worse.'

Freddie stopped on the drive and turned to her, taking both her hands. She could feel the heat of his skin through her fine leather gloves.

'Panning for gold with your grandfather in the wilds of Tasmania taught me how the best things in life come to those who wait,' he said. 'When I found you in Overshill, I found what I'd been looking for, a nugget of pure gold. As I've said before, I love you.'

'I love you too,' she said. She was certain of that now. 'Always and for ever.'

Chapter Twenty-Six

Nothing Ventured, Nothing Gained

The newlyweds spent three days in a hotel in Canterbury when they visited a school and set up a trust to fund the education of five street children, boys and girls, as well as paying a brief visit to Donald in gaol. In March, they travelled to New York, then in late May, Minnie was delivered of a healthy infant. The child, called Edith, was the sweetest little girl who looked like her mother with no trace of her father's features or character, a relief to Rose who'd been afraid that she would be reminded of Abel and the brickfield whenever she saw her.

Rose and Freddie celebrated the first anniversary of their marriage in December, then saw in the New Year of 1881 with Aunt Marjorie and a fair number of their neighbours whom they invited for dinner and dancing. It was a happy occasion, confirming that they'd become part of the community in Overshill. The only thing that would make her joy complete, Rose thought, was to see Arthur again. She often wondered how he and Tabby were, and what they were doing.

The winter was a cold one. The stream was frozen, thick frost adorned the cobwebs in the hedgerows, and the ground was solid underfoot when Rose walked with Minnie pushing the pram around the grounds. The days were short, making her long for spring.

January passed and February blustered in, accompanied by storms and rain.

One morning, when the east wind had blown through, bringing down one of the chestnut trees in the park, Rose was in the parlour choosing the week's menu at her meeting with Mrs Causton and Cook. Her confidence as mistress of the house was growing, thanks to Freddie's faith in her abilities.

'So the eggs florentine, veal and potatoes for Wednesday,' Cook was saying.

'Unless the butcher has another flitch of pork,' Rose said.

'Guess who's come to see us!' Minnie came rushing into the room.

'Oh, Minnie, please knock before you come in.' Rose smiled at how motherhood had made little alteration in her sister, her ways remaining very childlike. 'Can't you see that I'm with Cook?'

'I'm sorry, but you might wish to alter your plans,' Minnie exclaimed, her cheeks flushed pink. 'You'll never guess who's at the door with his wife and children. Oh, Rose, it's our brother, Arthur.'

'Arthur! How can that be?' Rose stood up, her heart overflowing with joy. 'This will have to wait. I believe we will order the fatted calf and throw a few more potatoes in the pot.' She almost ran after her sister out of the parlour and along to the hall where the butler, Rice, was standing with their visitors, a quizzical look on his face.

'This is Mr Arthur Fortune, ma'am. He says he is a relative of yours.'

She stared at her long-lost brother, dressed in a wool coat and polished leather boots, and holding a silk hat.

'Arthur, I'm so pleased to see you,' she said, throwing her arms around his neck. 'After all this time.'

'Rose, my dear sister.' Arthur tossed his hat to Minnie and hugged Rose back. 'As Pa would have said, it's monsterful to see you.'

'I can't believe you're here.' Rose smiled as he turned to his companions, Tabby and two small children, a girl in her arms and a boy holding her hand. 'Let me introduce you to my wife, our son Arthur, and daughter, Anne.'

'So you did get married! How wonderful.' Rose addressed the butler. 'Rice, please take their coats. Have you any luggage?'

'It's on the doorstep,' Arthur said. 'Mr Wild invited us to spend a few days with you.'

'Freddie did? How did he find you?'

'Your husband did some detective work, and found us living in Greenwich. Is it true that he was your grandfather's ward?'

'Yes, he knew Ma's father – they met on the other side of the world and now he's here, living the life of an English gentleman, except that he's better than any of them: kind, thoughtful and generous ... Oh, I know it's hard to believe, but he had proof of who he was: the other half of the sixpence that Ma left to me in her will. Why didn't you come and find us before? I was worried about you.'

'I'm sorry. I never stopped thinking of you and the twins, but I didn't want to intrude by turning up at your grandmother's. You remember when we last saw each other when we were leaving Willow Place, how I said I felt I didn't really belong, especially after Ma and Pa had gone.'

'Oh Arthur, why didn't you believe me when I said we were all part of the same family?' Rose said. 'We'll always be brother and sister.'

'I know,' he said, smiling. 'We have a lot of catchin' up to do.'

'What do you think of our home?'

Arthur gazed around the room, open-mouthed. 'You've gone up in the world.'

'As have you, by the looks of it.' She bit back tears of pride, realising how hard he must have strived to make a good living for himself, Tabby and their children. 'Let Rice take your coats. One of the footmen will collect your luggage and take it upstairs. We will sit in the parlour and talk until we are all talked out.'

'Where is Donald? Will he be back later?'

'I'm afraid that his escapades caught up with him,' Rose said awkwardly.

'He is gorn?' Arthur said, wide-eyed.

'Oh no, he's in gaol for thieving.'

'The little tyke!'

'Not now. Not in front of the littl'uns,' Rose said quickly. 'I'll explain later. In the meantime, you must meet the newest member of our family. Minnie, go and fetch Edith.'

Minnie hurried upstairs and came back down proudly holding Edith in her arms.

'This is your daughter, Rose?' Arthur said.

'Oh no. She is Minnie's daughter.'

A frown crossed his face.

'We wouldn't be without her. She brings much joy into our lives, including Aunt Marjorie's.'

'Aunt Marjorie? This is too much to take in.'

'She's our honorary nanny. You see, the only person missing is Donald. Come and take the weight off your feet. Tabby, you're welcome to use the nursery as you please. There are toys and games to keep the children occupied. I'll ask Cook to prepare soup and cold meats for luncheon.' Rose turned to the butler. 'Rice, would you fetch my husband, please?'

'Yes, ma'am,' he said.

Rose, Freddie and Arthur sat in the parlour while the others spent time in the nursery with the children. They took luncheon together and walked in the grounds before dinner. Rose found out that Bert had given Arthur work and a place to stay with Tabby. They'd married, and he'd completed an apprenticeship as a bricklayer before being promoted rapidly to foreman on various building sites all over London where the houses were springing up – in Arthur's words, like mushrooms.

In the dining room that night, Rose had a lump in her throat as she looked around the table. Only Donald was missing and it wouldn't be long until he was released from gaol, having served his sentence.

Arthur made a toast as Pa had done at Willow Place.

'Let's raise our glasses and drink to health and happiness, and the jolliest of times,' he said, standing up with a glass of claret in his hand. 'To Freddie and Rose for their hospitality, to Minnie, to Aunt Marjorie and last but not least, to my dear wife for her patience.'

'To health and happiness,' Rose said.

'And the jolliest of times,' Arthur repeated.

They drained their glasses, and Freddie responded by thanking their guests for joining them and suggesting a visit to Canterbury the following day.

It was quite an outing, Rose thought as her husband held her hand and helped her into the carriage early next morning.

'Tabby has decided to stay with Aunt Marjorie and the children. The younger one has a sniffle and she doesn't want him out in the cold,' she said as she took a seat and rested the bouquet of evergreens she'd had one of the gardener's boys cut for her across her lap. 'It is the four of us: you, me, Minnie and Arthur.' She wished Donald had been there with them – she'd wanted to see him, but it was too late to arrange a prison visit.

'Don't you want a blanket?' Minnie asked.

'Just a foot-warmer for now, please,' she said, moving along to make room for her husband.

The groom slammed the door shut and the four dapple-grey horses fidgeted, their hooves crunching in the gravel. The coachman cracked his whip and the carriage lumbered forward, picking up speed as the horses trotted down the drive with Jack, Freddie's manservant, riding alongside. Rose wasn't sure if it was something she'd eaten or the motion of the carriage, but she began to feel overheated and nauseous. She had thought that the worst of it was over, but it kept reappearing from time to time.

She pressed a lace handkerchief to her mouth.

'Are you well?' Freddie whispered.

'I'm not quite myself, but I'll be all right. Don't worry.'

Freddie held her hand, and the journey passed more quickly. Soon, they were approaching the Westgate.

'Look, there's the river,' Minnie said, pointing.

'Does this feel like home to you, Rose?' Freddie asked.

'Not any more,' she said wistfully, recalling good and bad times. 'I'm home when I'm with you, my dear. Thank you for bringing us here today.'

'It's my pleasure.' Smiling, he squeezed her fingers.

'To be truthful, I'm not looking forward to going to the cemetery. I haven't been there since our parents were buried.'

'I think I'll find it upsetting, but I have so much to tell them,' Minnie said.

'They know everything,' Arthur countered. 'They watch over us day and night. That's my belief anyway, and I find great comfort in it.'

The carriage came to a rumbling halt.

'What is going on?' Rose asked, hearing the sound of voices. Freddie opened the door. Rose looked past him at the crowd milling around outside the Weavers' House where the town crier, dressed in flamboyant robes, was ringing his hand-bell and yelling, 'Oyez, oyez, at twelve midday, two gentlemen from London are to cross the Channel in a balloon. Oyez, oyez, meet at Wincheap to marvel at their bravery. Oyez, oyez, don't delay!'

Even though the coachman tried to make his way through, they were stuck for a few minutes while the town crier moved up the road and the crowd began to disperse.

Freddie turned to Rose. 'Shall we go and see this historic event after we've paid our respects?'

'I'd like to,' Arthur cut in.

'I'm asking my wife in case she doesn't feel up to it.'

'I should like to observe this spectacle,' Rose said, 'but is it safe?'

'They're brave men,' Freddie said, 'but they're unlikely to get as far as the sea, let alone France. I've read about them in the newspapers this week – the flight has already failed twice when the wind shifted the wrong way.'

They travelled to the cemetery where Rose laid the evergreens at the foot of the shared headstone. Arthur bent down and pulled up a weed that had escaped the care-taker's attention and Minnie began to sob. As Rose cried with her, she felt Freddie's hand on her arm.

'My dear,' he whispered.

'Thank you. I'm sorry for embarrassing you like this.'

'I'd be more embarrassed if I thought you felt nothing.' He smiled. 'I'm glad we came. I never met your parents, but I feel closer to them now. I hope they would be proud of me, and happy to have me as their son-in-law.'

'Oh Freddie, they would have loved you almost as much as I do.' The sun crept out from behind the clouds, revealing the inscription on the gravestone: *Oliver Cheevers and Agnes Cheevers; Beloved by All Who Knew Them.* Rose swallowed hard. 'Let us go,' she said softly.

'We can stay as long as you wish.'

'I'm afraid I'm finding this too much to bear.' She removed one of her gloves, reached out and felt the cold marble beneath her fingertips. 'Goodbye, dear Ma and Pa. Until next time,' she whispered before turning back to her handsome husband. 'Let's go and watch this balloon. Pa wouldn't have missed something like this.'

They took the carriage to Wincheap but were forced to disembark a little way away because of the number of people gathering to watch. Suddenly, a young man emerged from the crowd and came running across to greet them.

'Mornin', Miss Cheevers, or should it be afternoon?' he said, taking off his cap. 'Fancy seein' you here!'

'Baxter! It's wonderful to meet you again, but I can assure you that it's still morning,' she said, smiling. 'And you can address me from now on as Mrs Freddie Wild. Allow me to introduce you to my husband.'

'Time moves on, don't it?' He scratched his head. 'I can't recall when I saw you last.'

'It was a couple of summers ago when we asked you to mind the barrow. I seem to remember that you drove a hard bargain.'

'If you don't ask, you don't get.' He grinned. 'I have news of my own – I've got a permanent job at the tannery, taking Mr Jones's place when he retires.'

'Congratulations,' Rose said.

'I've turned out better than expected, thanks to your schooling. Mr Milsom was impressed when he found out I'd mastered the basics of 'rithmetic. He said it would come in handy when working out how much bark to put in the pits, and measuring the size of the butts.'

'Do you still live with your family?'

'I support them now – Pa respects me for that.' He changed the subject. 'I don't know if you've heard about the Kingsleys?'

'Not recently,' Rose said.

'After they sold the tannery, Mr Kingsley lost his marbles through drink and Mrs Kingsley pegged it – I mean, she passed away, Mrs Wild, due to what rumour said was indiscreet and excessive use of sleeping drops. She looked awful poorly when I last saw her traipsing the streets of Can'erbury.'

'Are you all right?' Freddie asked, taking Rose's arm.

'I'm fine.' Aunt Temperance had received her comeuppance and she felt nothing, not an ounce of sorrow. 'Good day, Baxter.'

'Good day, Mrs Wild.' He put his cap back on, straightened it and sauntered off.

'He's turned out well, Freddie,' Rose said. 'He was one of our pupils. Do you remember him, Minnie?'

She smiled wryly. 'He used to pull my hair.'

'Did he? Oh, I wouldn't have put it past him back then.'

'Let's not hang around,' Arthur said. 'It can't be long before the balloon goes up.'

Freddie stopped to speak to a policeman. 'Where's the best place to see this?'

'From the promenade above the Dane John, or in the field beside the gasometer,' he said.

'Thank you, Constable,' Freddie said. 'We'll try the field.'

They paid a small admission at the gate and walked across the grass, lining up in front of a crowd of onlookers who had climbed on top of a stack of hop poles for a better view.

'Is that it?' Minnie said, her voice filled with excitement. 'I don't know why, but I thought the men would travel in the balloon.'

'No, they'll go in the car,' Arthur said.

The car was a tiny box, its dimensions no more than a few feet in each direction. It had a cork gunwale with *The Colonel* painted on the side, and was attached to the balloon, a delicate structure about eighty foot tall that trembled in the breeze as a couple of men filled it with gas from a long pipe leading from the gasworks. Several others hung on to the balloon via ropes. Every so often one would cry out as his feet lifted from the ground, and a member of the crowd would rush forward and grab on to his legs to pull him back down.

'We're here just in time,' Freddie observed, as the intrepid fliers shook hands with the mayor and sheriff and a few other gentlemen before squeezing themselves inside the car. 'That's Colonel Brice, and his companion, Mr Simmons.'

'They are madmen,' Rose said. 'There's nothing that would induce me to get into that tiny car and float away without any means of power except the force of nature, wind and gas.'

'What about travelling in a flying machine? Would you not go in one of those with me?' Freddie said.

'To die together?' she said.

'No, to fly together.'

'Are we not flying high right now?'

'Yes, I suppose we are, my dear wife,' Freddie said as a cheer went up and the men let go of the ropes. 'We are part of history.'

The balloon rose slowly into the sky to a point where it seemed to hang and quiver like a hovering bird, deciding whether to flap its wings or dive to the ground, before it started to drift slowly in the direction of France. The crowd sent up another cheer, their exhalations seeming to give the balloon an extra nudge.

'They have brandy, beer and cheese – at least they will die happy,' Freddie said before quickly adding, 'I'm joking. Nothing ventured, nothing gained. They are brave men indeed. Let's go and eat. My man has booked us a table at the Dining Rooms in Mercery Lane, not far from here. Unless you wish to go straight home, Rose?'

'I'll be all right,' she said, thankful for his consideration.

They had a late luncheon in the eatery, which was crowded with people talking of the balloon. Afterwards, as they took a tour of the cathedral, they heard a report that a carrier pigeon had arrived with the message that the Colonel and Mr Simmonds were halfway across the Channel, but they couldn't stay any longer to hear the outcome because the sky was darkening and the coachman didn't want to risk the horses in the pitch-black later in the evening.

It wasn't until the day after that the newspaper came with a report that the two men had been seen getting off the train from Dover on the same evening as they had left Canterbury in the balloon. Freddie read the article to Rose when they dined together.

'Apparently, most of their pigeons refused to fly – they kept coming back to settle on the car.'

'I didn't realise pigeons had so much sense,' Rose smiled.

'They ditched in the sea with good fortune, right beside the Calais mail steamer, *Foam*. The captain Jutelet helped them aboard and there was little damage. Their provisions were intact although the crew had had to cut a hole in the balloon to release the gas when it became entangled with the rigging. Ah, they will be able to try again.' He changed the subject. 'You've been a little out of sorts for a while – I thought you might be tiring of me.'

'Of course I'm not.'

'How are you now? I haven't asked.'

'You have asked me at least five times today,' she said with a chuckle, unable to contain herself any longer. 'I wanted to wait until I've seen the doctor, but I have no doubt. I don't need anyone else to confirm it.'

'What is it, my darling?' His voice quavered and he gazed into her eyes, his expression a mixture of hope tinged with apprehension. 'It's good news ...?'

Six months later Rose stood just inside the nursery door, playing with the sixpence on the silver chain at her throat. Ever thoughtful and romantic, Freddie had taken the two halves of the coin to a jeweller in Canterbury and had them mounted together, presenting the finished article to her as a gift to celebrate the birth of their first child.

Her breast filled with love and pride as she watched Freddie lift their son out of the crib to show him how the rays of the late summer sun caught the stained-glass butterfly set in one of the windows and cast its bright colours across the floor.

Donald was beside her, his arm around her shoulders.

'I wish you didn't have to go,' she said, turning to him. His chin was squarer and he'd grown taller than when she'd last seen him in gaol. 'You can stay as long as you like, you know.'

'I've been here long enough, and Arthur's expecting me to join him in London. I want a fresh start where people don't judge me for what I was before. I've changed, but there are many around here who can't accept that.'

'You will visit us, though?'

'Of course.' He grinned. 'If you'll have me.'

She laughed. 'You'll always be welcome – you're one of the family.'

She turned her attention to the table where Aunt Marjorie was sitting with Minnie, who was bouncing her daughter on her knee. Aunt Marjorie was peeling an apple for Edith, who was already fifteen months old.

'Be careful,' Minnie warned. 'Don't break the peel.'

'I won't. I've had plenty of practice.' Aunt Marjorie was fighting a losing battle against the grey whiskers growing on her chin, and her hands shook as she turned the paring knife against the apple until the peel dropped on to the table in one piece. 'There you go.'

Minnie picked up the peel and threw it down on the floor.

'What does it say? What letter does it make?' Aunt Marjorie said.

'It's a B.' Minnie frowned. 'I don't know anyone whose name begins with B.'

'There's Bill, the woodcutter,' Donald contributed.

Minnie's eyebrows shot up. 'Not that old bloke! I'm not marrying him. That can't be right. Aunt Marjorie, please can you peel another apple?'

'Not now,' she smiled. 'One apple a day keeps the doctor away. Two will have a detrimental effect on the digestion. No, you must wait until I've cut it into quarters and taken the pips out,' she added as Edith reached out to try to grab it. 'If you eat the pips, you'll end up with apple trees growing out of your ears.'

'No, you don't,' Donald said, smiling. 'I've eaten the pips hundreds of times.'

Aunt Marjorie looked up and gave him a playful glare.

'I'm sorry,' he said, backing down. 'Edith, you must do as Aunt Marjorie says. She has the wisdom that comes with advanced age.'

'Excuse me, we'll have less of the age.' Aunt Marjorie wagged her finger then started to cut into the peeled apple, the knife trembling in her hand.

'Let me do that.' Donald stepped up to the table to take over quartering the apple and removing the core and pips.

'Thank you, dear,' she said. 'You don't want to get old – it can be a terrible trial, although it does have its compensations: wisdom, as you've said; the satisfaction of reflecting on a life well-lived; the joy of knowing that Edith and little Matty have the best start possible' – her eyes sparkled with humour – 'with help from the manual of etiquette to guide them.'

As if to express his disapproval of the idea of learning etiquette in the future, the baby let out a fretful cry.

'I'll take him,' Rose said quickly as Freddie turned towards her, his expression one of mild panic.

'He needs his ma,' she said, walking across to her husband who gently placed their son into her arms.

'There, there,' she whispered, stroking his cheek. With his blue-green eyes and shock of blond hair, he was the most beautiful creature she'd ever seen. His face crumpled as if he was about to cry again, so she held him against her shoulder, cupping the back of his head and inhaling his sweet, milky scent as he settled. 'That's better.' She gazed out of the window, leaning back against Freddie as he slid his hands around her waist.

Rose couldn't believe her luck after all they'd been through. Her patchwork family had been unpicked by various unfortunate disasters – a few of their own making and some not their fault. It had been stitched back together, albeit in a different pattern, and as Pa would have said, there was nothing wrong in that. They were no ordinary family, but they were a happy one. She smiled to herself. Here in her beloved Freddie's arms with little Matty breathing softly against her ear, and her family around her, she had finally found a place to call home.

Acknowledgements

I should like to thank Laura at MBA Literary Agents, and Cass and the team at Penguin Random House UK for their enthusiasm and support.

I'm also very grateful to my family for their help with researching how life would have been in Victorian Canterbury and Faversham.